Laurence Sterne

A SENTIMENTAL JOURNEY
Through France and Italy

AND

CONTINUATION OF THE BRAMINE'S JOURNAL

WITH RELATED TEXTS

Laurence Sterne

A SENTIMENTAL JOURNEY
Through France and Italy

AND

CONTINUATION OF THE BRAMINE'S JOURNAL

WITH RELATED TEXTS

Edited, with Introduction and Notes, by
Melvyn New and W. G. Day

Hackett Publishing Company, Inc.
Indianapolis/Cambridge

06 07 08 09   1 2 3 4 5 6 7

For further information, please address
    Hackett Publishing Company, Inc.
    P.O. Box 44937
    Indianapolis, IN 46244-0937

    www.hackettpublishing.com

Cover design by Brian Rak and Abigail Coyle
Interior design by Elizabeth Wilson
Composition by William Hartman
Printed at Edwards Brothers, Inc.

Library of Congress Cataloging-in-Publication Data

Sterne, Laurence, 1713–1768.
    A sentimental journey through France and Italy ; and, Continuation of
    the Bramine's journal : with related texts / edited, with introduction and
    notes, by Melvyn New and W.G. Day.
        p. cm.
    Includes bibliographical references.
    ISBN 0-87220-800-1 (pbk.)
    I. New, Melvyn.   II. Day, Geoffrey.   III. Sterne, Laurence, 1713–1768.
Journal to Eliza.   IV. Title: Continuation of the Bramine's journal.   V. Title.

PR3714.S4 2006

                                                                2005026350

CONTENTS

ACKNOWLEDGMENTS

We are indebted to Gardner D. Stout's scholarly 1967 edition of *A Sentimental Journey* and to the University of California Press for its generous permission to quote as we deemed appropriate from that edition. We are most grateful to Professor Anne Bandry for her help with Sterne's idiosyncratic French. In preparing this edition, based on the Florida Edition, we were most usefully assisted by the careful work of Sue Gillmor and Laura M. Cecil.

INTRODUCTION

A Sentimental Journey through France and Italy was published in two volumes on February 27, 1768. Three weeks later, on Friday, March 18, Laurence Sterne's death was witnessed at 4:00 P.M. by a footman who had been sent to inquire after his health. Though Sterne was not given to false modesty—he declared that he wrote "not [to] be *fed*, but to be *famous*"[1]—he might well have been surprised to learn that this publication was to become not only one of the most frequently reprinted eighteenth-century English literary works, but also, in the late-eighteenth and early-nineteenth centuries, a text with which to rally nationalist support against occupying powers in such eastern European countries as Poland and Hungary, and a way of publishing subversive comment in 1792 on the Revolution in France.[2]

This may be seen as all the more remarkable in view of the evidence that suggests the text is incomplete; into subscribers' copies of the first edition was inserted a loose leaf apology for the author's failure to deliver the four volumes they had been promised, and to which there had been references in correspondence as early as July 1766:

> THE Author begs leave to acknowledge to his Subscribers, that they have a further claim upon him for Two Volumes more than these delivered to them now, and which nothing but ill health could have prevented him, from having ready along with these.
>
> The Work will be compleated and delivered to the Subscribers early the next Winter.

The nature of the two extant volumes of *A Sentimental Journey* is such, however, that it would probably be an error to suggest that, apart from Italian place names, Sterne's tour of Italy would have been different from his tour of France. Nonetheless, as was true throughout the nineteenth century, it has remained something of a donnée with Sterne's modern critics, starting with the biographer Wilbur Cross at the beginning of the twentieth century, that Sterne's travels were a template for *A Sentimental Journey*. As recently as 2004 an edition of *Tristram Shandy* was published with a biographical note that states emphatically: "His sole remaining work, *A Sentimental Journey*, was published

---

[1] Lewis Perry Curtis, ed., *Letters of Laurence Sterne* (Oxford: Clarendon Press, 1935), 90; hereafter referred to as *Letters. A Sentimental Journey* is hereafter referred to as *ASJ;* and *Bramine's Journal* as *BJ.*

[2] See Peter de Voogd and John Neubauer, eds., *The Reception of Laurence Sterne in Europe* (London and New York: Thoemmes Continuum, 2004).

in February 1768; it was based on Sterne's escapades during a seven-month tour by coach through France and Italy."[3] This opinion is not supported by what is known of Sterne's tours, of which there were two, both lasting more than seven months.

Sterne's Own Travels through France and Italy

1762–1764

Sterne departed from London on January 2, 1762, the day that George III declared war on Spain, in the party of George Pitt, Envoy Extraordinary and Minister Plenipotentiary to the Court of Turin (the capital of the Kingdom of Sardinia). Pitt had been appointed to negotiate a peace treaty to terminate the Seven Years' War; the Treaty of Paris was eventually signed on February 10, 1763, so that, for the first thirteen months of his travels, Sterne was living in what was technically enemy territory. Because France's borders were closed in 1762, the only safe and legal way of gaining entry was by being in a diplomatic party.

On arriving in France the group stayed in Calais at the Lyon d'Argent inn run by Pierre Quillac, more commonly known as Dessein, under which name he appears in the first pages of the *Journey* (see pp. 12, 18ff.). They arrived in Paris in mid-January, and on the 31st Sterne applied for a passport so that he could travel separately. Within days, the *British Chronicle* (February 1–3) reported his death. It was subsequently denied, but the error was perhaps excusable; Sterne was, throughout his time abroad, plagued by the chronic illness that had first manifested itself when he was a student at Cambridge, and that now had caused him to leave England to seek a milder climate. He immediately set about learning French. Richard Phelps, Pitt's secretary in the diplomatic mission, noted that Sterne was inclined to "talk more bad French in one day, than would serve a reasonable man a whole Month. He talks à tort et à travers to whoever sits next to him wherever he happens to be."[4] Sterne himself claimed to "speak it fast and fluent, but incorrect both in accent and phrase" (*Letters* 155). This lack of accuracy is evident throughout the text of *A Sentimental Journey*, where the spelling of French words is erratic and the use of the acute and grave accents is neither consistent nor accurate; and we may assume from the frequency with which he literally anglicizes French idioms, that he could well have employed the same procedure in reverse.

---

[3] Robert Folkenflik, ed., *Tristram Shandy* (New York: Modern Library, 2004), vii. (This is a biographical note copyrighted on the verso of the title page by Random House, 1995, and is not here ascribed to the editor.)

[4] Arthur H. Cash, *Laurence Sterne: The Later Years* (London and New York: Methuen, 1986), 130; hereafter referred to as *LY*. Much of the biographical material in this Introduction is derived from Cash.

On July 8 he was joined by his wife and daughter, and in the middle of the month they set off for Toulouse by an unspecified route that took three weeks. In June of the following year they traveled to Bagnères, but returned to Toulouse and then set off in the direction of Nice—it is not known whether they got that far— and visited Marseilles and Aix, arriving finally in Montpellier in November 1763. There they encountered Tobias Smollett, who was gathering materials for his own description of France and Italy. On January 4, Sterne set off on horseback for Pézenas but failed to complete the journey, and in March he returned to Paris, leaving Elizabeth and Lydia in Montauban. In Paris an anecdote circulated about Sterne's witty comparison of the French to worn coins, a variant of which is found in the *Journey* (p. 126). He arrived back in London at the end of May 1764.

1765–1766

Leaving London on October 10, 1765, Sterne stayed again in Calais with Dessein, but this time in the landlord's new establishment, the Hôtel d'Angleterre. When he passed through Paris a few days later, John "Fish" Craufurd, son of the Laird of Errol, is said to have told Sterne the anecdote that was to become the basis for the final "Case of Delicacy" in the *Journey* (pp. 169–73). At the end of October Sterne set out for Lyons. Though there is no hard evidence of Sterne's route, Arthur Cash, in his attempt to establish a direct connection between the actual and fictional travels, suggests that it included Auxerre, Moulins, and Tavare.

In early November Sterne departed Lyons, and traveled via Pont-de-Beauvoisin and the Mont Cenis Pass to Turin, where he arrived in mid-November. By November 28 he was in Milan, the location of the story of the Marquesina di F*** (pp. 81–2), and on December 18, in Florence. It is particularly salutary to note that Sterne's principal intention in Florence was not one shared by most visitors. They would have been in the city to see either the Duomo or Michelangelo's *David;* his stated purpose was to visit three Englishmen he had not previously met: "I stay here three days to dine with our Plenipo—Ld Tit[c]hfield & Cowper" (*Letters* 266). The "Plenipo" was Sir Horace Mann, Envoy Extraordinary and Minister Plenipotentiary to the court of Florence since 1740, and the well-known correspondent of Horace Walpole. Sterne's desire to establish contact with English circles is one of many differences between the author and his fictional Yorick, who believes that *"an English man does not travel to see English men"* (p. 17).

During the Christmas season, Sterne reached Rome, where he almost certainly visited the Pantheon and where he met Joseph Nollekens, who carved the magnificent portrait bust of the author, reproduced in the frontispiece to his daughter's 1775 edition of his letters. Leaving Rome on January 10, 1766, Sterne traveled to Naples, where he remained until early March, and then returned, via Monte Cassino, to Rome, arriving on the ides of March. In early April he set out for France, spending some time wandering in the southern provinces in search of his wife and daughter, who had left Montauban; he eventually found them in

Franche Comté. During the course of May he spent a week in Dijon and arrived at Paris in the final week of that month. In Paris, he learned of the publication of Smollett's *Travels through France and Italy* and had firsthand experience of the French reaction. He finally returned to London in mid-June 1766, and may well have read there an anecdote in the *St. James's Chronicle*, supposedly about his time in Italy, which he would later include in *Tristram Shandy* (IX.24).

The Relationship of Sterne's Travels to *A Sentimental Journey*

The brief surveys presented above of Sterne's own travels are designed not to reinforce the view held by many of his biographers and critics that the fiction was based on actual experience, but, on the contrary, to emphasize just how very little of his own experience of traveling permeates *A Sentimental Journey*. Apart from the description of Dessein and the necessity to acquire a passport for travel in enemy territory, there is virtually nothing which necessarily derives from the two journeys. Indeed, it is notable how few of the places Sterne refers to in the *Journey* are to be found among those we know he visited. At the most extreme, he does not appear at any point to have come within 215 miles of Rennes, the location of the affecting story of the sword. Craufurd's anecdote could just as easily have been heard in England as in Paris; and the attempts of previous Sterne scholars to identify the original of the Marquesina di F*** seem to us to be almost willful in the turning of a blind eye to the clearly indecent implications of the asterisks. As evidence of an almost cavalier disregard of his surroundings, we may usefully draw attention to the description of Calais in *Tristram Shandy* (VII.5), where Sterne explicitly denies any personal knowledge of the town and resorts to copying out of a guidebook written by Piganiol de la Force (1724). This may be set alongside the indication cited above of his apparent lack of interest in what, for most other travelers, were the primary motives for visiting Florence. For the creative forces actually behind the *Journey* we need thus to consider those ideas that his writings reveal were uppermost in his mind during the final years of his life—writing a travelogue was definitely not one of those ideas.

Tristram Shandy and *A Sentimental Journey*

The ill health to which he refers in the loose-leaf advertisement to the *Journey* had plagued Sterne since his days at Cambridge. The motivation for his first continental tour had been to find a milder climate, and throughout that journey he had had several relapses: on May 10, 1762, for example, he wrote to Archbishop Drummond that he had had "a fever, which has ended the worst way it could for me, in a *defluxion Poitrine* as the french Physicians call it—it is generally fatal to weak

Lungs" (*Letters* 164); and six or seven weeks later, to his close friend John Hall-Stevenson, he disclosed an even more serious second episode, in which "I bled the bed full, and finding in the morning I was likely to bleed to death, I immediately sent for a surgeon" (*Letters* 180). This recurrent hemorrhaging from the lungs is generally accepted to be the driving force behind the flight from death so graphically described in volume VII of *Tristram Shandy,* some of which may have been written in France during his first sojourn there. In the Appendix we have provided an excerpt from the first chapter of that volume to illustrate this point.

When volumes VII and VIII of *Tristram Shandy* were published in January 1765, one of the most notable comments—by Ralph Griffiths in the *Monthly Review* (February 1765)—reechoed forcefully sentiments that had been expressed about earlier volumes:

> One of our gentlemen once remarked, in *print,* Mr. Shandy—that he thought your excellence lay in the PATHETIC. I think so too. In my opinion, the little story of Le Fevre has done you more honour than every thing else you have wrote, except your Sermons. Suppose you were to strike out a new plan? Give us none but amiable or worthy, or exemplary characters. . . . Paint Nature in her loveliest dress—her native simplicity. Draw natural scenes, and interesting situations—In fine, Mr. Shandy, do, for surely you can, excite our passions to *laudable* purposes—awake our affections, engage our hearts—arouze, transport, refine, improve us.

It is possible to see the *Journey* as Sterne's acquiescence to Griffiths' suggestions and a conscious switch to "sentimentalism" as a commercially attractive mode; on the other hand, it is just as easy to offer the counterargument—namely, that Sterne's employment of the pathetic was ironically manipulative. We have provided in the Appendix an extended excerpt from chapter 43 of volume VII of *Tristram Shandy,* in which the material describing the peasant dance conspicuously prefigures "The Grace" in the *Journey* (pp. 167–68) and allows the reader to consider the degree to which Sterne employs the ironic mode. What is undoubtedly true is that in volumes VII and VIII Sterne, for the first time, made fictional use of his travels, suggesting that he was already moving in a different direction. And this direction is reinforced by a letter written in July 1766 that claims, "I am in my peaceful retreat, writing the ninth volume of Tristram and shall publish but one this year, and the next I shall begin a new work of four volumes" (*Letters* 284). This new work is clearly the *Journey.*

The ninth volume of *Tristram Shandy,* published in January 1767, provides further light for our reading of the *Journey.* Three examples should demonstrate this. First, there is the sympathetic description of the "poor negro girl" that appears in the midst of a discussion of a courtship conducted while sausage-making (IX.7). Sterne, as so often happens, seems unwilling to separate serious topics from an inclination toward comic bawdiness; it is a hoary tradition, with roots in the classical writings of Petronius and Lucian, and branches in Chaucer, Rabelais, Cervantes, and Swift, among many others. Second, it may be argued that the pervasive topic of volume IX is "love"—as in the relationships of Trim's brother and the Jew's widow, Trim himself and Bridget, Toby and the Widow Wadman, and, significantly, Tristram and Jenny. Love, and especially its physical manifestations, is, for Sterne, an essential motivating force, as will be seen in his relationship with Eliza Draper, discussed below. Thirdly, and possibly more precisely demonstrable, there is in volume IX a preview of the *Journey* in the account of Tristram's meeting with Maria, the forsaken maid driven mad by an unfaithful lover; a lengthy excerpt from the relevant chapter is provided for comparison in the Appendix. There are some minor improvements—the pet goat is replaced by the faithful Sylvio (although see our annotations to this passage for the possibility of parodic intent). The detail perhaps most important to notice, however, is that in *Tristram Shandy* the chapter begins with an invocation to "the easy pen of my beloved CER-VANTES," and we would wish to argue that the cervantick tone is as good a candidate for the guiding muse of *A Sentimental Journey* as any, and that no word better defines Sterne's affair with Eliza Draper than *quixotic*.

The Importance of Sterne's Sermons

Having returned to London to see volumes VII and VIII of *Tristram Shandy* through the press, Sterne decided to edit two more volumes of his sermons, which he published in January 1766. It is necessary to keep in mind that Sterne was a clergyman who took his vocation seriously, as may be seen both from his detailed responses to Archbishop Herring's Visitation queries in 1743[5] and from his extant sermons. We have therefore included in our Appendix lengthy extracts from three of Sterne's sermons: "Philanthropy recommended" (vol. I, 1760), "The prodigal son" (vol. III, 1766), and "Our conversation in heaven" (vol. V, 1769 [published posthumously]), all of which, although probably written many years earlier, may be seen as providing important glosses on *A Sentimental Journey*. Perhaps the most obvious in this regard is "The prodigal son," taken from the volume that Sterne was actively editing when he first seems to have thought seriously about what was to become the *Journey*. This sermon is a celebration of the affective Christianity (in recounting the joy that greets the homecoming of the prodigal) that resonates throughout the *Journey*: "When the affections so kindly break loose, Joy, is another name for Religion. . . . Was it not for this that GOD gave man musick to strike upon the kindly passions; that nature taught the feet to dance to its movements" (*Sermons* 4:190–91).[6] Moreover, the concluding comments in this sermon (probably added during his editing in 1765) may be

---

[5] S. L. Ollard and P. C. Walker, "Archbishop Herring's Visitation Returns, 1743"; reprinted in *Letters,* 21–22.

[6] Melvyn New, ed., *The Sermons of Laurence Sterne,* Volume 4 of the *University of Florida Press Edition of the Works of Sterne* (Gainesville: University Press of Florida, 1996).

seen as contributing to contemporary discussions of travel—and may be directly compared with the opening remarks of the *Journey*—but may equally be taken as an expression of Sterne's traditional Christian view that the full experience of life, properly considered, is a "joyous gift from God": "this desire for travelling . . . is no way bad,——but as others are,——in it's mismanagement or excess;—— order it rightly the advantages are worth the pursuit; the chief of which are—— to learn the languages, the laws and customs, and understand the government and interest of other nations,——to acquire an urbanity and confidence of behaviour, and fit the mind more easily for conversation and discourse . . . by tasting perpetually the varieties of nature, to know what *is good*——by observing the address and arts of men, to conceive what *is sincere,*——and by seeing the difference of so many various humours and manners,——to look into ourselves and form our own" (4:192).

Literary Influences

It can be claimed that the *Journey* has as a major influence Tobias Smollett's notably splenetic *Travels through France and Italy* (1766), and that in the voice of Yorick, Sterne created a response to the voice of Smollett, whom he had met in Montpellier in 1763 and whose work was being debated in Paris during his May 1766 visit. We have tried to indicate in the notes all points of intersection between the two works. In contrast to *Tristram Shandy,* where there are many examples of direct verbal borrowing from a wide range of texts, in the *Journey* such a compositional device is relatively infrequent. There are clear allusions to Shakespeare, and there are a few individual borrowings from Robert Burton's *Anatomy of Melancholy* (1621), Montaigne's *Essays* (1580, 1588), transmuted though Charron's *Of Wisdome* (1612), *Don Quixote* (1605, 1615), and Bishop Joseph Hall (1574–1656), but some of the major sources of *Tristram Shandy*— Rabelais, Chambers' *Cyclopaedia*, and Tindal's *History of England*—are conspicuous in their absence. We have indicated Sterne's indebtedness to the first critic of John Locke's *Essay Concerning Human Understanding,* John Norris of Bemerton (1657–1711), whose influence on Sterne has only recently begun to be explored.

Continuation of the Bramine's Journal

Sterne and Eliza

The genesis of *A Sentimental Journey* is intertwined not only with the sermons and the final volumes of *Tristram Shandy,* but also with the writing of *Continuation of the Bramine's Journal,* which overlapped the writing of the *Journey.* A matter of weeks before the final volume of *Tristram Shandy* appeared in January 1767, Sterne made the acquaintance of Commodore William James and his wife, Anne, in London. James was the retired commander-in-chief of the East India Company's marine forces and had retired to London in 1759, where he had married in 1765 the daughter of another East India Company official. Their house became a center for Company officials on leave, and there Sterne met Eliza Draper, née Sclater, a twenty-two-year-old married mother, who had sailed to England in 1763 with her husband and children for the benefit of Mr. Draper's health and was now preparing to rejoin him in Bombay, since he had returned the year before.

Born in India in 1744, Eliza Sclater had been educated in England but had returned to the subcontinent to marry the thirty-nine-year-old Daniel Draper when she was fourteen. Though by modern standards this is rather young, it was not at all uncommon: in 1760 Eliza's sister Mary, also at the age of fourteen, married Rawson Hart Boddam, who subsequently became Governor of Bombay. However, the Draper marriage does not appear to have been happy: Cash records that Daniel Draper was "exceedingly ugly, as we know from an existing portrait, and a man who knew nothing of the world except the colonial service to which he had been born" (*LY* 271–72). Eventually Eliza left him, but not until five years after Sterne's death. When Sterne first met her, in late January or early February 1767, Eliza Draper had only a few months left with her children in London, a city she seems to have loved, before returning to India and her husband, neither of which ranked high in her affections. She was in a vulnerable state. Sterne, temporarily alone (Mrs. Sterne and daughter Lydia were in France) and permanently ill, was equally vulnerable, and especially to a woman's attentions, as indeed he seems to have been for much of his life.

As is clear from the opening chapters of the *Journey,* Sterne had a penchant for parading both his vulnerabilities and his affections, and this flamboyant behavior contributed to the cottage industry that grew up after his death and produced a stream of letters claiming to be authentic remains of the correspondence between Yorick and Eliza. Among these forgeries and pastiches, there are a few genuine pieces. In 1773 appeared ten letters from Sterne under the title *Letters from Yorick to Eliza,* which Curtis argues to be the only certifiably authentic remains of their exchanges.[7] Dated in the weeks just before he started the *Bramine's Journal* and *A Sentimental Journey,* the ten letters give a useful portrait of Sterne's state of mind at the time, and we have provided excerpts from two of them in the Appendix. They reinforce the notion that Sterne was disposed to be passionately in love, and that he tended to fantasize about Eliza as his muse: "Was your husband in England, I wou'd freely give him £500 (if money cou'd purchase the acquisition) to let you only sit by me two hours in the day, while I wrote my sentimental journey—I am sure the work wou'd sell so much the better for it" (Appendix, pp. 251). When he came to draft an exculpatory letter to Daniel Draper, however, Sterne appears to have had some difficulty in describing the relationship: "I <am> fell <really dear

[7] Melvyn New and Peter de Voogd, eds., "The 1773 Edition of *Letters from Yorick to Eliza:* A Facsimile," *Shandean* 15 (2004): 79–105.

Sir> in Love with y^r Wife—but tis a Love, You would honour me for—for tis so like that I bear my own daughter who is a good creature, that I <can> scarse distinguish a difference between it" (*Letters* 349; pointed brackets mark deletions); fortunately, the letter does not appear ever to have been sent.

Primarily from the evidence provided by Sterne's ten letters to Eliza, Cash has reconstructed the generation of the *Bramine's Journal.* Early in their acquaintance they agreed to keep echoing journals. Sterne's first installment was sent to Eliza in March, when her ship was at anchor—an inference based on the claim, "I began a new journal this morning" (*Yorick to Eliza* 25). Several weeks later in the first entry of *Bramine's Journal,* he tells Eliza that he is sending her a second part—"the Journal kept from the day we parted" (*BJ* 177). Thus, Cash concludes, the *Continuation* here printed is the third part. It opens with an entry dated Sunday, April 13, which is a misdate; in 1767 April 13 fell on a Monday. Entries are regular until mid-July when Sterne appears to have rejoined his friends in the Yorkshire social scene. There is a gap between July 19 and 27, the latter date being the day when he writes that he has received from Eliza a packet of letters she dispatched from the Cape Verde Islands.

Up to this point in the *Journal,* it has been noticeable that Sterne always assumes his anguish over their separation is being exactly mirrored by Eliza, so that his reticence in describing the contents of her epistles as "the most interesting Acc^t" (*BJ* 228) is telling. Five days later he seems to have received a second packet of letters, conveyed by a Dutch vessel that had crossed paths with Eliza's ship, and abruptly on August 4 the journal stops, with the claim that Sterne is occupied by the imminent arrival of his wife and daughter, though, in fact, they were not expected for another month. There is one final entry, dated November 1. We assume that whatever Eliza had written, it did not match Sterne's expectations of mirrored anguish, and that his *Journal* remark, that her counterpart journal is "worth reading" (*BJ* 176) is a compliment so cool as to be a mere cover for a document he could not bring himself to destroy, but which, equally, he could no longer bring himself to continue.

Continuation of the Bramine's Journal: The History of the Manuscript

The whereabouts of the manuscript of *Continuation of the Bramine's Journal* immediately after Sterne's death are unknown, and the possibility of his daughter, Lydia, having access to it while she prepared her 1775 edition of his *Letters* has divided Sterne scholars, including the current editors. Curtis (*Letters* 12–16) maintains that she not only saw the manuscript but also used it to fabricate at least one of the letters Sterne supposedly wrote to his wife in their courtship year (1740–1741); Cash (*EMY* 81–82) disagrees, and tentatively suggests a more complicated alternative: that Lydia copied a letter to Eliza, which Sterne had written simultaneously with the *Journal*, altered the date, readdressed it, and then destroyed the letter. There are further possible explanations—including Sterne's apparent penchant for recycling earlier letters, a practice he perhaps parodies in La Fleur's all-purpose love letter (*ASJ* 67–8)—but the matter will almost certainly remain undecided. What is known is that the manuscript was effectively lost until well into the nineteenth century, when an eleven-year-old boy, Thomas Washbourne Gibbs, while playing in a storeroom used by his family to store wastepaper "to cut up into spills to light candles with," had the preternatural presence of mind to rescue the manuscript because he had recognized Sterne's name. Some years later he rather less presciently lent the manuscript to William Makepeace Thackeray, who, in his 1851 lecture on Sterne (published in *English Humorists* [1853]) delivered what Cash rightly calls the first of a series of "vicious and unscholarly" attacks based on his archetypical Victorian response to the *Journal* (*LY* 284, n. 68).[8] The manuscript was bequeathed by Gibbs to the British Museum (now the British Library) and deposited in 1894. The name "Journal to Eliza" appears to have been first bestowed on this work by Wilbur Cross in his 1904 edition, with the explicit intention of suggesting a parallel with Swift's *Journal to Stella*. We believe this analogy to be highly misleading and have reverted to Sterne's own title.

A Sentimental Journey: The Copy-Text

Our copy-text is the first edition, published in London by T. Becket and P. A. Dehondt. Twenty-five hundred copies were printed in the same small octavo format (cut size, approximately 95 x 150 mm.) used for *Tristram Shandy* and the first four volumes of Sterne's sermons. A further 150 copies were printed, principally for the 105 subscribers who had opted for a total of 135 copies of what had been advertised as "imperial" copies, on a slightly larger sheet (cut size, approximately 105 x 175 mm., and with uncut copies recorded up to 180 mm. in height). We have had access to copies in both formats, and have collated them; we have also collated the first edition with the second edition (March 1768), and a new (third) edition (July–August, 1768). Further complications arise as a result of the fact that the two volumes of the *Journey* were printed by different printers: the first, by William Strahan, whose ledgers provide valuable details; and the second, by an unknown printer who was rather less accurate in composition. Those readers—and especially those scholars—who wish to be informed of all emendations, sub-

---

[8] Thackeray likely committed a cardinal scholarly sin by placing "x" marks (and perhaps underscorings and marginal brackets as well) at certain places in the manuscript to express his shocked outrage. We would, at any rate, like to believe these are Thackeray's marks, if only to lay blame where it gives satisfaction to do so. We have retained these superscript "x" marks in our text so that readers can perhaps discover another—and better—explanation of their existence.

stantive and accidental variants, line-end hyphenations, and the like, are strongly recommended to consult and cite the scholarly Florida Edition (volume 6 of the *Works of Sterne*),[9] rather than a textbook edition.

The holograph manuscript used by the compositor of volume I has survived and is held in the British Library (Egerton MS. 1610); a second manuscript in two hands (neither of them Sterne's) is to be found in the J. Pierpont Morgan Library (MA 1046–47). These manuscripts have also been collated and a full discussion is to be found in the Florida Edition.

Continuation of the Bramine's Journal: The Copy-Text

Sterne's holograph manuscript of *Bramine's Journal,* which is the copy-text for this edition, is held in the British Library (Add. MSS. 34527), and is made up of thirty-nine leaves (319 x 200 mm.) and a fragment at the end containing the final six words of the journal. We have opted to publish a clean text and have recorded a few interesting insertions, rewritings, and erasures in the footnotes, which we hope will encourage those interested in Sterne's process of composition, perhaps nowhere more on display than in this daily journal-keeping, to consult the full record in the Florida Edition. We have tried to record as faithfully as possible Sterne's accidentals, including his occasional lowercase letters at the beginning of sentences and much of his erratic punctuation, including the handwritten dashes of varying length. Superscript abbreviations have been retained, though the period often placed under the superscript letter(s) has been silently removed, because it is likely to lead the modern reader into assuming it to be a closing period. Datings have not been normalized, and we have, following Sterne's practice, treated the line after a date as a slash rather than underscoring. On those occasions where Sterne has left a gap in the manuscript, indicative either of a break in his thought or in the actual time of writing, we have also left a gap. Again, as with *A Sentimental Journey,* readers who wish to explore further the ramifications of the deletions and insertions in the copy-text are strongly advised to consult the extensive bibliographical appendixes to be found in volume 6 of the Florida Edition.

The Annotations

The annotations are designed to elucidate rather than interpret. Readers will notice that both in this introduction and in our notes we have eschewed any

---

[9] Melvyn New and W. G. Day, eds., *A Sentimental Journey through France and Italy* and *Continuation of Bramine's Journal,* Volume 6 of the *University of Florida Press Edition of the Works of Sterne* (Gainesville: University Press of Florida, 2002).

extended discussion of what are perceived as keywords—"sentiment," "sensibility," "sensation," "feeling," and the like—words that are conventionally discussed at some length in trade editions of *A Sentimental Journey.* There is an extensive and thoughtful literature on these topics, and we have included those titles we regard as the most useful in the list of further reading. As these words are so pervasive in the eighteenth century, any study of, say, "sentimental," inevitably becomes a study of the century rather than of the particular text. Within the necessarily limited space of this Introduction we have therefore opted to provide a survey of the history and composition of these two texts; and in the annotations we have addressed the notion of "sentimental" and its many associated ideas as localized and text-derived issues, with no attempt to offer a unified perception of Sterne's contribution to the ongoing debates, much less a unified theory of eighteenth-century sentimentalism.

SUGGESTED ADDITIONAL READING

The most complete edition of *A Sentimental Journey* and *Bramine's Journal*, including extensive textual commentary and annotative materials, is volume 6 (2002) of the *University of Florida Press Edition of the Works of Laurence Sterne*, upon which this present edition is based. Sterne's other writings comprise the earlier volumes of the *Florida Edition*, volumes 1–3 (1978, 1984) containing the text and annotations for *Tristram Shandy*, and volumes 4–5 (1996), the text and annotations for *Sermons*. The Penguin Classics edition of *Tristram Shandy* (1997, reprint ed., 2003) is based on the *Florida Edition*. Much useful information about Laurence Sterne and his writings can be found in *The Shandean: The Annual of the Laurence Sterne Trust*, which began publication in 1989. Since 1986, *The Scriblerian* has included reviews of almost every essay and monograph published about Sterne. The *New Dictionary of National Biography* (2004–2005) contains an entry on Sterne's life and writings by Melvyn New, encapsulating Arthur H. Cash's invaluable biographical study, *Laurence Sterne: The Early and Middle Years* (Methuen, 1975) and *Laurence Sterne: The Later Years* (Methuen, 1986). For Sterne's correspondence see Lewis Perry Curtis, *Letters of Laurence Sterne* (Oxford: Clarendon, 1935); a new edition, volumes 7 and 8 of the *Florida Edition*, is in preparation. Among the many collections of essays on Sterne, see *Critical Essays on Laurence Sterne*, ed. Melvyn New (New York: G. K. Hall, 1998) and *Laurence Sterne* (Longman Critical Readers), ed. Marcus Walsh (London: Longman, 2002).

Barker-Benfield, G. J. *The Culture of Sensibility: Sex and Society in Eighteenth-Century Britain* (Chicago: U of Chicago P, 1992).

Battestin, Martin C. "Sterne among the *Philosophes*: Body and Soul in *A Sentimental Journey*," *ECF* 7 (1994):17–36.

Brissenden, R. F. *Virtue in Distress: Studies in the Novel of Sentiment from Richardson to Sade* (London: Macmillan, 1974).

Cash, Arthur H. *Sterne's Comedy of Moral Sentiments: The Ethical Dimension of the "Journey"* (Pittsburgh: Duquesne UP, 1966).

———. "Sterne, Hall, Libertinism, and *A Sentimental Journey*," *Age of Johnson* 12 (2001):291–327.

Chadwick, Joseph. "Infinite Jest: Interpretation in Sterne's *A Sentimental Journey*," *ECS* 12 (1978):190–205.

Descargues, Madeleine. "*A Sentimental Journey*, or 'The Case of (In)delicacy,'" *Critical Essays on Laurence Sterne*, 243–53.

Dussinger, John A. "Yorick and the 'Eternal Fountain of our Feelings,'" *Psychology and Literature in the Eighteenth Century,* ed. C. Fox (New York: AMS, 1987), 259–76.

Ellis, Markman. *The Politics of Sensibility: Race, Gender, and Commerce in the Sentimental Novel* (Cambridge: Cambridge UP, 1996).

Franssen, Paul. "'Great Lessons of Political Instruction': The Earl of Clonmell Reads Sterne," *Shandean* 2 (1990):152–201.

Gerard, W. B. "Benevolent Vision: The Ideology of Sentimentality in Contemporary Illustrations of *A Sentimental Journey* and *The Man of Feeling,*" *ECF* 14 (2002):533–74.

Howes, Alan B. *Laurence Sterne: The Critical Heritage* (London: Routledge, 1974).

Keymer, Tom. *Sterne, The Moderns, and the Novel* (Oxford: Oxford UP, 2002).

Kraft, Elizabeth. *Laurence Sterne Revisited* (New York: Twayne, 1996).

———. "The Pentecostal Moment in *A Sentimental Journey,*" *Critical Essays on Laurence Sterne,* 292–310.

Lamb, Jonathan. "Language and Hartleian Associationism in *A Sentimental Journey,*" *ECS* 13 (1980):285–312.

Loveridge, Mark. *Laurence Sterne and the Argument about Design* (Totowa, N.J.: Barnes and Noble, 1982).

Markley, Robert. "Sentimentality as Performance: Shaftesbury, Sterne, and the Theatrics of Virtue," *The New Eighteenth Century,* ed. F. Nussbaum and L. Brown (London: Methuen, 1987), 210–30; reprinted in *Critical Essays on Laurence Sterne,* 270–91.

Mullan, John. *Sentiment and Sociability: The Language of Feeling in the Eighteenth Century* (Oxford: Clarendon, 1988).

New, Melvyn. "Proust's Influence on Sterne: Remembrance of Things to Come," *MLN* 103 (1988):1031–55; reprinted in *Critical Essays on Laurence Sterne,* 177–97.

———. "Job's Wife and Sterne's Other Women," *Out of Bounds: Male Writers and Gender(ed) Criticism,* ed. L. Claridge and E. Langland (Amherst, Mass.: U of Massachusetts P, 1990), 55–74; reprinted in *Laurence Sterne* (Longman), 69–90.

———. "The Odd Couple: Laurence Sterne and John Norris of Bemerton," *PQ* 75 (1996):361–85.

———. "Reading Sterne through Proust and Levinas," *Age of Johnson* 12 (2001):329–60; reprinted in *In Proximity: Emmanuel Levinas and the Eighteenth Century,* ed. M. New, et al. (Lubbock: Texas Tech UP, 2001), 111–40.

Parnell, Tim. "A Story Painted to the Heart? *Tristram Shandy* and Sentimentalism Reconsidered," *Shandean* 9 (1997):122–35.

Pfister, Manfred. *Laurence Sterne.* "British Writers and their Work" (Horndon, Devon: Northcote House, 2001).

Putney, Rufus. "The Evolution of *A Sentimental Journey,*" *PQ* 19 (1940):349–67.

Seidel, Michael. "Narrative Crossings: Sterne's *A Sentimental Journey,*" *Genre* 18 (1985):1–22.

Tadié, Alexis. " *Translating* French Looks and Attitudes into Plain English: The Language of Gestures in Laurence Sterne's *A Sentimental Journey,*" *BSEAA* 38 (1994):217–32.

Van Sant, Ann Jessie. *Eighteenth-Century Sensibility and the Novel: The Senses in Social Context* (Cambridge: Cambridge U P, 1993).

Wehrs, Donald R. "Levinas and Sterne: From the Ethics of the Face to the Aesthetics of Unrepresentability," *Critical Essays on Laurence Sterne,* 311–29; reprinted in *In Proximity: Emmanuel Levinas and the Eighteenth Century,* 141–65.

KEY TO SHORT TITLES IN THE NOTES

All journals are abbreviated as in the *PMLA* Bibliography. Classical quotations and translations are taken from the Loeb Classical Library, Harvard UP, unless otherwise indicated. Shakespeare is quoted from *The Riverside Shakespeare,* ed. G. Blakemore Evans, et al. (Houghton Mifflin, 1974). Scripture is quoted from the King James Version.

Footnotes are numbered consecutively within each chapter of *A Sentimental Journey;* and consecutively for each month of *Bramine's Journal,* with the few additional entries after July 31 numbered with that month. An italic question mark before a word or words indicates a conjectural alternative reading. The place of publication before 1800 is understood to be London, unless otherwise indicated. Assertion that a phrase is "proverbial" is based on its appearance in *The Oxford Dictionary of English Proverbs,* 3d ed. rev. F. P. Wilson (1970) or Morris Palmer Tilley, *A Dictionary of the Proverbs in England in the Sixteenth and Seventeenth Centuries* (Ann Arbor: U of Michigan P, 1950).

This edition is based on the text and annotations in volume 6 of the *Florida Edition of the Works of Laurence Sterne,* ed. Melvyn New and W. G. Day (Gainesville: UP of Florida, 2002); as our notes make clear, we are particularly indebted to the scholarly edition edited by Gardner D. Stout, Jr. (Berkeley: U of California P, 1967).

Sterne's other writings are cited from volumes 1–5 of the *Florida Edition.* For *Tristram Shandy,* indicated by *TS,* reference is to volume, chapter, and page number (e.g., VII.7.777), ed. Melvyn New and Joan New (1978). For the annotations to *Tristram Shandy,* the notes refer to volume 3, ed. Melvyn New, with Richard A. Davies and W. G. Day (1984). For Sterne's sermons, reference is to title and consecutive number, 1–45, in *Sermons,* volume 4, and for the annotations to the sermons, volume 5, ed. Melvyn New (1996). Sterne's letters are quoted from the valuable edition of Lewis Perry Curtis (Oxford: Clarendon, 1935), cited as *Letters.* Other works often referred to have been given short titles as follows:

Cash, *EMY*	Arthur H. Cash, *Laurence Sterne: The Early and Middle Years* (London: Methuen, 1975).
Cash, *LY*	Arthur H. Cash, *Laurence Sterne: The Later Years* (London: Methuen, 1986).
Cervantes	Miguel de Cervantes, *Don Quixote,* tr. Peter Motteux, rev. John Ozell, 7th ed., 4 vols. (1743).

Cole, *Journal*

Rev. William Cole, *A Journal of My Journey to Paris in the Year 1765,* ed. Francis G. Stokes (London: Constable, 1931).

Cross, *Life*

Wilbur L. Cross, *The Life and Times of Laurence Sterne,* 3d ed. (New Haven: Yale UP, 1929).

Cross, *Works*

Wilbur L. Cross, ed., *Works of Laurence Sterne,* 12 vols. (New York: J. F. Taylor, 1904).

Cunnington

C. Willett Cunnington and Phillis Cunnington, *Handbook of English Costume in the Eighteenth Century* (Boston: Plays, 1972).

Franssen

Paul Franssen, "'Great Lessons of Political Instruction': The Earl of Clonmell Reads Sterne," *Shandean* 2 (1990):152–201.

Goring

Paul Goring, ed., *A Sentimental Journey* (London: Penguin, 2001).

Johnson, *Dictionary*

Samuel Johnson, *A Dictionary of the English Language,* 2 vols. (1755).

Keymer

Tom Keymer, ed., *A Sentimental Journey and Other Writings* (London: Everyman, 1994).

Le Roux

Philibert Joseph Le Roux, *Dictionnaire comique, satyrique, critique, burlesque, libre et proverbial* (Paris, 1718).

OED

The Oxford English Dictionary (Oxford: Oxford UP, 1992).

Parnell

Ian Jack and Tim Parnell, eds., *A Sentimental Journey and Other Writings* (Oxford: Oxford UP, 2003).

Smollett, *Travels*

Tobias Smollett, *Travels through France and Italy,* 2 vols. (1766).

A

SENTIMENTAL JOURNEY

THROUGH

FRANCE AND ITALY.

BY

MR. YORICK.

VOL. I.

LONDON:

Printed for T. BECKET and P. A. DE HONDT,
in the Strand. MDCCLXVIII.

A
SENTIMENTAL JOURNEY,
&c. &c.

_____T HEY order, said I, this matter better in France—[1]

—You have been in France? said my gentleman, turning quick upon me with the most civil triumph in the world.—Strange! quoth I, debating the matter with myself, That one and twenty miles sailing, for 'tis absolutely no further from Dover to Calais, should give a man these rights—I'll look into them: so giving up the argument—I went straight to my lodgings, put up half a dozen shirts and a black pair of silk breeches[2]—"the coat I have on, said I, looking at the sleeve, will do"—took a place in the Dover stage; and the packet sailing at nine the next morning—by three I had got sat down to my dinner upon a fricassee'd chicken[3] so incontestably in France, that had I died that night of an indigestion, the whole world could not have suspended the effects of the *_Droits d'aubaine_[4]— my shirts, and black pair of silk breeches—portmanteau and all must have gone

---

*All the effects of strangers (Swiss and Scotch excepted) dying in France, are seized by virtue of this law, tho' the heir be upon the spot——the profit of these contingencies being farm'd,[5] there is no redress.

---

[1] Martin C. Battestin, "Sterne Among the _Philosophes_: Body and Soul in _A Sentimental Journey_," _ECF_ 7 (1994):17–36, argues that Sterne is setting out to investigate the materialistic thinking of the _philosophes_. Cf. Michael Seidel, "Narrative Crossings: Sterne's _A Sentimental Journey_," _Genre_ 18 (1985):2: "Any reader so 'obtuse' as to try to gauge the zero degree point of Sterne's precise narrative angle into France—what exactly it is that is better ordered—has indeed come in too late . . . ."

[2] Cf. _TS,_ IX.24.780, where Tristram also travels with only six shirts; and "Slawkenbergius's Tale," where Don Diego, a most sentimental traveler, has nothing in his cloak-bag but "two shirts—a crimson-sattin pair of breeches, and a fringed—Dear Julia!" (IV.S.T.300).

[3] The fricassees and ragouts of French cuisine were deplored by the English, who favored roast beef; Sterne had mocked the French diet in _TS,_ VII.17.599–600: "Ho! 'tis the time of sallads.——O rare! sallad and soup—soup and sallad—sallad and soup, _encore._"

[4] I.e., in English law, the right to take property subject to escheat. Smollett recorded his view of the French law in similar language: "If a foreigner dies in France, the king seizes all his effects, even though his heir should be upon the spot; and this tyranny is called the _droit d'aubaine_" (_Travels,_ letter 2, 1:16). In 1766, William Cole censured the practice (_Journal_ 83–4) as "sufficient to stigmatize them for greater Barbarians & more inhospitable Savages than any of their Neighbours."

[5] French tax collectors were called _fermiers généraux_ (farmers-general), and hence "farmers" of taxes.

to the King of France[6]—even the little picture which I have so long worn, and so often have told thee, Eliza, I would carry with me into my grave, would have been torn from my neck.[7]—Ungenerous!—to seize upon the wreck of an unwary passenger, whom your subjects had beckon'd to their coast—by heaven! SIRE, it is not well done; and much does it grieve me, 'tis the monarch of a people so civilized and courteous, and so renown'd for sentiment and fine feelings, that I have to reason with——

But I have scarce set foot in your dominions——

---

[6] Louis XV (1710–1774), great-grandson of Louis XIV. Complaints about French taxes on travelers were commonplace, but Sterne had a real experience with the *droit d'aubaine* while living in Toulouse in 1763. Cash, *LY*, 161–62, records Sterne's defiance of the demand on the death of a young acquaintance, George Oswald, and his ultimate success; see also Archibald Bolling Shepperson, "Yorick as Ministering Angel," *VQR* 30 (1954):54–66; and Peter de Voogd, "The Oswald Papers," *Shandean* 10 (1998):80–91.

[7] Cf. *BJ* (June 13): "L[d] Spencer has loaded me with a grand Ecritoire of 40 Guineas—I am to recieve . . . a gold Snuff Box . . .—I have a present of a portrait, (which by the by, I have immortalized in my Sentimental Journey) worth them both . . ."; and *BJ* (June 17): "I have brought y[r] name *Eliza!* and Picture into my work—where they will remain—when You & I are at rest for ever—Some Annotator or explainer of my works in this place will take occasion, to speak of the Friendship w[ch] Subsisted so long & faithfully betwixt Yorick & the Lady he speaks of . . . ."

For Sterne's relationship with Elizabeth Sclater Draper (1744–1778), see Introduction (pp. xiii–xv). Sterne mentions this miniature portrait of Eliza on numerous occasions in *BJ*; e.g., on April 16 and again on April 25. Its whereabouts is unknown, but see Appendix (pp. 249–51), Sterne's letter to Eliza.

Sterne was in the habit of showing Eliza's portrait to his acquaintances, including Lady Spencer (*BJ* May 16), the Demoniacs (*BJ* June 26, July 13), and, surprisingly, to the Archbishop of York, Robert Hay Drummond, and his wife (*BJ* May 23).

Eliza's own words (April 15, 1772) suggest that Sterne was perhaps not singular in admiring her appearance: "I am a good deal altered . . . since you used to view me . . . but, my Head and Heart, if Self Love does not mislead me, are both much improved and the Qualities of Reflection and tenderness, are no bad substitutes for that clearness of Complection, and Je-ne-scai-quoi Air, which my flatterers used to say entitled me to the Apellation of Belle Indian" (Cross, *Journal,* in *Works,* 188).

CALAIS.

WHEN I had finish'd my dinner, and drank the King of France's health,[1] to satisfy my mind that I bore him no spleen, but, on the contrary, high honour for the humanity of his temper—I rose up an inch taller for the accommodation.

—No—said I—the Bourbon is by no means a cruel race: they may be misled like other people; but there is a mildness in their blood. As I acknowledged this, I felt a suffusion of a finer kind upon my cheek—more warm and friendly to man, than what Burgundy (at least of two livres a bottle, which was such as I had been drinking) could have produced.

—Just God! said I, kicking my portmanteau aside, what is there in this world's goods which should sharpen our spirits, and make so many kind-hearted brethren of us, fall out so cruelly as we do by the way?

When man is at peace with man, how much lighter than a feather is the heaviest of metals in his hand! he pulls out his purse, and holding it airily and uncompress'd, looks round him, as if he sought for an object to share it with—In doing this, I felt every vessel in my frame dilate—the arteries beat all chearily together, and every power which sustained life, perform'd it with so little friction, that 'twould have confounded the most *physical precieuse*[2] in France: with all her materialism, she could scarce have called me a machine—[3]

I'm confident, said I to myself, I should have overset her creed.

---

[1] Cf. Philip Thicknesse, *Useful Hints to Those Who Make the Tour of France* (1768), 283: "The king's health is never drank in France, nor is it deemed polite for a stranger to drink it. To Frenchmen it is very unusual, or rather wrong, to drink the health of any person, male or female."

[2] The original *précieuses* were associated with Madame de Rambouillet (1588–1665), Madame de Sévigné (1626–1696), and Madeleine de Scudéry (1607–1701), and immortalized by Molière in *Les précieuses ridicules* (1659); Keymer, 151, notes that the play had recently been translated by Samuel Foote as *The Conceited Ladies* (1762). Sterne, however, is probably thinking more of eighteenth-century descendants of the original *précieuses* — those associated with the Encyclopédists, and—given the adjective "*physical*"—with Julien Offray de La Mettrie (1709–1751), author of *L'homme machine* (1747), the epitome of mechanistic theorizing in the century.

[3] Stout, 68–69, quotes at length from sermon 5 ("The case of Elijah and the widow of Zerephath") to reinforce his consideration of this passage as "a characteristic expression of Sterne's belief in the interaction of benevolence and physical well-being": "one might further maintain, exclusive of the happiness which the mind itself feels in the exercise of [charity], that the very body of man is never in a better state than when he is most inclined to do good offices . . . . What divines say of the mind, naturalists have observed of the body; that there is no passion so natural to it as love, which is the principle of doing good . . ." (*Sermons* 4:48–50). Cf. *TS*, III.4.189: "A Man's body and his mind, with the utmost reverence to both I speak it, are exactly like a jerkin, and a jerkin's lining;—rumple the one—you rumple the other"; and IX.13.764: "the soul and body are joint-sharers in every thing they get."

The accession of that idea, carried nature, at that time, as high as she could go—I was at peace with the world before, and this finish'd the treaty with myself—

—Now, was I a King of France, cried I—what a moment for an orphan to have begg'd his father's portmanteau of me!

Having established this homiletic context for the passage, it is noteworthy, on this first of many such occasions, that a quite different context is established by recalling Sterne's bawdiness in *TS;* "heaviest of metals in his hand," "his purse," which is pulled out and held "airily and uncompress'd," the desire to share it with "an object," the arteries beating and performing with "so little friction," as to "overset" the *précieuse,* and, finally, nature being carried "as high as she could go," all impregnate the moment with eroticism. In the ms. Sterne has "mettles," an interchangeable spelling, but one that more clearly points to innuendo, as in *TS,* IV.S.T.293.1–4. Eric Partridge lists *purse* as colloquial for "scrotum" and "female pudend" (*A Dictionary of Slang and Unconventional English,* ed. Paul Beale [New York: Macmillan, 1984]).

THE MONK.
CALAIS.

I HAD scarce utter'd the words, when a poor monk of the order of St. Francis[1] came into the room to beg something for his convent. No man cares to have his virtues the sport of contingencies—or one man may be generous, as another man is puissant—*sed non, quo ad hanc*[2]—or be it as it may—for there is no regular reasoning upon the ebbs and flows of our humours;[3] they may depend upon the same causes, for ought I know, which influence the tides themselves—'twould oft be no discredit to us, to suppose it was so: I'm sure at least for myself, that in many a case I should be more highly satisfied, to have it said by the world, "I had had an affair with the moon, in which there was neither sin nor shame," than have it pass altogether as my own act and deed, wherein there was so much of both.

—But be this as it may. The moment I cast my eyes upon him, I was predetermined not to give him a single sous; and accordingly I put my purse into my pocket—button'd it up—set myself a little more upon my centre, and advanced up gravely to him: there was something, I fear, forbidding in my look: I have his figure this moment before my eyes, and think there was that in it which deserved better.

The monk, as I judged from the break in his tonsure, a few scatter'd white hairs upon his temples, being all that remained of it, might be about seventy—but from his eyes, and that sort of fire which was in them, which seemed more temper'd by courtesy than years, could be no more than sixty—Truth might lie between—He was certainly sixty-five; and the general air of his countenance,

---

[1] Sterne establishes a certain closeness with his fellow-cleric by naming him Lorenzo, the Italian equivalent of his own name. Thomas Jefferson has an interesting comment on this episode in a letter dated 1771: "We neither know nor care whether [he] really went to France, whether he was there accosted by the poor Franciscan . . . or whether the whole be not a fiction. In either case we are equally sorrowful at the rebuke, and secretly resolve *we* will never do so: we are pleased with the subsequent atonement, and view with emulation a soul candidly acknowledging it's fault, and making a just reparation" (*The Papers of Thomas Jefferson*, ed. Julian P. Boyd [Princeton, N.J.: Princeton UP, 1950], 1:77). Jefferson famously labeled the "writings of Sterne" the "best course of morality that ever was written" (see *Writings*, ed. Merrill D. Peterson [New York: Library of America, 1984], 902).

[2] Sterne's Latin is puzzling, but seems to translate best as "but not so determined for that [reason or cause]," the intention of which is perhaps caught by "be it as it may."

[3] A commonplace in Sterne's writings, e.g., *TS,* II.17.164: "the ebbs and flows of his own passions"; VIII.11.669: "the passions . . . ebb and flow ten times in a minute"; *Sermons,* 4:37.1–2 (sermon 4, "Self knowledge"): "the various ebbs and flows of their passions and desires"; and *Letters,* 402: "we are all born with passions which ebb and flow."

notwithstanding something seem'd to have been planting wrinkles[4] in it before their time, agreed to the account.

It was one of those heads, which Guido[5] has often painted—mild, pale—penetrating, free from all common-place ideas of fat contented ignorance looking downwards upon the earth—it look'd forwards; but look'd, as if it look'd at something beyond this world. How one of his order came by it, heaven above, who let it fall upon a monk's shoulders, best knows: but it would have suited a Bramin,[6] and had I met it upon the plains of Indostan, I had reverenced it.

The rest of his outline may be given in a few strokes;[7] one might put it into the hands of any one to design, for 'twas neither elegant or otherwise, but as character and expression made it so: it was a thin, spare form, something above the common size, if it lost not the distinction by a bend forwards in the figure—but it was the attitude of Intreaty; and as it now stands presented to my imagination, it gain'd more than it lost by it.

When he had enter'd the room three paces, he stood still; and laying his left hand upon his breast, (a slender white staff with which he journey'd being in his right)—when I had got close up to him, he introduced himself with the little story of the wants of his convent, and the poverty of his order—and did it with so simple a grace—and such an air of deprecation was there in the whole cast of his look and figure—I was bewitch'd not to have been struck with it—

—A better reason was, I had predetermined not to give him a single sous.

---

[4] Cf. *Letters,* 321 (to Eliza, March 30, 1767): "May no anguish of heart plant a wrinkle upon thy face, till I behold it again!"

[5] Guido Reni (1575–1642), Italian painter. In Tristram's parody of the connoisseur (*TS,* III.12.214), the "airs of *Guido*" are noted. Cf. Roger de Piles, *The Art of Painting, and the Lives of the Painters . . . done from the French* (1706): "As for his *Heads,* they yield no manner of precedence to those of *Raphael,* either for Correctness of *Design,* or Delicacy of *Expression* . . ." (230). Sterne could have viewed at least thirteen Guidos when he visited the gallery of the Palais-Royal in 1762.

[6] The term looks in two directions, apropos of his affair with Eliza, alluding to his own priesthood (the Brahmins are the priestly caste among Hindus) and to Eliza's India connections. "Indostan" is Sterne's version of "Hindustan," usually thought of as the northern part of India. Keymer, 152, calls attention to the proverbial status of the Bramin as wise and austere, as in Pope's *Epistle to Bathurst* (1733), lines 185–86: "If Cotta liv'd on pulse, it was no more / Than Bramins, Saints, and Sages did before."

[7] This construction, with its reference to drawing or painting, is a favorite with Sterne for introducing characters; cf. *TS,* II.5.109: "I have but one more stroke to give to finish Corporal *Trim*'s character . . ."; II.9.121: "Such were the out-lines of Dr. *Slop*'s figure, which,—if you have read *Hogarth*'s analysis of beauty . . . you must know, may as certainly be. . . convey'd to the mind by three strokes as three hundred"; and II.12.131: "I could not give the reader this stroke in my uncle *Toby*'s picture."

THE MONK.
CALAIS.

— 'TIS very true, said I, replying to a cast upwards with his eyes, with which he had concluded his address—'tis very true—and heaven be their resource who have no other but the charity of the world, the stock of which, I fear, is no way sufficient for the many *great claims* which are hourly made upon it.

As I pronounced the words *great claims,* he gave a slight glance with his eye downwards upon the sleeve of his tunick—I felt the full force of the appeal—I acknowledge it, said I—a coarse habit, and that but once in three years, with meagre diet —are no great matters; and the true point of pity is, as they can be earn'd in the world with so little industry, that your order should wish to procure them by pressing upon a fund which is the property of the lame, the blind, the aged and the infirm[1]—the captive who lies down counting over and over again the days of his afflictions, languishes also for his share of it;[2] and had you been of the *order of mercy,*[3] instead of the order of St. Francis, poor as I am, continued I, pointing at my portmanteau, full chearfully should it have been open'd to you, for the ransom of the unfortunate—The monk made me a bow—but of all others, resumed I, the unfortunate of our own country, surely, have the first rights; and I have left thousands in distress upon our own shore—The monk gave a cordial wave with his head—as much as to say, No doubt, there is misery enough in every corner of the world, as well as within our convent—But we distinguish, said I, laying my hand upon the sleeve of his tunick, in return for his appeal—we distinguish, my good Father! betwixt those who wish only to eat the bread of their own labour—and those who eat the bread of other people's, and have no other plan in life, but to get through it in sloth and ignorance, *for the love of God.*[4]

---

[1] Cf. Luke 14:21: "bring in hither the poor, and the maimed, and the halt, and the blind."

[2] Cf., below, "The Captive," pp. 103–4.

[3] Cf. *TS,* V.1.412: "One denier, cried the order of mercy—one single denier, in behalf of a thousand patient captives, whose eyes look towards heaven and you for their redemption." Stout, 73, notes: "The Order of Our Lady of Mercy, founded in Spain, in 1218, to solicit funds for ransoming Christians captured by the Moors; the members were called Mercedarians (from Maria des Mercedes). A branch of the order was established for women in 1568."

[4] The opening sentence of this passage glances at Genesis 3:19: "In the sweat of thy face shalt thou eat bread." The final phrase translates "pour l'amour de Dieu," the standard accompaniment of an appeal for alms; cf. below, p. 52 and nn. 7, 9. Cf. John Moore, M.D., *A Journal During a Residence in France* (new corr. ed., 1794), 2:489: "I do not know whether it will be considered as a sign that a sense of religion is declining among the French, that the beggars in asking charity no longer add *pour l'amour de Dieu,* but instead of that, generally cry *Vive la nation* . . . ."

The poor Franciscan made no reply: a hectic[5] of a moment pass'd across his cheek, but could not tarry—Nature seemed to have had done with her resentments in him; he shewed none—but letting his staff fall within his arm, he press'd both his hands with resignation upon his breast, and retired.

Sterne's Anglican hostility to Roman Catholicism is evident throughout his sermons and *TS,* but nowhere more starkly than here, because Yorick's hostility is now contrasted to Sterne's quite sympathetic portrait of the monk; a greater toleration of a Catholic country and of Roman Catholicism is foreshadowed. His earlier position is epitomized by a sentence in sermon 6 ("Pharisee and publican in the temple"): "'Tis to be feared the buffooneries of the Romish church, bid fair to [bring about] . . . the disgrace and utter ruin of christianity wherever popery is established" (*Sermons* 4:64). Cf. sermon 19 ("Felix's behaviour towards Paul"): "Consider popery well; you will be convinced, that the truest definition which can be given of it, is,——That it is a pecuniary system, well contrived to operate upon men's passions and weakness, whilst their pockets are o'picking . . ." (4:184).

In *TS,* the anti-Catholicism is more humorous, but equally pervasive, from mockery of Dr. Slop, and numerous barbs against nuns and monks in "Slawkenbergius's Tale" (vol. IV), to the whirlwind tour of France (vol. VII), and the fair Beguine (vol. VIII). Most apropos to this passage is this comment on Walter Shandy (VII.27.619): "he hated a monk and the very smell of a monk worse than all the devils in hell."

[5] *OED*'s first example of a figurative use; s.v. B.b.3: "A hectic flush; *transf.* a flush or heightened colour on the cheek."

10

THE MONK.
CALAIS.

MY heart smote me the moment he shut the door—Psha! said I with an air of carelessness, three several times—but it would not do: every ungracious syllable I had utter'd, crouded back into my imagination: I reflected, I had no right over the poor Franciscan, but to deny him; and that the punishment of that was enough to the disappointed without the addition of unkind language—I consider'd his grey hairs—his courteous figure seem'd to re-enter and gently ask me what injury he had done me?—and why I could use him thus—I would have given twenty livres[1] for an advocate—I have behaved very ill; said I within myself; but I have only just set out upon my travels; and shall learn better manners as I get along.[2]

---

[1] The lowest denomination of French coin was the *denier,* three of which made one *liard;* four *liards* made a *sou;* twenty *sous* made one *livre* (roughly equivalent to ten pence in Sterne's day). Twenty-four *livres* equaled one *Louis d'or* (about one guinea). A crown (*ecu*) contained three *livres* (sometimes denominated a half-crown); a double crown, six (sometimes denominated a crown).

[2] The ethical implications of this passage are explored by Donald R. Wehrs, "Levinas and Sterne: From the Ethics of the Face to the Aesthetics of Unrepresentability," *Critical Essays on Laurence Sterne,* ed. Melvyn New (New York: G. K. Hall, 1998), 311–29.

THE DESOBLIGEANT.
CALAIS.

WHEN a man is discontented with himself, it has one advantage however, that it puts him into an excellent frame of mind for making a bargain. Now there being no travelling through France and Italy without a chaise[1]—and nature generally prompting us to the thing we are fittest for, I walk'd out into the coach yard to buy or hire something of that kind to my purpose: an old *Desobligeant[2] in the furthest corner of the court, hit my fancy at first sight, so I instantly got into it, and finding it in tolerable harmony with my feelings, I ordered the waiter to call Monsieur Dessein[3] the master of the hôtel—but Monsieur Dessein being gone to vespers, and not caring to face the Franciscan whom I saw on the opposite side of the court, in conference with a lady just arrived, at the inn—I drew the taffeta curtain betwixt us, and being determined to write my journey, I took out my pen and ink, and wrote the preface to it in the *Desobligeant.*

*A chaise, so called in France, from its holding but one person.

---

[1] Sterne made the same point to his wife as she was preparing to sail to Calais (May 31, 1762): "'Tis well I bought you a chaise—there is no getting one in Paris now, but at an enormous price—for they are all sent to the army, and such a one as yours we have not been able to match for forty guineas . . ." (*Letters* 171); see below, p. 38, n. 1.

[2] *OED* cites this passage as its first example. Stout (plate 5) provides an illustration and notes that "this type of chaise was apparently so called primarily because it was too narrow to hold two persons comfortably, and the occupant could not conveniently offer to accommodate another person" (76).

[3] Pierre Quillacq (1726–1793), *dit* Dessein (i.e., *design*). Cf. Stout, 87: "in 1762, the year of Yorick's *Journey* . . . Dessein was master of the Lyon d'Argent in Calais, and Sterne probably stopped there in January 1762 on his first trip to Paris" (cf. *Letters*, 177: "at Calais at the Lyon D'Argent—the master a Turk in grain"). This inn burned down in 1764, and when Sterne returned to Calais in October 1765, he stayed at Dessein's newly built Hôtel d'Angleterre.

On Dessein's fame (and fortune) after being immortalized by Sterne, cf. Frederic Reynolds's report of comments made by the innkeeper in 1782: "Your countryman, Monsieur Sterne, von great, von vary great man, and he carry me vid him to posterity. He gain moche money by his Journey of Sentiment—mais moi—I—make more through de means of dat, than he, by all his ouvrages reunies——Ha, ha!" (*Life and Times of Frederic Reynolds, Written by Himself* [London, 1826], 1:180).

PREFACE[1]
In the DESOBLIGEANT.

IT must have been observed by many a peripatetic philosopher,[2] That nature has set up by her own unquestionable authority certain boundaries and fences to circumscribe the discontent of man: she has effected her purpose in the quietest and easiest manner by laying him under almost insuperable obligations to work out his ease, and to sustain his sufferings at home. It is there only that she has provided him with the most suitable objects to partake of his happiness, and bear a part of that burden which in all countries and ages, has ever been too heavy for one pair of shoulders. 'Tis true we are endued with an imperfect power of spreading our happiness sometimes beyond *her* limits, but 'tis so ordered, that from the want of languages, connections, and dependencies, and from the difference in education, customs and habits, we lie under so many impediments in communicating our sensations out of our own sphere, as often amount to a total impossibility.

It will always follow from hence, that the balance of sentimental commerce[3] is always against the expatriated[4] adventurer: he must buy what he has little occasion for at their own price—his conversation[5] will seldom be taken in exchange for theirs without a large discount—and this, by the by, eternally driving him

---

[1] As Stout and others have noted, Sterne anticipates some of the observations here in both *TS* (where the "Author's Preface" appears in III.20, i.e., well into the second installment) and sermon 20, "The prodigal son" (Appendix, pp. 238–42). His ideas on travel may have derived from John Locke's *Some Thoughts Concerning Education* (1693) and Bishop Joseph Hall's *Quo Vadis?* (1617; see below, pp. 16–17, nn. 18, 19).

[2] As Keymer, 152, notes, Sterne humorously puns on Yorick as a traveler and the so-called peripatetic school of philosophy—i.e., Aristotle and his students, whose classroom was the covered walks of the Lyceum.

[3] Cf. sermon 41 ("Follow peace"), which celebrates "peaceful commerce" between human beings: "There is no man so liberally stocked with earthly blessings, as to be able to live without another man's aid.—God, in his wisdom, has so dispensed his gifts, in various kinds and measures, as to render us helpful, and make a social intercourse indispensable" (4:388). The sermon is an important gloss on *ASJ*, echoing the message of countless eighteenth-century sermons: peaceableness, good citizenship, mutual responsibility, and charity.

[4] First example recorded in *OED*.

[5] Cf. p. 70: "converse sweet, etc."; a commonplace euphemism for sexual union, as in Henry Fielding, *Tom Jones* (1749), ed. Martin C. Battestin and Fredson Bowers (Middletown, CT: Wesleyan UP, 1975), XIII.7: "It would be tedious to give the particular Conversation which consisted of very common and ordinary Occurrences, and which lasted from two till six o'Clock in the Morning" (2:717; see also XIII.9, 2:726). Cf. *BJ* (May 17): "one Evening *so spent,* as the *Saturday's* wch preceded our *Separation*—would sicken all the *Conversation* of the world—I relish no *Converse* since . . . ."

into the hands of more equitable brokers for such conversation as he can find, it requires no great spirit of divination to guess at his party—

This brings me to my point; and naturally leads me (if the see-saw of this *Desobligeant* will but let me get on) into the efficient as well as the final causes of travelling—[6]

Your idle people that leave their native country and go abroad for some reason or reasons which may be derived from one of these general causes—

> Infirmity of body,
> Imbecility of mind, or
> Inevitable necessity.

The first two include all those who travel by land or by water, labouring with pride, curiosity, vanity or spleen, subdivided and combined *in infinitum.*

The third class includes the whole army of peregrine[7] martyrs; more especially those travellers who set out upon their travels with the benefit of the clergy,[8] either as delinquents travelling under the direction of governors recommended by the magistrate—or young gentlemen transported by the cruelty of parents and guardians, and travelling under the direction of governors recommended by Oxford, Aberdeen and Glasgow.[9]

There is a fourth class, but their number is so small that they would not deserve a distinction, was it not necessary in a work of this nature to observe the greatest precision and nicety, to avoid a confusion of character. And these men I

---

[6] Continuing his play on the "peripatetic philosopher" (cf., p. 13, n. 2), Sterne alludes to two of Aristotle's four causes, i.e., the efficient, the material, the formal, and the final. See also James Gow's suggestion that Sterne was familiar with Sir Thomas Palmer's encyclopedic *An Essay of the Means how to make our Trauailes into forraine Countries, the more profitable and honourable* (1606), punctuated by repetition of the phrase "efficient and final" causes ("Scholia" in *Scriblerian*, 37 [2004–2005]).

[7] *OED* cites this passage as its last illustration of an obsolete usage: "Upon a pilgrimage; upon one's travels; travelling abroad."

[8] "Literally, clerical exemption from the jurisdiction of the ordinary courts of the law; Yorick turns the phrase to the practice of sending young aristocrats on the Grand Tour under clerical supervision" (Keymer 152).

[9] Tristram promises a "most delectable narrative" of his travels "with Mr. *Noddy*'s eldest son, whom, in the year 1741, I accompanied as governor" (I.11.26). According to John Croft, "Sterne said that his first Plan, was to travell his Hero . . . all over Europe . . . and at length to return Tristram well informed and a compleat English Gentleman" ("Anecdotes of Sterne," *The Whitefoord Papers*, ed. W. A. S. Hewins [Oxford: Oxford UP, 1898], 228). While we have no evidence that Sterne ever served as a traveling companion, he expressed some interest in doing so between 1761 and 1765, when facing the expenses of a European sojourn in search of better health (*Letters* 140, 257, 288). In Sterne's list of universities, the absence of his alma mater, Cambridge, is conspicuous.

speak of, are such as cross the seas and sojourn in a land of strangers[10] with a view of saving money for various reasons and upon various pretences:[11] but as they might also save themselves and others a great deal of unnecessary trouble by saving their money at home—and as their reasons for travelling are the least complex of any other species of emigrants, I shall distinguish these gentlemen by the name of

Simple Travellers.

Thus the whole circle of travellers may be reduced to the following *Heads.*[12]

Idle Travellers,
Inquisitive Travellers,
Lying Travellers,
Proud Travellers,
Vain Travellers,
Splenetic Travellers.

Then follow the Travellers of Necessity.
The delinquent and felonious Traveller,[13]
The unfortunate and innocent Traveller,
The simple Traveller,
And last of all (if you please) The

Sentimental Traveller (meaning thereby myself) who have travell'd, and of which I am now sitting down to give an account—as much out of *Necessity,* and the *besoin de* Voyager,[14] as any one in the class.

---

[10] See 1 Maccabees 4:22: "They fled every one into the land of strangers."

[11] Cf. sermon 20, "The prodigal son" (Appendix, p. 241), where Sterne belittles cheap bear-leaders, as traveling companions were called.

[12] Cataloging traveler types was a standard trope in travel literature from Palmer (see n. 6 above) to Josiah Tucker, *Instructions for Travellers* (1757; New York: Johnson Reprint, n.d.), 3: "Persons who propose to themselves a Scheme for Travelling, generally do it with a View to obtain one, or more of the following Ends, *viz. First,* To make curious Collections as Natural Philosophers, Virtuosos, or Antiquarians. *Secondly,* To improve in Painting, Statuary, Architecture, and Music. *Thirdly,* To obtain the Reputation of being Men of Vertù . . . . *Fourthly,* to acquire foreign Airs . . . . Or, *Fifthly,* to rub off local Prejudices . . . ."

[13] Stout, 81: "In Boulogne (a gathering-place for 'delinquent and felonious' Britishers compelled to flee abroad), Tristram encounters 'a jolly set' of 'debtors and sinners' who assume that he is pursued by the authorities for debt, murder, treason, or some other crime" (quoting *TS* VII.7.585–86).

[14] The urge or need to travel, wanderlust.

I am well aware, at the same time, as both my travels and observations will be altogether of a different cast from any of my fore-runners;[15] that I might have insisted upon a whole nitch entirely to myself—but I should break in upon the confines of the *Vain* Traveller, in wishing to draw attention towards me, till I have some better grounds for it, than the mere *Novelty of my Vehicle.*[16]

It is sufficient for my reader, if he has been a traveller himself, that with study and reflection hereupon he may be able to determine his own place and rank in the catalogue—it will be one step towards knowing himself; as it is great odds, but he retains some tincture and resemblance, of what he imbibed or carried out, to the present hour.

The man who first transplanted the grape of Burgundy to the Cape of Good Hope (observe he was a Dutch man) never dreamt of drinking the same wine at the Cape, that the same grape produced upon the French mountains—he was too phlegmatic for that—but undoubtedly he expected to drink some sort of vinous liquor; but whether good, bad, or indifferent—he knew enough of this world to know, that it did not depend upon his choice, but that what is generally called *chance* was to decide his success: however, he hoped for the best; and in these hopes, by an intemperate confidence in the fortitude of his head, and the depth of his discretion, *Mynheer* might possibly overset both in his new vineyard; and by discovering his nakedness, become a laughing-stock to his people.[17]

Even so it fares with the poor Traveller, sailing and posting through the politer kingdoms of the globe in pursuit of knowledge and improvements.

Knowledge and improvements[18] are to be got by sailing and posting for that purpose; but whether useful knowledge and real improvements, is all a lottery—and even where the adventurer is successful, the acquired stock must be used with caution and sobriety to turn to any profit—but as the chances run prodigiously

---

[15] Cf. Tristram's account of his father on the Grand Tour (VII.27.617–18): "his remarks and reasonings upon the characters, the manners and customs of the countries . . . were so opposite to those of all other mortal men . . . That the whole put together, it appears of so different a shade and tint from any tour of Europe, which was ever executed . . . ."

[16] Sterne uses the same phrase in dedicating his first published sermon ("The case of Elijah and the widow of Zerephath," 1747), and calls both *A Political Romance* and *Tristram Shandy* a "vehicle"; here, however, his genius for literalizing a figurative expression should be noted.

[17] Stout, 331–32, suggests an allusion to Jan Van Riebeeck, governor of the Cape from 1652 to 1662, whose interest in establishing vineyards is discussed in *The Present State of the Cape of Good-Hope . . . by Peter Kolben,* tr. Guido Medley, 2 vols. (1731, 1:20–21), and indicates several reprintings of this popular account of the Dutch settlement of the Cape.

The phrase "discovering his nakedness" ties the vineyard to Noah's drunkenness in Genesis 9:20–22. But, as Stout also notes, 83, there are many other references in Scripture to the discovering of nakedness—e.g., Exodus 20:26, Ezekiel 16:36, 22:10, 23:18.

[18] Sterne borrows heavily here from *Quo Vadis? A Just Censure of Travel* (1617), written by one of his favorite authors, Bishop Joseph Hall (1574–1656).

the other way both as to the acquisition and application, I am of opinion, That a man would act as wisely, if he could prevail upon himself, to live contented without foreign knowledge or foreign improvements, especially if he lives in a country that has no absolute want of either—and indeed, much grief of heart has it oft and many a time cost me, when I have observed how many a foul step the inquisitive Traveller has measured to see sights and look into discoveries; all which, as Sancho Pança said to Don Quixote,[19] they might have seen dry-shod at home. It is an age so full of light, that there is scarce a country or corner of Europe whose beams are not crossed and interchanged with others—Knowledge in most of its branches, and in most affairs, is like music in an Italian street, whereof those may partake, who pay nothing—But there is no nation under heaven—and God is my record, (before whose tribunal I must one day come and give an account of this work)—that I do not speak it vauntingly—But there is no nation under heaven abounding with more variety of learning—where the sciences may be more fitly woo'd, or more surely won than here—where art is encouraged, and will so soon rise high—where Nature (take her all together) has so little to answer for—and, to close all, where there is more wit and variety of character to feed the mind with—Where then, my dear countrymen, are you going—

—We are only looking at this chaise, said they—Your most obedient servant, said I, skipping out of it, and pulling off my hat—We were wondering, said one of them, who, I found, was an *inquisitive traveller*—what could occasion its motion.—'Twas the agitation, said I coolly, of writing a preface—I never heard, said the other, who was a *simple traveller*, of a preface wrote in a *Desobligeant.*—It would have been better, said I, in a *Vis a Vis.*[20]

—*As an English man does not travel to see English men,*[21] I retired to my room.

---

[19] Cf. *Don Quixote,* II.III.5 (3:46), Sancho's lament in parting from his wife (and not to Don Quixote, as Sterne suggests): "wou'd Heaven but be pleas'd to let me live at home dry-shod, in Peace and Quietness, without gadding over Hill and Dale, thro' Brambles and Briars." The immediate source is Hall's *Quo Vadis?:* "some grave and painful author hath collected into one view whatsoever his country affords worthy of mark; having measured many a foul step for that which we may see dryshod . . ." (*Works,* ed. Philip Wynter [Oxford, 1863], 9:540; sec. 10).

[20] *OED*'s earliest recorded usage is in Horace Walpole's correspondence (1753): "a light carriage for two persons sitting face-to-face."

[21] Stout, 85–86, notes a parallel observation in Smollett: "This sort of reserve seems peculiar to the English disposition. When two natives of any other country chance to meet abroad, they run into each other's embrace like old friends, even though they have never heard of one another till that moment; whereas two Englishmen in the same situation maintain a mutual reserve and diffidence, and keep without the sphere of each other's attraction, like two bodies endowed with a repulsive power" (*Travels,* letter 41, 2:261). Cf. his observation of an Englishman taking "a solitary walk on the beach, avoiding us with great care, although he knew we were English . . . . This is a character truly British" (letter 35, 2:188).

CALAIS.

I Perceived that something darken'd the passage more than myself, as I stepp'd along it to my room; it was effectually[1] Mons. Dessein, the master of the hôtel, who had just return'd from vespers, and, with his hat under his arm, was most complaisantly following me, to put me in mind of my wants. I had wrote myself pretty well out of conceit with the *Desobligeant;* and Mons. Dessein speaking of it, with a shrug, as if it would no way suit me, it immediately struck my fancy that it belong'd to some *innocent traveller,* who, on his return home, had left it to Mons. Dessein's honour to make the most of. Four months had elapsed since it had finish'd its career of Europe in the corner of Mons. Dessein's coach-yard; and having sallied out from thence but a vampt-up business at the first, though it had been twice taken to pieces on Mount Sennis,[2] it had not profited much by its adventures—but by none so little as the standing so many months unpitied in the corner of Mons. Dessein's coach-yard. Much indeed was not to be said for it—but something might—and when a few words will rescue misery out of her distress, I hate the man who can be a churl of them.

—Now was I the master of this hôtel, said I, laying the point of my fore-finger on Mons. Dessein's breast, I would inevitably make a point of getting rid of this unfortunate *Desobligeant*—it stands swinging reproaches at you every time you pass by it—

Mon Dieu! said Mons. Dessein—I have no interest—Except the interest, said I, which men of a certain turn of mind take, Mons. Dessein, in their own sensations—I'm persuaded, to a man who feels for others as well as for himself, every rainy night, disguise it as you will, must cast a damp upon your spirits—You suffer, Mons. Dessein, as much as the machine—

I have always observed, when there is as much *sour* as *sweet* in a compliment, that an Englishman is eternally at a loss within himself, whether to take it, or let it alone: a Frenchman never is: Mons. Dessein made me a bow.

C'est bien vrai,[3] said he—But in this case I should only exchange one disquietude for another, and with loss: figure to yourself, my dear Sir,[4] that in giving you a chaise which would fall to pieces before you had got half way to Paris—figure to

---

[1] *OED*'s last illustration of a usage deemed obsolete: "In effect; in fact, in reality." It may instead be Sterne's own anglicization of *en effet.*

[2] Samuel Sharp (see below, p. 41, n. 18), *Letters from Italy* (1767), describes this method of crossing the Alps at Mount Cenis, connecting Lyons and Turin: "Both going and returning, when you arrive at the foot of the hill, your coach, or chaise, is taken to pieces, and carried upon mules to the other side, and you yourself are transported by two men, on a common straw elbow chair, without any feet to it, fixed upon two poles, like a sedan chair" (290). Sterne describes this practice again at the end of *ASJ;* see below, p. 169.

[3] You're quite right.

[4] Sterne's attempt to anglicize French phrasing—i.e., *figurez-vous mon cher monsieur.*

yourself how much I should suffer, in giving an ill impression of myself to a man of honour, and lying at the mercy, as I must do, *d'un homme d'esprit.*[5]

The dose was made up exactly after my own prescription; so I could not help taking it—and returning Mons. Dessein his bow, without more casuistry we walk'd together towards his Remise,[6] to take a view of his magazine of chaises.

---

[5] Of a man of wit. See below, p. 93 and n. 4, the description of the Count de B**** as "*un Esprit fort*"; and p. 153.

[6] Carriage-house. Familiar in eighteenth-century English as was its alternative usage as the carriage itself (see p. 104).

IN THE STREET.
CALAIS.

IT must needs be a hostile kind of a world, when the buyer (if it be but of a sorry post-chaise) cannot go forth with the seller thereof into the street to terminate the difference betwixt them, but he instantly falls into the same frame of mind and views his conventionist[1] with the same sort of eye, as if he was going along with him to Hyde-park corner to fight a duel.[2] For my own part, being but a poor sword's-man, and no way a match for Monsieur *Dessein,* I felt the rotation of all the movements within me, to which the situation is incident—I looked at Monsieur *Dessein* through and through—ey'd him as he walked along in profile—then, *en face*[3]—thought he look'd like a Jew—then a Turk[4]—disliked his wig—cursed him by my gods—wished him at the devil—

—And is all this to be lighted up in the heart for a beggarly account of three or four louisd'ors, which is the most I can be over-reach'd in?—Base passion! said I, turning myself about, as a man naturally does upon a sudden reverse of sentiment—base, ungentle passion! thy hand is against every man, and every man's hand against thee[5]—heaven forbid! said she, raising her hand up to her forehead, for I had turned full in front upon the lady whom I had seen in conference with the monk—she had followed us unperceived—Heaven forbid indeed! said I,

---

[1] First example recorded in *OED:* "one who enters into a convention or contract."

[2] Among the many duelists who resorted to Hyde Park in Sterne's day, Sterne would have been most familiar with John Wilkes, who had been severely wounded there by Samuel Martin, Secretary to the Treasury, in 1763. Sterne knew Wilkes before then, and certainly spent time with him in Paris in the winter of 1764, while he was still recovering from his wound.

[3] Full in the face, with the implication "straight in the eye."

[4] Cf. *Letters,* 177, wherein Sterne warns his wife about Dessein: "at Calais [lodge] at the Lyon D'Argent—the master a Turk in grain." With both "Jew" and "Turk," Sterne seems to perpetuate stereotypes, but they are so ingrained in the Christian culture of the eighteenth century that caution should be exercised before accusing Sterne of special animosity. Indeed, the thrust of the passage is a step away from hostilities among people, including strangers.

[5] Cf. Genesis 16:12: "And he [Ishmael] will be a wild man; his hand will be against every man, and every man's hand against him." Melinda Alliker Rabb, "Engendering Accounts in Sterne's *A Sentimental Journey,*" in *Johnson and His Age,* ed. James Engell (Cambridge: Harvard UP, 1984), 542, notes Sterne's pervasive use of "hands" in *ASJ* "as synecdoches for the intricacies of sentimental commerce." Cf. Anne Bandry, "Les livres de Sterne: Suites et fins," *BSEAA* 50 (2000):132–33, who notes the word's high frequency in *ASJ,* where it occurs more often than any other common noun except "man."

Clonmell comments on this passage: "True delicate double entendre is not where yᵉ Word bears two meanings but where a modest Expression leaves incidentally a Lewd Idea upon yᵉ Mind" (Franssen 166).

offering her my own—she had a black pair of silk gloves open only at the thumb and two fore-fingers,[6] so accepted it without reserve—and I led her up to the door of the Remise.

Monsieur *Dessein* had *diabled*[7] the key above fifty times before he found out he had come with a wrong one in his hand: we were as impatient as himself to have it open'd; and so attentive to the obstacle, that I continued holding her hand almost without knowing it; so that Monsieur *Dessein* left us together with her hand in mine, and with our faces turned towards the door of the Remise, and said he would be back in five minutes.

Now a colloquy of five minutes, in such a situation, is worth one of as many ages, with your faces turned towards the street: in the latter case, 'tis drawn from the objects and occurrences without—when your eyes are fixed upon a dead blank—you draw purely from yourselves. A silence of a single moment upon Monsieur *Dessein*'s leaving us, had been fatal to the situation—she had infallibly turned about—so I began the conversation instantly.—

—But what were the temptations, (as I write not to apologize for the weaknesses of my heart in this tour,—but to give an account of them)—shall be described with the same simplicity, with which I felt them.

---

[6] Cunnington, 175–76, notes that *"Gloves with open finger-tips* were occasionally worn," and cites mentions of gloves that are "open-fingered" (1740) or "cut fingered" (1719).

[7] Cf. the French expression *le dessein du diable* (the designs of the devil). *OED,* s.v. *diable,* lists Sterne's usage in *TS,* VII.8.587, as its second illustration, but no entry is offered for the form used here. See also p. 54, n. 4.

THE REMISE DOOR.
CALAIS.

WHEN I told the reader that I did not care to get out of the *Desobligeant*, because I saw the monk in close conference with a lady just arrived at the inn—I told him the truth; but I did not tell him the whole truth; for I was full as much restrained by the appearance and figure of the lady he was talking to. Suspicion crossed my brain, and said, he was telling her what had passed: something jarred upon it within me—I wished him at his convent.

When the heart flies out before the understanding, it saves the judgment a world of pains—I was certain she was of a better order of beings—however, I thought no more of her, but went on and wrote my preface.

The impression returned, upon my encounter with her in the street; a guarded frankness with which she gave me her hand, shewed, I thought, her good education and her good sense; and as I led her on, I felt a pleasurable ductility about her, which spread a calmness over all my spirits—[1]

—Good God! how a man might lead such a creature as this round the world with him!—

I had not yet seen her face—'twas not material; for the drawing was instantly set about, and long before we had got to the door of the Remise, *Fancy* had finished the whole head, and pleased herself as much with its fitting her goddess, as if she had dived into the TIBER for it[2]—but thou art a seduced, and a seducing slut;[3] and albeit thou cheatest us seven times a day with thy pictures and images,

---

[1] Stout, 91, calls attention to Sterne's letter to Elizabeth Vesey (probably June 1766) exploring the nature of immediate impressions: "surely the most penetrating of her sex need not be told that intercourses of this kind . . . can be measured only by the degrees of penetration by wch we discover Characters at first sight, or by the openess and frankness of heart wch lets the by-stander into it, without the pains of reflection . . ." (*Letters* 137).

The dichotomy of head and heart is one of Sterne's and his century's most persistent ideas. Cf. his early letter (1750): "this Impertinence of his . . . had Issued not so much from his Heart, as from his Head" (*Letters* 27); and the last letter he ever wrote (March 1768): "cherish the remembrance of me, and forget the follies which you so often condemn'd—which my heart, not my head betray'd me into" (419). See also the preface to the *Sermons,* where his sermons are said to proceed "more from the heart than the head" (4:2).

[2] The bed of the Tiber (running through Rome) was the repository of many archaeological finds; Yorick compares the operations of Fancy to the archaeologists' practice of searching for the missing heads of statues of gods and goddesses at the bottom of the Tiber.

[3] As *OED* notes (s.v. *slut, sb.,* 2.b.), the word was in playful use, without serious imputation of bad qualities, throughout the eighteenth century.

yet with so many charms dost thou do it, and thou deckest out thy pictures in the shapes of so many angels of light,[4] 'tis a shame to break with thee.

When we had got to the door of the Remise, she withdrew her hand from across her forehead, and let me see the original—it was a face of about six and twenty—of a clear transparent brown, simply set off without rouge or powder[5]— it was not critically handsome, but there was that in it, which in the frame of mind I was in, which attached me much more to it—it was interesting; I fancied it wore the characters of a widow'd look,[6] and in that state of its declension, which had passed the two first paroxysms of sorrow, and was quietly beginning to reconcile itself to its loss—but a thousand other distresses might have traced the same lines; I wish'd to know what they had been—and was ready to enquire, (had the same *bon ton*[7] of conversation permitted, as in the days of Esdras)—*"What aileth thee? and why art thou disquieted? and why is thy understanding troubled?"*[8]—In a word, I felt benevolence for her; and resolved some way or other to throw in my mite[9] of courtesy—if not of service.[10]

---

[4] Cf. 2 Corinthians 11:13–14: "For such are false apostles, deceitful workers, transforming themselves into the apostles of Christ. And no marvel; for Satan himself is transformed into an angel of light." The scriptural "seven times a day" (e.g., Proverbs 24:16, Matthew 18:21–22, Luke 17:4), gives the entire passage an undercurrent of seriousness.

[5] Cf. *Letters,* 391–92, where Sterne instructs his daughter, before her return home, to "throw all your rouge pots into the Sorgue . . . I will have no rouge put on in England." French women were thought to use cosmetics to excess.

[6] Behind the suggestion of widowhood are two opposing tropes: first, the scriptural injunction to charity and compassion, where widows and orphans are the most consistently invoked objects; and second, the supposed sexual "easiness" of widows, a tradition Sterne exploits with widow Wadman in *TS*. In annotating "interesting," Parnell, 227, cites Cash, *LY,* 27: "The *OED* cites [this passage] as its earliest example of this word in its second meaning—appealing to or able to arouse emotions."

Sterne lost his way in this long sentence, resulting in a superfluous "which" before "attached."

[7] *OED* cites Lord Chesterfield (1747) as its first example: "*arch.* Good style, good breeding; polite or fashionable society; the fashionable world." Sterne uses the term in a letter to Garrick (April 1762): "there is scarce a woman who understands the *bon ton,* but is seven times in a day in downright extasy . . ." (*Letters* 161–62).

[8] Cf. 2 Esdras 10:31: "What aileth thee? and why art thou so disquieted? and why is thine understanding troubled . . .?"

[9] Another scriptural echo; cf. Mark 12:42 (Luke 21:2): "And there came a certain poor widow, and she threw in two mites."

[10] The bawdy implication of *service* would not escape Sterne's readers; Clonmell points to it in summarizing this chapter: "The conduct of this Chapter is remarkable[.] . . . The Rhapsody on fancy is beautifull & gives you time to admire ye first part & prepare y^rself for Pity in ye Succeeding part . . . Which fits you for receiving ye last part of ye Description delicately lascivious" (Franssen 166). Cf. *TS,* IX.33.807: "My father . . . was obliged to keep a Bull for the service of the Parish . . . ."

Such were my temptations—and in this disposition to give way to them, was I left alone with the lady with her hand in mine, and with our faces both turned closer to the door of the Remise than what was absolutely necessary.

THE REMISE DOOR.
CALAIS.

THIS certainly, fair lady! said I, raising her hand up a little lightly as I began, must be one of Fortune's whimsical doings: to take two utter strangers by their hands—of different sexes, and perhaps from different corners of the globe, and in one moment place them together in such a cordial situation, as Friendship herself could scarce have atchieved for them, had she projected it for a month—

—And your reflection upon it, shews how much, Monsieur, she has embarrassed you by the adventure.—

When the situation is, what we would wish, nothing is so ill-timed as to hint at the circumstances which make it so: you thank Fortune, continued she—you had reason[1]—the heart knew it, and was satisfied; and who but an English philosopher would have sent notices of it to the brain to reverse the judgment?

In saying this, she disengaged her hand with a look which I thought a sufficient commentary upon the text.

It is a miserable picture which I am going to give of the weakness of my heart, by owning, that it suffered a pain, which worthier occasions could not have inflicted.—I was mortified with the loss of her hand, and the manner in which I had lost it carried neither oil nor wine to the wound:[2] I never felt the pain of a sheepish inferiority so miserably in my life.

The triumphs of a true feminine heart are short upon these discomfitures. In a very few seconds she laid her hand upon the cuff of my coat, in order to finish her reply; so some way or other, God knows how, I regained my situation.

—She had nothing to add.

I forthwith began to model a different conversation for the lady, thinking from the spirit as well as moral of this, that I had been mistaken in her character; but upon turning her face towards me, the spirit which had animated the reply was fled—the muscles relaxed, and I beheld the same unprotected look of distress which first won me to her interest[3]—melancholy! to see such sprightliness the prey of sorrow.—I pitied her from my soul; and though it may seem ridiculous enough to a torpid heart,—I could have taken her into my arms, and cherished her, though it was in the open street, without blushing.

---

[1] I.e., *vous avez eu raison*. Another literal anglicization.

[2] Reinforcing Stout's observation, 96, that "the English were popularly regarded by the French as a philosophical, serious people," is the fact that Sterne's language here echoes Luke's account of the good Samaritan (Luke 10:33–34); Sterne employs it again below, p. 161, in his account of Yorick's meeting with Maria, and in sermon 3, "Philanthropy recommended" (Appendix, p. 233).

[3] Sterne continues to pursue a scientific (mechanistic) description of the relationship between the body and sympathy, as he had done in sermon 20, "The prodigal son" (Appendix, p. 238).

The pulsations of the arteries along my fingers pressing across hers, told her what was passing within me:[4] she looked down—a silence of some moments followed.

I fear, in this interval, I must have made some slight efforts towards a closer compression of her hand, from a subtle sensation I felt in the palm of my own—not as if she was going to withdraw hers—but, as if she thought about it—and I had infallibly lost it a second time, had not instinct more than reason directed me to the last resource in these dangers—to hold it loosely, and in a manner as if I was every moment going to release it, of myself; so she let it continue, till Monsieur *Dessein* returned with the key; and in the mean time I set myself to consider how I should undo the ill impressions which the poor monk's story, in case he had told it her, must have planted in her breast against me.

---

[4] *OED* credits Sterne, perhaps erroneously, with the first recorded *figurative* usage of *pulsation,* in *TS,* VIII.16.676–77, where widow Wadman removes Toby's pipe from his hand, thus ensuring contact with her own finger, because, Tristram observes, since "there was no arterial or vital heat in the end of the tobacco-pipe, it could excite no sentiment——it could neither give fire by pulsation——or receive it by sympathy"; whereas, on the contrary, by "following my uncle Toby's forefinger with hers, . . . touching it here——then there, and so on——it set something at least in motion." Surely in *ASJ* the usage is not figurative, and probably not in the passage from *TS;* cf. the chapter "The Pulse," below, p. 73*ff.*

THE SNUFF-BOX.[1]
CALAIS.

THE good old monk was within six paces of us, as the idea of him cross'd my mind; and was advancing towards us a little out of the line, as if uncertain whether he should break in upon us or no.—He stopp'd, however, as soon as he came up to us, with a world of frankness; and having a horn snuff-box in his hand, he presented it open to me—You shall taste mine—said I, pulling out my box (which was a small tortoise one) and putting it into his hand—'Tis most excellent, said the monk; Then do me the favour, I replied, to accept of the box and all, and when you take a pinch out of it, sometimes recollect it was the peace-offering of a man who once used you unkindly, but not from his heart.

The poor monk blush'd as red as scarlet.[2] *Mon Dieu!* said he, pressing his hands together—you never used me unkindly.—I should think, said the lady, he is not likely. I blush'd in my turn; but from what movements, I leave to the few who feel to analyse—Excuse me, Madame,[3] replied I—I treated him most unkindly; and from no provocations—'Tis impossible, said the lady.—My God! cried the monk, with a warmth of asseveration which seemed not to belong to him—the fault was in me, and in the indiscretion of my zeal—the lady opposed it, and I joined with her in maintaining it was impossible, that a spirit so regulated as his, could give offence to any.

I knew not that contention could be rendered so sweet and pleasurable a thing to the nerves as I then felt it.—We remained silent, without any sensation of that foolish pain which takes place, when in such a circle you look for ten minutes in one another's faces without saying a word. Whilst this lasted, the monk rubb'd his horn box upon the sleeve of his tunick; and as soon as it had acquired a little air of brightness by the friction—he made a low bow, and said, 'twas too late to say

---

[1] The exchange of snuff-boxes in this chapter formed the basis of so-called Lorenzo cults in Germany, described by Alan B. Howes, ed., *Sterne: The Critical Heritage* (London: Routledge & Kegan Paul, 1974), 429; and by J. C. T. Oates, *Shandyism and Sentiment, 1760–1800* (Cambridge: Cambridge Bibliographical Society, 1968), 23: "We now come to the lunatic fringe of Sterneana. In Germany, where societies of sentimentalists did honour to Sterne's Father Lorenzo by exchanging snuff from boxes made of horn . . . ." However, the cults may have been journalistic fantasy: see W. G. Day, "Sternean Material Culture," *The Reception of Laurence Sterne in Europe,* ed. Peter de Voogd and John Neubauer (London: Thoemmes, 2004), 250–52.

[2] Cf. the Commination service in the *Book of Common Prayer:* "For tho' our sins be as red as scarlet, they shall be made white as snow" (cf. Isaiah 1:18); the simile may well be a commonplace, but is unrecorded as such.

[3] Stout, 311–15, makes a cogent argument, based on different manuscript versions, that from "Excuse me" to the end of the next paragraph, Sterne did a careful rewriting; see also Florida *ASJ,* 6:427, n. to 26.17–27.10.

whether it was the weakness or goodness of our tempers which had involved us in this contest—but be it as it would—he begg'd we might exchange boxes—In saying this, he presented his to me with one hand, as he took mine from me in the other; and having kiss'd it—with a stream of good nature in his eyes he put it into his bosom—and took his leave.

I guard this box, as I would the instrumental parts of my religion,[4] to help my mind on to something better: in truth, I seldom go abroad without it; and oft and many a time have I called up by it the courteous spirit of its owner to regulate my own, in the justlings of the world;[5] they had found full employment for his, as I learnt from his story, till about the forty-fifth year of his age, when upon some military services ill requited, and meeting at the same time with a disappointment in the tenderest of passions, he abandon'd the sword and the sex together, and took sanctuary, not so much in his convent as in himself.

I feel a damp upon my spirits, as I am going to add, that in my last return through Calais, upon inquiring after Father Lorenzo, I heard he had been dead near three months, and was buried, not in his convent, but, according to his desire, in a little cimetiery belonging to it, about two leagues off: I had a strong desire to see where they had laid him—when, upon pulling out his little horn box, as I sat by his grave, and plucking up a nettle or two at the head of it,[6] which had no business to grow there, they all struck together so forcibly upon my affections, that I burst into a flood of tears—but I am as weak as a woman; and I beg the world not to smile, but pity me.

---

[4] A stock phrase for the rituals and laws of religious practice (also, "instrumental duties"). Cf. sermon 6 ("Pharisee and publican"), where Sterne preaches against being misled by "the pomp of such external parts of religion," but, typically enough, finds middle ground in his conclusion: "the instrumental duties of religion are duties of unquestionable obligation to us——yet they are still but INSTRUMENTAL DUTIES, conducive to the great end of all religion—which is to purify our hearts—and conquer our passions—and in a word, to make us wiser and better . . ." (*Sermons* 4:63–64). In *TS*, VIII.31.715, Tristram ridicules Hilarion the hermit, and "his abstinence, his watchings, flagellations, and other instrumental parts of his religion"; Yorick's tolerance manifests a more accepting attitude.

[5] Cf. sermon 25, "Humility": "THE great business of man, is the regulation of his spirit; the possession of such a frame and temper of mind, as will lead us peaceably through this world, and in the many weary stages of it, afford us, what we shall be sure to stand in need of,——*Rest unto our souls*" (*Sermons* 4:235).

The "justlings" of the world is a favorite metaphor for Sterne; cf. *TS*, IV.8.333: "the sudden jerks and hard jostlings . . . in this rugged journey [of life]"; *Sermons*, 4:12: "this uneasy journey of life, . . . the ruggedness of the road, and the many hard justlings he is sure to meet with"; 4:100: "How many justlings and hard struggles do we undergo, in making our way in the world"; and 4:350: "the many shocks and hard jostlings, which we are sure to meet with in our way."

[6] Cf. *TS*, VI.25.544–45, Tristram's homage to Trim: "Weed his grave clean, ye men of goodness,—for he was your brother . . . ." The grave-side scene is archetypically sentimental.

THE REMISE DOOR.
CALAIS.

I HAD never quitted the lady's hand all this time; and had held it so long, that it would have been indecent to have let it go, without first pressing it to my lips: the blood and spirits, which had suffer'd a revulsion from her, crouded back to her, as I did it.[1]

Now the two travellers who had spoke to me in the coach-yard, happening at that crisis to be passing by, and observing our communications, naturally took it into their heads that we must be *man and wife* at least; so stopping as soon as they came up to the door of the Remise, the one of them, who was the inquisitive traveller, ask'd us, if we set out for Paris the next morning?—I could only answer for myself, I said; and the lady added, she was for Amiens.—We dined there yesterday, said the simple traveller—You go directly through the town, added the other, in your road to Paris. I was going to return a thousand thanks for the intelligence, *that Amiens was in the road to Paris;* but, upon pulling out my poor monk's little horn box to take a pinch of snuff—I made them a quiet bow, and wishing them a good passage to Dover—they left us alone—

—Now where would be the harm, said I to myself, if I was to beg of this distressed lady to accept of half of my chaise?—and what mighty mischief could ensue?

Every dirty passion, and bad propensity in my nature, took the alarm, as I stated the proposition—It will oblige you to have a third horse,[2] said AVARICE, which will put twenty livres out of your pocket.—You know not who she is, said CAUTION—or what scrapes the affair may draw you into, whisper'd COWARDICE—

Depend upon it, Yorick! said DISCRETION, 'twill be said you went off with a mistress, and came by assignation to Calais for that purpose—[3]

---

[1] *OED,* s.v. *revulsion,* 2, records this passage to illustrate the "action of drawing, or the fact of being drawn back or away. In later use only *fig.*"; it seems more likely, however, that Sterne uses it as a medical word, s.v. *revulsion,* 1: "The action or practice of diminishing a morbid condition in one part of the body by operating or acting upon another." Why the "blood and spirits" have retreated is difficult to say; perhaps the emotions of the snuffbox exchange had overwhelmed her sensibilities, or perhaps Yorick has been holding her hand too tightly, too long.

[2] Stout, 105, cites *The Gentleman's Guide* (1770), 18: "the regulations governing travel by post-chaise in France required that a chaise occupied by one person had to have two horses, and one occupied by two persons had to have a third horse."

[3] Sterne here re-creates the character of Yorick described in the opening pages of *TS,* the enemy to hypocrisy, caution, gravity, and discretion: "in plain truth, he was a man unhackneyed and unpractised in the world, and was altogether as indiscreet and foolish on every other subject of discourse where policy is wont to impress restraint" (I.11.29). Cf. sermon

—You can never after, cried HYPOCRISY aloud, shew your face in the world—or rise, quoth MEANNESS, in the church—or be any thing in it, said PRIDE, but a lousy prebendary.[4]

—But 'tis a civil thing, said I—and as I generally act from the first impulse,[5] and therefore seldom listen to these cabals, which serve no purpose, that I know of, but to encompass the heart with adamant[6]—I turn'd instantly about to the lady—

—But she had glided off unperceived, as the cause was pleading, and had made ten or a dozen paces down the street, by the time I had made the determination; so I set off after her with a long stride, to make her the proposal with the best address I was master of; but observing she walk'd with her cheek half resting upon the palm of her hand—with the slow, short-measur'd step of thoughtfulness, and with her eyes, as she went step by step, fix'd upon the ground, it struck me, she was trying the same cause herself.—God help her! said I, she has some mother-in-law, or tartufish[7] aunt, or nonsensical old woman, to consult upon the occasion, as well as

---

17, "The case of Hezekiah and the messengers": "there is scarce any character so rare, as a man of a real open and generous integrity,——who carries his heart in his hand,——who says the thing he thinks; and does the thing he pretends. Tho' no one can dislike the character,——yet, Discretion generally shakes her head,—and the world soon lets him into the reason" (*Sermons* 4:164).

[4] Not coincidentally, the portrait of Yorick as indiscreet leads Sterne to his own disappointments as a cleric, his failure to rise in the Church establishment, a persistent theme in his writings.

[5] Cf. Tristram's account of his writing practice: "A sudden impulse comes across me——drop the curtain, *Shandy*—I drop it——Strike a line here across the paper, *Tristram*—I strike it . . ." (*TS* IV.10.336); and again, VIII.2.656: "I am confident my own way of [writing] is the best——I'm sure it is the most religious——for I begin with writing the first sentence——and trusting to Almighty God for the second."

[6] Cf. Zechariah 7:10, 12: "And oppress not the widow, nor the fatherless, the stranger, nor the poor . . . . Yea, they made their hearts as an adamant stone, lest they should hear the law."

[7] Tartuffe, the sanctimonious hypocrite in Molière's eponymous comedy (1664), uses a mask of religious conviction to conceal numerous vices, particularly lust and avarice. He appears often in Sterne's writings—e.g., see below, p. 88, where the French officer explains the cry "*Haussez les mains, Monsieur l'Abbe*" as having "begun in the theatre about the time the Tartuffe was given in it"; *TS*, V.1.408–9, where Tristram leaves his chain of reasoning, on the "affair of *Whiskers*," as a legacy to "Prudes and Tartufs, to enjoy and make the most of"; VIII.2.657, where Tristram rejects "the errantest TARTUFFE, in science—in politics—or in religion . . ."; and a letter Sterne wrote just before his death to an American admirer, Dr. John Eustace: "It is too much to write books and find heads to understand them. The world, however, seems to come into a better temper about them, the people of genius here being, to a man, on its side. . . . A few Hypocrites and Tartufe's, whose approbation could do it nothing but dishonor, remain unconverted" (*Letters* 411). For a further account of these allusions, see the chapter "Tartuffery," in Melvyn New, *"Tristram Shandy": A Book for Free Spirits* (New York: Twayne, 1994), 113–34, esp. 118–20.

myself: so not caring to interrupt the processe, and deeming it more gallant to take her at discretion than by surprize, I faced about, and took a short turn or two before the door of the Remise, whilst she walk'd musing on one side.

IN THE STREET.
CALAIS.

HAVING, on first sight of the lady, settled the affair in my fancy, "that she was of the better order of beings"—and then laid it down as a second axiom, as indisputable as the first, That she was a widow, and wore a character of distress—I went no further; I got ground enough for the situation which pleased me—and had she remained close beside my elbow till midnight, I should have held true to my system, and considered her only under that general idea.

She had scarce got twenty paces distant from me, ere something within me called out for a more particular inquiry—it brought on the idea of a further separation—I might possibly never see her more—the heart is for saving what it can; and I wanted the traces thro' which my wishes might find their way to her, in case I should never rejoin her myself: in a word, I wish'd to know her name—her family's—her condition; and as I knew the place to which she was going, I wanted to know from whence she came: but there was no coming at all this intelligence: a hundred little delicacies stood in the way. I form'd a score different plans—There was no such thing as a man's asking her directly—the thing was impossible.

A little French *debonaire*[1] captain, who came dancing down the street, shewed me, it was the easiest thing in the world; for popping in betwixt us, just as the lady was returning back to the door of the Remise, he introduced himself to my acquaintance, and before he had well got announced, begg'd I would do him the honour to present him to the lady—I had not been presented myself—so turning about to her, he did it just as well by asking her, if she had come from Paris?— No: she was going that rout, she said.—*Vous n'etez pas de Londre?*[2]—She was not, she replied.—Then Madame must have come thro' Flanders.—*Apparamment vous etez Flammande?* said the French captain.—The lady answered, she was.— *Peutetre, de Lisle?* added he—She said, she was not of Lisle.—Nor Arras?—nor Cambray?—nor Ghent?—nor Brussels? She answered, she was of Brussels.

---

[1] In eighteenth-century French, *débonnaire* meant primarily "gracious," "courteous," "mild," "easygoing," but could also have negative connotations, from "jaunty" to "foolish." *OED* considers the word "very common in ME., but obsolescent from the 16th c., and now a literary archaism"; its citation from Cowper's *Table Talk* (1782) suggests a meaning close to Sterne's usage: "The Frenchman, easy, debonair, and brisk." Cf. below, p. 107: "with all the gaity and debonairness in the world" (*OED*'s last illustration of the form until several twentieth-century occurrences).

[2] You are not from London? (Properly, *Vous n'êtes pas de Londres?*) "*Apparamment vous etez Flammande?*" Then you are Flemish? (Properly, *Apparemment vous êtes Flammande or Flamande?*) "*Peutetre, de Lisle?*" Perhaps from Lille? (Properly, *Peut-être de Lille?*) "*pour cela*": for that. "*Et Madame a son Mari?*" And Madame has her husband? (Idiomatically, he would seem to be asking whether Yorick, standing beside her, is her husband, but since Yorick has already indicated that he does not know her, it is perhaps Sterne's awkward attempt at "And is Madame married?")

He had had the honour, he said, to be at the bombardment of it last war[3]— that it was finely situated, *pour cela*—and full of noblesse when the Imperialists were driven out by the French (the lady made a slight curtsy)—so giving her an account of the affair, and of the share he had had in it—he begg'd the honour to know her name—so made his bow.

—*Et Madame a son Mari?*—said he, looking back when he had made two steps—and without staying for an answer—danced down the street.

Had I served seven years apprenticeship to good breeding, I could not have done as much.[4]

---

[3] The French took Brussels from the Imperialist allies (i.e., the supporters of the Empress Maria Theresa of Austria) in February 1746 in the War of the Austrian Succession (1740–1748); England was aligned with the Dutch and Austrians against France.

[4] Stout, 108, cites an apropos description of French manners from Smollett, *Travels,* letter 7, 1:110, 121–22: "Of all the coxcombs on the face of the earth, a French *petit maitre* is the most impertinent: and they are all *petit maitres* . . . . Vanity, indeed, predominates among all ranks, to such a degree, that they are the greatest *egotists* in the world . . . . Neither conscious poverty nor disgrace will restrain him [from] . . . making his addresses to the finest lady, whom he has the smallest opportunity to approach . . . . It is all one to him whether he himself has a wife . . . or the lady a husband . . . . He takes it for granted that his addresses cannot but be acceptable . . . ."

THE REMISE.
CALAIS.

A S the little French captain left us, Mons. Dessein came up with the key of the
Remise in his hand, and forthwith let us into his magazine of chaises.

The first object which caught my eye, as Mons. Dessein open'd the door of the
Remise, was another old tatter'd *Desobligeant:* and notwithstanding it was the
exact picture of that which had hit my fancy so much in the coach-yard but an
hour before—the very sight of it stirr'd up a disagreeable sensation within me
now; and I thought 'twas a churlish beast into whose heart the idea could first
enter, to construct such a machine; nor had I much more charity for the man
who could think of using it.

I observed the lady was as little taken with it as myself: so Mons. Dessein led
us on to a couple of chaises which stood abreast, telling us as he recommended
them, that they had been purchased by my Lord A. and B. to go the *grand tour,*[1]
but had gone no further than Paris, so were in all respects as good as new—They
were too good—so I pass'd on to a third, which stood behind, and forthwith
began to chaffer for the price—But 'twill scarce hold two, said I, opening the
door and getting in—Have the goodness, Madam,[2] said Mons. Dessein, offering
his arm, to step in—The lady hesitated half a second, and stepp'd in; and the
waiter that moment beckoning to speak to Mons. Dessein, he shut the door of
the chaise upon us, and left us.

---

[1] Sterne's italicizing suggests he wants us to think of this as French, not English.

[2] In French, *ayez la bonté, Madame;* see the same phrasing below, p. 73.

THE REMISE.
CALAIS.

C'EST bien comique,[1] 'tis very droll, said the lady smiling, from the reflection that this was the second time we had been left together by a parcel of non-sensical contingencies—*c'est bien comique,* said she—

—There wants nothing, said I, to make it so, but the comick use which the gallantry of a Frenchman would put it to—to make love the first moment, and an offer of his person the second.

'Tis their *fort.*[2] replied the lady.

It is supposed so at least—and how it has come to pass, continued I, I know not; but they have certainly got the credit of understanding more of love, and making it better than any other nation upon earth:[3] but for my own part I think them errant bunglers,[4] and in truth the worst set of marksmen that ever tried Cupid's patience.

—To think of making love by *sentiments!*[5]

I should as soon think of making a genteel suit of cloaths out of remnants:—and to do it—pop—at first sight by declaration—is submitting the offer and

---

[1] 'Tis very comical, or, as in the next phrase, "very droll."

[2] I.e., *c'est leur fort. OED's* first illustration of English usage (*fort* or *forte*) is dated 1682: "the strong point (of a person), that in which he excels."

[3] Cf. Smollett's letter 7 (see above, p. 33, n. 4): "he piques himself upon being polished above the natives of any other country by his conversation with the fair sex. In the course of this communication, with which he is indulged from his tender years, he learns like a parrot, by rote, the whole circle of French compliments, which you know are a set of phrases, ridiculous even to a proverb; and these he throws out indiscriminately to all women, without distinction, in the exercise of that kind of address, which is here distinguished by the name of gallantry: it is no more than his making love to every woman who will give him the hearing" (*Travels* 1:112).

[4] Although usage was confused before the nineteenth century, Sterne's meaning here leans toward our present-day *arrant* rather than *errant.* Cf. Johnson, *Dictionary,* s.v. *arrant:* "[a word of uncertain etymology, but probably from *errant,* which being at first applied to its proper signification to vagabonds, as an *errant* or *arrant* rogue, that is, a *rambling rogue,* lost, in time, its original signification, and being by its use understood to imply something bad, was applied at large to any thing that was mentioned with hatred or contempt.] Bad in a high degree."

[5] Cf. *TS,* IX.25.787, where Tristram sets about correcting "an error which the bulk of the world lie under——but the French, every one of 'em to a man, who believe in it, almost as much as the REAL PRESENCE, '*That talking of love, is making it*'." And cf. *Letters,* 256 (?August 23, 1765): "I myself must ever have some dulcinea in my head—it harmonises the soul . . . but I carry on my affairs quite in the French way, sentimentally." Cf. below, p. 48.

themselves with it, to be sifted, with all their *pours* and *contres*,[6] by an unheated mind.

The lady attended as if she expected I should go on.

Consider then, madam, continued I, laying my hand upon hers—

That grave people hate Love for the name's sake—[7]

That selfish people hate it for their own—

Hypocrites for heaven's—

And that all of us both old and young, being ten times worse frighten'd than hurt by the very *report*—What a want of knowledge in this branch of commerce a man betrays, whoever lets the word come out of his lips, till an hour or two at least after the time, that his silence upon it becomes tormenting. A course of small, quiet attentions, not so pointed as to alarm—nor so vague as to be misunderstood,—with now and then a look of kindness, and little or nothing said upon it—leaves Nature for your mistress, and she fashions it to her mind.—[8]

Then I solemnly declare, said the lady, blushing—you have been making love to me all this while.

---

[6] Sterne seems to be translating literally "pros and cons," but it is not a French expression. Anne Bandry has suggested to us a possible nod to *Le pour et contre,* the Anglophile periodical conducted by the abbé Prévost from 1733 to 1740; Prévost had died in 1763. For a second use of the term, see below, p. 88.

[7] Stout, 111, suggests a borrowing from Burton, *The Anatomy of Melancholy,* preface to the third partition, on "love-melancholy" (5th ed. [1638], 402): "There will not bee wanting . . . one or other that will much discommend some part of this Treatise of Love Melancholy, and object . . . *that it is too light for a Divine, too Comicall a subject* . . . [and that] the very name of love is odious to *Chaster* eares; And therefore some againe out of an affected gravity, will dislike all for the names sake before they read a word . . . ." For Sterne's admiration of Burton, see *Notes* to *TS,* 3:14–15 and passim; and see below, "The Fragment" (pp. 49–50), an extensive borrowing from this section of *Anatomy.*

[8] Cf. Clonmell: "I think this Paragraph yᵉ truest Investigation of yᵉ Heart & most Adequately described of any Passage I ever met in any Book in any Language" (Franssen 159).

THE REMISE.
CALAIS.

MONSIEUR *Dessein* came back to let us out of the chaise, and acquaint the lady, the Count de L——— her brother was just arrived at the hotel. Though I had infinite good will for the lady, I cannot say, that I rejoiced in my heart at the event—and could not help telling her so—for it is fatal to a proposal, Madam, said I, that I was going to make you—

—You need not tell me what the proposal was, said she, laying her hand upon both mine, as she interrupted me.—A man, my good Sir, has seldom an offer of kindness to make to a woman, but she has a presentiment of it some moments before—

Nature arms her with it, said I, for immediate preservation—But I think, said she, looking in my face, I had no evil to apprehend—and to deal frankly with you, had determined to accept it.—If I had—(she stopped a moment)—I believe your good will would have drawn a story from me, which would have made pity the only dangerous thing in the journey.

In saying this, she suffered me to kiss her hand twice, and with a look of sensibility mixed with a concern she got out of the chaise—and bid adieu.

IN THE STREET.
CALAIS.

I NEVER finished a twelve-guinea bargain[1] so expeditiously in my life: my time
seemed heavy upon the loss of the lady, and knowing every moment of it
would be as two, till I put myself into motion—I ordered post horses directly,
and walked towards the hotel.

Lord! said I, hearing the town clock strike four, and recollecting that I had
been little more than a single hour in Calais—[2]

—What a large volume of adventures may be grasped within this little span of
life by him who interests his heart in every thing,[3] and who, having eyes to see,
what time and chance are perpetually holding out to him[4] as he journeyeth on his

---

[1] Yorick is not a wealthy traveler; cf. Philip Thicknesse, *Observations on the Customs and Manners of the French Nation* (1766), 109: "it will be necessary to hire a chaise upon your arrival here, and M. Dessin will provide one for you to Paris . . . but as you intend making a long tour, you will do well to purchase one; and there will be no difficulty in meeting with a tolerably good chaise for twenty guineas."

[2] Sterne's interest in the difference between clock time and the mind's sense of its own duration is broached several times in *TS*, most especially, III.18.222–23, where Toby recites, without understanding it, Locke's analysis in book II, ch. 14, "Of Duration and Its Simple Modes," in *Essay Concerning Human Understanding*.

The text of this paragraph to the end of the chapter was originally positioned between "The Remise Door. Calais" (p. 29) and "In the Street. Calais" (p. 32); see Stout, 300–7, and Florida *ASJ*, 6:429, n. to 36.7ff.

[3] This chapter elaborates on Sterne's often-stated belief in the plentitude of the world and the ethical and aesthetic meaning of that abundance. It occurs early in *TS*, and, as here, is linked to the metaphor of life as a journey:

> Could a historiographer drive on his history, as a muleteer drives on his mule,—straight forward . . . he might venture to foretell you to an hour when he should get to his journey's end;-----but the thing is, morally speaking, impossible: For, if he is a man of the least spirit, he will have fifty deviations from a straight line to make with this or that party as he goes along, which he can no ways avoid. (I.14.41)

Sterne returns to the idea in *TS*, VII.42–43, in which he crosses the plains of Languedoc on a mule and finds "adventures" and "human nature" in abundance. At the end of this chapter he invokes Mundungus as the opposite sort of traveler (see below, p. 41).

Behind these passages Stout, 119, suggests sermon 3 ("Philanthropy recommended"); see Appendix, pp. 233–37, esp. p. 234. The idea is, however, a commonplace in the century, with a particularly fine example in Johnson's *Idler* 97 (February 23, 1760).

[4] Sterne joins two scriptural phrases: Mark 8:18: "Having eyes, see ye not?" (cf. Matthew 13:13 and Luke 8:10), with Ecclesiastes 9:11: "time and chance happeneth to them all." The last text is one of Sterne's favorites, frequently occurring in the sermons, e.g., 4:94.15, 146.3, 210.22, 369.25–26, 389.19; for Sterne and his age, it often leads to an assertion that all accident and chance are providentially directed, although we may not have "the eyes" to comprehend God's workings.

way, misses nothing he can *fairly*[5] lay his hands on.—

—If this won't turn out something—another will—no matter —'tis an assay upon human nature—I get my labour for my pains[6]—'tis enough—the pleasure of the experiment has kept my senses, and the best part of my blood awake, and laid the gross to sleep.[7]

I pity the man who can travel from *Dan* to *Beersheba*,[8] and cry, 'Tis all barren—and so it is; and so is all the world to him who will not cultivate the fruits it offers. I declare, said I, clapping my hands chearily together, that was I in a desert, I would find out wherewith in it to call forth my affections—If I could not do better, I would fasten them upon some sweet myrtle, or seek some melancholy cypress[9] to connect myself to—I would court their shade, and greet them kindly for their protection—I would cut my name upon them, and swear they were the loveliest trees throughout the desert: if their leaves wither'd, I would teach myself to mourn, and when they rejoiced, I would rejoice along with them.[10]

The learned SMELFUNGUS[11] travelled from Boulogne to Paris—from Paris to Rome—and so on—but he set out with the spleen and jaundice, and every object

---

[5] Sterne's italics suggest a typical bawdiness even in the midst of his scriptural references, one that begins with "adventures"; David A. Brewer, "Scholia" in *Scriblerian* 29–30 (1997):294–95, points to a similar use of "adventures" in *TS*, I.20.65, suggesting "illicit sexual encounters," a common usage throughout the century.

[6] Sterne uses this proverbial phrase again in *Letters,* 394; see Tilley, L1: "He has his LABOR for his pains"; and *ODEP,* 438.

[7] Cf. sermon 18, "The Levite and his concubine": "a good heart wants some object to be kind to——and the best parts of our blood, and the purest of our spirits suffer most under the destitution" (*Sermons* 4:170).

[8] A scriptural formula (Judges 20:1, 2 Samuel 24:2); Dan and Beersheba are at the northern and southern extremities of Canaan. In *TS,* VII.27.617, Walter Shandy is a traveler who "would have found fruit even in a desert"; and in VII.43.648, Tristram reports that the "barren" plains of Languedoc provided the "most fruitful and busy period" of his life.

[9] The myrtle was held sacred to Venus; the cypress was associated with death and cemeteries. Cf. *Letters,* 19 (?1739–1740, to his future wife): "Thou wilt leave thy name upon the myrtle-tree.—If trees . . . could compose an elegy, I should expect a very plaintive one . . ."; and *TS,* VI.32.556: "O brother! 'tis one thing for a soldier to gather laurels,—and 'tis another to scatter cypress.——[*Who told thee, my dear* Toby, *that cypress was used by the ancients on mournful occasions?*]"

[10] Stout, 116, draws a parallel to Don Quixote's conduct in the desert of the Sierra Morena, where, in the manner of a true knight-errant, he mourns over imaginary cruelties inflicted on him by Dulcinea (*Don Quixote,* I.III.11; 1:247–71). Cf. also Quixote's praise (II.III.17; 2:151–52) of the nobility of the "Knight-Errant, who . . . wanders through Desarts, through solitary Wildernesses . . . in Quest of perilous Adventures, resolv'd to bring them to a happy Conclusion."

[11] I.e., Tobias Smollett; see Introduction, p. xiii.

he pass'd by was discoloured or distorted—He wrote an account of them, but 'twas nothing but the account of his miserable feelings.[12]

I met Smelfungus in the grand portico of the Pantheon—he was just coming out of it—'*Tis nothing but a huge cock-pit**, said he—I wish you had said nothing worse of the Venus of Medicis, replied I[13]—for in passing through Florence, I had heard he had fallen foul upon the goddess, and used her worse than a common strumpet, without the least provocation in nature.

I popp'd upon Smelfungus again at Turin, in his return home;[14] and a sad tale of sorrowful adventures had he to tell, "wherein he spoke of moving accidents by flood and field, and of the cannibals which each other eat: the Anthropophagi"[15]—he had been flea'd alive, and bedevil'd, and used worse than St. Bartholomew,[16] at every stage he had come at—

*Vide S——'s Travels.

---

[12] Cf. the headnote to *BJ*, p. 176, where Sterne calls it "a Diary of the miserable feelings of a person separated from a Lady for whose Society he languish'd"; and again, on August 4, when he tells Eliza: "all I can write would be but the History of my miserable feelings" (p. 231).

[13] Sterne met Smollett in Montpellier in November 1763, when both families were staying there; Smollett's letter from Montpellier (letter 11, November 12), mentions an account he had of a medical case from "Mrs. St——e who was on the spot" (1:190). They did not, however, meet in Rome; when Sterne finally reached Italy, on his second trip to the continent three years later, Smollett was back in England. Sterne wrote from Florence in December 1765, that he intended "in 5 days [to] tread the Vatican, and be introduced to all the Saints in the Pantheon" (*Letters* 266); since he did, in fact, visit Rome, there is every reason to believe he carried out this intention.

Of the Pantheon, Smollett wrote: "I was much disappointed at sight of the Pantheon, which, after all that has been said of it, looks like a huge cockpit, open at top" (letter 31, 2:122–23); and of the *Venus de Medici*: "Without all doubt, the limbs and proportions of this statue are elegantly formed . . . and the back parts especially are executed so happily, as to excite the admiration of the most indifferent spectator" (letter 28, 2:63–64).

[14] In letter 38, Smollett recounts his excursion from Nice to Turin and back, "the greater part of the way lying over frightful mountains covered with snow" (*Travels* 2:210); it is a vivid description of the real dangers of a journey that probably should not have been undertaken in February.

[15] See *Othello*, I.iii.134–35, 143–44: "Wherein I spoke of most disastrous chances: / Of moving accidents by flood and field / . . . And of the Cannibals that each [other] eat, / The Anthropophagi." Cf. *BJ* (July 27), where Sterne again recalls a line from Othello's famous speech (I.iii.167); see below, p. 229, n. 42 and cf. p. 208, n. 34.

[16] One of the twelve apostles, said to have been flayed alive at Albanopolis in Armenia in A.D. 44. Smollett mentions him in listing the "shocking subjects of the martyrology" that occupy Roman Catholic painters: ". . . Bartholomew fleaed alive, and a hundred other pictures equally frightful, which can only serve to . . . encourage a spirit of religious fanaticism" (*Travels*, letter 31, 2:121).

—I'll tell it, cried Smelfungus, to the world. You had better tell it, said I, to your physician.[17]

Mundungus,[18] with an immense fortune, made the whole tour; going on from Rome to Naples—from Naples to Venice—from Venice to Vienna—to Dresden, to Berlin, without one generous connection or pleasurable anecdote to tell of; but he had travell'd straight on looking neither to his right hand or his left, lest Love or Pity should seduce him out of his road.

Peace be to them! if it is to be found; but heaven itself, was it possible to get there with such tempers, would want objects to give it—every gentle spirit would come flying upon the wings of Love to hail their arrival—Nothing would the souls of Smelfungus and Mundungus hear of, but fresh anthems of joy, fresh raptures of love, and fresh congratulations of their common felicity—I heartily pity them: they have brought up no faculties for this work; and was the happiest mansion in heaven to be allotted to Smelfungus and Mundungus, they would be so far from being happy, that the souls of Smelfungus and Mundungus would do penance there to all eternity.[19]

Keymer, 153, calls attention to the probable pun on Smollett's many complaints about flea-ridden inns. Cf. *TS,* IV.S.T.302: "the several sisterhoods had scratch'd and mawl'd themselves all to death—they got out of their beds almost flead alive."

[17] Smollett was a licensed member of the medical profession. In addition to the humor of Sterne's advice, cf. Luke 4:23: "Ye will surely say unto me this proverb, Physician, heal thyself."

[18] Mundungus has traditionally been identified as Dr. Samuel Sharp (1700?–1778), who published *Letters from Italy, Describing the Customs and Manners of That Country, in the Years 1765, and 1766* (1766, 2d ed. 1767). Like Smollett, Sharp was ill, and critical of the Italians, but he was (excepting his anti-Roman Catholicism) a more evenhanded traveler than most: "I wish I could always write panegyric; for, speaking as an *Englishman,* every partiality allowable should be admitted in their favour. I assure you, the politeness of the *Italians* towards our nation, is very extraordinary" (131–32).

Stout and others have stressed the definition of *mundungus* as "offal, refuse." But Sterne may have had its more common eighteenth-century usage in mind, "bad-smelling tobacco" (Johnson's *Dictionary:* "stinking tobacco"). Among its examples, *OED* cites Samuel Paterson, *Another Traveler* (1767), 1:192: "The Flemish tobacco is the poorest Mundungus in the world."

[19] This passage, which begins with a scriptural tag from Luke 24:36 (cf. John 20:19), "Peace be unto you," borrows its idea from John Norris (1657–1711), *Practical Discourses upon the Beatitudes* (1690). For its appearance in sermon 29, "Our conversation in heaven," see Appendix, pp. 242–45 below. Sterne is not contrasting Smelfungus's failure to enjoy the world with Yorick's delight in it, but rather his intense worldliness, which prevents him from rising above mundane concerns, even if doing so is the only path to heaven. Norris, a Christian platonist, argues not for heightened sensibility toward the world, but the opposite: the journey through life must be a purgation of the senses. For further discussion, see the Florida *ASJ,* 6:273–75, n. to 38.4–13; and Melvyn New, "The Odd Couple: Laurence Sterne and John Norris of Bemerton," *PQ* 75 (1996):361–85.

MONTRIUL.[1]

I HAD once lost my portmanteau from behind my chaise, and twice got out in the rain, and one of the times up to the knees in dirt, to help the postilion to tie it on, without being able to find out what was wanting[2]—Nor was it till I got to Montriul, upon the landlord's[3] asking me if I wanted not a servant, that it occurred to me, that that was the very thing.

A servant! That I do most sadly, quoth I—Because, Monsieur, said the landlord, there is a clever young fellow, who would be very proud of the honour to serve an Englishman[4]—But why an English one, more than any other?—They are so generous, said the landlord—I'll be shot if this is not a livre out of my pocket, quoth I to myself, this very night—But they have wherewithal to be so, Monsieur, added he—Set down one livre more for that, quoth I—It was but last night, said the landlord, *qu'un my Lord Anglois presentoit un ecu a la fille de chambre—Tant pis, pour Mad^lle Janatone,* said I.[5]

---

[1] Sterne consistently misspells Montreuil in *ASJ;* it is correctly spelled in *TS,* VII.9.588.

[2] Tristram makes a similar observation, namely that after the "sixth, seventh, eighth, ninth, and tenth time" it happened, he was ready to make a "national reflection of it":

> That something is always wrong in a French post-chaise upon first setting out.
> Or the proposition may stand thus.
> A French postilion has always to alight before he has got three hundred yards out of town. (*TS* VII.8.587)

Sterne's own experience on the road is captured in a letter that might have been written by Smollett: "Can you conceive a worse accident than that in such a journey, in the hottest day and hour of it . . . we should break a hind wheel into ten thousand pieces . . . —To mend the matter, my two postillions were two dough-hearted fools, and fell a crying—Nothing was to be done! By heaven, quoth I, pulling off my coat and waistcoat, something shall be done, for I'll thrash you both within an inch of your lives . . ." (*Letters* 183).

[3] Stout, 121, notes the identification made by John Poole (1786–1872?), author of *Paul Pry* (1825) and other forgotten plays, that the landlord was a Monsieur Varennes, master of the Hôtel de la Cour de France ("Sterne at Calais and Montreuil," *London Magazine and Review* 1 [January 1825]:44–45). Poole's account of his retracing of Yorick's journey (January, 38–46; March, 387–94) is a witty and intelligent appreciation of Sterne.

[4] Cf. Smollett, *Travels,* letter 6, 1:85–86: "Nothing gives me such chagrin, as the necessity I am under to hire a *valet de place* . . . . You cannot conceive with what eagerness and dexterity those rascally valets exert themselves in pillaging strangers. . . . He produces recommendations from his former masters, and the people of the house vouch for his honesty. The truth is, those fellows are very handy, useful, and obliging; and so far honest, that they will not steal in the usual way . . . ."

[5] That an English lord [correctly, *milord Anglois;* Sterne lapses into English] gave the chambermaid an ecu—so much the worse, for Miss Janatone. An ecu was worth sixty sous, or three livres (see above, p. 11, n. 1), a sum large enough to raise suspicion. *Janatone* is probably Sterne's phonetic transcription of *Jeanneton,* a diminutive of *Jeannette,*

Now Janatone being the landlord's daughter, and the landlord supposing I was young in French, took the liberty to inform me, I should not have said *tant pis*— but, *tant mieux. Tant mieux, toujours, Monsieur,*[6] said he, when there is any thing to be got—*tant pis,* when there is nothing. It comes to the same thing, said I. *Pardonnez moi,*[7] said the landlord.

I cannot take a fitter opportunity to observe once for all, that *tant pis* and *tant mieux* being two of the great hinges in French conversation, a stranger would do well to set himself right in the use of them, before he gets to Paris.

A prompt French Marquis at our ambassador's table demanded of Mr. H——, if he was H—— the poet? No, said H—— mildly—*Tant pis*, replied the Marquis.[8]

It is H—— the historian, said another—*Tant mieux,* said the Marquis. And Mr. H——, who is a man of an excellent heart, return'd thanks for both.

When the landlord had set me right in this matter, he called in La Fleur,[9]

---

itself a diminutive of *Jeanne,* a common name for an inn-servant or girl of loose morals in French folksongs. In *TS,* VII.9.588, Janatone is the innkeeper's daughter at Montreuil who, Tristram warns, may "go off like a hussy" and lose herself (590).

[6] I.e., "I should not have said *so much the worse*—but, *so much the better. So much the better, always.*" Sterne uses *tant pis* at least once in his correspondence: "there is an acc[t] here that the great Rock of Gibraltor is overthrown by an earthquake—tant pis pour nous: we could only defend the place ag[st] men" (*Letters* 273).

[7] Pardon me. The landlord's tone may be indignant or merely puzzled; Yorick calls attention to a possible lapse on Janatone's part (and perhaps puns: being paid for nothing [no *thing*] is to be paid for something), but the landlord's response is noncommittal. In the anecdote following, *tant pis* might best be translated "too bad" and *tant mieux,* "all the better."

[8] David Hume (1711–1776), the philosopher and historian, and John Home (1722–1808), the author of the successful tragedy *Douglas* (1756), pronounced their names exactly alike. Hume was in Paris from 1763 to 1765 as secretary to the Earl of Hertford, ambassador to the Court of France. He met Sterne on several occasions, including a dinner party at which they supposedly debated about the sermon Sterne had delivered earlier in the day, and the question of miracles; see *Sermons,* 5:194–95, and *Letters,* 218–19. That Sterne praises him here for the elegance of his response is consonant with his epistolary assessment of Hume (1764): "in my life, did I never meet with a being of a more placid and gentle nature; and it is this amiable turn of his character, that has given more consequence and force to his scepticism, than all the arguments of his sophistry" (218). Some years after Sterne's death, in 1773, Hume wrote to William Strahan, the publisher: "England is so sunk in Stupidity . . . that you may as well think of Lapland for an author. The best Book, that has been writ by any English these thirty Years . . . is *Tristram Shandy* bad as it is. A Remark which may astonish you; but which you will find true on Reflection" (*Letters of David Hume,* ed. J. Y. T. Greig [Oxford: Oxford UP, 1932], 2:269).

[9] Stout, 342–43, dismisses the claims of an actual La Fleur and is also correct to dismiss claims that Sterne found the name in Bayle's *Dictionary.* More probable is Curtis's suggestion (*Letters* 268, n. 2), that he found the name in Philippe Néricault-Destouches, *Le glorieux* (1732), where it belongs to a servant. However, *La Fleur* (the Flower) may simply have struck Sterne (and others) as an appropriate name for a French valet.

which was the name of the young man he had spoke of—saying only first, That as for his talents, he would presume to say nothing—Monsieur was the best judge what would suit him; but for the fidelity of La Fleur, he would stand responsible in all he was worth.

The landlord deliver'd this in a manner which instantly set my mind to the business I was upon—and La Fleur, who stood waiting without, in that breathless expectation which every son of nature of us have felt in our turns, came in.

MONTRIUL.

I AM apt to be taken with all kinds of people at first sight; but never more so, than when a poor devil comes to offer his service to so poor a devil as myself; and as I know this weakness, I always suffer my judgment to draw back something on that very account—and this more or less, according to the mood I am in, and the case—and I may add the gender too, of the person I am to govern.

When La Fleur enter'd the room, after every discount I could make for my soul, the genuine look and air of the fellow determined the matter at once in his favour; so I hired him first—and then began to inquire what he could do: But I shall find out his talents, quoth I, as I want them—besides, a Frenchman can do every thing.

Now poor La Fleur could do nothing in the world but beat a drum, and play a march or two upon the fife. I was determined to make his talents do; and can't say my weakness was ever so insulted by my wisdom, as in the attempt.

La Fleur had set out early in life, as gallantly as most Frenchmen do, with *serving* for a few years; at the end of which, having satisfied the sentiment, and found moreover, That the honour of beating a drum was likely to be its own reward, as it open'd no further track of glory to him—he retired *a ses terres,* and lived *comme il plaisoit a Dieu*[1]—that is to say, upon nothing.

—And so, quoth *Wisdome,* you have hired a drummer to attend you in this tour of your's thro' France and Italy! Psha! said I, and do not one half of our gentry go with a hum-drum *compagnon du voiage*[2] the same round, and have the piper and the devil and all to pay besides? When man can extricate himself with an *equivoque*[3] in such an unequal match—he is not ill off—But you can do something else, La Fleur? said I—*O qu'oui!*[4]—he could make spatterdashes, and play a little upon the fiddle—Bravo! said Wisdome—Why, I play a bass myself, said I[5]—we shall do very well.—You can shave, and dress a wig a little, La Fleur?—He had all the dispositions in the world[6]—It is enough for heaven! said I, interrupting him—and ought to be enough for me—So supper coming in, and having a frisky English spaniel on one side of my chair, and a French valet, with

---

[1] He deserted and lived at God's pleasure (literally, he retired to his estate; correctly, *dans ses terres*).

[2] Traveling companion (correctly, *de voyage;* Sterne's spelling was obsolete).

[3] "An expression capable of more than one meaning; a play upon words, a pun"; *OED* lists English usages from the seventeenth century. The pun here is, of course, on "hum-*drum*."

[4] Yes, indeed.

[5] Cf. Cash, *EMY,* 208: "Readers of *Tristram Shandy* readily assume that Sterne knew a great deal about music, so common are the musical images. In the 'Memoirs' he said he enjoyed 'fiddling.' . . . When Sterne died he left behind a bass viol."

[6] A literal translation of the French: *il avait toutes les dispositions du monde.*

as much hilarity in his countenance as ever nature painted in one, on the other—
I was satisfied to my heart's content with my empire; and if monarchs knew what
they would be at, they might be as satisfied as I was.

MONTRIUL.

A S La Fleur went the whole tour of France and Italy with me, and will be often upon the stage, I must interest the reader a little further in his behalf, by saying, that I had never less reason to repent of the impulses which generally do determine me, than in regard to this fellow—he was a faithful, affectionate, simple soul as ever trudged after the heels of a philosopher; and notwithstanding his talents of drum-beating and spatterdash-making, which, tho' very good in themselves, happen'd to be of no great service to me, yet was I hourly recompenced by the festivity of his temper—it supplied all defects—I had a constant resource in his looks in all difficulties and distresses of my own—I was going to have added, of his too; but La Fleur was out of the reach of every thing; for whether 'twas hunger or thirst, or cold or nakedness, or watchings, or whatever stripes of ill luck La Fleur met with in our journeyings,[1] there was no index in his physiognomy to point them out by—he was eternally the same; so that if I am a piece of a philosopher,[2] which Satan now and then puts it into my head I am—it always mortifies the pride of the conceit, by reflecting how much I owe to the complexional philosophy of this poor fellow, for shaming me into one of a better kind. With all this, La Fleur had a small cast of the coxcomb—but he seemed at first sight to be more a coxcomb of nature than of art; and before I had been three days in Paris with him—he seemed to be no coxcomb at all.

---

[1] Cf. Paul's description of his sufferings in 2 Corinthians 11:23–27: "in stripes above measure . . . In journeyings often . . . in watchings . . . in hunger and thirst . . . in cold and nakedness."

[2] Cf. Sterne's discussion in sermon 15 ("Job's expostulation with his wife") of the role of classical philosophy in teaching us to endure the misfortunes of life: "in most modern languages, the patient enduring of affliction has by degrees obtained the name of philosophy, and almost monopolized the word to itself, as if it was the chief end, or compendium of all the wisdom which philosophy had to offer" (*Sermons* 4:143).

MONTRIUL.

THE next morning La Fleur entering upon his employment, I delivered to him the key of my portmanteau with an inventory of my half a dozen shirts and silk pair of breeches; and bid him fasten all upon the chaise—get the horses put to—and desire the landlord to come in with his bill.

C'est un garçon de bonne fortune,[1] said the landlord, pointing through the window to half a dozen wenches who had got round about La Fleur, and were most kindly taking their leave of him, as the postilion was leading out the horses. La Fleur kissed all their hands round and round again, and thrice he wiped his eyes, and thrice he promised he would bring them all pardons from Rome.

The young fellow, said the landlord, is beloved by all the town, and there is scarce a corner in Montriul where the want of him will not be felt:[2] he has but one misfortune in the world, continued he, "He is always in love."—I am heartily glad of it, said I,—'twill save me the trouble every night of putting my breeches under my head. In saying this, I was making not so much La Fleur's eloge, as my own, having been in love with one princess or another almost all my life, and I hope I shall go on so, till I die, being firmly persuaded, that if ever I do a mean action, it must be in some interval betwixt one passion and another: whilst this interregnum lasts, I always perceive my heart locked up—I can scarce find in it, to give Misery a sixpence; and therefore I always get out of it as fast as I can, and the moment I am rekindled, I am all generosity and good will again;[3] and would do any thing in the world either for, or with any one, if they will but satisfy me there is no sin in it.

—But in saying this—surely I am commending the passion—not myself.

---

[1] Le Roux, *Dictionnaire,* has an entry for "Homme à bonne fortune," defined as "lucky in love."

[2] The bawdy suggestiveness gives point to the pardons La Fleur promises to bring back from Rome.

[3] Yorick shares a view Sterne had embraced in a letter to a friend in 1765: "I am glad that you are in love—'twill cure you (at least) of the spleen, which has a bad effect on both man and woman—I myself must ever have some dulcinea in my head—it harmonises the soul"; see above, p. 35, and n. 5. Cf. *TS,* VIII.26.709: "I call not love a misfortune, from a persuasion, that a man's heart is ever the better for it." Parnell, 230, quotes Adam Smith, *The Theory of Moral Sentiments* (1759): "The sentiment of love is, in itself, agreeable to the person who feels it. It sooths and composes the breast, seems to favour the vital motions, and to promote the heathful state of the human constitution . . ." (ed. D. D. Raphael and A. L. Macfie [Oxford: Oxford UP, 1979], I.ii.4.2, p. 39).

A FRAGMENT.[1]

————THE town of Abdera, notwithstanding Democritus lived there trying all the powers of irony and laughter to reclaim it, was the vilest and most profligate town in all Thrace.[2] What for poisons, conspiracies and assassinations—libels, pasquinades and tumults, there was no going there by day—'twas worse by night.

Now, when things were at the worst, it came to pass, that the Andromeda of Euripides[3] being represented at Abdera, the whole orchestra was delighted with it: but of all the passages which delighted them, nothing operated more upon their imaginations, than the tender strokes of nature which the poet had wrought up in that pathetic speech of Perseus,

O Cupid, prince of God and men, &c.

Every man almost spoke pure iambics the next day, and talk'd of nothing but Perseus his pathetic address—"O Cupid! prince of God and men"—in every street of Abdera, in every house—"O Cupid! Cupid!"—in every mouth, like the natural notes of some sweet melody which drops from it whether it will or no—nothing but "Cupid! Cupid! prince of God and men"—The fire caught—and the whole city, like the heart of one man, open'd itself to Love.

No pharmacopolist could sell one grain of helebore[4]—not a single armourer had a heart to forge one instrument of death—Friendship and Virtue met together, and kiss'd each other in the street—the golden age return'd, and hung o'er the town of Abdera—every Abderite took his oaten pipe, and every

---

[1] Sterne borrows his "fragment" directly from Burton, *The Anatomy of Melancholy,* 3.2.3.4 (481), but as Stout, 130, notes, Burton copied it from the classical satirist, Lucian (b.c. 120), the opening of "The Way to Write History" (*Works* 6:2–5). Sterne's borrowing was first noted by John Ferriar, *Illustrations of Sterne,* 2d ed. (1812), 1:118–20.

[2] Abdera, a town in southern Thrace; the inhabitants were proverbially stupid or mad. Democritus (c. 460–c. 357 B.C.), Greek physical philosopher and the source of Burton's use of the pseudonym "Democritus Junior." In his introduction to *Anatomy,* Burton writes: "After a wandring life, he setled at *Abdera* a town in *Thrace,* and was sent for thither to be their Law-maker, Recorder or Town-clerke, as some will; or as others, he was there bred and born. Howsoever it was, there he lived . . . a private life, *saving that sometimes he would walk down to the haven, and laugh heartily at such varietie of ridiculous objects, which there he saw*" (2); hence Democritus's title, "the laughing philosopher." Cf. *Notes* to *TS,* 3:336–37, on Sterne's epigraphs to volumes V and VI, borrowed from "Democritus Junior."

[3] The play, produced in 412 B.C., is not extant; Euripides (c. 485–406 B.C.), the third and last great Greek tragedian.

[4] Hellebore was conventionally believed to cure madness, particularly love madness.

49

Abderitish[5] woman left her purple web, and chastly sat her down and listen'd to the song—

'Twas only in the power, says the Fragment, of the God whose empire extendeth from heaven to earth, and even to the depths of the sea, to have done this.[6]

---

[5] Sterne's own nonce-word.

[6] Sterne adds this to Burton, recalling, perhaps, the praise of God in the Morning Prayer of the *Book of Common Prayer*, beginning with the words of the Lord's Prayer ("Thy will be done in earth, As it is in heaven") and Psalm 95:5: "In his hand are all the corners of the earth . . . The sea is his and he made it."

MONTRIUL.

WHEN all is ready, and every article is disputed and paid for in the inn, unless you are a little sour'd by the adventure, there is always a matter to compound at the door, before you can get into your chaise; and that is with the sons and daughters of poverty, who surround you.[1] Let no man say, "let them go to the devil"—'tis a cruel journey to send a few miserables, and they have had sufferings enow without it: I always think it better to take a few sous out in my hand; and I would counsel every gentle traveller to do so likewise: he need not be so exact in setting down his motives for giving them—they will be register'd elsewhere.

For my own part, there is no man gives so little as I do; for few that I know have so little to give: but as this was the first publick act of my charity in France, I took the more notice of it.

A well-a-way! said I. I have but eight sous in the world, shewing them in my hand, and there are eight poor men and eight poor women for 'em.

A poor tatter'd soul without a shirt on instantly withdrew his claim, by retiring two steps out of the circle, and making a disqualifying bow on his part. Had the whole parterre cried out, *Place aux dames*,[2] with one voice, it would not have conveyed the sentiment of a deference for the sex with half the effect.

Just heaven! for what wise reasons hast thou order'd it, that beggary and urbanity,[3] which are at such variance in other countries, should find a way to be at unity in this?

—I insisted upon presenting him with a single sous, merely for his *politesse*.[4]

---

[1] The scene was common for travelers in France; cf. Cole, *Journal*, 45: "It is incredible how troublesome the Beggars are to you: if you stop in a Coach, or Post Chaise, you have presently 10 or a Dozen about you . . . ." Cf. Henry Peckham, *Tour of Holland . . . and Part of France* (1772), 228: "The whole kingdom [of France] swarms with beggars . . . . This observation was confirmed at every inn I came to, by crowds of wretches, whose appearance spake their misery. I have often passed from the inn-door to my chaise through a file of twenty or thirty of them."

[2] Ladies first. For "parterre" see below, p. 83, n. 2.

[3] In *TS*, VII.17.599, Sterne ironically labels Paris the "SCHOOL of URBANITY herself": "Ha!——and no one gives the wall!——but in the SCHOOL of URBANITY herself, if the walls are besh—t—how can you do otherwise?" Cf. below, p. 125, where the Count questions Yorick on the vaunted urbanity of the French.

[4] Courtesy. Early in his sojourn, Cole, *Journal*, 27–29, scorns "all their boasted Politeness & good Manners to Strangers," because in all his time in a carriage to Paris, he could never "see the least . . . obliging Behaviour of that Sort . . . ." And, he comments ironically, "before the End of the Journey I fully experienced the French *Politesse* . . . a contemptuous Reserve in Respect to myself; & tho' they were not absolutely rude, yet the French Officer could not contain more than once having a malitious Fling at the English Nation . . . ."

A poor little dwarfish brisk fellow, who stood over-against me in the circle, putting something first under his arm, which had once been a hat, took his snuff-box out of his pocket, and generously offer'd a pinch on both sides of him: it was a gift of consequence, and modestly declined—The poor little fellow press'd it upon them with a nod of welcomeness—*Prenez en—prenez,*[5] said he, looking another way; so they each took a pinch—Pity thy box should ever want one! said I to myself; so I put a couple of sous into it—taking a small pinch out of his box, to enhance their value, as I did it—He felt the weight of the second obligation more than that of the first—'twas doing him an honour—the other was only doing him a charity—and he made me a bow down to the ground for it.

—Here! said I to an old soldier with one hand, who had been campaign'd and worn out to death in the service—here's a couple of sous for thee—*Vive le Roi!*[6] said the old soldier.

I had then but three sous left: so I gave one, simply *pour l'amour de Dieu,*[7] which was the footing on which it was begg'd—The poor woman had a dislocated hip; so it could not be well, upon any other motive.

Mon cher et tres charitable Monsieur[8]—There's no opposing this, said I.

My Lord Anglois—the very sound was worth the money—so I gave *my last sous for it.* But in the eagerness of giving, I had overlook'd a *pauvre honteux,*[9] who had no one to ask a sous for him, and who, I believed, would have perish'd, ere he could have ask'd one for himself: he stood by the chaise a little without the circle, and wiped a tear from a face which I thought had seen better days—Good God! said I—and I have not one single sous left to give him—But you have a thousand! cried all the powers of nature, stirring within me—so I gave him—no matter what—I am ashamed to say *how much,* now—and was ashamed to think, how little, then: so if the reader can form any conjecture of my disposition, as these two

---

[5] Take some; idiomatically, help yourself.

[6] Long live the King!

[7] For the love of God.

[8] My dear and very charitable Sir.

[9] A poor man ashamed to beg. A significant parallel to this encounter may be found in an anonymous pamphlet published almost sixty years earlier, *Occasional Reflections in a Journey from London to Norwich & Cambridge* (1711), noted in *European Magazine* (1797), 240–41; and much later, by Arthur Sherbo, "More from the *Gentleman's Magazine,*" *SB* 40 (1987):164–74. The description of a confrontation with a beggar, while not an actual source for Sterne, indicates how firmly fixed "sentimentalism" was from one end of the century to the other: "I HAVE little Compassion, for Common Beggars: But, there are some Men, I cannot pass, without an Alms. One of These I overtook, this Morning . . . . He ask't me Nothing. Indeed there was no Occasion for it; his Countenance sufficiently Exprest his Wants. . . . He had lost one of his Eyes, by Sickness; and the same Distemper had Impair'd the Other. The best Service, they could do him, Now, was, to Weep withal: Which he did . . ." (6–7). See below, p. 58, n. 6, another passage in which Sterne's "sentimentalism" is paralleled by this earlier text.

fixed points are given him, he may judge within a livre or two what was the precise sum.

I could afford nothing for the rest, but, *Dieu vous benisse—Et le bon Dieu vous benisse encore*[10]—said the old soldier, the dwarf, &c. The *pauvre honteux* could say nothing—he pull'd out a little handkerchief, and wiped his face as he turned away—and I thought he thank'd me more than them all.

---

[10] God bless you—And, again, the good Lord bless you. As Le Roux, *Dictionnaire,* points out, *Dieu vous benisse* was a term used to dismiss beggars and hence a possible error or irony on Sterne's part.

THE BIDET.[1]

HAVING settled all these little matters, I got into my post-chaise with more ease than ever I got into a post-chaise in my life; and La Fleur having got one large jack-boot[2] on the far side of a little *bidet**, and another on this (for I count nothing of his legs)—he canter'd away before me as happy and as perpendicular[3] as a prince.—

—But what is happiness! what is grandeur in this painted scene of life! A dead ass, before we had got a league, put a sudden stop to La Fleur's career—his bidet would not pass by it—a contention arose betwixt them, and the poor fellow was kick'd out of his jack-boots the very first kick.

La Fleur bore his fall like a French christian, saying neither more or less upon it, than, Diable![4] so presently got up and came to the charge again astride his bidet, beating him up to it as he would have beat his drum.

The bidet flew from one side of the road to the other, then back again—then this way—then that way, and in short every way but by the dead ass.—La Fleur insisted upon the thing—and the bidet threw him.

What's the matter, La Fleur, said I, with this bidet of thine?—*Monsieur*, said he, *c'est un cheval le plus opiniatré du monde*[5]—Nay, if he is a conceited beast, he must go his own way, replied I—so La Fleur got off him, and giving him a good

*Post horse.

---

[1] Stout, 135–36, suggests a humorous reference to the small size of French post-horses, as noted by Sterne in *TS*, VII.20.605: "I hate to hear a person . . . complain that we do not get on so fast in France as we do in England; whereas we get on much faster . . . if you . . . consider their puny horses." The small size of French horses was often ridiculed by English travelers.

We might suspect a bawdy play on a second meaning of "bidet" (a low basin for the washing of the private parts), which attracted much attention among Sterne's fellow-travelers; see, e.g., Smollett, *Travels*, letter 5, 1:64: "Will custom exempt from the imputation of gross indecency a French lady, who shifts her frowsy smock in presence of a male visitant, and talks to him of her *lavement*, her *medicine*, and her *bidet!*" While this second usage may not seem quite appropriate to the chapter, La Fleur astride his "bidet" encountering a dead "ass" may not be entirely innocent of innuendo. And cf. Le Roux, *Dictionnaire*, where *bidet* is said to also be used for "le membre viril"; see n. 3 below.

[2] See Cunnington, 81: "These reached above the knees with slightly spreading 'bucket tops'; the toes blocked and square . . . . Heels square and massive but not very high . . . . Made of very strong leather."

[3] *OED*'s first illustration of usage to refer to a person: "of erect figure or attitude when standing or riding . . . ."

[4] Deuce take it! "*Le Diable*" (p. 55) is perhaps a foreshortening for *Que le Diable l'emporte* (Let the Devil take it); and see above, "*diabled*" (p. 21).

[5] It is the most stubborn horse in the world (correctly, *le cheval le plus opiniâtre*).

sound lash, the bidet took me at my word, and away he scamper'd back to Mon-triul.—*Peste!*[6] said La Fleur.

It is not *mal a propos*[7] to take notice here, that tho' La Fleur availed himself but of two different terms of exclamation in this encounter—namely, *Diable!* and *Peste!* that there are nevertheless three, in the French language; like the positive, comparative, and superlative, one or the other of which serve for every unexpected throw of the dice in life.

Le Diable! which is the first, and positive degree, is generally used upon ordinary emotions of the mind, where small things only fall out contrary to your expectations—such as—the throwing once doublets[8]—La Fleur's being kick'd off his horse, and so forth—cuckoldom, for the same reason, is always—*Le Diable!*

But in cases where the cast has something provoking in it, as in that of the bidet's running away after, and leaving La Fleur aground in jack-boots—'tis the second degree.

'Tis then *Peste!*

And for the third—[9]

—But here my heart is wrung with pity and fellow-feeling, when I reflect what miseries must have been their lot, and how bitterly so refined a people must have smarted, to have forced them upon the use of it.—

Grant me, O ye powers which touch the tongue with eloquence in distress!—whatever is my *cast*, Grant me but decent words to exclaim in, and I will give my nature way.[10]

---

[6] What a plague! Despite Yorick's ranking it as stronger than *Diable*, it is a milder oath, perhaps equal to "bless me!"

[7] Unseasonable, amiss (correctly, à).

[8] *OED*, s.v. *doublets*, 3.a., considers it a dicing term: "the same number turning up on both the dice at a throw." It may refer more specifically to a pair (doublets) of ones ("aces" or "snake eyes" in craps) in a game where the object is to make a high score; in hazard, e.g., double one is an automatic losing throw.

[9] Readers of *TS* will likely think of *foutre* (to fuck)—as does Serge Soupel (*Le voyage sentimental* [Paris: Flammarion, 1981], 91, n. 49)—or *bouger* (to move, with an allusion to *bougre*, to bugger; cf. *TS* VII.25.613–14). Sterne refers to France as "foutre-land" (*Letters* 214).

[10] Cf. Wisdom 10:21: "For wisdom opened the mouth of the dumb, and made the tongues of them that cannot speak eloquent"; see also Isaiah 32:4, 35:6, Ezekiel 24:27, 33:22, Matthew 9:33, 15:31, etc., for variations of this scriptural commonplace. Sterne invokes it in sermon 10, "Job's account of the shortness and troubles of life": "the words of that being, who first inspired man with language, and taught his mouth to utter, who opened the lips of the dumb, and made the tongue of the infant eloquent" (*Sermons* 4:91). That Sterne has Scripture in mind is indicated by his first version of this passage, "Grant me but religious & decent words . . . ."

Cf. *TS*, VII.20.605, where Tristram considers ways to tell us the two "magic" words that can move a French post-horse: "My ink burns my finger to try."

—But as these were not to be had in France, I resolved to take every evil just as it befell me without any exclamation at all.

La Fleur, who had made no such covenant with himself, followed the bidet with his eyes till it was got out of sight—and then, you may imagine, if you please, with what word he closed the whole affair.

As there was no hunting down a frighten'd horse in jack-boots, there remained no alternative but taking La Fleur either behind the chaise, or into it.—

I preferred the latter, and in half an hour we got to the post-house at Nampont.

NAMPONT.
THE DEAD ASS.[1]

—AND this, said he, putting the remains of a crust into his wallet—and this, should have been thy portion, said he, hadst thou been alive to have shared it with me. I thought by the accent, it had been an apostrophe to his child; but 'twas to his ass, and to the very ass we had seen dead in the road, which had occasioned La Fleur's misadventure. The man seemed to lament it much; and it instantly brought into my mind Sancho's lamentation for his; but he did it with more true touches of nature.

The mourner was sitting upon a stone bench at the door, with the ass's pannel[2] and its bridle on one side, which he took up from time to time—then laid them down—look'd at them and shook his head. He then took his crust of bread out of his wallet again, as if to eat it; held it some time in his hand—then laid it upon the bit of his ass's bridle—looked wistfully at the little arrangement he had made—and then gave a sigh.

The simplicity of his grief drew numbers about him, and La Fleur amongst the rest, whilst the horses were getting ready; as I continued sitting in the post-chaise, I could see and hear over their heads.

—He said he had come last from Spain, where he had been from the furthest borders of Franconia;[3] and had got so far on his return home, when his ass died. Every one seem'd desirous to know what business could have taken so old and poor a man so far a journey from his own home.

It had pleased heaven, he said, to bless him with three sons, the finest lads in all Germany; but having in one week lost two of the eldest of them by the small-pox,

---

[1] Sterne introduces an ass in *TS*, VII.32 ("—But with an ass, I can commune for ever"), and here challenges himself further: could he wax sentimental about an ass, while simultaneously keeping alert to the ludicrousness of doing so? His model was Cervantes' similar exercise in Sancho Panza's lamentation when his ass Dapple is stolen: "finding himself depriv'd of that dear Partner of his Fortunes, and best Comfort in his Peregrinations, he broke out into the most pitiful and sad Lamentations in the World" (I.III.9; 1:222).

This chapter became the basis for an unfortunate anecdote circulated about Sterne, that he had neglected his mother. Horace Walpole gave it epigrammatic longevity: "Her son had too much sentiment to have any feeling. A dead ass was more important to him than a living mother." Byron's version has even more bite: "Ah, I am as bad as that dog Sterne, who preferred whining over 'a dead ass to relieving a living mother'" (see Alan B. Howes, *Yorick and the Critics: Sterne's Reputation in England, 1760–1868* [New Haven: Yale UP, 1958], 89–90).

[2] *OED*, s.v. *panel*, I.2: "A kind of saddle: generally applied to a rough treeless pad; but formerly sometimes to an ass's wooden saddle." Sancho's Dapple is so equipped.

[3] The area of southwest Germany constituting parts of present-day Baden, Wurttemberg, and northern Bavaria.

and the youngest falling ill of the same distemper, he was afraid of being bereft of them all; and made a vow, if Heaven would not take him from him also, he would go in gratitude to St. Iago in Spain.[4]

When the mourner got thus far on his story, he stopp'd to pay nature her tribute—and wept bitterly.

He said, Heaven had accepted the conditions; and that he had set out from his cottage with this poor creature, who had been a patient partner of his journey—that it had eat the same bread with him all the way, and was unto him as a friend.[5]

Every body who stood about, heard the poor fellow with concern—La Fleur offered him money.—The mourner said, he did not want it—it was not the value of the ass—but the loss of him.—The ass, he said, he was assured loved him—and upon this told them a long story of a mischance upon their passage over the Pyrenean mountains which had separated them from each other three days; during which time the ass had sought him as much as he had sought the ass, and that they had neither scarce eat or drank till they met.

Thou hast one comfort, friend, said I, at least in the loss of thy poor beast; I'm sure thou hast been a merciful master to him.—Alas! said the mourner, I thought so, when he was alive—but now that he is dead I think otherwise.—I fear the weight of myself and my afflictions together have been too much for him—they have shortened the poor creature's days, and I fear I have them to answer for.—Shame on the world! said I to myself—Did we love each other, as this poor soul but loved his ass—'twould be something.—[6]

---

[4] "[T]he shrine of the apostle St. James (the greater) in Santiago de Compostela, in northwest Spain; the supposed site of St. James's tomb and one of the chief shrines of Christendom" (Stout 139).

[5] Cf. 2 Samuel 12:3. As does Nathan in these verses, Sterne begins with love for an animal and moves in the course of *ASJ* to love between people; the gist of the lesson, however, is the blindness caused by self-love; see below, p. 161, n. 2.

[6] It is worth recalling that for Sterne *ass* is embedded in passion, reminding us of both the body and our capacity to make fools of ourselves. In *TS,* VIII.31–32.715ff., we are told that Walter, "for many years . . . never used the word *passions* once—but *ass* ['meaning his body'] always instead of them"; thus, when he inquires about Toby's affair with widow Wadman, he asks: "how goes it with your ASSE?"

On the other hand, Elizabeth Kraft, *Laurence Sterne Revisited* (New York: Twayne, 1996), 112, hears an echo of "the second 'great commandment' (Matthew 22:36–39): Each of us should love the world as he loves his own ass. More decorously put, in the words of Christ, we should love our neighbor as we love ourselves."

An interesting anticipation of this passage occurs in *Occasional Reflections . . . Cambridge* (1711), where the traveler comments on a whipped horse: "Dumb Creatures . . . cannot plead for themselves: And Our Statutes assign no Council, for such *Paupers*. The Bar is Silent . . . as the Pulpit is. Could Asses but Drop Gold, at Pleasure, They would not want an Advocate in Either Place" (3–4). See p. 52, n. 9.

NAMPONT.
THE POSTILLION.[1]

THE concern which the poor fellow's story threw me into, required some attention: the postillion paid not the least to it, but set off upon the *pavè*[2] in a full
gallop.

The thirstiest soul in the most sandy desert of Arabia could not have wished
more for a cup of cold water,[3] than mine did for grave and quiet movements; and
I should have had an high opinion of the postillion had he but stolen off with me
in something like a pensive pace.—On the contrary, as the mourner finished his
lamentation, the fellow gave an unfeeling lash to each of his beasts, and set off
clattering like a thousand devils.

I called to him as loud as I could, for heaven's sake to go slower—and the
louder I called the more unmercifully he galloped.—The deuce take him and his
galloping too—said I—he'll go on tearing my nerves to pieces till he has worked
me into a foolish passion, and then he'll go slow, that I may enjoy the sweets of it.

The postillion managed the point to a miracle: by the time he had got to the
foot of a steep hill about half a league from Nampont,—he had put me out of
temper with him—and then with myself, for being so.

My case then required a different treatment; and a good rattling gallop would
have been of real service to me.—

—Then, prithee get on—get on, my good lad, said I.

---

[1] Cf. Cole, *Journal*, 326–27: "Their Postilions are generally great rough, rude, Fellows, of no
Sort of Behaviour & are never contented with what you give them. . . . I never saw more
clownish, brutal People in my Life."

Stout, 142, points here to one of Sterne's favorite themes—"the relationship between
motion and emotion," often expressed "in terms of the interaction between a traveler's
motions and his feelings." Among the passages cited are *TS*, V.1.407: "IF it had not been for
those two mettlesome tits, and that madcap of a postilion, who drove them from Stilton to
Stamford [not only French postilions had a bad reputation], the thought had never entered
my head. He flew like lightning . . . the motion was most rapid—most impetuous—'twas
communicated to my brain—my heart partook of it"; and VII.13.593: "so much of motion,
is so much of life, and so much of joy—— . . . to stand still, or get on but slowly, is death
and the devil."

[2] Pavement, highway (correctly, *pavé*).

[3] Cf. *Letters*, 117 (?June 1760): "An urn of cold water in the driest stage of the driest Desert
in Arabia, pour'd out by an angel's hand to a thirsty Pilgrim, could not have been more
gratefully received than Miss Macartny's Letter——pray is that Simile too warm? or con-
ceived too orientally?" Behind the phrasing is Proverbs 25:25: "As cold waters to a thirsty
soul, so is good news from a far country."

The postillion pointed to the hill—I then tried to return back to the story of the poor German and his ass—but I had broke the clue[4]—and could no more get into it again, than the postillion could into a trot.—

—The deuce go, said I, with it all! Here am I sitting as candidly disposed to make the best of the worst, as ever wight was, and all runs counter.

There is one sweet lenitive at least for evils, which nature holds out to us; so I took it kindly at her hands, and fell asleep; and the first word which roused me was *Amiens.*

—Bless me! said I, rubbing my eyes—this is the very town where my poor lady is to come.

---

[4] *OED*, s.v. *clue*, 3.a., uses this passage to illustrate the meaning: "Any figurative 'thread': a. the thread of a discourse, of thought, of history, tendency, etc."

AMIENS.

THE words were scarce out of my mouth, when the Count de L***'s post-chaise, with his sister in it, drove hastily by: she had just time to make me a bow of recognition—and of that particular kind of it, which told me she had not yet done with me. She was as good as her look; for, before I had quite finished my supper, her brother's servant came into the room with a billet, in which she said, she had taken the liberty to charge me with a letter, which I was to present myself to Madame R*** the first morning I had nothing to do at Paris. There was only added, she was sorry, but from what *penchant*[1] she had not considered, that she had been prevented telling me her story—that she still owed it me; and if my rout should ever lay through Brussels, and I had not by then forgot the name of Madame de L***—that Madame de L*** would be glad to discharge her obligation.

Then I will meet thee, said I, fair spirit! at Brussels—'tis only returning from Italy through Germany to Holland, by the rout of Flanders, home—'twill scarce be ten posts[2] out of my way; but were it ten thousand! with what a moral delight[3] will it crown my journey, in sharing in the sickening incidents of a tale of misery told to me by such a sufferer? to see her weep! and though I cannot dry up the fountain of her tears, what an exquisite sensation is there still left, in wiping them away from off the cheeks[4] of the first and fairest of women, as I'm sitting with my handkerchief in my hand in silence the whole night besides her.[5]

---

[1] John Dryden includes *penchant* in a list of fashionable French words in *Marriage à la Mode* (1672), III.i; it was in the process of becoming naturalized by the mid–eighteenth century.

[2] A post was approximately six miles; Yorick makes a deliberately comical miscalculation.

[3] Stout, 145, annotates "moral delight" with a passage from sermon 23, "The parable of the rich man and Lazarus": "let ['even the most insensible man'] . . . comfort the captive, or cover the naked with a garment, and he will feel what is meant by that moral delight arising in the mind from the conscience of a humane action" (*Sermons* 4:222). The idea that good deeds create joyful feelings is a commonplace in eighteenth-century Anglican theology, but Clonmell's annotation, "Nothing gives such a Zest to Lewdness as a Dash of piety or at least of Decency" (Franssen 186), reminds us that "moral delight" in sitting up the "whole night" by a woman's bedside may not be quite the same act of charity the clerics (including Sterne) had in mind.

[4] Cf. Isaiah 25:8: "the Lord God will wipe away tears from off all faces"; and Revelation 7:17, 21:4. Sterne uses the phrase in his two sermons on Job (10 and 15); see *Sermons*, 4:102.10–11, 147.12–13; and in *BJ*, p. 231; cf. *TS*, IX.3.741: "[Uncle Toby] knew not . . . the right end of a Woman from the wrong, and therefore was never altogether at his ease near any one of them——unless in sorrow or distress; then infinite was his pity; nor would the most courteous knight of romance have gone further . . . to have wiped away a tear from a woman's eye . . . ."

[5] Cf. *BJ*, April 28; and again, June 15.

There was nothing wrong in the sentiment; and yet I instantly reproached my heart with it in the bitterest and most reprobate[6] of expressions.

It had ever, as I told the reader, been one of the singular blessings of my life, to be almost every hour of it miserably in love with some one; and my last flame[7] happening to be blown out by a whiff of jealousy on the sudden turn of a corner, I had lighted it up afresh at the pure taper of Eliza but about three months before—swearing as I did it, that it should last me through the whole journey—Why should I dissemble the matter? I had sworn to her eternal fidelity[8]—she had a right to my whole heart—to divide my affections was to lessen them—to expose them, was to risk them: where there is risk, there may be loss—and what wilt thou have, Yorick! to answer to a heart so full of trust and confidence—so good, so gentle and unreproaching?

—I will not go to Brussels, replied I, interrupting myself—but my imagination went on—I recall'd her looks at that crisis of our separation when neither of us had power to say Adieu! I look'd at the picture she had tied in a black ribband about my neck[9]—and blush'd as I look'd at it—I would have given the world to have kiss'd it,—but was ashamed—And shall this tender flower, said I, pressing it between my hands—shall it be smitten to its very root—and smitten, Yorick! by thee, who hast promised to shelter it in thy breast?

Eternal fountain of happiness! said I, kneeling down upon the ground—be thou my witness—and every pure spirit which tastes it, be my witness also, That

---

[6] Sterne's awkward phrasing here illustrates a usage considered obsolete by *OED*, s.v. *reprobate, a.* 6: "deserving or worthy of condemnation or reproof; appropriate to reprobates."

[7] One possible candidate for this role has been identified as Lady Anne Stuart, Lady Warkworth, third daughter of the Earl of Bute. Sterne wrote at least one bawdy letter to her that has survived, probably in April 1767. And cf. *BJ* (May 1) where he records for Eliza his encounter with a former love interest identified only as "Sheba." Without making a definite claim that "my last flame" or "Sheba" is Lady Warkworth, it is possible that Sterne here, and in *BJ*, records this particular flirtation.

However, when Yorick tells us he has "been in love with one princess or another" almost all his life (p. 48), he only partially captures Sterne's own practice, which was to be in love with as many women as possible, as often as possible. The language of love for Sterne—the language permeating *BJ*—was the inherited one of faithfulness and jealousy, but his practice was most characterized by an ironic awareness of fugacity; see Melvyn New, "Job's Wife and Sterne's Other Women," in *Out of Bounds: Male Writers and Gender(ed) Criticism*, ed. Laura Claridge and Elizabeth Langland (Amherst, Mass.: U of Massachusetts P, 1990), 55–74, esp. 62–64.

[8] See Introduction, pp. xiii–xv, for a discussion of Sterne's relationship with Eliza, which began in January 1767; since Yorick's *Journey* takes place in 1762, there is an obvious anachronism.

[9] See p. 4 and n. 7, and p. 226.

I would not travel to Brussels, unless Eliza went along with me, did the road lead me towards heaven.[10]

In transports of this kind, the heart, in spite of the understanding, will always say too much.[11]

---

[10] Cf. sermon 22, "The history of Jacob": "Grant me, gracious GOD! to go chearfully on, the road which thou hast marked out;——I wish it neither more wide or more smooth. . . ——I will kneel upon the ground seven times a day, to seek the best track I can with it——and having done that, I will trust myself and the issue of my journey to thee, who art the fountain of joy . . ." (*Sermons* 4:208–9). See also *TS,* I.22.82, "fountain of health"; and VII.1.575, "fountain of life." And see below, p. 162, "eternal fountain of our feelings."

[11] Cf. sermon 18, "The Levite and his concubine": "'tis a story on which the heart cannot be at a loss for what to say, or the imagination for what to suppose—the danger is, humanity may say too much" (*Sermons* 4:168).

THE LETTER.
AMIENS.

FORTUNE had not smiled upon La Fleur; for he had been unsuccessful in his feats of chivalry—and not one thing had offer'd to signalize his zeal for my service from the time he had enter'd into it, which was almost four and twenty hours. The poor soul burn'd with impatience; and the Count de L***'s servant's coming with the letter, being the first practicable occasion which offered, La Fleur had laid hold of it; and in order to do honour to his master, had taken him into a back parlour in the Auberge,[1] and treated him with a cup or two of the best wine in Picardy; and the Count de L***'s servant in return, and not to be behind hand in politeness with La Fleur, had taken him back with him to the Count's hôtel. La Fleur's *prevenancy*[2] (for there was a passport in his very looks) soon set every servant in the kitchen at ease with him; and as a Frenchman, whatever be his talents, has no sort of prudery in shewing them, La Fleur, in less than five minutes, had pull'd out his fife, and leading off the dance himself with the first note, set the *fille de chambre*, the *maitre d'hotel*,[3] the cook, the scullion, and all the houshold, dogs and cats, besides an old monkey, a-dancing: I suppose there never was a merrier kitchen since the flood.

Madame de L***, in passing from her brother's apartments to her own, hearing so much jollity below stairs, rung up her *fille de chambre* to ask about it; and hearing it was the English gentleman's servant who had set the whole house merry with his pipe, she order'd him up.

As the poor fellow could not present himself empty, he had loaden'd himself in going up stairs with a thousand compliments to Madame de L***, on the part of his master—added a long apocrypha of inquiries after Madame de L***'s health—told her, that Monsieur his master was *au desespoire*[4] for her re-establishment from the fatigues of her journey—and, to close all, that Monsieur had received the letter which Madame had done him the honour——And he has

---

[1] Inn, hostelry. Hôtel was beginning to be used in its modern manner, although still retaining its French meaning of mansion or large town house.

[2] Sterne's usage is cited as the *OED*'s only illustration; it is based on the French *prévenance:* "courteous anticipation of the desires or needs of others; an obliging manner; complaisance."

   Cf. Clonmell: "Prevenancy . . . is One of ye greatest Constitutionall Qualities of a Politician or Man of ye World, this Pasport Countenance" (Franssen 180).

[3] Steward, butler (correctly, *maître d'hôtel*).

[4] In despair, disconsolate (correctly, *au désespoir*).

done me the honour, said Madame de L***, interrupting La Fleur, to send a billet in return.[5]

Madame de L*** had said this with such a tone of reliance upon the fact, that La Fleur had not power to disappoint her expectations—he trembled for my honour—and possibly might not altogether be unconcerned for his own, as a man capable of being attach'd to a master who could be a wanting *en egards vis a vis d'une femme;*[6] so that when Madame de L*** asked La Fleur if he had brought a letter—*O qu'oui,*[7] said La Fleur: so laying down his hat upon the ground, and taking hold of the flap of his right side pocket with his left hand, he began to search for the letter with his right—then contrary-wise—*Diable!*—then sought every pocket—pocket by pocket, round, not forgetting his fob—*Peste!*—then La Fleur emptied them upon the floor—pulled out a dirty cravat—a handkerchief— a comb—a whip lash—a night-cap—then gave a peep into his hat—*Quelle etourderie!*[8] He had left the letter upon the table in the Auberge—he would run for it, and be back with it in three minutes.

I had just finished my supper when La Fleur came in to give me an account of his adventure: he told the whole story simply as it was; and only added, that if Monsieur had forgot *(par hazard)*[9] to answer Madame's letter, the arrangement gave him an opportunity to recover the *faux pas*[10]—and if not, that things were only as they were.

Now I was not altogether sure of my *etiquette,*[11] whether I ought to have wrote or no; but if I had—a devil himself could not have been angry: 'twas but the officious zeal of a well-meaning creature for my honour; and however he might have mistook the road—or embarrassed me in so doing—his heart was in no fault—I was under no necessity to write—and what weighed more than all—he did not look as if he had done amiss.

—'Tis all very well, La Fleur, said I.—'Twas sufficient. La Fleur flew out of the room like lightening, and return'd with pen, ink, and paper, in his hand; and coming up to the table, laid them close before me, with such a delight in his countenance, that I could not help taking up the pen.

---

[5] Another example of literal anglicization: *la lettre dont Madame lui avait fait l'honneur—Et il m'a fait l'honneur . . . d'envoyer un billet en retour."*

[6] Wanting in consideration (or attentions) to a woman (correctly, *égards vis à vis*).

[7] Yes, indeed.

[8] How absent-minded of me! How thoughtless! (correctly, *étourderie*).

[9] By chance.

[10] *OED* lists naturalized usage from 1676.

[11] Sterne's italics suggest he still considers this a French word; *OED* cites this passage as its first illustration, with the definition: "The conventional rules of personal behaviour observed in the intercourse of polite society; the ceremonial observances prescribed by such rules."

I begun and begun again; and though I had nothing to say, and that nothing might have been express'd in half a dozen lines, I made half a dozen different beginnings, and could no way please myself.

In short, I was in no mood to write.

La Fleur stepp'd out and brought a little water in a glass to dilute my ink— then fetch'd sand and seal-wax—It was all one: I wrote, and blotted, and tore off, and burnt, and wrote again—*Le Diable l'emporte!*[12] said I half to myself—I cannot write this self-same letter; throwing the pen down despairingly as I said it.

As soon as I had cast down the pen, La Fleur advanced with the most respectful carriage up to the table, and making a thousand apologies for the liberty he was going to take, told me he had a letter in his pocket wrote by a drummer in his regiment to a corporal's wife, which, he durst say, would suit the occasion.

I had a mind to let the poor fellow have his humour—Then prithee, said I, let me see it.

La Fleur instantly pull'd out a little dirty pocket-book cramm'd full of small letters and billet-doux in a sad condition, and laying it upon the table, and then untying the string which held them all together, run them over one by one, till he came to the letter in question—*La voila!*[13] said he, clapping his hands: so unfolding it first, he laid it before me, and retired three steps from the table whilst I read it.

---

[12] Let the devil take it! See p. 54, n. 4.
[13] Here it is! (correctly, *voilà*).

THE LETTER.[1]

MADAME,

JE suis penetré de la douleur la plus vive, et reduit en même temps au desespoir par ce retour imprevû du Corporal qui rend notre entrevue de ce soir la chose du monde la plus impossible.

Mais vive la joie! et toute la mienne sera de penser a vous.

L'amour n'est *rien* sans sentiment.

Et le sentiment est encore *moins* sans amour.[2]

On dit qu'on ne doit jamais se desesperer.

On dit aussi que Monsieur le Corporal monte la garde Mecredi:[3] alors ce sera mon tour.

---

[1] I.e.,

MADAM,

I am filled with the most acute pain and, at the same time, reduced to despair by the unexpected return of the Corporal, which makes our meeting this evening the most impossible thing in the world.

But long live joy! and all my joy will be to think of you.

Love is *nothing* without sentiment.

And sentiment is still *less* without love.

They say that one should never despair.

They also say that the Corporal will mount guard on Wednesday: then it will be my turn.

Everyone has his turn.

Meanwhile, long live love! and long live bagatelle!

I am MADAM,
with the most respectful and tender sentiments, entirely yours,

[2] The sentiment is first recorded in a letter written in 1765: "but I carry on my affairs quite in the French way, sentimentally—'*l'amour*' (say they) '*n'est rien sans sentiment*'" (*Letters* 256). If Sterne had a particular source for the sentiment (i.e., "say they"), we have not located it.

[3] Considered an acceptable spelling in Sterne's day, along with *mercredi,* the only accepted spelling today.

Chacun a son tour.[4]

En attendant—Vive l'amour! et vive la bagatelle![5]

> Je suis, MADAME,
> Avec toutes les sentiments les
> plus respecteux et les plus
> tendres tout a vous,
> JAQUES ROQUE.

It was but changing the Corporal into the Count—and saying nothing about mounting guard on Wednesday—and the letter was neither right or wrong—so to gratify the poor fellow, who stood trembling for my honour, his own, and the honour of his letter,—I took the cream gently off it, and whipping it up in my own way—I seal'd it up and sent him with it to Madame de L***—and the next morning we pursued our journey to Paris.

---

[4] Since Sterne's accenting is always haphazard, one might suspect a should be à, in which case, the translation would be "Everyone in his turn."

[5] Sterne uses this phrase in *TS,* I.19.60, in discussing Walter's hobby-horse: "for he had a thousand little sceptical notions of the comick kind to defend,——most of which notions . . . at first enter'd upon the footing of mere whims, and of a *vive la Bagatelle* . . . ." The phrase is closely associated with Swift; see *Notes* to *TS,* 3:100, n. to 60.22–23. One might translate the phrase as "long live trifling," but *bagatelle* had significantly entered the English language before Sterne's usage.

PARIS.

WHEN a man can contest the point by dint of equipage, and carry all on floundering before him with half a dozen lackies and a couple of cooks—'tis very well in such a place as Paris—he may drive in at which end of a street he will.[1]

A poor prince who is weak in cavalry, and whose whole infantry does not exceed a single man, had best quit the field; and signalize himself in the cabinet,[2] if he can get up into it—I say *up into it*—for there is no descending perpendicular amongst 'em with a "*Me voici! mes enfans*"[3]—here I am—whatever many may think.

I own my first sensations, as soon as I was left solitary and alone in my own chamber in the hotel, were far from being so flattering as I had prefigured them. I walked up gravely to the window in my dusty black coat, and looking through the glass saw all the world in yellow, blue, and green, running at the ring of pleasure.—The old with broken lances, and in helmets which had lost their vizards—the young in armour bright which shone like gold, beplumed with each gay feather of the east—all—all tilting at it like fascinated knights in tournaments of yore for fame and love.—[4]

---

[1] Almost every traveler to Paris commented on the narrowness of the streets, including Sterne in *TS*, VII.17.600: "don't you see, friend, the streets are so villainously narrow, that there is not room in all Paris to turn a wheel-barrow?"

[2] A commonplace distinction in the century; cf. *TS*, II.17.165 (and *Notes* 3:188–89), apropos of the English clergy writing fine sermons but delivering them poorly: "But, alas! . . . like *French* politicians in this respect, what they gain in the cabinet they lose in the field"; cf. III.25.250 and VII.27.619. And see below, p. 107: "if in the field—why not face to face in the cabinet too?"

[3] Here I am, my children. Cf. p. 118, where Yorick uses "*Me, Voici*" to point to himself in *Hamlet*. *Me voici* is the French translation of the important scriptural phrase rendered in English as "Here I am," the response to divine summons, first spoken by Abraham and often repeated by patriarchs and the prophets. Perhaps most apposite to Yorick's entrance into Paris, however, is Isaiah 6:5–8: "Then said I, Woe is me! for I am undone; because I am a man of unclean lips, and I dwell in the midst of a people of unclean lips . . . . Also I heard the voice of the Lord, saying, Whom shall I send, and who will go for us? Then said I, Here am I; send me."

[4] Melvyn New, "Proust's Influence on Sterne: Remembrance of Things to Come," *MLN* 103 (1988):1032, calls this passage "typical of Sterne's most mature writing—a virtuoso mingling of heretofore incompatible intentions, most obviously the pathetic and the bawdy. . . . The accumulation of pathos is too rich to be unintentional, but so is the accumulation of bawdiness."

Among the bawdy openings, we might note the "ring of pleasure" (cf. *TS* VII.43.649: "They are running at the ring of pleasure, said I, giving [my mule] a prick"), originally indicating a chivalric exercise in which a rider attempts to pass his lance through a suspended ring (*OED*). Rabelais anticipated Sterne's usage: "Some other puffes did swell in length by the member . . . in such sort, that it grew marvellous long, plump, jolly, . . . : you would

Alas, poor Yorick![5] cried I, what art thou doing here? On the very first onset of all this glittering clatter, thou art reduced to an atom—seek—seek some winding alley, with a tourniquet[6] at the end of it, where chariot never rolled or flambeau[7] shot its rays—there thou mayest solace thy soul in converse sweet with some kind *grisset*[8] of a barber's wife, and get into such coteries!—[9]

—May I perish! if I do, said I, pulling out the letter which I had to present to Madame de R***.—I'll wait upon this lady, the very first thing I do. So I called La Fleur to go seek me a barber directly—and come back and brush my coat.

---

have taken them for men that had their lances settled on their rest, to run at the ring, or tilting quintain" (*Works*, tr. Thomas Urquhart and Peter Motteux, with notes by John Ozell, 5 vols. [1750], II.1.9–10). The bawdiness continues with "broken lances," "lost vizards" (an allusion to damage wrought to noses by the chemical treatment of venereal disorders), and the young "in armour," i.e., in condoms (22). And cf. *Letters*, 294 (?January 1767): "I'll put off my Cassoc & turn Knight Errant for you, & say the kindest things of you to Dulcinea that Dulcinea ever heard—if she has a Champion . . . Ill enter the Lists with him and break a spear in your behalf; tho by the by, mine is half rusty, and should be hung up in the old family hall amongst Pistols without Cocks, and Helmets which have lost their Vizards."

[5] Sterne reprises his use of the line in *TS*, I.12.35–36, where it serves as Yorick's epitaph and elegy, set off by the black page. Originally Hamlet's address to Yorick's skull (V.i.184), there is, in its use here, much of the memento-mori tone of Sterne's (and Shakespeare's) earlier use. Cf. *BJ* (May 29–30): "confined to my bed—so emaciated, and unlike what I was . . . Alas! Poor Yorick!"

[6] A turnstile; *OED* considers the usage rare and lists this occurrence as its second illustration. The word is, of course, French, but Sterne's lack of italics, if not inadvertent, may indicate familiarity with the word in English. Sterne begins here a metaphorical—but hardly subtle—bit of bawdy, climaxing in *coteries*.

[7] English since the seventeenth century.

[8] Shop-girl (correctly, *grisette*).

[9] This passage provides the second illustration in *OED* for the definition: "A circle of persons associated together and distinguished from 'outsiders.'" The first illustration (*Common Sense*, 1738) perhaps leads to Sterne's meaning: "beware of Select Coteries, where, without an Engagement, a Lady passes but for an odd Body"—but the word was also gaining a political connotation, for which an illustration dated 1766 is significant: "The word *cotterie*, of which so much has been said of late." Le Roux, *Dictionnaire*, states that the word frequently has a connotation of debauchery ("compagnie de débauche"). See also p. 154.

THE WIG.
PARIS.[1]

WHEN the barber came, he absolutely refused to have any thing to do with my wig: 'twas either above or below his art: I had nothing to do, but to take one ready made of his own recommendation.

—But I fear, friend! said I, this buckle[2] won't stand.—You may immerge it, replied he, into the ocean, and it will stand—

What a great scale is every thing upon in this city! thought I—The utmost stretch of an English periwig-maker's ideas could have gone no further than to have "dipped it into a pail of water"—What difference! 'tis like time to eternity.

I confess I do hate all cold conceptions, as I do the puny ideas which engender them; and am generally so struck with the great works of nature, that for my own part, if I could help it, I never would make a comparison less than a mountain at least.

All that can be said against the French sublime[3] in this instance of it, is this— that the grandeur is *more* in the *word;* and *less* in the *thing.* No doubt the ocean fills the mind with vast ideas; but Paris being so far inland, it was not likely I should run post a hundred miles out of it, to try the experiment—the Parisian barber meant nothing.—

---

[1] Cf. Tristram's remark (VII.17.600) on the numerous barbers in Paris, a tribute to the French belief that *"the periwig maketh the man."* Sterne comments on the subject in a letter to Robert Foley, his Paris banker (*Letters* 260; October 7, 1765): "It is a terrible thing to be in Paris without a perriwig to a man's head!" Cf. Curtis, *Letters,* 260, n. 2, quoting Boswell, *Life:* "even Johnson, while travelling in France in 1775, 'was furnished with a Paris-made wig, of handsome construction.'"

Smollett too comments on the sartorial makeover required to appear in Parisian society: "when an Englishman comes to Paris, he cannot appear until he has undergone a total metamorphosis. At his first arrival he finds it necessary to send for the taylor, peruquier, hatter, shoemaker, and every other tradesman concerned in the equipment of the human body . . ." (*Travels,* letter 6, 1:97–98).

[2] Cunnington, 245: "The side curls [of wigs] . . . were rigid hollow rolls, lying horizontally, and frequently described as 'buckles,' from the French 'boucle.'" Cf. *TS,* IX.2.738, where Toby's wig is described: "it curl'd every where but where the Corporal would have it; and where a buckle or two, in his opinion, would have done it honour, he could as soon have raised the dead." Clearly, the state of one's wig led to hyperbole, whether the barber was French or English.

[3] Sterne's discussion, ending with his invocation of the "sublime," recalls *TS,* IV.10.337–38, where he attacks "cold conceits" with an appeal to Longinus's discussion of "frigid Expressions" in *On the Sublime,* tr. William Smith (1739), 113; see *Notes* to *TS,* 3:306–7. Cf. *TS,* IX.8.763, where Tristram laments having fallen into "a cold unmetaphorical vein of infamous writing."

The pail of water standing besides the great deep, makes certainly but a sorry figure in speech—but 'twill be said—it has one advantage—'tis in the next room, and the truth of the buckle may be tried in it without more ado, in a single moment.

In honest truth, and upon a more candid revision of the matter, *The French expression professes more than it performs.*[4]

I think I can see the precise and distinguishing marks of national characters more in these nonsensical *minutiæ,* than in the most important matters of state; where great men of all nations talk and stalk so much alike, that I would not give nine-pence to chuse amongst them.[5]

I was so long in getting from under my barber's hands, that it was too late to think of going with my letter to Madame R*** that night: but when a man is once dressed at all points for going out, his reflections turn to little account, so taking down the name of the Hotel de Modene[6] where I lodged, I walked forth without any determination where to go—I shall consider of that, said I, as I walk along.

---

[4] Cf. *Letters,* 161–62, Sterne to Garrick during his first visit to Paris: "I hear no news of you, or your *empire,* I would have said *kingdom*—but here every thing is hyperbolized—and if a woman is but simply pleased—'tis *Je suis charmée*—and if she is charmed 'tis nothing less, than that she is *ravi*-sh'd—and when ravi-sh'd, (which may happen) there is nothing left for her but to fly to the other world for a metaphor, and swear, qu'elle etoit toute *extasiée* . . . ."

[5] Cf. sermon 31, "St. Peter's character": "I would sooner form a judgment of a man's temper from his behaviour on such little occurrences of life . . . than from the more weighed and important actions, where a man is more upon his guard . . ." (*Sermons* 4:297). Cf. *TS,* VI.5.497: "There are a thousand unnoticed openings, continued my father, which let a penetrating eye at once into a man's soul; and I maintain it, added he, that a man of sense does not lay down his hat in coming into a room . . . but something escapes, which discovers him."

[6] John Poole (see above, p. 42, n. 3) located the hotel in the Rue Jacob (the "English quarter"), Faubourg St. Germain, by using the instructions of the grisette. Cf. Peckham, *Tour of Holland,* 131–32: "we drove to the Hotel de l'Imperatrice in the Rue Jacob, where we have an elegant dining-room, with two bed chambers . . . . I confess the lodgings are dear, but the situation is good . . . ." And he continues, in Sterne's manner, "Add to this that Mademoiselle Brunett is young, sprightly, and handsome . . . ."

THE PULSE.
PARIS.

HAIL ye small sweet courtesies of life, for smooth do ye make the road of it! like grace and beauty which beget inclinations to love at first sight; 'tis ye who open this door and let the stranger in.

—Pray, Madame, said I, have the goodness[1] to tell me which way I must turn to go to the Opera comique:[2]—Most willingly, Monsieur, said she, laying aside her work—

I had given a cast with my eye into half a dozen shops as I came along in search of a face not likely to be disordered by such an interruption; till at last, this hitting my fancy, I had walked in.

She was working a pair of ruffles as she sat in a low chair on the far side of the shop facing the door—

—*Tres volentieres*,[3] most willingly, said she, laying her work down upon a chair next her, and rising up from the low chair she was sitting in, with so chearful a movement and so chearful a look, that had I been laying out fifty louis d'ors with her, I should have said—"This woman is grateful."

You must turn, Monsieur, said she, going with me to the door of the shop, and pointing the way down the street I was to take—you must turn first to your left hand—*mais prenez guarde*[4]—there are two turns; and be so good[5] as to take the second—then go down a little way and you'll see a church, and when you are past it, give yourself the trouble to turn directly to the right, and that will lead you to the foot of the *pont neuf*, which you must cross—and there, any one will do himself the pleasure to shew you—[6]

---

[1] In French, *ayez la bonté.*

[2] See Stout, 161: "On 3 Feb. 1762, soon after Sterne reached Paris on his first trip abroad . . . , the new Comédie Italienne, popularly called the Opéra Comique, opened at the Hôtel de Bourgogne in the Rue Mauconseil . . . . This company had been formed through a merger of the Opéra Comique, which had presented a mixture of comedy, song, and vaudeville, with the impoverished Comédiens Italiens, which had presented comic operas."

[3] Most willingly (correctly, *volontiers*).

[4] But be careful (correctly, *garde*).

[5] The grisette's "English" suggests further attempts on Sterne's part to anglicize French; e.g., "be so good as" is *ayez la bonté de;* "give yourself the trouble" is *donnez-vous la peine de;* "will do himself the pleasure to shew you" is *se fera le (un) plaisir de vous montrer.*

[6] Despite Poole's claim (see above, p. 72, n. 6) that he had followed these instructions to find the Hotel de Modene, Stout, 162, was unable to arrive at the same destination. One suspects Sterne does not want readers concentrating on the grisette's actual instructions any better than did Yorick. Stout also suggests that the church mentioned may be the Chapelle du Collège des Quatre Nations on the Rue de Seine. The *"pont neuf"* is one of the primary

She repeated her instructions three times over to me with the same good natur'd patience the third time as the first;—and if *tones and manners* have a meaning, which certainly they have, unless to hearts which shut them out[7]—she seem'd really interested, that I should not lose myself.[8]

I will not suppose it was the woman's beauty, notwithstanding she was the handsomest grisset, I think, I ever saw, which had much to do with the sense I had of her courtesy; only I remember, when I told her how much I was obliged to her, that I looked very full in her eyes,—and that I repeated my thanks as often as she had done her instructions.

I had not got ten paces from the door, before I found I had forgot every tittle of what she had said—so looking back, and seeing her still standing in the door of the shop as if to look whether I went right or not—I returned back, to ask her whether the first turn was to my right or left—for that I had absolutely forgot.— Is it possible! said she, half laughing.—'Tis very possible, replied I, when a man is thinking more of a woman, than of her good advice.

As this was the real truth—she took it, as every woman takes a matter of right, with a slight courtesy.

—*Attendez!*[9] said she, laying her hand upon my arm to detain me, whilst she called a lad out of the back-shop to get ready a parcel of gloves. I am just going to send him, said she, with a packet into that quarter, and if you will have the complaisance to step in, it will be ready in a moment, and he shall attend you to the place.—So I walk'd in with her to the far side of the shop, and taking up the ruffle in my hand which she laid upon the chair, as if I had a mind to sit,[10] she sat down herself in her low chair, and I instantly sat myself down besides her.

---

bridges across the Seine, completed in the early seventeenth century; see the typical British observation in Peckham, 138: "The Pont-neuf is the most esteemed [of Paris's bridges], which in fact is as pitiful as the river it is built over."

[7] Stout, 162–63, compares sermon 43, "[Efficacy of prayer]," where Sterne argues the interconnectedness of body and soul: "in the present state we are in, we find such a strong sympathy and union between our souls and bodies, that the one cannot be touched or sensibly affected, without producing some corresponding emotion in the other.—Nature has assigned a different look, tone of voice, and gesture, peculiar to every passion and affection we are subject to . . ." (*Sermons* 4:402).

Sterne's view was shared by philosophers *and* clerics throughout the century and does not indicate a belief in the materiality of the soul. Indeed, for many, the harmony of body and soul was evidence for the soul's immateriality, an entity precisely not body.

[8] Cf. Tristram's fear that Janatone may "go off like a hussy—and lose thyself" (*TS* VII.9.590).

[9] Wait!

[10] Sterne's ms. gives us a chance to note how carefully he shaped his sentences. He originally wrote "as if to sit down," altered it to "as if she had a mind to sit," and finally produced the present reading.

—He will be ready, Monsieur, said she, in a moment—And in that moment, replied I, most willingly would I say something very civil to you for all these courtesies. Any one may do a casual act of good nature, but a continuation of them shews it is a part of the temperature;[11] and certainly, added I, if it is the same blood which comes from the heart, which descends to the extremes (touching her wrist) I am sure you must have one of the best pulses of any woman in the world—Feel it, said she, holding out her arm. So laying down my hat, I took hold of her fingers in one hand, and applied the two fore-fingers of my other to the artery—

—Would to heaven! my dear Eugenius,[12] thou hadst passed by, and beheld me sitting in my black coat, and in my lack-a-day-sical manner, counting the throbs of it, one by one, with as much true devotion as if I had been watching the critical ebb or flow of her fever—How wouldst thou have laugh'd and moralized upon my new profession?—and thou shouldst have laugh'd and moralized on—Trust me, my dear Eugenius, I should have said, "there are worse occupations in this world *than feeling a woman's pulse.*"—But a Grisset's! thou wouldst have said—and in an open shop! Yorick—

—So much the better: for when my views are direct, Eugenius, I care not if all the world saw me feel it.

---

[11] I.e., temperament; cf. *TS*, I.1.1, where Tristram laments his parents' lack of concentration despite the fact that the "happy formation and temperature of his body . . ." were concerned in his procreation.

[12] The name *Eugenius* was traditionally applied as a compliment in the eighteenth century; cf. *Spectator* 177: "*Eugenius* is a Man of an Universal Good-nature, and Generous beyond the Extent of his Fortune, but withal so prudent in the Oeconomy of his Affairs, that what goes out in Charity is made up by Good Management" (ed. Donald F. Bond [Oxford: Clarendon, 1965], 2:198). Sterne's use of the name for his longtime friend, John Hall-Stevenson (1718–1795), here and as the confidant of Yorick in *TS* (see esp. I.12), was almost certainly gently ironic. They had met at Jesus College, Cambridge, and appear to have remained close friends thereafter, keeping in relatively frequent contact during Sterne's travels, a correspondence that provides context for Hall-Stevenson's appearance here: e.g., in October 1762, Sterne wrote from Toulouse: "the ground work of my *ennui* is more to the eternal platitude of the French characters—little variety, no originality in it at all—than to any other cause . . ." (*Letters* 186); and in May 1764, from Paris: "We have been talking and projecting about setting out from this city of seductions every day this month . . . . I have been for eight weeks smitten with the tenderest passion that ever tender wight underwent" (213); it is in this letter that Sterne applies the term "foutre-land" to France (214).

Thicknesse, *Useful Hints*, 161, is livid about Paris, a "city of seduction": "Paris . . . is the wickedest city in the universe. The principal manufacture is *ready-made love* . . . ."

THE HUSBAND.
PARIS.

I HAD counted twenty pulsations, and was going on fast towards the fortieth, when her husband coming unexpected from a back parlour into the shop, put me a little out in my reckoning—'Twas no body but her husband, she said—so I began a fresh score—Monsieur is so good, quoth she, as he pass'd by us, as to give himself the trouble of feeling my pulse—The husband took off his hat, and making me a bow, said, I did him too much honour—and having said that, he put on his hat and walk'd out.

Good God! said I to myself, as he went out—and can this man be the husband of this woman?

Let it not torment the few who know what must have been the grounds of this exclamation, if I explain it to those who do not.

In London a shopkeeper and a shopkeeper's wife seem to be one bone and one flesh:[1] in the several endowments of mind and body, sometimes the one, sometimes the other has it, so as in general to be upon a par, and to tally with each other as nearly as man and wife need to do.

In Paris, there are scarce two orders of beings more different: for the legislative and executive powers of the shop not resting in the husband, he seldom comes there—in some dark and dismal room behind, he sits commerceless[2] in his thrum night-cap, the same rough son of Nature that Nature left him.

The genius of a people where nothing but the monarchy is *salique*,[3] having ceded this department, with sundry others, totally to the women—by a continual higgling with customers of all ranks and sizes from morning to night, like so many rough pebbles shook long together in a bag, by amicable collisions, they have worn down their asperities and sharp angles, and not only become round and smooth, but will receive, some of them, a polish like a brilliant[4]—Monsieur

---

[1] Cf. Genesis 2:23: "And Adam said, This is now bone of my bones, and flesh of my flesh."

[2] *OED* quotes this passage as its first usage.

[3] See *OED,* s.v. *salic:* "the alleged fundamental law of the French monarchy, by which females were excluded from succession to the crown; hence *gen.,* a law excluding females from dynastic succession. In this sense often *Salique.*"

[4] As noted by Mark Loveridge, *Laurence Sterne and the Argument about Design* (Totowa, N.J.: Barnes and Noble, 1982), 187, Sterne borrows his metaphor from Anthony Ashley Cooper, 3d Earl of Shaftesbury, *Characteristics of Men, Manners, Opinions, Times* (1711), "An Essay on the Freedom of Wit and Humour," I.2: "All Politeness is owing to Liberty. We polish one another, and rub off our Corners and rough Sides by a sort of *amicable Collision.* To restrain this, is inevitably to bring a Rust upon Mens Understandings. 'Tis a destroying of Civility, Good Breeding, and even Charity it-self . . ." ([Indianapolis: Liberty Fund, 2001], I:42). Cf. below, p. 126, where Yorick uses coins in his pocket to make the same point about French manners, but with a negative import.

le Mari[5] is little better than the stone under your foot—

—Surely—surely man! it is not good for thee to sit alone[6]—thou wast made for social intercourse and gentle greetings, and this improvement of our natures from it, I appeal to, as my evidence.

—And how does it beat, Monsieur? said she.—With all the benignity, said I, looking quietly in her eyes, that I expected—She was going to say something civil in return—but the lad came into the shop with the gloves—*A propos,* said I; I want a couple of pair myself.

[5] Monsieur Husband.

[6] See Genesis 2:18: "And the Lord God said, It is not good that the man should be alone; I will make him an help meet for him." Cf. sermon 18, "The Levite and his concubine": "notwithstanding all we meet with in books . . . Yet still, *'it is not good for man to be alone:'* nor can all which the cold-hearted pedant stuns our ears with upon the subject, ever give one answer of satisfaction to the mind; in the midst of the loudest vauntings of philosophy, Nature will have her yearnings for society and friendship . . ." (*Sermons* 4:169–70).

THE GLOVES.
PARIS.

THE beautiful Grisset rose up when I said this, and going behind the counter, reach'd down a parcel and untied it: I advanced to the side over-against her: they were all too large. The beautiful Grisset measured them one by one across my hand—It would not alter the dimensions—She begg'd I would try a single pair, which seemed to be the least—She held it open—my hand slipp'd into it at once—It will not do, said I, shaking my head a little—No, said she, doing the same thing.

There are certain combined looks of simple subtlety—where whim, and sense, and seriousness, and nonsense, are so blended, that all the languages of Babel set loose together could not express them—they are communicated and caught so instantaneously, that you can scarce say which party is the infecter.[1] I leave it to your men of words to swell pages about it—it is enough in the present to say again, the gloves would not do; so folding our hands within our arms, we both loll'd upon the counter—it was narrow, and there was just room for the parcel to lay between us.

The beautiful Grisset look'd sometimes at the gloves, then side-ways to the window, then at the gloves—and then at me. I was not disposed to break silence—I follow'd her example: so I look'd at the gloves, then to the window, then at the gloves, and then at her—and so on alternately.

I found I lost considerably in every attack—she had a quick black eye, and shot through two such long and silken eye-lashes with such penetration, that she look'd into my very heart and reins—It may seem strange, but I could actually feel she did—[2]

—It is no matter, said I, taking up a couple of the pairs next me, and putting them into my pocket.

I was sensible the beautiful Grisset had not ask'd a single livre above the price—I wish'd she had ask'd a livre more, and was puzzling my brains how to bring the matter about—Do you think, my dear Sir, said she, mistaking my embarrassment, that I could ask a *sous* too much of a stranger—and of a stranger

---

[1] *OED,* s.v. *infector,* records this as its second of three illustrations, but fails to differentiate Sterne's figurative usage from the literal; under *infecter,* with the same definition, Johnson (notes to *Timon of Athens,* 1765) is cited: "This alludes to an opinion in former times . . . that the venereal infection transmitted to another, left the infecter free."

[2] Sterne was a shrewd observer of the role of eyes in these matters; cf. earlier comments in this scene, including Yorick's acknowledgment that "I looked very full in her eyes," and again, "looking quietly in her eyes"; and, most importantly, the extensive discussion of widow Wadman's eyes in *TS,* VIII.24–25.705–8, eyes "full of gentle salutations——and soft responses."

whose politeness, more than his want of gloves, has done me the honour to lay himself at my mercy?—*M'en croyez capable?*[3]—Faith! not I, said I; and if you were, you are welcome—So counting the money into her hand, and with a lower bow than one generally makes to a shopkeeper's wife, I went out, and her lad with his parcel followed me.

---

[3] Can you think me capable of that? (Correctly, *m'en croyez-vous capable?*)

THE TRANSLATION.[1]
PARIS.

THERE was no body in the box I was let into but a kindly old French officer.[2] I love the character, not only because I honour the man whose manners are softened by a profession which makes bad men worse; but that I once knew one—for he is no more—and why should I not rescue one page from violation by writing his name in it, and telling the world it was Captain Tobias Shandy,[3] the dearest of my flock and friends, whose philanthropy I never think of at this long distance from his death—but my eyes gush out with tears. For his sake, I have a predilection for the whole corps of veterans; and so I strode over the two back rows of benches, and placed myself beside him.

The old officer was reading attentively a small pamphlet, it might be the book of the opera, with a large pair of spectacles. As soon as I sat down, he took his spectacles off, and putting them into a shagreen case, return'd them and the book into his pocket together. I half rose up, and made him a bow.

Translate this into any civilized language in the world—the sense is this:

"Here's a poor stranger come in to the box—he seems as if he knew no body; and is never likely, was he to be seven years in Paris, if every man he comes near keeps his spectacles upon his nose—'tis shutting the door of conversation absolutely in his face—and using him worse than a German."[4]

---

[1] Sterne anticipates the idea of "translation" in *TS,* when Toby and widow Wadman differ on exactly where she will lay her finger (IX.20.773):

> I will not touch it, however, quoth Mrs. Wadman to herself.
> This requires a second *translation:*—it shews what little knowledge is got by mere words—we must go up to the first springs. (Our italics.)

It is important to note that Sterne does not limit "translating" to simply putting gestures into words; the concept is more inclusive: what we *say* and what we *do* are *both* subject to "translation" into what we *mean.*

[2] Cf. Thicknesse, *Observations,* 14–15: "I have often heard asserted, that a French Officer, turn'd of forty, makes one of the most agreeable companions in the world."

[3] Sterne refers to Uncle Toby of *TS;* he is never called "Tobias" there, but doing so here gives credence to the idea that the apocryphal "Tobias" (a model of chastity) had some role in his creation. Yorick's speaking of a "long distance" from Toby's death is a confusion caused by the resurrection of Yorick from *TS,* where he dies in 1748, to the traveler of *ASJ,* voyaging abroad in 1762. We are never told exactly when Toby dies, although a eulogy is delivered in VI.25.545. Sterne was certainly not seeking narrative consistency in linking the two works but, rather, authorial identity.

[4] Stout, 171: "At the time of Yorick's *Journey,* the Seven Years War, in which the French and the Prussians were on opposing sides, was still in progress . . . ."

The French officer might as well have said it all aloud; and if he had, I should in course have put the bow I made him into French too, and told him, "I was sensible of his attention, and return'd him a thousand thanks for it."

There is not a secret so aiding to the progress of sociality, as to get master of this *short hand,* and be quick in rendering the several turns of looks and limbs, with all their inflections and delineations, into plain words. For my own part, by long habitude, I do it so mechanically, that when I walk the streets of London, I go translating all the way; and have more than once stood behind in the circle,[5] where not three words have been said, and have brought off twenty different dialogues with me, which I could have fairly wrote down and sworn to.

I was going one evening to Martini's concert at Milan,[6] and was just entering the door of the hall, when the Marquesina di F***[7] was coming out in a sort of a hurry—she was almost upon me before I saw her; so I gave a spring to one side to let her pass—She had done the same, and on the same side too; so we ran our heads together: she instantly got to the other side to get out: I was just as unfortunate as she had been; for I had sprung to that side, and opposed her passage again—We both flew together to the other side, and then back—and so on—it was ridiculous; we both blush'd intolerably; so I did at last the thing I should have done at first—I stood stock still, and the Marquesina had no more difficulty. I had no power to go into the room, till I had made her so much reparation as to wait and follow her with my eye to the end of the passage—She look'd back twice, and walk'd along it rather side-ways, as if she would make room for any one coming up stairs to pass her—No, said I—that's a vile translation: the Marquesina has a right to the best apology I can make her; and that opening is left for me to do it in—so I ran and begg'd pardon for the embarrassment I had given

---

[5] See *OED,* s.v. *circle, sb.* 20: "A number of persons standing or seated round a person or object of interest; 'an assembly surrounding the principal person' (J[ohnson]), as at Court, at a Drawing-room or Levée, etc."

[6] Sterne was in Italy from November 1765 to April or May 1766 and in Milan in early December; see Cash, *LY,* 233–49. He mentions his stay in *TS,* IX.24.780, in a way that may reflect on the "connection" made with the Marquesina di F*** (see n. 7): "My shirts! . . . I never had but six, and a cunning gypsey of a laundress at Milan cut me off the *fore*-laps of five—To do her justice, she did it with some consideration—for I was returning *out* of Italy"; see *Notes* to *TS,* 3:541–42, n. to 780.14–17, for the suggestion that this alludes to venereal discharges.

Martini: perhaps Giovanni Battista Martini (1706–1784), musician, composer, and scholar (Grove's *Dictionary of Music and Musicians*).

[7] Beginning with a comment by Arthur Young in *Travels during the Years 1787, 1788, and 1789* (1792), 203, the Marquesina has been identified as "the beautiful Marchesa Fagnani, née Costanza Brusati in Milan, who became mistress to George Selwyn and to the fourth Duke of Queensbury." Stout is almost certainly correct in dismissing this as speculation, but perhaps does not go far enough: any woman Sterne names F*** surely need not be assigned a "real" identity to be meaningful, especially not a woman with whom the "connection" gives Yorick "more pleasure than any one" he makes in Italy.

A Sentimental Journey

her, saying it was my intention to have made her way. She answered, she was guided by the same intention towards me—so we reciprocally thank'd each other. She was at the top of the stairs; and seeing no *Chichesbeo*[8] near her, I begg'd to hand her to her coach—so we went down the stairs, stopping at every third step to talk of the concert and the adventure—Upon my word, Madame, said I when I had handed her in, I made six different efforts to let you go out—And I made six efforts, replied she, to let you enter—I wish to heaven you would make a seventh, said I—With all my heart, said she, making room—Life is too short to be long about the forms of it[9]—so I instantly stepp'd in, and she carried me home with her—And what became of the concert, St. Cecilia,[10] who, I suppose, was at it, knows more than I.

I will only add, that the connection which arose out of that translation, gave me more pleasure than any one I had the honour to make in Italy.

---

[8] Few aspects of Italian society attracted more attention among English travelers than the Italian custom of providing married women a *cicisbeo,* an escort, and often a lover as well. Sharp, *Letters from Italy,* frequently alludes to the practice—e.g., "that abominable and infernal fashion of taking a Cicesbeo so soon after they have quitted the altar . . . . Many people in *England* imagine the majority of Cicesbeos to be an innocent kind of dangling fribble; but they are utterly mistaken" (73).

[9] Perhaps an ironic glance at Hippocrates' famous aphorism, *"Ars longa, vita brevis"* (life is short, the art [of healing] long), attacked by Walter Shandy in *TS,* V.34.473.

[10] Patron saint of music; her festival on November 22, the celebration of which began sometime before 1683 (the first for which a record exists), was an annual event for about twenty years thereafter, known to us primarily because of Dryden's two great St. Cecilia odes, written for the occasion in 1687 and 1697. Cf. *Oxford Companion to Music,* 10th ed., s.v.

THE DWARF.
PARIS.

I HAD never heard the remark made by any one in my life, except by one;[1] and who that was, will probably come out in this chapter; so that being pretty much unprepossessed, there must have been grounds for what struck me the moment I cast my eyes over the *parterre*[2]—and that was, the unaccountable sport of nature in forming such numbers of dwarfs—No doubt, she sports at certain times in almost every corner of the world; but in Paris, there is no end to her amusements[3]—The goddess seems almost as merry as she is wise.

As I carried my idea out of the *opera comique* with me, I measured every body I saw walking in the streets by it[4]—Melancholy application! especially where the size was extremely little—the face extremely dark—the eyes quick—the nose long—the teeth white—the jaw prominent—to see so many miserables, by force of accidents driven out of their own proper class into the very verge of another, which it gives me pain to write down—every third man a pigmy!—some by ricketty heads and hump backs—others by bandy legs—a third set arrested by the hand of Nature in the sixth and seventh years of their growth—a fourth, in their perfect and natural state, like dwarf apple-trees; from the first rudiments and stamina of their existence, never meant to grow higher.[5]

---

[1] I.e., Smollett's opinion; see below, nn. 6 and 7.

[2] Cf. pp. 57, 85, 88, where "parterre" is not italicized. *OED* cites Addison (1711) as its first illustration for this section in the theater, "the part of the ground-floor of the auditorium of a theatre behind the orchestra . . . . Also, The occupants of this part."

[3] Cf. *TS*, IV.S.T.308, where the Nosarians and anti-Nosarians argue about the possibility of Don Diego's nose: "there was a just and geometrical arrangement and proportion of the several parts of the human frame to its several destinations, offices, and functions, which could not be transgressed but within certain limits—that nature, though she sported—she sported within a certain circle;—and they could not agree about the diameter of it." Cf. Thicknesse, *Observations*, 80: "I cannot account for it, but [France] abounds more with human deformity, than any part of the world I have ever seen."

[4] Sterne's slip; the appearance of dwarfs in the audience triggers Yorick's thoughts about them on the street, which, in turn, trigger his anecdote about the dwarf in the theater (see pp. 85–6); Sterne seems to forget that Yorick has left the theater.

[5] Sterne returns to the learned debate in "Slawkenbergius's Tale," *TS*, IV.S.T.306: "And if a suitable provision of veins, arteries, &c. said they, was not laid in, for the due nourishment of such a nose, in the very first stamina and rudiments of its formation before it came into the world (bating the case of Wens) it could not regularly grow and be sustained afterwards." Clearly Sterne is thinking about the gigantic nose of "Slawkenbergius's Tale" as he writes about dwarfs.

Cf. Ephraim Chambers, *Cyclopædia: or, an Universal Dictionary of Arts and Sciences*, 5th ed., 2 vols. (1741, 1743), s.v. *Stamina*: "those simple, original parts, which existed first

A medical traveller might say, 'tis owing to undue bandages—a splenetic one, to want of air[6]—and an inquisitive traveller, to fortify the system, may measure the height of their houses—the narrowness of their streets, and in how few feet square in the sixth and seventh stories such numbers of the *Bourgoisie* eat and sleep together;[7] but I remember, Mr. Shandy the elder, who accounted for nothing like any body else,[8] in speaking one evening of these matters, averred, that children, like other animals, might be increased almost to any size, provided they came right into the world;[9] but the misery was, the citizens of Paris were so coop'd up, that they had not actually room enough to get them—I do not call it getting any thing, said he—'tis getting nothing—Nay, continued he, rising in his argument, 'tis getting worse than nothing, when all you have got, after twenty or five and twenty years of the tenderest care and most nutritious aliment bestowed upon it, shall not at last be as high as my leg. Now, Mr. Shandy being very short,[10] there could be nothing more said upon it.

---

in the embryo, or even in the seed; and by whose distinction, augmentation, and accretion by additional juices, the human body, at its utmost bulk is supposed to be formed."

[6] Cf. Smollett, *Travels,* letter 30, 2:98–99, commenting on the *enfans trouvés* (swaddled infants) in Paris and elsewhere, who were "so swathed with bandages, that the very sight of them made my eyes water . . . . The circulation of the blood, in such a case, must be obstructed on the whole surface of the body . . . . What are the consequences . . . ? the limbs are wasted; the joints grow rickety; the brain is compressed, and a hydrocephalus, with a great head and sore eyes, ensues. I take this abominable practice to be one great cause of the bandy legs, diminutive bodies, and large heads, so frequent in the south of France, and in Italy."

[7] Sterne continues to consult Smollett, this time a passage on ancient Rome (2:96): "we must naturally conclude they were strangely crouded together, and that in general they were a very frowzy generation. That they were crouded together appears from the height of their houses, which the poet Rutilius compared to towers made for scaling heaven."

[8] Sterne alludes to several descriptions of Walter Shandy in *TS,* most apropos, VII.27.617–18, his comments when accompanying Tristram on the Grand Tour: "his road seemed to lie so much on one side of that, wherein all other travellers had gone before him . . . and his remarks and reasonings upon the characters, the manners and customs of the countries we pass'd over, were so opposite to those of all other mortal men, . . . so odd, so mixed and tragicomical a contexture . . . ." Walter never offers this theory of dwarfs in *TS,* however; Sterne's joke is in aligning Smollett with Walter, on the one hand, and, more subtly, with the learned doctors in "Slawkenbergius's Tale," on the other.

[9] Sterne alludes to Walter's theory concerning birth and the location of the soul: "What is it to me which end of my son comes foremost into the world, provided all goes right after, and his cerebellum escapes uncrushed?" (II.19.177); and to the debate in Slawkenbergius as well: "In the triumph of which theory [of nutriment], they went so far as to affirm, that there was no cause in nature, why a nose might not grow to the size of the man himself" (IV.S.T.307).

[10] A source of some puzzlement to him, since Tristram is "very tall for his age"; see *TS,* VI.18.526.

As this is not a work of reasoning, I leave the solution as I found it, and content myself with the truth only of the remark, which is verified in every lane and by-lane of Paris. I was walking down that which leads from the Carousal[11] to the Palais Royal, and observing a little boy in some distress at the side of the gutter, which ran down the middle of it, I took hold of his hand, and help'd him over. Upon turning up his face to look at him after, I perceived he was about forty—Never mind, said I; some good body will do as much for me when I am ninety.

I feel some little principles within me, which incline me to be merciful towards this poor blighted part of my species, who have neither size or strength to get on in the world—I cannot bear to see one of them trod upon; and had scarce got seated beside my old French officer, ere the disgust was exercised, by seeing the very thing happen under the box we sat in.

At the end of the orchestra, and betwixt that and the first side-box, there is a small esplanade[12] left, where, when the house is full, numbers of all ranks take sanctuary. Though you stand, as in the parterre, you pay the same price as in the orchestra. A poor defenceless being[13] of this order had got thrust some how or other into this luckless place—the night was hot, and he was surrounded by beings two feet and a half higher than himself. The dwarf suffered inexpressibly on all sides; but the thing which incommoded him most, was a tall corpulent German,[14] near seven feet high, who stood directly betwixt him and all possibility of his seeing either the stage or the actors. The poor dwarf did all he could to get a peep at what was going forwards, by seeking for some little opening betwixt the German's arm and his body, trying first one side, then the other; but the German stood square in the most unaccommodating posture that can be imagined—the dwarf might as well have been placed at the bottom of the deepest draw-well in Paris; so he civilly reach'd up his hand to the German's sleeve, and told him his distress—The German turn'd his head

---

[11] The street mentioned (correctly, Carrousel) is now the Rue de Rivoli. The Carrousel was the inner court of the Tuileries, and the Palais-Royal was the royal residence.

[12] Originally a technical term from fortification; it came to mean, from the late seventeenth century onward, any level open space, as here and at p. 167 below.

[13] As John Ferriar, *Illustrations of Sterne*, 1:66–69, first pointed out, Sterne borrows his anecdote from Paul Scarron's *Roman comique* (1651), translated by Tom Brown and others. In Scarron's version, however, the "dwarf" is the butt of the joke and ends in a sewer drain under the theater seats; as Ferriar notes, "for the mean and disgusting turn which this story receives in the *Roman Comique*, Sterne has substituted a rich and beautiful chain of incidents . . ." (69).

[14] See above, p. 80, n 4. Cf. Le Roux, *Dictionnaire*, s.v. *Querelle d'Allemand*: "Pour une querelle mauvaise, injuste, qui a été suscité pour une bagatelle, pour un rien, commencée avec quelqu'un brutalement, et sans sujet ni raison" (A German quarrel: a bad, unjust quarrel, started over a trifle, for nothing, begun brutally, without rhyme or reason).

back, look'd down upon him as Goliah did upon David—and unfeelingly resumed his posture.

I was just then taking a pinch of snuff out of my monk's little horn box—And how would thy meek and courteous spirit, my dear monk! so temper'd to *bear and forbear!*[15]—how sweetly would it have lent an ear to this poor soul's complaint!

The old French officer seeing me lift up my eyes with an emotion, as I made the apostrophe, took the liberty to ask me what was the matter—I told him the story in three words; and added, how inhuman it was.

By this time the dwarf was driven to extremes, and in his first transports, which are generally unreasonable, had told the German he would cut off his long queue with his knife—The German look'd back coolly, and told him he was welcome if he could reach it.

An injury sharpened by an insult,[16] be it to who it will, makes every man of sentiment a party: I could have leaped out of the box to have redressed it.—The old French officer did it with much less confusion; for leaning a little over, and nodding to a centinel,[17] and pointing at the same time with his finger to the distress—the centinel made his way up to it.—There was no occasion to tell the grievance—the thing told itself; so thrusting back the German instantly with his musket—he took the poor dwarf by the hand, and placed him before him.[18]— This is noble! said I, clapping my hands together—And yet you would not permit this, said the old officer, in England.

---

[15] Cf. *Letters,* 174: "to bear and forbear will ever be my maxim." Cf. Stobaeus's fragment on Epictetus: "*Epictetus . . . was in the habit of saying* that there were two vices which are far more severe and atrocious than all others, . . . when we do not . . . bear the wrongs which we have to bear, or do not . . . forbear those matters and pleasures which we ought to forbear. 'And so,' he says, '. . . a man should take to heart these two words . . . ἀνέχου [bear] and ἀπέχου [forbear]" (*Epictetus* 2:455).

[16] The playwright Edward Moore (1712–1757) is credited with originating this expression (*The Foundling* [1748], V.v.: "This is adding Insult to Injuries" [60]), although it has classical roots. Cf. *BJ,* p. 180: "thou wilt be repaid with Injuries & Insults!"

[17] According to Anne Vincent-Buffault (*The History of Tears: Sensibility and Sentimentality in France,* tr. Teresa Bridgeman [New York: St. Martin's Press, 1991], 55), the "participation of the Pit in the French playhouse 'occurred to such a degree that in 1751 the French Guards were posted there in an attempt to moderate the critical ardour of the pit'"; she is quoting *Anecdotes dramatiques par J. B. Clément de Dijon* (1775). Cf. Peckham, *Tour of Holland,* 174–75: "You are never interrupted with riots and disturbances, as in England; for sentinels with their bayonets fixed, stand in different parts of the theatre, who on the least tumult, drag out the delinquent . . . ."

[18] The scene reenacts what Sterne describes as the fate of self-pride in sermon 24, "Pride": "if I exalt myself, I have no prospect of escaping;——with this vice I stand swoln up in every body's way, and must unavoidably be thrust back: which ever way I turn . . . I press unkindly upon some one, and in return, must prepare myself for such mortifying repulses, as will bring me down . . . ." (*Sermons* 4:228).

—In England, dear Sir, said I, *we sit all at our ease.*[19]

The old French officer would have set me at unity with myself, in case I had been at variance,—by saying it was a *bon mot*—and as a *bon mot* is always worth something at Paris, he offered me a pinch of snuff.

---

[19] Yorick perhaps alludes only to the installation of seats in all sections of London theaters during the seventeenth century, but may also be recalling *Romeo and Juliet,* II.iv.31–35: "*Mercutio:* Why, is not this a lamentable thing, grandsire, that we should be thus afflicted with . . . these fashion-mongers, these [pardon-]me's, who stand so much on the new form, that they cannot sit at ease on the old bench."

THE ROSE.
PARIS.

IT was now my turn to ask the old French officer "What was the matter?" for a cry of *"Haussez les mains, Monsieur l'Abbe,"*[1] re-echoed from a dozen different parts of the parterre, was as unintelligible to me, as my apostrophe to the monk had been to him.

He told me, it was some poor Abbe in one of the upper loges, who he supposed had got planted perdu[2] behind a couple of grissets in order to see the opera, and that the parterre espying him, were insisting upon his holding up both his hands during the representation.—And can it be supposed, said I, that an ecclesiastick would pick the Grisset's pockets? The old French officer smiled, and whispering in my ear, open'd a door of knowledge which I had no idea of—

Good God! said I, turning pale with astonishment—is it possible, that a people so smit with sentiment should at the same time be so unclean, and so unlike themselves—*Quelle grossierte!*[3] added I.

The French officer told me, it was an illiberal sarcasm at the church, which had begun in the theatre about the time the Tartuffe was given in it, by Moliere[4]—but, like other remains of Gothic manners, was declining—Every nation, continued he, have their refinements and *grossiertes,* in which they take the lead, and lose it of one another by turns—that he had been in most countries, but never in one where he found not some delicacies, which others seemed to want. *Le* POUR, *et le* CONTRE *se trouvent en chaque nation;*[5] there is a balance, said he, of good and bad every where; and nothing but the knowing it is so can emancipate one half of the world from the prepossessions which it holds against the other—that the advantage of travel, as it regarded the *sçavoir vivre,*[6] was by seeing a great deal both of men and manners; it taught us mutual toleration; and mutual toleration, concluded he, making me a bow, taught us mutual love.

---

[1] Put your hands up (i.e., up in the air), Monsieur Priest (correctly, *Abbé*).

[2] *Perdu* was familiar throughout the eighteenth century in English, although Sterne probably thought it gave a French flavor in the present instance. *Loge* was becoming anglicized and this passage is *OED*'s second illustration, but Sterne had altered its other occurrences in his ms. to "box" (see p. 80).

[3] What coarseness! (correctly, *grossièreté*). In light of American usage, "How gross!" may be a more apt translation.

[4] See above, p. 30, n. 7.

[5] Good and bad are found in every country. Cf. *Letters,* 201: "I'm more than half tired of France, as fine a Country as it is—but there is the *Pour* & the *Contre* for every place,—all wch being ballanced, I think Old England preferable to any Kingdome in the world—."

[6] Knowledge of the world; good breeding (correctly, *savoir-vivre*). Cf. *Letters,* 151 (to Garrick, January 31, 1762, after two weeks in Paris): "I hope in a fortnight to break through, or rather from the delights of this place, which in the *scavoir vivre,* exceed all the places, I believe, in this section of the globe."

The old French officer delivered this with an air of such candour and good sense, as coincided with my first favourable impressions of his character—I thought I loved the man; but I fear I mistook the object—'twas my own way of thinking—the difference was, I could not have expressed it half so well.

It is alike troublesome to both the rider and his beast—if the latter goes pricking up his ears, and starting all the way at every object which he never saw before—I have as little torment of this kind as any creature alive; and yet I honestly confess, that many a thing gave me pain, and that I blush'd at many a word the first month—which I found inconsequent and perfectly innocent the second.

Madame de Rambouliet,[7] after an acquaintance of about six weeks with her, had done me the honour to take me in her coach about two leagues out of town—Of all women, Madame de Rambouliet is the most correct; and I never wish to see one of more virtues and purity of heart—In our return back, Madame de Rambouliet desired me to pull the cord—I ask'd her if she wanted any thing—*Rien que pisser*,[8] said Madame de Rambouliet—

Grieve not, gentle traveller, to let Madame de Rambouliet p--ss on—And, ye fair mystic nymphs! go each one *pluck your rose*,[9] and scatter them in your path— for Madame de Rambouliet did no more—I handed Madame de Rambouliet out of the coach; and had I been the priest of the chaste CASTALIA,[10] I could not have served at her fountain with a more respectful decorum.

END OF VOL. I.

---

[7] Stout, 181–82, suggests an ironic allusion to "the ideal of refinement in language and manners made fashionable by the *précieuses* who frequented the salon" of Catherine de Vivonne, Marquise de Rambouillet (see p. 5, n. 2), and "whose extravagant *préciosité* Molière satirized in *Les Précieuses ridicules* (1659)."

[8] Only to urinate. *Pisser* does not have the impolite connotation of the English *piss,* the word Sterne first wrote before deleting it in favor of the French.

[9] Stout, 183–84: "a euphemism for easing oneself . . . . Partridge notes that the expression probably originated from the fact that the rural privy was often in the garden (*Dictionary of Slang and Unconventional English*). . . ." Sterne's illustration of cultural difference is well chosen since much was made by English travelers of what they perceived to be the indecency of other nations in such matters. Smollett, *Travels,* letter 5, 1:63–64, offers one of countless examples: "If there is no cleanliness among these people, much less shall we find delicacy . . . . Will custom exempt from the imputation of gross indecency a French lady, who shifts her frowsy smock in presence of a male visitant, and talks to him of her *lavement,* her *medicine,* and her *bidet!* . . . [cf. p. 54, n. 1] I have known a lady handed to the house of office by her admirer, who stood at the door, and entertained her with *bons mots* all the time she was within."

[10] In Greek myth, the nymph who, when pursued by Apollo, throws herself into a spring on Mt. Parnassus, near Delphi. The Castalian spring was thereafter credited by Greeks and Romans with powers of poetic inspiration. Pilgrims to the shrine of Apollo at Delphi purified themselves in its waters before consulting the oracle.

A

SENTIMENTAL JOURNEY

THROUGH

FRANCE AND ITALY,

BY

MR. YORICK.

VOL. II.

LONDON:

Printed for T. BECKET and P. A. DE HONDT,
in the Strand. MDCCLXVIII.

THE FILLE DE CHAMBRE.
PARIS.

WHAT the old French officer had deliver'd upon travelling, bringing Polonius's advice[1] to his son upon the same subject into my head—and that bringing in Hamlet; and Hamlet, the rest of Shakespear's works, I stopp'd at the Quai de Conti in my return home, to purchase the whole set.

The bookseller said he had not a set in the world—*Comment!*[2] said I; taking one up out of a set which lay upon the counter betwixt us.——He said, they were sent him only to be got bound, and were to be sent back to Versailles in the morning to the Count de B****.[3]

—And does the Count de B****, said I, read Shakespear? *C'est un Esprit fort;*[4] replied the bookseller.—He loves English books; and what is more to his honour, Monsieur, he loves the English too. You speak this so civilly, said I, that 'tis enough to oblige an Englishman to lay out a Louis d'or or two at your shop—the bookseller made a bow, and was going to say something, when a young decent girl of about twenty, who by her air and dress, seemed to be *fille de chambre* to some devout woman of fashion, came into the shop and asked for *Les Egarments du Cœur & de l'Esprit:*[5] the bookseller gave her the book directly; she pulled out a

---

[1] In *Hamlet,* I.iii.55–81; if Sterne had any particular line in mind, perhaps line 69: "Take each man's censure, but reserve thy judgment."

[2] How can that be! Explain yourself! Yorick believes he has caught the bookseller in a lie, since a set is in plain sight.

[3] See p. 114, n. 1.

[4] He's a man of genius. Cf. p. 19, n. 5. That a few lines later the *fille de chambre* asks for Crébillon's *Les égarements du cœur et de l'esprit* (see next n.) is perhaps not accidental.

[5] A novel (1736–1738) by Claude-Prosper Jolyot de Crébillon (1707–1777), known as Crébillon *fils*. Sterne met him in Paris in 1762, and informed Garrick that "Crebillion . . . has agreed to write me an expostulat[o]ry letter upon the indecorums of T. Shandy—which is to be answered by recrimination upon the liberties in his own works—these are to be printed together—Crebillion against Sterne—Sterne against Crebellion— . . . the money equally divided" (*Letters* 162); no such work has surfaced.

Sterne used the first part of the title to explain his theory of the hobby-horse to a correspondent in 1760: "The ruleing passion *et les egarements du cœur,* are the very things which mark, and distinguish a man's character;—in which I would as soon leave out a man's head as his hobby-horse" (*Letters* 88). He refers to the entire title in a letter possibly written to Lady Warkworth (see above, p. 62, n. 7): "I . . . carry about me the golden headed pencil & pinch-beck Ruler which [you] . . . put into my hands at parting . . . to mark . . . my back-slidings and my fore-slidings—*les egarments de mon coeur, & mon esprit pendent mon exile!*" (245).

There is no evidence that Sterne was influenced by the contents of the work (translated as *The Wanderings of the Heart and Mind* in 1751; more recently as *The Wayward Head and Heart,* tr. Barbara Bray [London: Oxford UP, 1963]), but the title seems lodged in his

little green sattin purse run round with a ribband of the same colour, and putting her finger and thumb into it, she took out the money, and paid for it. As I had nothing more to stay me in the shop, we both walked out at the door together.

——And what have you to do, my dear, said I, with *The Wanderings of the Heart,* who scarce know yet you have one? nor till love has first told you it, or some faithless shepherd has made it ache, can'st thou ever be sure it is so.—*Le Dieu m'en guard!*[6] said the girl.—With reason, said I—for if it is a good one, 'tis pity it should be stolen: 'tis a little treasure to thee, and gives a better air to your face, than if it was dress'd out with pearls.

The young girl listened with a submissive attention, holding her sattin purse by its ribband in her hand all the time—'Tis a very small one, said I, taking hold of the bottom of it—she held it towards me—and there is very little in it, my dear, said I; but be but as good as thou art handsome, and heaven will fill it: I had a parcel of crowns in my hand to pay for Shakespear; and as she had let go the purse intirely, I put a single one in; and tying up the ribband in a bow-knot, returned it to her.[7]

The young girl made me more a humble courtesy than a low one—'twas one of those quiet, thankful sinkings where the spirit bows itself down—the body does no more than tell it. I never gave a girl a crown in my life which gave me half the pleasure.

My advice, my dear, would not have been worth a pin to you, said I, if I had not given this along with it: but now, when you see the crown, you'll remember it—so don't, my dear, lay it out in ribbands.

Upon my word, Sir, said the girl, earnestly, I am incapable—in saying which, as is usual in little bargains of honour, she gave me her hand—*En verite, Monsieur, je mettrai cet argent apart,*[8] said she.

When a virtuous convention is made betwixt man and woman, it sanctifies their most private walks: so notwithstanding it was dusky, yet as both our roads

---

mind. The work itself is epitomized in two sentences: "it is less dangerous to be found wanting in heart than in manners" and "what is called knowledge of the world only makes us wiser insomuch as it makes us more corrupt" (Bray 159, 201).

But perhaps one of its opening remarks comes closest to capturing that aspect of Sterne that most baffles us: "I tried in vain to deaden the inner longing that oppressed me; only the society of women could dispel it. . . . I went to infinite trouble to seek them out. I could not be long in their company without knowing that they alone could bestow on me that happiness, those sweet delusions of the heart, that no other distraction offered me" (Bray 4).

[6] Lord preserve me from it! (correctly, *Dieu m'en garde*).

[7] Purses and crowns are never innocent; the anonymous annotator of an 1803 edition of *ASJ* (London: T. Hurst and C. Chapple) was shocked: "Here again the imagination is played with—the reader is left to make his own comments, and led into a path which he can only blame himself for pursuing" (105).

[8] Truly, Sir, I will put this money apart (correctly, *vérité . . . à part*).

lay the same way, we made no scruple of walking along the Quai de Conti[9] together.

She made me a second courtesy in setting off, and before we got twenty yards from the door, as if she had not done enough before, she made a sort of a little stop to tell me again,—she thank'd me.

It was a small tribute, I told her, which I could not avoid paying to virtue, and would not be mistaken in the person I had been rendering it to for the world— but I see innocence, my dear, in your face—and foul befal the man who ever lays a snare in its way!

The girl seem'd affected some way or other with what I said—she gave a low sigh—I found I was not impowered to enquire at all after it—so said nothing more till I got to the corner of the Rue de Nevers,[10] where we were to part.

—But is this the way, my dear, said I, to the hotel de Modene? she told me it was—or, that I might go by the Rue de Guineygaude,[11] which was the next turn.—Then I'll go, my dear, by the Rue de Guineygaude, said I, for two reasons; first I shall please myself, and next I shall give you the protection of my company as far on your way as I can. The girl was sensible I was civil—and said, she wish'd the hotel de Modene was in the Rue de St. Pierre—You live there? said I.—She told me she was *fille de chambre* to Madame R****—Good God! said I, 'tis the very lady for whom I have brought a letter from Amiens—The girl told me that Madame R****, she believed expected a stranger with a letter, and was impatient to see him—so I desired the girl to present my compliments to Madame R****, and say I would certainly wait upon her in the morning.

We stood still at the corner of the Rue de Nevers whilst this pass'd—We then stopp'd a moment whilst she disposed of her *Egarments de Cœur,* &c. more commodiously than carrying them in her hand—they were two volumes; so I held the second for her whilst she put the first into her pocket; and then she held her pocket, and I put in the other after it.

'Tis sweet to feel by what fine-spun threads our affections are drawn together.

We set off a-fresh, and as she took her third step, the girl put her hand within my arm—I was just bidding her—but she did it of herself with that undeliberating simplicity, which shew'd it was out of her head that she had never seen me before. For my own part, I felt the conviction of consanguinity so strongly, that I

---

[9] A real street, but, as Kenneth Monkman notes in his review of Stout (*TLS,* December 12, 1968, 1410), a "possible" bit of bawdiness as well.

[10] Probably a bilingual pun (perhaps two of them) in this location; Sterne had already punned on "Nevers" in *TS,* V.2.416, where Walter, plotting Bobby's Grand Tour, reaches "Nevers" at the very moment he is told of Bobby's death.

[11] I.e., *Guénégaud.*

could not help turning half round to look in her face, and see if I could trace out any thing in it of a family likeness—Tut! said I, are we not all relations?[12]

When we arrived at the turning up of the Rue de Guineygaude, I stopp'd to bid her adieu for good an' all: the girl would thank me again for my company and kindness—She bid me adieu twice—I repeated it as often; and so cordial was the parting between us, that had it happen'd any where else, I'm not sure but I should have signed it with a kiss of charity, as warm and holy as an apostle.

But in Paris, as none kiss each other but the men—I did, what amounted to the same thing——

——I bid God bless her.

---

[12] Cf. *Letters,* 408: "I could not wish y^r happiness and the Successe of what*ever conduces* to it, more than I do, was I your Brother——but good god! are we not all brothers and Sisters, who are friendly & virtuous & good?" Stout, 190–91, also directs attention to Sterne's famous letter to the former slave, Ignatius Sancho, quoted below, p. 101, n. 7; and to sermon 41, "Follow peace" (see above, p. 13, n. 3): e.g., "THE great end and design of our holy religion, next to the main view of reconciling us to God, was to reconcile us to each other"; and "For, as men, we are allied together in the natural bond of brotherhood, and are members one of another" (*Sermons* 4:384, 388).

THE PASSPORT.
PARIS.

WHEN I got home to my hotel, La Fleur told me I had been enquired after by the Lieutenant de Police—The duce take it! said I——I know the reason. It is time the reader should know it, for in the order of things in which it happened, it was omitted; not that it was out of my head; but that had I told it then, it might have been forgot now—and now is the time I want it.

I had left London with so much precipitation, that it never enter'd my mind that we were at war with France;[1] and had reach'd Dover, and look'd through my glass at the hills beyond Boulogne, before the idea presented itself; and with this in its train, that there was no getting there without a passport.[2] Go but to the end of a street, I have a mortal aversion for returning back no wiser than I set out; and as this was one of the greatest efforts I had ever made for knowledge, I could less bear the thoughts of it: so hearing the Count de **** had hired the packet, I begg'd he would take me in his *suite*.[3] The Count had some little knowledge of me, so made little or no difficulty—only said, his inclination to serve me could reach no further than Calais; as he was to return by way of Brussels to Paris: however, when I had once pass'd there, I might get to Paris without interruption; but that in Paris I must make friends and shift for myself.—Let me get to Paris, Monsieur le Count, said I—and I shall do very well. So I embark'd, and never thought more of the matter.

When La Fleur told me the Lieutenant de Police had been enquiring after me—the thing instantly recurred—and by the time La Fleur had well told me, the master of the hotel came into my room to tell me the same thing, with this addition to it, that my passport had been particularly ask'd after: the master of the hotel concluded with saying, He hoped I had one.—Not I, faith! said I.

The master of the hotel retired three steps from me, as from an infected person, as I declared this—and poor La Fleur advanced three steps towards me, and with that sort of movement which a good soul makes to succour a distress'd one—the fellow won my heart by it; and from that single *trait*, I knew his character as perfectly, and could rely upon it as firmly, as if he had served me with fidelity for seven years.

---

[1] Stout, 192: "when Sterne reached Paris in January 1762, on his first trip abroad, England and France were still officially engaged in the Seven Years War (the Treaty of Paris was not signed until February 1763), although hostilities between them had ceased . . . ." Sterne was among the first to take advantage of this (see *Letters* 146, n. 2).

[2] Sterne too had to seek a passport, once he decided to stay in Paris for several months; see Cash, *LY,* 128–29, and below, p. 104, n. 8.

[3] Sterne's italics here and for *trait* below, suggest an effort to treat both words as French, despite their long acceptance as English words; Sterne does this on occasion throughout *ASJ.*

Mon seignior![4] cried the master of the hotel—but recollecting himself as he made the exclamation, he instantly changed the tone of it—If Monsieur, said he, has not a passport (*apparament*[5]) in all likelihood he has friends in Paris who can procure him one.—Not that I know of, quoth I, with an air of indifference.— Then *certes,* replied he, you'll be sent to the Bastile or the Chatelet,[6] *au moins.*[7] Poo! said I, the king of France is a good natured soul—he'll hurt no body.—*Cela n'empeche pas,*[8] said he—you will certainly be sent to the Bastile to-morrow morning.—But I've taken your lodgings for a month, answer'd I, and I'll not quit them a day before the time for all the kings of France in the world. La Fleur whisper'd in my ear, That no body could oppose the king of France.

Pardi! said my host, *ces Messieurs Anglois sont des gens tres extraordinaires*[9]—and having both said and sworn it—he went out.

---

[4] An honorific address (*Monseigneur*) that seems inappropriate in context; Anne Bandry has suggested to us that the master of the hotel might be thought to have exclaimed "Seigneur!" (Lord!), which to Sterne's ear became "My Lord!"

[5] Apparently (correctly, *apparamment*).

[6] Cf. Cole, *Journal,* 215: "the Bastile, which consists of a sort of Square Building, with 8 roundish high Towers about it, & none or few Windows from it: so that it must be a very gloomy Habitation for the unhappy People who live in it . . . . It was built as a Fortress & Defence of the City in the 14th Century, & now serves as a Prison for State Criminals." The Châtelet was a fortified bridge-tower built in the ninth century and used chiefly for criminals.

[7] Certainly . . . at the very least.

[8] That makes no difference; that doesn't matter (correctly, *n'empêche*).

[9] By Heaven! . . . these English are certainly extraordinary people. If we may believe Thicknesse, *Useful Hints,* 178, the landlord was not an innocent bystander: "The hotel wherever you lodge durst not let you sleep one night there without giving in your name to . . . [the police]."

THE PASSPORT.
The Hotel at Paris.

I COULD not find in my heart to torture La Fleur's with a serious look upon the subject of my embarrassment, which was the reason I had treated it so cavalierly: and to shew him how light it lay upon my mind, I dropt the subject entirely; and whilst he waited upon me at supper, talk'd to him with more than usual gaiety about Paris, and of the opera comique.—La Fleur had been there himself, and had followed me through the streets as far as the bookseller's shop; but seeing me come out with the young *fille de chambre,* and that we walk'd down the Quai de Conti together, La Fleur deem'd it unnecessary to follow me a step further—so making his own reflections upon it, he took a shorter cut——and got to the hotel in time to be inform'd of the affair of the Police against my arrival.

As soon as the honest creature had taken away, and gone down to sup himself, I then began to think a little seriously about my situation.—

—And here, I know, Eugenius, thou wilt smile at the remembrance of a short dialogue which pass'd betwixt us the moment I was going to set out——I must tell it here.

Eugenius, knowing that I was as little subject to be overburthen'd with money as thought,[1] had drawn me aside to interrogate me how much I had taken care for; upon telling him the exact sum, Eugenius shook his head, and said it would not do; so pull'd out his purse in order to empty it into mine.—I've enough in conscience, Eugenius, said I.——Indeed, Yorick, you have not, replied Eugenius—I know France and Italy better than you.——But you don't consider, Eugenius, said I, refusing his offer, that before I have been three days in Paris, I shall take care to say or do something or other for which I shall get clapp'd up into the Bastile, and that I shall live there a couple of months entirely at the king of France's expence.—I beg pardon, said Eugenius, drily: really, I had forgot that resource.

Now the event I treated gaily came seriously to my door.

Is it folly, or nonchalance, or philosophy, or pertinacity—or what is it in me, that, after all, when La Fleur had gone down stairs, and I was quite alone, that I could not bring down my mind to think of it otherwise than I had then spoken of it to Eugenius?

---

[1] Sterne may be paying tribute to some generous gesture by Hall-Stevenson, but the only evidence we have of his financial situation before departing London in 1762 comes from a letter to Garrick in late December: "upon reviewing my finances, this morning, wth some unforseen expences—I find I should set out with 20 p^{ds} less—than a prudent man ought—will You lend me twenty pounds" (*Letters* 146).

—And as for the Bastile! the terror is in the word—Make the most of it you can, said I to myself, the Bastile is but another word for a tower—and a tower is but another word for a house you can't get out of—Mercy on the gouty![2] for they are in it twice a year—but with nine livres a day, and pen and ink and paper and patience, albeit a man can't get out, he may do very well within—at least for a month or six weeks; at the end of which, if he is a harmless fellow his innocence appears, and he comes out a better and wiser man than he went in.

I had some occasion (I forget what) to step into the court-yard, as I settled this account; and remember I walk'd down stairs in no small triumph with the conceit of my reasoning—Beshrew the *sombre* pencil! said I vauntingly—for I envy not its powers, which paints the evils of life with so hard and deadly a colouring. The mind sits terrified at the objects she has magnified herself, and blackened: reduce them to their proper size and hue she overlooks them—'Tis true, said I, correcting the proposition—the Bastile is not an evil to be despised—but strip it of its towers[3]—fill up the fossè[4]—unbarricade the doors—call it simply a confinement, and suppose 'tis some tyrant of a distemper—and not of a man which holds you in it—the evil half vanishes, and you bear the other half without complaint.

I was interrupted in the hey-day of this soliloquy, with a voice which I took to be of a child, which complained "it could not get out."—I look'd up and down the passage, and seeing neither man, woman, or child, I went out without further attention.

In my return back through the passage, I heard the same words repeated twice over; and looking up, I saw it was a starling hung in a little cage.—"I can't get out—I can't get out," said the starling.[5]

---

[2] *OED's* earliest use of this absolute form is dated 1799.

[3] Cf. *TS,* V.3.425, Walter's oration on death: "There is no terror, brother *Toby,* in its looks, but what it borrows from groans and convulsions . . . . Strip it of these, what is it . . . ."

[4] Moat, ditch (correctly, *fossé*). Readers of *TS* will recognize the phrase as a commonplace of fortification.

[5] Stout, 197: "The appropriateness of the caged starling as an emblem of Yorick's threatened confinement in the Bastille may depend partly on an association between 'starling' and 'Sterne'"; see below, p. 106, n. 2. Jane Austen alludes to this passage in chapter 10 of *Mansfield Park:* "But unluckily that iron gate, that ha-ha, give me a feeling of restraint and hardship. I cannot get out, as the starling said" (*The Novels,* ed. R. W. Chapman [Oxford: Clarendon, 1934], 3:99). Possibly, as Stephen Derry has suggested ("*Mansfield Park,* Sterne's Starling, and Bunyan's Man of Despair," *N&Q* 44 [1997]:322–23), the origin of the lament is the Man in the Iron Cage in John Bunyan's *Pilgrim's Progress* (ed. Roger Sharrock [London: Oxford UP, 1966], 166): "I am *now* a Man of Despair, and am shut up in it, as in this Iron Cage. I cannot get out; O *now* I cannot." See also Maria Edgeworth, *Ennui* (1809), 188.

And cf. a story told by Thicknesse (*Useful Hints* 51) that may also have had some influence: "a young lady of my acquaintance, who being a pensioner at a convent, desired one of the nuns to set her right from a mistake she had made in her embroidery. The peevish sister refused her, and bid her wait till the mistress of that work was at leisure; adding, in a

I stood looking at the bird: and to every person who came through the passage it ran fluttering to the side towards which they approach'd it, with the same lamentation of its captivity—"I can't get out," said the starling—God help thee! said I, but I'll let thee out, cost what it will; so I turn'd about the cage to get to the door; it was twisted and double twisted so fast with wire, there was no getting it open without pulling the cage to pieces—I took both hands to it.

The bird flew to the place where I was attempting his deliverance, and thrusting his head through the trellis, press'd his breast against it, as if impatient—I fear, poor creature! said I, I cannot set thee at liberty—"No," said the starling—"I can't get out—I can't get out," said the starling.

I vow, I never had my affections more tenderly awakened; or do I remember an incident in my life, where the dissipated spirits, to which my reason had been a bubble, were so suddenly call'd home. Mechanical as the notes were, yet so true in tune to nature were they chanted, that in one moment they overthrew all my systematic reasonings upon the Bastile; and I heavily walk'd up stairs, unsaying every word I had said in going down them.[6]

Disguise thyself as thou wilt, still slavery! said I—still thou art a bitter draught; and though thousands in all ages have been made to drink of thee, thou art no less bitter on that account.[7]—'Tis thou, thrice sweet and gracious goddess,

---

flirting manner, you are *got out,* sister, and you cannot *get in!* 'It is true, replied the young lady; but it is still worse with you, sister: for you have *got in,* and you cannot *get out.'*"

[6] Stout, 198, calls attention to sermon 3 ("Philanthropy recommended") as a gloss on this passage (see Appendix, pp. 233–37); the echoes make clear that the eighteenth-century "man of feeling" was closely related to portrayals of Jesus in the period and should not be understood solely as a secularization of moral conduct.

[7] Cf. sermon 10, "Job's account . . ." (*Sermons* 4:99–100): "Consider slavery——what it is,——how bitter a draught, and how many millions have been made to drink of it;—which if it can poison all earthly happiness when exercised barely upon our bodies, what must it be, when it comprehends both the slavery of body and mind?" Responding to this passage, a former slave, Ignatius Sancho (1729–1780), wrote to Sterne asking that he "give one half-hour's attention to slavery . . . . That subject, handled in your striking manner, would ease the yoke (perhaps) of many" (*Letters of the Late Ignatius Sancho, an African,* 5th ed. [1803; first pub. 1782], 70–72). Sterne responded by calling attention to a passage in *TS* (IX.6) he said he was writing when Sancho's letter arrived (*Letters* 285–87) about "the sorrows of a friendless poor negro girl" and then added:

it is by the finest tints and most insensible gradations that nature descends from the fairest face about St James's, to the sootyest complexion in Africa: at which tint of these, is it, Sancho, that the ties of blood & nature cease? . . . tis no uncommon thing my good Sancho, for one half of the world to use the other half of it like brutes, and then endeavour to make 'em so.

. . . [I]t casts, a great Shade upon the world, that so great a part of it, are, and have been so long bound down in chains of darkness & in chains of misery.

See Madeleine Descargues, "Ignatius Sancho's *Letters,*" *Shandean* 3 (1991):145–66.

addressing myself to LIBERTY,[8] whom all in public or in private worship, whose taste is grateful, and ever wilt be so, till NATURE herself shall change—no *tint*[9] of words can spot thy snowy mantle, or chymic power turn thy sceptre into iron—with thee to smile upon him as he eats his crust, the swain is happier than his monarch, from whose court thou art exiled—Gracious heaven! cried I, kneeling down upon the last step but one in my ascent—grant me but health,[10] thou great Bestower of it, and give me but this fair goddess as my companion—and shower down thy mitres, if it seems good unto thy divine providence, upon those heads which are aching for them.[11]

---

[8] Cf. *TS*, VII.34.635–36, where the imposition of a tax on his travel leads Tristram to celebrate English "freedom": "O England! England! thou land of liberty, and climate of good sense, thou tenderest of mothers—and gentlest of nurses, cried I, kneeling upon one knee, as I was beginning my apostrophè." Cf. II.17.164: "this land of liberty and good sense"; and III.12.212: "this land of liberty of ours."

[9] Cf. sermon 19, "Felix's behaviour towards Paul" (*Sermons* 4:180): "each one lends it something of its own complexional tint and character." *OED*, s.v. *tint, sb.* 1.b. *fig.*, offers Sterne's two usages as its first two illustrations: "a slight imparted or modifying character, a 'tinge' *of* something."

[10] Given Sterne's ill health, this wish is hardly platitudinous; he repeats the notion throughout *TS*—e.g., V.33.471: "O Blessed health! cried my father . . . thou art above all gold and treasure." Tristram invokes "the fountain of health" (I.22.82) and, again, "the fountain of life to bless me so long with health and good spirits" (VII.1.575).

[11] Sterne alludes to Sancho Panza's reply to the idea of his wife's being a Queen: "I doubt of it . . . for I can't help believing, that though it should rain Kingdoms down upon the Face of the Earth, not one of them would sit well upon *Mary Gutierez*'s Head" (*Don Quixote* I.I.7, 1:58). Sterne often returns to this image in his writings when confronting his failure to rise in the clerical hierarchy; see, e.g., *TS*, I.12.34; and also *BJ*, p. 231. See above, p. 30 and n. 4.

THE CAPTIVE.
PARIS.

THE bird in his cage pursued me into my room; I sat down close to my table, and leaning my head upon my hand, I began to figure to myself the miseries of confinement. I was in a right frame for it, and so I gave full scope to my imagination.

I was going to begin with the millions of my fellow creatures born to no inheritance but slavery;[1] but finding, however affecting the picture was, that I could not bring it near me, and that the multitude of sad groups in it did but distract me—

—I took a single captive,[2] and having first shut him up in his dungeon, I then look'd through the twilight of his grated door to take his picture.[3]

I beheld his body half wasted away with long expectation and confinement,[4] and felt what kind of sickness of the heart it was which arises from hope deferr'd.[5] Upon looking nearer I saw him pale and feverish: in thirty years the western

---

[1] Cf. Ignatius Sancho's (see above, p. 101, n. 7) comment: "in me, you behold the uplifted hands of Millions of my moorish brethren—Grief (you pathetically observe) is eloquent—figure to yourselves their attitudes—hear their supplicatory address—humanity must comply" (*Letters* 283); and sermon 10, "Job's account" (*Sermons* 4:101): "Millions of our fellow-creatures, born to no inheritance but poverty and trouble, forced by the necessity of their lots to drudgery and painful employments . . . ."

[2] Sterne had described captivity in several sermons, most notably in "Abuses of conscience" (see *TS* II.17), that of the prisoner of the Inquisition whom Trim identifies as his brother. See also sermon 7, "Vindication of human nature": "[A man] cannot stop his ears against the cries of the unfortunate . . . . *The sorrowful sighing of the prisoners will come before him* [Psalm 79:11, Psalter version]; and a thousand other untold cases of distress to which the life of man is subject, find a way to his heart" (*Sermons* 4:71). Stout (201) suggests that "Yorick's choice of an imprisoned captive to exemplify slavery may owe something" to Matthew 25:36: "[I was] Naked, and ye clothed me: I was sick, and ye visited me: I was in prison, and ye came unto me" and quotes Sterne's use of the verse in sermon 3, "Philanthropy recommended" (see Appendix, p. 237).

Dugald Stewart, *Elements of the Philosophy of the Human Mind* (1792), offers this passage as "beautifully illustrat[ing]" his point that "what we commonly call sensibility, depends, in a great measure, on the power of imagination" (500–2).

[3] Cf. a similar setting in *TS*, IX.24.780, Tristram's invocation of Cervantes toward the end of the work: "GENTLE Spirit of sweetest humour, who erst didst sit upon the easy pen of my beloved CERVANTES; Thou who glided'st daily through his lattice, and turned'st the twilight of his prison into noon-day brightness by thy presence"; Cervantes was said to have written *Don Quixote* in prison. *OED*'s first illustration of *grated* is dated 1786.

[4] Sterne echoes his picture of the victim of the Inquisition in "Abuses of conscience" (sermon 27): "Behold this helpless victim . . . . His body so wasted with sorrow and long confinement" (*Sermons* 4:265).

[5] An echo of Proverbs 13:12: "Hope deferred maketh the heart sick."

breeze had not once fann'd his blood—he had seen no sun, no moon in all that time—nor had the voice of friend or kinsman breathed through his lattice—his children—

—But here my heart began to bleed—and I was forced to go on with another part of the portrait.

He was sitting upon the ground upon a little straw, in the furthest corner of his dungeon, which was alternately his chair and bed: a little calender of small sticks were laid at the head notch'd all over with the dismal days and nights he had pass'd there—he had one of these little sticks in his hand, and with a rusty nail he was etching another day of misery to add to the heap. As I darkened the little light he had, he lifted up a hopeless eye towards the door, then cast it down—shook his head, and went on with his work of affliction. I heard his chains upon his legs, as he turn'd his body to lay his little stick upon the bundle—He gave a deep sigh—I saw the iron enter into his soul[6]—I burst into tears—I could not sustain the picture of confinement which my fancy had drawn—I startled up from my chair, and calling La Fleur, I bid him bespeak me a *remise*,[7] and have it ready at the door of the hotel by nine in the morning.

—I'll go directly, said I, myself to Monsieur Le Duke de Choiseul.[8]

La Fleur would have put me to bed; but not willing he should see any thing upon my cheek, which would cost the honest fellow a heart ache—I told him I would go to bed by myself—and bid him go do the same.

---

[6] Sterne conflates Psalm 105:18, "Whose feet they hurt with fetters: he was laid in iron," with the Psalter version, "Whose feet they hurt in the stocks: the iron entered into his soul." He repeats his description of Joseph's captivity from sermon 12, "Joseph's history": "besides the anguish of suspected virtue, he had felt that of a prison, where he had long lain neglected in a friendless condition; . . . the Psalmist acquaints us that his sufferings were still grievous;——*That his feet were hurt with fetters,* and the iron entered *even into his soul*" (*Sermons* 4:117).

Keymer, 156, calls attention to Joseph Wright's rendition of *The Captive* (1774), reproduced in Judy Egerton, *Wright of Derby* (London: Tate Gallery, 1990), 108. For a useful discussion of several illustrators who found visual inspiration in *ASJ*, see W. B. Gerard, "Benevolent Vision: The Ideology of Sentimentality in Contemporary Illustrations of *A Sentimental Journey* and *The Man of Feeling*," *ECF* 14 (2002):533–74.

[7] See above, p. 19, n. 6.

[8] Cf. *Letters,* 151 (January 31, 1762, from Paris): "My application to the Count de Choisuiel goes on swimmingly, for not only Mr. Pelletiere . . . has undertaken my affair, but the Count de Limbourgh [and] the Baron d'Holbach . . . ." Curtis, 152, n. 4, identifies the Count as César-Gabriel de Choiseul (1712–1785), Minister of Foreign Affairs, "to whom Sterne applied for a passport." However, Cash, *LY,* 128, is probably correct in suggesting it is his cousin, Étienne-François de Choiseul-Stainville (1719–1785), Duc de Choiseul, who was not only Secretary of State for Foreign Affairs, but effectively Prime Minister; five years after the fact, Sterne himself perhaps did not recall to which Duc de Choiseul he was most indebted.

THE STARLING.
ROAD to VERSAILLES.

I GOT into my *remise* the hour I proposed: La Fleur got up behind, and I bid the coachman make the best of his way to Versailles.

As there was nothing in this road, or rather nothing which I look for in travelling, I cannot fill up the blank better than with a short history of this self-same bird, which became the subject of the last chapter.

Whilst the Honourable Mr. **** was waiting for a wind at Dover it had been caught upon the cliffs before it could well fly, by an English lad who was his groom; who not caring to destroy it, had taken it in his breast into the packet—and by course of feeding it, and taking it once under his protection, in a day or two grew fond of it, and got it safe along with him to Paris.

At Paris the lad had laid out a livre in a little cage for the starling, and as he had little to do better the five months his master stay'd there, he taught it in his mother's tongue the four simple words—(and no more)—to which I own'd myself so much it's debtor.

Upon his master's going on for Italy—the lad had given it to the master of the hotel—But his little song for liberty, being in an *unknown* language at Paris—the bird had little or no store set by him—so La Fleur bought both him and his cage for me for a bottle of Burgundy.

In my return from Italy I brought him with me to the country in whose language he had learn'd his notes—and telling the story of him to Lord A—Lord A begg'd the bird of me—in a week Lord A gave him to Lord B—Lord B made a present of him to Lord C—and Lord C's gentleman sold him to Lord D for a shilling—Lord D gave him to Lord E—and so on—half round the alphabet—From that rank he pass'd into the lower house, and pass'd the hands of as many commoners——But as all these wanted to *get in*[1]—and my bird wanted to get out—he had almost as little store set by him in London as in Paris.

It is impossible but many of my readers must have heard of him; and if any by mere chance have ever seen him—I beg leave to inform them, that that bird was my bird—or some vile copy set up to represent him.

---

[1] In alluding to Parliament, and underscoring the words, Sterne gives *"get in"* a particular political bite, i.e., a reflection on the ambition of place-seekers.

I have nothing further to add upon him, but that from that time to this, I have borne this poor starling as the crest to my arms.[2]—Thus:

——And let the heralds officers twist his neck about if they dare.

---

[2] Cf. Stout, 205–6: "Yorick is probably daring the[m] to do away with the starling on his arms, by twisting about (i.e., wringing) its neck because he has placed it . . . illegally, without the authority of the heralds officers . . . presumably . . . because of an association between 'starling'—dialectical *starn* (fr. OE *stearn*), Latin *sturnus*—and 'Sterne.'" Stout believes that while Sterne's great-grandfather Richard Sterne (1596?–1683), Archbishop of York (1664–1683), had a right to the arms, Sterne's branch of the family did not. But Michael J. O'Shea, "Laurence Sterne's Display of Heraldry," *Shandean* 3 (1991):61–69, argues that while Sterne's line was not demonstrably entitled to the arms, "*Burke's General Armory* [nevertheless] records the use of these arms . . . by 'the author of "Tristram Shandy"' . . . ." O'Shea also reads the "twisting" of the neck somewhat differently, suggesting that Sterne may have thought the bird looked left and hence might be taken as a sign of bastardy (cf. the "bend sinister" on the Shandy coat of arms, *TS* IV.25.372–73). In actuality, since the shield is always described from the bearer's viewpoint, the bird is indeed looking right, as is proper.

THE ADDRESS.
VERSAILLES.

I SHOULD not like to have my enemy take a view of my mind, when I am going to ask protection of any man: for which reason I generally endeavour to protect myself; but this going to Monsieur Le Duc de C***** was an act of compulsion—had it been an act of choice, I should have done it, I suppose, like other people.

How many mean plans of dirty address, as I went along, did my servile heart form! I deserved the Bastile for every one of them.

Then nothing would serve me, when I got within sight of Versailles, but putting words and sentences together, and conceiving attitudes and tones to wreath myself into Monsieur Le Duc de C*****'s good graces—This will do——said I—Just as well, retorted I again, as a coat carried up to him by an adventurous taylor, without taking his measure—Fool! continued I—see Monsieur Le Duc's face first—observe what character is written in it; take notice in what posture he stands to hear you—mark the turns and expressions of his body and limbs—And for the tone—the first sound which comes from his lips will give it you; and from all these together you'll compound an address at once upon the spot, which cannot disgust the Duke—the ingredients are his own, and most likely to go down.

Well! said I, I wish it well over—Coward again! as if man to man was not equal, throughout the whole surface of the globe; and if in the field—why not face to face in the cabinet too?[1] And trust me, Yorick, whenever it is not so, man is false to himself; and betrays his own succours ten times, where nature does it once. Go to the Duc de C***** with the Bastile in thy looks—My life for it, thou wilt be sent back to Paris in half an hour, with an escort.

I believe so, said I—Then I'll go to the Duke, by heaven! with all the gaity and debonairness[2] in the world.—

—And there you are wrong again, replied I—A heart at ease, Yorick, flies into no extremes—'tis ever on its center.—Well! well! cried I, as the coachman turn'd in at the gates—I find I shall do very well: and by the time he had wheel'd round the court, and brought me up to the door, I found myself so much the better for my own lecture, that I neither ascended the steps like a victim to justice, who was to part with life upon the topmost,—nor did I mount them with a skip and a couple of strides, as I do when I fly up, Eliza! to thee, to meet it.

As I enter'd the door of the saloon, I was met by a person who possibly might be the maitre d'hotel, but had more the air of one of the under secretaries, who told me the Duc de C***** was busy—I am utterly ignorant, said I, of the forms

---

[1] Cf. p. 69, n. 2.
[2] Cf. p. 32, n. 1.

of obtaining an audience, being an absolute stranger, and what is worse in the present conjuncture of affairs, being an Englishman too.——He replied, that did not increase the difficulty.—I made him a slight bow, and told him, I had something of importance to say to Monsieur Le Duc. The secretary look'd towards the stairs, as if he was about to leave me to carry up this account to some one—But I must not mislead you, said I—for what I have to say is of no manner of importance to Monsieur Le Duc de C*****—but of great importance to myself.—*C'est une autre affaire,*[3] replied he——Not at all, said I, to a man of gallantry.—But pray, good sir, continued I, when can a stranger hope to have *accesse?*[4] In not less than two hours, said he, looking at his watch. The number of equipages in the court-yard seem'd to justify the calculation, that I could have no nearer a prospect—and as walking backwards and forwards in the saloon, without a soul to commune with, was for the time as bad as being in the Bastile itself, I instantly went back to my *remise,* and bid the coachman drive me to the *cordon bleu,*[5] which was the nearest hotel.

I think there is a fatality in it—I seldom go to the place I set out for.

---

[3] That's another story (i.e., that changes the situation).

[4] Sterne's word is neither French (*accès*) nor English, but his own French-appearing invention. See below, p. 125, *excesse.*

[5] Blue Ribbon. Its usage to designate a "first-class cook" may not have been known to Sterne; *OED* has only nineteenth-century examples. On the other hand, no establishment in Versailles with that name has been found, which may indicate Sterne already associated the term with dining.

LE PATISSER.[1]
VERSAILLES.

BEFORE I had got half-way down the street, I changed my mind: as I am at Versailles, thought I, I might as well take a view of the town; so I pull'd the cord, and ordered the coachman to drive round some of the principal streets—I suppose the town is not very large, said I.—The coachman begg'd pardon for setting me right, and told me it was very superb, and that numbers of the first dukes and marquises and counts had hotels[2]—The Count de B****,[3] of whom the bookseller at the Quai de Conti had spoke so handsomely the night before, came instantly into my mind.—And why should I not go, thought I, to the Count de B****, who has so high an idea of English books, and Englishmen—and tell him my story? so I changed my mind a second time—In truth it was the third; for I had intended that day for Madame de R**** in the Rue St. Pierre, and had devoutly sent her word by her *fille de chambre* that I would assuredly wait upon her—but I am govern'd by circumstances—I cannot govern them:[4] so seeing a man standing with a basket on the other side of the street, as if he had something to sell, I bid La Fleur go up to him and enquire for the Count's hotel.

La Fleur return'd a little pale; and told me it was a Chevalier de St. Louis[5] selling *patès*[6]—It is impossible, La Fleur! said I.—La Fleur could no more account for the phenomenon than myself; but persisted in his story: he had seen the croix

---

[1] The pastry-maker (correctly, *pâtissier*).

[2] Sterne is ironically dismissive of Versailles, as he was of Fontainbleau in *TS*, VII.27.616. Smollett, on the other hand, was dismissive without irony: "In spite of all the ornaments that have been lavished on Versailles, it is a dismal habitation. The apartments are dark, ill-furnished, dirty, and unprincely. . . . [A] most fantastic composition of magnificence and littleness, taste, and foppery" (*Travels*, letter 6, 1:88–89).

Versailles, on the outskirts of Paris, had been the seat of government since Louis XIV; in the eighteenth century many new homes were built surrounding the royal palace.

[3] See p. 114, n. 1.

[4] Sterne's most characteristic posture, both as an author and a social creature; see, e.g., *Letters*, 193–94: "in all things I am governed by circumstances"; and 394: "The truth is this—that my pen governs me—not me my pen"; and *TS*, I.5.8–9: "I have been the continual sport of what the world calls Fortune . . ."; and VI.6.500: "But this is neither here nor there—why do I mention it?——Ask my pen,—it governs me,—I govern not it."

[5] The order of St. Louis was instituted in 1693 by Louis XIV to reward military officers. Chevalier (Knight) was the highest of the three grades, and those chosen had to be Catholic. Members of the order were called *Cordons-rouges* (i.e., Red-ribbons; hence his "red ribband" in his button-hole).

[6] Pies, pastries (correctly, *pâtés*). *OED* lists its first English appearance in 1706, with the second illustration being this passage. Sterne's misaccenting may suggest the word was still foreign to him—or, conversely, that it had already become anglicized (as in "a *pat* of butter"); or it may be his usual unconcern with the niceties of French accents.

set in gold, with its red ribband, he said, tied to his button-hole—and had look'd into the basket and seen the *patès* which the Chevalier was selling; so could not be mistaken in that.

Such a reverse in man's life awakens a better principle than curiosity: I could not help looking for some time at him as I sat in the *remise*—the more I look'd at him—his croix and his basket, the stronger they wove themselves into my brain—I got out of the *remise* and went towards him.

He was begirt with a clean linen apron which fell below his knees, and with a sort of a bib went half way up his breast; upon the top of this, but a little below the hem, hung his croix. His basket of little *patès* was cover'd over with a white damask napkin; another of the same kind was spread at the bottom; and there was a look of *propreté*[7] and neatness throughout, that one might have bought his *patès* of him, as much from appetite as sentiment.

He made an offer of them to neither; but stood still with them at the corner of a hotel, for those to buy who chose it, without solicitation.

He was about forty-eight—of a sedate look, something approaching to gravity. I did not wonder.—I went up rather to the basket than him, and having lifted up the napkin and taken one of his *patès* into my hand—I begg'd he would explain the appearance which affected me.

He told me in a few words, that the best part of his life had pass'd in the service, in which, after spending a small patrimony, he had obtain'd a company and the croix with it; but that at the conclusion of the last peace,[8] his regiment being reformed, and the whole corps, with those of some other regiments, left without any provision—he found himself in a wide world without friends, without a livre—and indeed, said he, without any thing but this—(pointing, as he said it, to his croix)—The poor chevalier won my pity, and he finish'd the scene, with winning my esteem too.

The king, he said, was the most generous of princes, but his generosity could neither relieve or reward every one,[9] and it was only his misfortune to be amongst the number. He had a little wife,[10] he said, whom he loved, who did the *patisserie;* and added, he felt no dishonour in defending her and himself from want in this way—unless Providence had offer'd him a better.

It would be wicked to with-hold a pleasure from the good, in passing over what happen'd to this poor Chevalier of St. Louis about nine months after.

---

[7] Cleanliness, neatness.

[8] Stout, 210: "presumably the Treaty of Aix-la-Chapelle, ending, in 1748, the War of the Austrian Succession. The Treaty of Paris, ending the Seven Years War, was not signed until 1763, and Yorick's *Journey* takes place in 1762."

[9] According to Thicknesse, the Order of St. Louis was, at this time, "as common as acorns in an oak forest" (*Useful Hints* 211).

[10] Not an anticipation of the modern slight, but a literal translation of *une petite femme*, a phrase of endearment; see below, p. 140, n. 10.

It seems he usually took his stand near the iron gates which lead up to the palace, and as his croix had caught the eye of numbers, numbers had made the same enquiry which I had done—He had told them the same story, and always with so much modesty and good sense, that it had reach'd at last the king's ears—who, hearing the Chevalier had been a gallant officer, and respected by the whole regiment as a man of honour and integrity—he broke up his little trade by a pension of fifteen hundred livres a year.

As I have told this to please the reader, I beg he will allow me to relate another out of its order, to please myself—the two stories reflect light upon each other,—and 'tis a pity they should be parted.

THE SWORD.
RENNES.[1]

WHEN states and empires have their periods of declension, and feel in their turns what distress and poverty is—I stop not to tell the causes which gradually brought the house d'E**** in Britany into decay. The Marquis d'E**** had fought up against his condition with great firmness; wishing to preserve, and still shew to the world some little fragments of what his ancestors had been—their indiscretions had put it out of his power. There was enough left for the little exigencies of *obscurity*—But he had two boys who look'd up to him for *light*—he thought they deserved it. He had tried his sword—it could not open the way—the *mounting*[2] was too expensive—and simple œconomy was not a match for it—there was no resource[3] but commerce.

In any other province in France, save Britany, this was smiting the root for ever of the little tree his pride and affection wish'd to see reblossom—But in Britany, there being a provision for this,[4] he avail'd himself of it; and taking an occasion when the states were assembled at Rennes, the Marquis, attended with his two boys, enter'd the court; and having pleaded the right of an ancient law of the duchy, which, though seldom claim'd, he said, was no less in force; he took his sword from his side—Here—said he—take it; and be trusty guardians of it, till better times put me in condition to reclaim it.

The president accepted the Marquis's sword—he stay'd a few minutes to see it deposited in the archives of his house—and departed.

---

[1] A town in the west of France, capital of the ancient province of Brittany, some 230 miles east-southeast of Paris.

[2] Sterne's underscoring probably indicates a pun, as Stout, 212, suggests: hilt of a sword; more generally, a soldier's "outfit or 'kit'" (*OED*); and, perhaps, the expense of a commission.

[3] Sterne perhaps meant "recourse."

[4] Louis T. Milic, "An Annotated Critical Edition of Sterne's *Sentimental Journey*" (Columbia University, 1950), 90–91: "Engaging in retail commerce, mechanical craftsmanship, and farming of others' lands for hire, were considered fatal to a nobleman's quality. However, in Brittany, under a custom . . . dating back to 1451 . . . nobles wishing to engage in the forbidden activities were privileged to suspend their nobility . . . . The nobles, or their descendants . . . could reclaim their nobility by ceasing from the ignoble activity, making a declaration before the nearest Judge-Royal . . . ." Where Sterne came across the story (if it were not fully invented) or information about the *déroger à noblesse* (as the tradition was called: "stooping from nobility") is unknown; he might have become familiar with it from a scene in Samuel Foote's most popular play, *The Minor* (1760), where Sir George Wealthy, who scorns those in trade, nevertheless recollects "an edict in favour of Britany; that when a man of distinction engages in commerce, his nobility is suffer'd to sleep. . . . And upon his quitting the contagious connexion, he is permitted to resume his rank" (act 2, p. 58).

The Marquis and his whole family embarked the next day for Martinico,[5] and in about nineteen or twenty years of successful application to business, with some unlook'd for bequests from distant branches of his house—return'd home to reclaim his nobility and to support it.

It was an incident of good fortune which will never happen to any traveller, but a sentimental one, that I should be at Rennes at the very time of this solemn requisition:[6] I call it solemn—it was so to me.

The Marquis enter'd the court with his whole family: he supported his lady—his eldest son supported his sister, and his youngest was at the other extreme of the line next his mother—he put his handkerchief to his face twice—

—There was a dead silence. When the Marquis had approach'd within six paces of the tribunal, he gave the Marchioness to his youngest son, and advancing three steps before his family—he reclaim'd his sword. His sword was given him, and the moment he got it into his hand he drew it almost out of the scabbard—'twas the shining face of a friend he had once given up—he look'd attentively along it, beginning at the hilt, as if to see whether it was the same—when observing a little rust which it had contracted near the point, he brought it near his eye, and bending his head down over it—I think I saw a tear fall upon the place:[7] I could not be deceived by what followed.

"I shall find," said he, "some *other way,* to get it off."

When the Marquis had said this, he return'd his sword into its scabbard, made a bow to the guardians of it—and, with his wife and daughter and his two sons following him, walk'd out.

O! how I envied him his feelings!

---

[5] I.e., Martinique, an island of the Lesser Antilles, a French colonial interest from 1635.

[6] We have no evidence that Sterne ever visited Rennes; it would have been quite off the track of the two journeys to France that we do know about.

[7] The scene is the culmination of Sterne's use of the single tear in his own writing, if not in all sentimental writing; see Alfred G. Engstrom, "The Single Tear: A Stereotype of Literary Sensibility," *PQ* 42 (1963):106–9, and Vincent-Buffault, *The History of Tears* (see above, p. 86, n. 17).

THE PASSPORT.
VERSAILLES.

I FOUND no difficulty in getting admittance to Monsieur Le Count de B****. The set of Shakespears was laid upon the table, and he was tumbling them over.[1] I walk'd up close to the table, and giving first such a look at the books as to make him conceive I knew what they were—I told him I had come without any one to present me, knowing I should meet with a friend in his apartment who, I trusted, would do it for me—it is my countryman the great Shakespear, said I, pointing to his works—*et ayez la bontè, mon cher ami,* apostrophizing his spirit, added I, *de me faire cet honneur la.*[2]——

The Count smil'd at the singularity of the introduction; and seeing I look'd a little pale and sickly,[3] insisted upon my taking an arm-chair: so I sat down; and to save him conjectures upon a visit so out of all rule, I told him simply of the incident in the bookseller's shop, and how that had impell'd me rather to go to him with the story of a little embarrassment I was under, than to any other man in France—And what is your embarrassment? let me hear it, said the Count. So I told him the story just as I have told it the reader—

—And the master of my hotel, said I, as I concluded it, will needs have it, Monsieur le Count, that I shall be sent to the Bastile—but I have no apprehensions, continued I—for in falling into the hands of the most polish'd people in the world, and being conscious I was a true man, and not come to spy the nakedness of the land,[4] I scarce thought I laid at their mercy.—It does not suit the gallantry of the French, Monsieur le Count, said I, to shew it against invalids.

An animated blush came into the Count de B****'s cheeks, as I spoke this—*Ne craignez rien*[5]—Don't fear, said he—Indeed I don't, replied I again—besides, continued I a little sportingly—I have come laughing all the way from London to

---

[1] Cf. *Letters,* 151 (January 31, 1762): "'Twas an odd incident when I was introduced to the Count de Bissie . . . I found him reading Tristram." Cf. Cash, *LY,* 128: "the person who actually got [the passport] for him in all probability was the anglophile general, Claude de Thiard, Comte de Bissy [1721–1810]."

[2] And have the goodness, my dear friend . . . to do me the honor (correctly, *bonté . . . honneur là*).

[3] Cf. Sterne's description of himself in *Letters,* 155 (Paris, March 1762): "I have got a colour into my face now, though I came with no more than there is in a dishclout"; and of Tristram, in *TS,* VII.34.636: "a person in black, with a face as pale as ashes . . . looking still paler by the contrast and distress of his drapery." Yorick will recall this pallor in his meeting with Maria, below, p. 159.

[4] Cf. Genesis 42:9: "And Joseph . . . said unto them, Ye are spies; to see the nakedness of the land ye are come." In November 1763, Sterne commented that he had "traversed the South of France so often" that he "ran a risk of being taken up for a Spy" (*Letters* 205).

[5] Sterne translates himself.

Paris, and I do not think Monsieur le Duc de Choiseul is such an enemy to mirth, as to send me back crying for my pains.

——My application to you, Monsieur le Compte de B**** (making him a low bow) is to desire he will not.

The Count heard me with great good nature, or I had not said half as much—and once or twice said—*C'est bien dit.*[6] So I rested my cause there—and determined to say no more about it.

The Count led the discourse: we talk'd of indifferent things;—of books and politicks, and men—and then of women—God bless them all! said I, after much discourse about them—there is not a man upon earth who loves them so much as I do: after all the foibles I have seen, and all the satires I have read against them, still I love them; being firmly persuaded that a man who has not a sort of an affection for the whole sex, is incapable of ever loving a single one as he ought.

Hèh bien![7] *Monsieur l'Anglois,* said the Count, gaily—You are not come to spy the nakedness of the land—I believe you—*ni encore,*[8] I dare say, *that* of our women—But permit me to conjecture—if, *par hazard,*[9] they fell in your way—that the prospect would not affect you.

I have something within me which cannot bear the shock of the least indecent insinuation: in the sportability of chit-chat[10] I have often endeavoured to conquer it, and with infinite pain have hazarded a thousand things to a dozen of the sex together—the least of which I could not venture to a single one, to gain heaven.[11]

Excuse me, Monsieur Le Count, said I—as for the nakedness of your land, if I saw it, I should cast my eyes over it with tears in them—and for that of your women (blushing at the idea he had excited in me) I am so evangelical in this,

---

[6] Well said.

[7] Well!

[8] Nor; nor still.

[9] By chance.

[10] Cf. *TS,* IX.6.748: "he had lost the sportable key of his voice which gave sense and spirit to his tale"; *OED* lists both passages as first illustrations. Sportability: "Capacity for being sportive or playful." The entire paragraph echoes Tristram's ironic claim that although "the world has revenged itself upon me for leaving so many openings to equivocal strictures,—and for depending . . . upon the cleanliness of my reader's imaginations," he will continue always to take the clean road—and then defines "nose" with as many "indecent insinuations" as possible (*TS* III.31.257–58). Cf. below, p. 172 and n. 10; and, also, the anonymous annotator of the 1803 edition (see above, p. 94, n. 7): "No man ever hazarded more things of this nature than our author; if he never breaks down the fence of decency, it often shakes under his grasp" (136).

[11] Cf. above, pp. 62–3, where Yorick vows he will not visit Madame de L*** in Brussels unless Eliza accompanies him, "did the road lead me towards heaven."

and have such a fellow-feeling for what ever is *weak* about them, that I would cover it with a garment, if I knew how to throw it on[12]—But I could wish, continued I, to spy the *nakedness* of their hearts,[13] and through the different disguises of customs, climates, and religion, find out what is good in them, to fashion my own by—and therefore am I come.[14]

It is for this reason, Monsieur le Compte, continued I, that I have not seen the Palais royal—nor the Luxembourg—nor the Façade of the Louvre—nor have attempted to swell the catalogues we have of pictures, statues, and churches[15]—I conceive every fair being as a temple,[16] and would rather enter in, and see the

---

[12] Stout, 217, suggests an allusion to Genesis 9:23: "And Shem and Japheth took a garment . . . and covered the nakedness of their father; and their faces were backward, and they saw not their father's nakedness." Cf. "Preface," above, p. 16, n. 17.

[13] Cf. *TS,* I.23.82: "If the fixure of *Momus*'s glass, in the human breast . . . had taken place . . . nothing more would have been wanting, in order to have taken a man's character, but to have . . . look'd in,--view'd the soul stark naked;---observ'd all her motions,—her machinations . . . "; and sermon 2 ("The house of feasting"): "could we see [the heart] . . . naked as it is—stripped of all its passions, unspotted by the world" (*Sermons* 4:20).

[14] Cf. Mark 1:38: "And he [Jesus] said unto them, Let us go into the next towns, that I may preach there also: for therefore came I forth." Or, more ironically from Sterne, Luke 14:20, the refusal of an invitee to attend a wedding: "I have married a wife, and therefore I cannot come."

The passage has a somewhat different sense in the copyist's version: "disguises & customs, climates and religion." The sentiment is echoed in sermon 20, "The prodigal son" (see Appendix, p. 241).

[15] Cf. Smollett, *Travels,* letter 6, 1:84: "I could not leave Paris, without carrying my wife and the girls to see the most remarkable places in and about this capital, such as the Luxemburg, the Palais-Royal, the Thuilleries, the Louvre." Sterne visited the Palais-Royal in January 1762: "the Count de Bissie . . . gives me leave to go a private way through his apartments into the palais royal, to view the Duke of Orleans' collections, every day I have time" (*Letters* 151).

Sterne commented on the "Façade of the Louvre" in *TS,* VII.18.603:

——Then you will have seen——
——but, 'tis what no one needeth to tell you, for you will read it yourself upon the portico of the Louvre, in these words,
*EARTH NO SUCH FOLKS!—NO FOLKS E'ER SUCH A TOWN
AS PARIS IS!—SING, DERRY, DERRY, DOWN.

[16] Cf. sermon 17, "The case of Hezekiah": "It is a pleasing allusion the scripture makes use of in calling us sometimes a house, and sometimes a temple, according to the more or less exalted qualities of the spiritual guest which is lodged within us" (*Sermons* 4:164). The relevant scriptural verses include John 2:21, 1 Corinthians 3:16–17 and 6:19, and 2 Corinthians 6:16. That Yorick's metaphor is not totally spiritual is suggested by a parallel usage in *Letters,* 157: "I have been introduced to one half of their best Goddesses, and in a month more shall be admitted to the shrines of the other half—but I neither worship—or fall (much) upon my knees before them."

original drawings and loose sketches[17] hung up in it, than the transfiguration of Raphael itself.[18]

The thirst of this, continued I, as impatient as that which inflames the breast of the connoisseur, has led me from my own home into France—and from France will lead me through Italy—'tis a quiet journey of the heart in pursuit of NATURE, and those affections which rise out of her, which make us love each other—and the world, better than we do.[19]

The Count said a great many civil things to me upon the occasion; and added very politely how much he stood obliged to Shakespear for making me known to him—but, *a-propos*, said he—Shakespear is full of great things—He forgot a small punctillio of announcing your name—it puts you under a necessity of doing it yourself.

---

[17] Cf. *Letters*, 99, where Sterne requests from Hogarth "the loosest Sketch in Nature, of Trim's reading the Sermon." Stout, 219, calls attention to *Letters*, 316 (to Eliza, March 1767), wherein Sterne celebrates the "loose touches of an honest heart," by which his letters "speak more than the most studied periods; and will give thee more ground of trust and reliance upon Yorick, than all that laboured eloquence could supply."

[18] The *Transfiguration of Christ* (illustrating Matthew 17:1–18, Mark 9:2–8, Luke 9:28–42) in the Vatican was left unfinished by Raphael (1483–1520), though still considered one of his greatest achievements.

[19] Cf. *Letters*, 400–401 (November 12, 1767), describing *A Sentimental Journey:* "I told you my design in it was to teach us to love the world and our fellow creatures better than we do—so it runs most upon those gentler passions and affections, which aid so much to it."

THE PASSPORT.
VERSAILLES.

THERE is not a more perplexing affair in life to me, than to set about telling any one who I am—for there is scarce any body I cannot give a better account of than of myself;[1] and I have often wish'd I could do it in a single word—and have an end of it. It was the only time and occasion in my life, I could accomplish this to any purpose—for Shakespear lying upon the table, and recollecting I was in his books, I took up Hamlet, and turning immediately to the grave-diggers scene in the fifth act, I lay'd my finger upon YORICK, and advancing the book to the Count, with my finger all the way over the name—*Me, Voici!*[2] said I.

Now whether the idea of poor Yorick's skull was put out of the Count's mind, by the reality of my own,[3] or by what magic he could drop a period of seven or eight hundred years, makes nothing in this account—'tis certain the French conceive better than they combine—I wonder at nothing in this world, and the less at this; inasmuch as one of the first of our own church, for whose candour and paternal sentiments I have the highest veneration, fell into the same mistake in the very same case.—"He could not bear," he said, "to look into sermons wrote by the king of Denmark's jester."[4]—Good, my lord! said I—but there are two Yoricks. The Yorick your lordship thinks of, has been dead and buried eight hundred years ago; he flourish'd in Horwendillus's court[5]—the other Yorick is myself,

---

[1] Cf. *TS*, VII.33.633, where Tristram addresses the commissary sent to collect his fees:

> ——My good friend, quoth I——as sure as I am I—and you are you——
> ——And who are you? said he.——Don't puzzle me; said I.

[2] Here I am! Cf. p. 69, n. 3. At first sight the comma is an obvious error, but whether Sterne's or the compositor's cannot be determined; it is just possible, however, that the punctuation is deliberate, thus making "*Me*" English, a further example of Sterne's intermingling of English and French.

[3] That Yorick appears in *Hamlet*, V.i, only as a skull in the graveyard scene served Sterne well in *TS*, where the relationship between jester and death is established at the outset, most specifically in the description of Yorick's riding a horse (Rosinante) upon which "he could . . . meditate as delightfully *de vanitate mundi et fugâ sæculi,* as with the advantage of a death's head before him" (*TS* I.10.20); and, of course, with the black page (I.12.37–38).

[4] Stout, 222, is certainly correct in identifying a reference "to the furor caused by Sterne's publication of Vols. I and II of the *Sermons*" with dual title-pages, the first giving the author as "Mr. Yorick," the second as "Laurence Sterne, A. M., Prebendary of York, and Vicar of Sutton on the Forest" (see *Sermons* 5:2). He is also correct in suggesting that if Sterne is alluding to anyone specific, the obvious candidate is William Warburton, Bishop of Gloucester (1698–1779); see Melvyn New, "Sterne, Warburton, and the Burden of Exuberant Wit," *ECS* 15 (1982):245–74.

[5] Cf. *TS*, I.11.25–26, on the genealogy of "Yorick": "the family was originally of *Danish* extraction, and had been transplanted into *England* as early as in the reign of *Horwendillus,*

who have flourish'd my lord in no court—He shook his head—Good God! said I, you might as well confound Alexander the Great, with Alexander the Copper-smith, my lord[6]——'Twas all one, he replied—

—If Alexander king of Macedon could have translated your lordship, said I—I'm sure your Lordship would not have said so.

The poor Count de B**** fell but into the same *error*—

——*Et, Monsieur, est il Yorick?* cried the Count.—*Je le suis,* said I.—*Vous?*—*Moi—moi qui ai l'honneur de vous parler, Monsieur le Compte—Mon Dieu!* said he, embracing me——*Vous etes Yorick.*[7]

The Count instantly put the Shakespear into his pocket—and left me alone in his room.

---

king of *Denmark,* in whose court it seems, an ancestor of this Mr. *Yorick's* . . . held a consid-erable post." Shakespeare's eighteenth-century editors acknowledged *Hamlet's* origins in the *Gesta Danorum* of Saxo Grammaticus (c. 1200), published in 1514. Since the story is not historical, Sterne's dating it "eight hundred years ago" is a futile guess.

[6] Keymer, 157, cites 2 Timothy 4:14: "Alexander the coppersmith did me much evil: the Lord reward him according to his works." Stout, 223, suggests Sterne recalls the graveyard scene in *Hamlet,* V.i.185–205, and Hamlet's question: "Dost thou think Alexander looked a' this fashion i' th' earth?" The clever melding of Scripture and Shakespeare is worth noting.

[7] And are you Yorick? cried the Count.—I am, said I.—You?—Me—myself who has the honor of addressing your Lordship.—My God! said he . . . You are Yorick.

THE PASSPORT.
VERSAILLES.

I COULD not conceive why the Count de B**** had gone so abruptly out of the room, any more than I could conceive why he had put the Shakespear into his pocket—*Mysteries which must explain themselves, are not worth the loss of time, which a conjecture about them takes up:* 'twas better to read Shakespear; so taking up "*Much Ado about Nothing*," I transported myself instantly from the chair I sat in to Messina in Sicily,[1] and got so busy with Don Pedro and Benedick and Beatrice, that I thought not of Versailles, the Count, or the Passport.

Sweet pliability of man's spirit, that can at once surrender itself to illusions, which cheat expectation and sorrow of their weary moments!—long—long since had ye number'd out my days,[2] had I not trod so great a part of them upon this enchanted ground:[3] when my way is too rough for my feet, or too steep for my strength, I get off it, to some smooth velvet path which fancy has scattered over with rose-buds of delights;[4] and having taken a few turns in it, come back strengthen'd and refresh'd—When evils press sore upon me, and there is no retreat from them in this world, then I take a new course—I leave it—and as I have a clearer idea of the elysian fields than I have of heaven, I force myself, like Eneas, into them—I see him meet the pensive shade of his forsaken Dido[5]—and

---

[1] While Sterne alludes to one play (in which Don Pedro, Benedick, and Beatrice are characters), he may, in fact, have another Shakespearean passage in mind, viz., the memorable prologue to act II of *Henry V,* ll.34–39: "The King is set from London, and the scene / Is now transported, gentles, to Southampton; / There is the playhouse now, there you must sit, / And thence to France shall we convey you safe, / And bring you back, charming the Narrow Seas / To give you gentle pass . . . ."

[2] See Psalm 90:12: "So teach us to number our days, that we may apply our hearts unto wisdom."

[3] Stout, 224, cites *Letters*, 234: "we must bring three parts in four of the treat along with us—In short we must be happy within—and then few things without us make much difference—This is my Shandean philosophy"; and 139: "if God, for my consolation under [my miseries], had not poured forth the spirit of Shandeism into me, which will not suffer me to think two moments upon any grave subject, I would else, just now lay down and die—die——and yet, in half an hour's time, I'll lay a guinea, I shall be as merry as a monkey—and as mischievous too, and forget it all." See also *TS,* VII.1.575–76; and VIII.31.716, Tristram's definition of the hobby-horse as "*any thing,* which a man makes a shift to get a stride on, to canter it away from the cares and solicitudes of life—'Tis as useful a beast as is in the whole creation—nor do I really see how the world could do without it."

[4] Cf. sermon 15, "Job's expostulation": "as if all their paths had been strewed with rose buds of delight" (*Sermons* 4:148); and sermon 23, "The rich man and Lazarus": "have all his paths strewed with rose-buds of delight" (4:218).

[5] Virgil, *Aeneid,* VI, ll. 450–76, tells of Aeneas's meeting with Dido in Hades and her turning away from him in silence; and in VI, ll. 635–36, of Aeneas's entry into the Elysian fields.

wish to recognize it—I see the injured spirit wave her head, and turn off silent from the author of her miseries and dishonours—I lose the feelings for myself in hers—and in those affections which were wont to make me mourn for her when I was at school.[6]

Surely this is not walking in a vain shadow—nor does man disquiet himself in vain, *by it*[7]—he oftener does so in trusting the issue of his commotions to reason only.—I can safely say for myself, I was never able to conquer any one single bad sensation in my heart so decisively, as by beating up as fast as I could for some kindly and gentle sensation, to fight it upon its own ground.[8]

When I had got to the end of the third act, the Count de B**** entered with my Passport in his hand. Mons. le Duc de C*****,[9] said the Count, is as good a prophet, I dare say, as he is a statesman—*Un homme qui rit,* said the duke, *ne sera jamais dangereuz.*[10]—Had it been for any one but the king's jester, added the Count, I could not have got it these two hours.—*Pardonnez moi,* Mons. Le Compte, said I—I am not the king's jester.—But you are Yorick?—Yes.—*Et vous*

Cf. *BJ,* p. 179: "I look forwards towards the Elysium we have so often and rapturously talk'd of"; and next note.

[6] Cf. *TS,* VI.32.556, Toby's apologetical oration: "was I not as much concerned for the destruction of the *Greeks* and *Trojans* as any boy of the whole school? . . . Did any one of you shed more tears for *Hector?*" See Elizabeth Kraft, "The Pentecostal Moment in *A Sentimental Journey,*" in *Critical Essays on Laurence Sterne,* 307: "the terms with which he describes his compassionate reaction forge a connection between [the elysian fields and heaven], a connection severed . . . by St. Augustine in his *Confessions.* . . . In weeping for Dido, he says, 'I committed fornication against Thee . . . *for the friendship of this world is fornication against Thee'*" (tr. E. B. Pusey [London: Dent, 1907], 13). Sterne, Kraft argues, rejects this stark dichotomizing; at times, both human language and bodily desires "can reveal to us the union of body and soul."

[7] Sterne combines Psalm 39:6: "Surely every man walketh in a vain shew: surely they are disquieted in vain" with its Psalter version (39:7): "For man walketh in a vain shadow, and disquieteth himself in vain."

[8] Stout, 226, cites *Letters,* 76: "One Passion is only to be combated by Another."

[9] Choiseul; see above, p. 104, n. 8. We have a brief picture of Sterne in the salons in a March 1762 letter: "I Shandy it away fifty times more than I was ever wont, talk more nonsense than ever you heard me talk in your days—and to all sorts of people. *Qui le diable est ce homme là*—said Choiseul, t'other day—ce Chevalier Shandy—You'll think me as vain as a devil, was I to tell you the rest of the dialogue" (*Letters* 157); and again, the following month: "I laugh 'till I cry, and in the same tender moments *cry 'till I laugh.* I Shandy it more than ever, and verily do believe . . . I fence as much against infirmities, as I do by the benefit of air and climate" (163).

[10] A man who laughs will never be dangerous (correctly, *dangereux,* as in the copyist's ms.)

plaisantez?[11]—I answered, Indeed I did jest—but was not paid for it—'twas entirely at my own expence.[12]

We have no jester at court, Mons. Le Compte, said I, the last we had was in the licentious reign of Charles the IId[13]—since which time our manners have been so gradually refining, that our court at present is so full of patriots, who wish for *nothing* but the honours and wealth of their country[14]—and our ladies are all so chaste, so spotless, so good, so devout—there is nothing for a jester to make a jest of—

Voila un persiflage![15] cried the Count.

---

[11] And do you joke? are you joking? The question seems to have both general and specific application—do you joke as part of your role as a jester, and are you joking now?

[12] Probably a glance at Sterne's sense that his jesting and bawdy had had repercussions for his clerical career; see, e.g., the account of Yorick's death in *TS,* I.11.29: "he had but too many temptations in life, of scattering his wit and his humour,—his gibes and his jests about him.----They were not lost for want of gathering."

[13] Stout, 227, suggests a possible reference to Thomas Killigrew (1612–1683), a favorite companion of Charles II, appointed master of the revels in 1673. More generally, Sterne is commenting on the morals of the Restoration, as he did on several occasions in *Sermons*— e.g., sermon 45, "The ingratitude of Israel": "a licentious king introduced a licentious age.—The court of Charles the Second first brake in upon, and, I fear, has almost demolished the out-works of religion, of modesty, and of sober manners" (4:421).

[14] Stout, 227: "an ironic thrust at those professing a disinterested zeal for England's welfare in order to further their own ambitions. After the 'patriots' led by Pulteney, Carteret, the elder Pitt, et al. came to power in 1742, after Walpole's resignation, their conduct brought professions of 'patriotism' into disrepute . . . ." Cf. *TS,* III.7.195; and V.2.416: "——PATRIOT is sold, said *Obadiah.*"

[15] Aha! you are joking! *OED* records Lord Chesterfield (1757) for its first illustration: "light banter or raillery . . . a frivolous manner of treating any subject," but Sterne perhaps associated the word particularly with Crébillon *fils* (see above, p. 93, n. 5), and with Parisian society; *persiflage* was au courant in French salons and theatrical circles, derived from the title character of the play *Persiflès* by Nicolas Ragot de Grandval (1676–1753) and popularized by his son, the comedian François-Charles Ragot de Grandval (1710–1784); see Élisabeth Bourguinat, *Le siècle du persiflage: 1734–1789* (Paris: Presses Universitaires de France, 1998).

And cf. *Letters,* 248 (May 29, 1765): "the duce take these bellows of mine [i.e., his lungs]; I must get 'em stop'd, or I shall never live to *persifler* Lord Effingham again."

THE PASSPORT.
VERSAILLES.

AS the Passport was directed to all lieutenant governors, governors, and commandants of cities, generals of armies, justiciaries, and all officers of justice, to let Mr. Yorick, the king's jester, and his baggage, travel quietly along—I own the triumph of obtaining the Passport was not a little tarnish'd by the figure I cut in it—But there is nothing unmixt in this world; and some of the gravest of our divines have carried it so far as to affirm, that enjoyment itself was attended even with a sigh—and that the greatest *they knew of,* terminated *in a general way,* in little better than a convulsion.[1]

I remember the grave and learned Bevoriskius,[2] in his commentary upon the generations from Adam, very naturally breaks off in the middle of a note to give

---

[1] Cf. sermon 10, "Job's account": "When we reflect that this span of life, short as it is, is chequered with so many troubles, that there is nothing in this world springs up, or can be enjoyed without a mixture of sorrow, how insensibly does it incline us to turn our eyes and affections from so gloomy a prospect, and fix them upon that happier country, where afflictions cannot follow us, and where God will wipe away all tears from off our faces for ever and ever?" (*Sermons* 4:102); and cf. sermon 22, "The history of Jacob," 4:212. The notion is a Christian commonplace, but Sterne's particular bawdy rendition almost certainly derives from Pierre Charron's *Of Wisdome,* one of his more important sources in *TS* (see Françoise Pellan, "Laurence Sterne's Indebtedness to Charron," *MLR* 67 [1972]:752–55; and Melvyn New, *"Tristram Shandy": A Book for Free Spirits,* 77–78, 83–84). Charron writes: "Good things, delights and pleasures cannot be enioyed without some mixture of euil and discommodity . . . . The highest pleasure that is, hath a sigh and a complaint to accompany it; and being come to perfection is but debility, a deiection of the minde, languishment" (tr. Samson Lennard [London, 1630], 130–31). As is often the case, Charron is paraphrasing his mentor, Montaigne, in this instance the essay "That we taste nothing pure"; see Melvyn New, "Some Sterne Borrowings from Four Renaissance Authors," *PQ* 71 (1992):302.

[2] Edward W. West (*N&Q* 12 [1885]:425–26) identified Sterne's "Bevoriskius" as Johan van Beverwyck *or* Beverwijck *or* Beverwych, called Beverovicius (1594–1647), "a Dutch physician and magistrate," and the "commentary upon the generations from Adam" as the beginning of *Joh. Van Beverwiick's Schat der Gesontheydt Met Veersen verçiert door de Heer Jacob Cats, Ridder* (Amsterdam, 1652). Stout believes he found this edition or one very similar and notes that in book III, ch. xiv—entitled "Of Birds"—there is a discussion of the stimulating power of sparrows: "Arabic physicians forbid [sparrow] as a food, because of [the sparrow's] short life and lecherousness. Many believe that it therefore stimulates . . . a phlegmatic man." In an expanded discussion in 1672, there is more that might have triggered Sterne's commentary: "*Orus in Hieroglyph* writes that [sparrows] copulate . . . seven times in one hour. *J. C. Scaliger* has seen a sparrow do it ten times in one day, and *Aldrouandus* twenty times during a brief part of a day" (quoted by Stout, 351, from *Schat der Gesonthey[d]t* [1672], 155–56; we use the translation provided).

As Stout notes, the passage seems to be what Sterne had in mind when crediting Bevoriskius with the observation, but we remain stymied as to where Sterne encountered this material in a language he could read.

an account to the world of a couple of sparrows upon the out-edge[3] of his window, which had incommoded him all the time he wrote, and at last had entirely taken him off from his genealogy.

—'Tis strange! writes Bevoriskius; but the facts are certain, for I have had the curiosity to mark them down one by one with my pen—but the cock-sparrow during the little time that I could have finished the other half this note, has actually interrupted me with the reiteration of his caresses three and twenty times and a half.

How merciful, adds Bevoriskius, is heaven to his creatures!

Ill fated Yorick! that the gravest of thy brethren should be able to write that to the world, which stains thy face with crimson, to copy in even thy study.[4]

But this is nothing to my travels—So I twice—twice beg pardon for it.

---

[3] OED records two examples (s.v. out- in comb. 3), the first of which is in TS, I.13.39, "the very out-edge" of the village; and the second, this passage.

[4] Cf. Letters, 412: "the women will read this book [ASJ] in the parlour, and Tristram in the bed-chamber"; and TS, VII.20.605: "though their reverences may laugh at it in the bed-chamber—full well I wot, they will abuse it in the parlour." All these passages allude to Montaigne's comment in "Upon Some Verses of Virgil"—"I am vexed that my Essays only serve the Ladies for a common moveable, a Book to lie in the Parlour Window; this Chapter shall prefer me to the Closet"—to which Sterne called attention early in TS, I.4.5; see Notes, 3:49.

CHARACTER.
VERSAILLES.

A ND how do you find the French? said the Count de B****, after he had given me the Passport.

The reader may suppose that after so obliging a proof of courtesy, I could not be at a loss to say something handsome to the enquiry.

—*Mais passe, pour cela*[1]—Speak frankly, said he; do you find all the urbanity in the French which the world give us the honour of?—I had found every thing, I said, which confirmed it—*Vraiment,* said the count—*Les François sont polis.*[2]—To an excess, replied I.

The count took notice of the word *excesse;*[3] and would have it I meant more than I said. I defended myself a long time as well as I could against it—he insisted I had a reserve, and that I would speak my opinion frankly.

I believe, Mons. Le Compte, said I, that man has a certain compass,[4] as well as an instrument; and that the social and other calls have occasion by turns for every key in him; so that if you begin a note too high or too low, there must be a want either in the upper or under part, to fill up the system of harmony.—The Count de B**** did not understand music, so desired me to explain it some other way. A polish'd nation, my dear Count, said I, makes every one its debtor; and besides, urbanity itself, like the fair sex, has so many charms, it goes against the heart to say it can do ill; and yet, I believe, there is but a certain line of perfection, that man, take him altogether, is empower'd to arrive at—if he gets beyond, he rather exchanges qualities, than gets them. I must not presume to say, how far this has affected the French in the subject we are speaking of—but should it ever be the case of the English, in the progress of their refinements, to arrive at the same polish which distinguishes the French, if we did not lose the *politesse de cœur,*[5] which inclines men more to humane actions, than courteous ones—we should at least

---

[1] But you don't need to answer this.

[2] Truly . . . the French are polite (civil, refined).

[3] Correctly, *excès;* see above, p. 108, n. 4.

[4] Sterne demonstrates his own understanding of music by using *compass* in its technical sense as a musical term; see *OED,* s.v. *compass,* 10: "Music. The full range of tones which a voice or musical instrument is capable of producing." Cf. p. 45, n. 5.

[5] See above, p. 51, n. 4. Sterne's bilingual play here involves the similar sounds of polite/polish and *cœur*/courteous.

Cf. *Letters,* 391: "I will shew you more real politesses than any you have met with in France," he wrote to Lydia in August 1767, perhaps at the very time he was writing this chapter, "as mine will come warm from the heart." A few months later he used the term with heavy irony in relation to his wife's return to Coxwold: "My wife is come to pay me a sentimental visit as far as from Avignon—and the *politesses* arising from such a proof of her urbanity, has robb'd me of a month's writing" (December 1767; *Letters* 405).

lose that distinct variety and originality of character, which distinguishes them, not only from each other, but from all the world besides.[6]

I had a few of King William's shillings[7] as smooth as glass in my pocket; and foreseeing they would be of use in the illustration of my hypothesis, I had got them into my hand, when I had proceeded so far—

See, Mons. Le Compte, said I, rising up, and laying them before him upon the table—by jingling and rubbing one against another for seventy years together in one body's pocket or another's, they are become so much alike, you can scarce distinguish one shilling from another.[8]

The English, like antient medals, kept more apart, and passing but few peoples hands, preserve the first sharpnesses which the fine hand of nature has given them—they are not so pleasant to feel—but in return, the legend is so visible, that at the first look you see whose image and superscription they bear.—But the French, Mons. Le Compte, added I, wishing to soften what I had said, have so many excellencies, they can the better spare this—they are a loyal, a gallant, a generous, an ingenious, and good temper'd people as is under heaven—if they have a fault—they are too *serious.*

Mon Dieu! cried the Count, rising out of his chair.

Mais vous plaisantez,[9] said he, correcting his exclamation.—I laid my hand upon my breast, and with earnest gravity assured him, it was my most settled opinion.

The Count said he was mortified, he could not stay to hear my reasons, being engaged to go that moment to dine with the Duc de C*****.

But if it is not too far to come to Versailles to eat your soup with me,[10] I beg,

---

[6] Although Sterne was at first charmed with French manners ("I am very well pleased with Paris—indeed I meet with so many civilities amongst the people here that I must sing their praises—the French have a great deal of urbanity in their composition . . ." [*Letters* 178; July 9, 1762]), by October he was already expressing an opinion close to that of Yorick; see the quotation from *Letters,* 186, above, p. 75, n. 12.

[7] Stout, 232: "issued during the reign of William III (1689–1702) and bearing his likeness."

[8] See above, p. 76 and n. 4. Cf. Cash, *LY,* 176–77, where an account is given of the antecedent of Sterne's metaphor: "According to Joseph Craddock [*Literary and Miscellaneous Memoirs,* 1828], French enthusiasm for Sterne as a person had cooled since 1762 [i.e., in 1764, when Sterne returned to Paris]. The French, he said, could not bear Sterne because of 'some keen ridicule which he had thrown on the Parisians.' . . . One sarcasm . . . made its way into the *London Chronicle* for April 16–18, 1765: . . . 'A French Gentleman asked him, If he had found in France no original characters that he could make use of in his history? *"No,"* replied he, *"The French resemble old pieces of coin, whose impression is worn out by rubbing".'"*

[9] But you are joking. Cf. p. 122, n. 11.

[10] Cf. *Histoire de l'alimentation,* ed. Jean-Louis Flandrin and Massimo Montanari (Paris: Fayard, 1996), 610: "The word 'soupe' was used for any meal that was not a snack: in all ranks of society, one would invite somebody over for a meal with, 'Come and eat soup with us/me'" (our translation); we thank Anne Bandry for providing the citation.

before you leave France, I may have the pleasure of knowing you retract your opinion—or, in what manner you support it.—But if you do support it, Mons. Anglois, said he, you must do it with all your powers, because you have the whole world against you.[11]—I promised the Count I would do myself the honour of dining with him before I set out for Italy—so took my leave.

---

[11] See Stout, 233: "the opinion Yorick expresses here runs counter to the popular view that, in comparison with the philosophic seriousness of the English . . . , the French were a gay people." He also notes, however, that Yorick later contradicts himself, apostrophizing the French as "Happy people! that once a week at least are sure to lay down all your cares together; and dance and sing and sport away the weights of grievance" (p. 140). As with all national stereotypes, the French character often refuses to conform—perhaps Sterne's wisdom is to point to that resistance by offering dubious generalizations on both sides.

THE TEMPTATION.
PARIS.

WHEN I alighted at the hotel, the porter told me a young woman with a band-box had been that moment enquiring for me.—I do not know, said the porter, whether she is gone away or no. I took the key of my chamber of him, and went up stairs; and when I had got within ten steps of the top of the landing before my door, I met her coming easily down.

It was the fair *fille de chambre* I had walked along the Quai de Conti with: Madame de R**** had sent her upon some commissions to a *merchande de modes*[1] within a step or two of the hotel de Modene; and as I had fail'd in waiting upon her, had bid her enquire if I had left Paris; and if so, whether I had not left a letter address'd to her.

As the fair *fille de chambre* was so near my door she turned back, and went into the room with me for a moment or two whilst I wrote a card.

It was a fine still evening in the latter end of the month of May—the crimson window curtains (which were of the same colour of those of the bed) were drawn close—the sun was setting and reflected through them so warm a tint into the fair *fille de chambre*'s face—I thought she blush'd—the idea of it made me blush myself—we were quite alone; and that super-induced a second blush before the first could get off.

There is a sort of a pleasing half guilty blush, where the blood is more in fault than the man—'tis sent impetuous from the heart, and virtue flies after it—not to call it back, but to make the sensation of it more delicious to the nerves—'tis associated—

————but I'll not describe it.—I felt something at first within me which was not in strict unison with the lesson of virtue I had given her the night before—I sought five minutes for a card—I knew I had not one.—I took up a pen—I laid it down again—my hand trembled—the devil was in me.

I know as well as any one, he is an adversary, whom if we resist, he will fly from us—but I seldom resist him at all; from a terror, that though I may conquer, I may still get a hurt in the combat—so I give up the triumph, for security; and instead of thinking to make him fly, I generally fly myself.[2]

---

[1] A draper's or mercer's shop (correctly, *marchande*).

[2] Cf. Sterne's "love letter" to Lady Warkworth (see above, p. 62, n. 7), *Letters*, 243: "It is but an hour ago, that I kneeled down and swore I never would come near you—and after saying my Lord's Prayer for the sake of the close, of not being led into temptation—out I sallied like any Christian hero, ready to take the field against the world, the flesh, and the devil; not doubting but I should finally trample them all down under my feet"; and a second letter, again possibly to Lady Warkworth: "fugitive as I am . . . it was not from Principles of rebellion,—but of virtue, that we made our escapes . . . . We ran headlong like a

The fair *fille de chambre* came close up to the bureau where I was looking for a card—took up first the pen I cast down, then offered to hold me the ink: she offer'd it so sweetly, I was going to accept it—but I durst not—I have nothing, my dear, said I, to write upon.—Write it, said she, simply, upon any thing.—

I was just going to cry out, Then I will write it, fair girl! upon thy lips.—

If I do, said I, I shall perish—so I took her by the hand, and led her to the door, and begg'd she would not forget the lesson I had given her—She said, Indeed she would not—and as she utter'd it with some earnestness, she turned about, and gave me both her hands, closed together, into mine—it was impossible not to compress them in that situation—I wish'd to let them go; and all the time I held them, I kept arguing within myself against it—and still I held them on.—In two minutes I found I had all the battle to fight over again—and I felt my legs and every limb about me tremble at the idea.

The foot of the bed was within a yard and a half of the place where we were standing—I had still hold of her hands—and how it happened I can give no account, but I neither ask'd her—nor drew her—nor did I think of the bed—but so it did happen, we both sat down.

I'll just shew you, said the fair *fille de chambre*, the little purse I have been making to-day to hold your crown. So she put her hand into her right pocket, which was next me, and felt for it for some time—then into the left—"She had lost it."—I never bore expectation more quietly—it was in her right pocket at last—she pulled it out; it was of green taffeta, lined with a little bit of white quilted sattin, and just big enough to hold the crown—she put it into my hand— it was pretty; and I held it ten minutes with the back of my hand resting upon her lap—looking sometimes at the purse, sometimes on one side of it.[3]

A stitch or two had broke out in the gathers of my stock[4]—the fair *fille de chambre*, without saying a word, took out her little hussive,[5] threaded a small needle, and sew'd it up—I foresaw it would hazard the glory of the day; and as she passed her hand in silence across and across my neck in the manœuvre, I felt the laurels shake which fancy had wreath'd about my head.

Ielemachus and a Mentor from a Calypso & her Nymphs, hastening as fast as our members would let us, from the ensnaring favours of an enchanting Court" (244–45).

[3] Cf. p. 94, n. 7. Little if anything in this chapter is "in strict unison with the lesson of virtue" Yorick had delivered the night before. At the same time, it is important to note that the passage remains inconclusive; it is impolite to peek behind a closed door.

[4] Cf. Cunnington, 75: "THE STOCK. From about 1735 onwards. It was a piece of linen or cambric folded to form a high neckband and sometimes stiffened with pasteboard. It was buckled behind, leaving the ruffled shirt front uncovered."

[5] *OED*, s.v. *housewife, sb.* 3: "A pocket-case for needles, pins, thread, scissors, etc. (In this sense still often spelt *huswife, hussive*)." The first illustration is dated 1749, and Sterne's uses here and in *TS*, V.16.445–46 ("[the *Tristrapædia*] might be rolled up in my mother's hussive"), are also cited.

A strap had given way in her walk, and the buckle of her shoe was just falling off—See, said the *fille de chambre,* holding up her foot—I could not for my soul but fasten the buckle in return, and putting in the strap—and lifting up the other foot with it, when I had done, to see if both were right—in doing it too suddenly—it unavoidably threw the fair *fille de chambre* off her center—and then—

THE CONQUEST.[1]

YES——and then—Ye whose clay-cold heads and luke-warm hearts can argue down or mask your passions—tell me, what trespass is it that man should have them? or how his spirit stands answerable, to the father of spirits, but for his conduct under them?

If nature has so wove her web of kindness, that some threads of love and desire are entangled with the piece—must the whole web be rent in drawing them out?—Whip me such stoics,[2] great governor of nature! said I to myself—Wherever thy providence shall place me for the trials of my virtue—whatever is my danger—whatever is my situation—let me feel the movements which rise out of it, and which belong to me as a man—and if I govern them as a good one—I will trust the issues to thy justice, for thou hast made us—and not we ourselves.[3]

---

[1] Sterne strikes the particular posture of moral tolerance evident in this chapter often in his writings, including *TS,* III.33.260–61: "Defend me, gracious heaven! from those persecuting spirits who make no allowances for these workings within us.—Never,—O never may I lay down in their tents, who cannot relax the engine, and feel pity for the force of education, and the prevalence of opinions long derived from ancestors!" See also V.9.435: "—Now I love you for this—and 'tis this delicious mixture within you which makes you dear creatures what you are—and he who hates you for it——all I can say of the matter, is—That he has either a pumkin for his head—or a pippin for his heart . . . ."

Sterne is not always so tolerant of human complexity, however; see, e.g., his discussion of character in sermon 17, "The case of Hezekiah": "We are a strange compound; and something foreign from what charity would suspect, so eternally twists itself into what we do . . . that whatever a man is about,——observe him,——he stands arm'd inside and out with two motives; an ostensible one for the world,——and another which he reserves for his own private use" (4:161–62). Like almost all moralists of the via media, Sterne can argue both sides of the question; the ambiguities of this chapter may be designed to reflect this refusal to dogmatize.

[2] Stout, 237, calls attention to a possible echo of *Othello,* I.i.49: "Whip me such honest knaves!"; cf. the apostrophe to Joy in sermon 20, "The prodigal son" (see Appendix, p. 240). Joyfulness was always connected to Christian belief (see below, p. 168 and n. 4).

[3] Sterne ends by quoting Psalm 100:3: "Know ye that the Lord he is God: it is he that hath made us, and not we ourselves." It is perhaps a passage such as this, with all its ambiguities, that led Joseph Cockfield to write (March 19, 1768) to the Reverend Weeden Butler: "I have seen the reverend Prebendary's new publication; in his former writings I saw evident marks of his genius and benevolence, but who that indulges serious reflection can read his obscenity and ill-applied passages of Holy Scripture, without horror" (quoted from John Nichols, *Illustrations* [1817], in *Sterne: The Critical Heritage,* 202).

As I finish'd my address,[4] I raised the fair *fille de chambre* up by the hand, and led her out of the room—she stood by me till I lock'd the door and put the key in my pocket—*and then*—the victory being quite decisive—and not till then, I press'd my lips to her cheek, and, taking her by the hand again, led her safe to the gate of the hotel.

---

[4] *OED* offers several possible meanings of *address:* (1) to order or arrange; (2) to stand erect or raise oneself; or (3) a discourse directed toward another. Keymer has called our attention to a letter from Richardson to Lady Bradshaigh (c. March 1751), in which the sexual connotation of *address* is readily evident: "[Colley Cibber] is as gay and lively at seventy-nine as he was at twenty-nine; and he . . . was noted for his address, and for his success, too, on two hundred and fifty occasions,—a little too many, I doubt, for a moderate rake: but then his long life must be considered" (*Correspondence of Samuel Richardson,* ed. A. L. Barbauld [London, 1804], 6:66–67).

THE MYSTERY.
PARIS.

IF a man knows the heart, he will know it was impossible to go back instantly to my chamber—it was touching a cold key with a flat third to it, upon the close of a piece of musick,[1] which had call'd forth my affections—therefore, when I let go the hand of the *fille de chambre,* I remain'd at the gate of the hotel for some time, looking at every one who pass'd by, and forming conjectures upon them, till my attention got fix'd upon a single object which confounded all kind of reasoning upon him.

It was a tall figure of a philosophic serious, adust[2] look, which pass'd and repass'd sedately along the street, making a turn of about sixty paces on each side of the gate of the hotel—the man was about fifty-two—had a small cane under his arm—was dress'd in a dark drab-colour'd coat, waistcoat, and breeches, which seem'd to have seen some years service—they were still clean, and there was a little air of frugal *propretè*[3] throughout him. By his pulling off his hat, and his attitude of accosting a good many in his way, I saw he was asking charity; so I got a sous or two out of my pocket ready to give him, as he took me in his turn—he pass'd by me without asking any thing—and yet did not go five steps further before he ask'd charity of a little woman—I was much more likely to have given of the two—He had scarce done with the woman, when he pull'd off his hat to another who was coming the same way.—An ancient gentleman came slowly—and, after him, a young smart one—He let them both pass, and ask'd nothing: I stood observing him half an hour, in which time he had made a dozen turns backwards and forwards, and found that he invariably pursued the same plan.

There were two things very singular in this, which set my brain to work, and to no purpose—the first was, why the man should *only* tell his story to the sex—and secondly—what kind of story it was, and what species of eloquence it could be, which soften'd the hearts of the women, which he knew 'twas to no purpose to practise upon the men.

There were two other circumstances which entangled this mystery—the one was, he told every woman what he had to say in her ear, and in a way which had much more the air of a secret than a petition—the other was, it was always

---

[1] Cf. Milic, 106: "A flat third is an interval short by half a tone of the natural [major] chord and has a dissonant and plaintive (to some displeasing) sound, especially at the end of a piece of music." Sterne's terms can refer to keyboard or non-keyboard instruments.

[2] *OED* indicates the origin of the word in medical descriptions (dryness, brown in color as if scorched by the sun or by fire); also, "sallow, gloomy in features or temperament." Cf. Pope, *Dunciad* (1743), II.37: "No meagre, muse-rid mope, adust and thin"; and Sterne's self-description in *Letters,* 241: "a thin, dry, hectic, unperspirable habit of Body."

[3] Cleanliness, neatness; correctly, *propreté.*

successful—he never stopp'd a woman, but she pull'd out her purse, and immediately gave him something.

I could form no system to explain the phenomenon.

I had got a riddle to amuse me for the rest of the evening, so I walk'd up stairs
to my chamber.

THE CASE OF CONSCIENCE.
PARIS.

I WAS immediately followed up by the master of the hotel, who came into my room to tell me I must provide lodgings elsewhere.—How so, friend? said I.— He answer'd, I had had a young woman lock'd up with me two hours that evening in my bed-chamber, and 'twas against the rules of his house.—Very well, said I, we'll all part friends then—for the girl is no worse—and I am no worse— and you will be just as I found you.——It was enough, he said, to overthrow the credit of his hotel.—*Voyez vous,*[1] *Monsieur,* said he, pointing to the foot of the bed we had been sitting upon.—I own it had something of the appearance of an evidence; but my pride not suffering me to enter into any detail of the case,[2] I exhorted him to let his soul sleep in peace, as I resolved to let mine do that night, and that I would discharge what I owed him at breakfast.

I should not have minded, *Monsieur,* said he, if you had had twenty girls—'Tis a score more, replied I, interrupting him, than I ever reckon'd upon—Provided, added he, it had been but in a morning.—And does the difference of the time of the day at Paris make a difference in the sin?—It made a difference, he said, in the scandal.—I like a good distinction in my heart; and cannot say I was intolerably out of temper with the man.—I own it is necessary, re-assumed[3] the master of the hotel, that a stranger at Paris should have the opportunities presented to him of buying lace and silk stockings and ruffles, *et tout cela*[4]—and 'tis nothing if a woman comes with a band box.——O' my conscience, said I, she had one; but I never look'd into it.—Then, *Monsieur,* said he, has bought nothing.—Not one earthly thing, replied I.—Because, said he, I could recommend one to you who would use you *en conscience.*[5]—But I must see her this night, said I.—He made me a low bow and walk'd down.

Now shall I triumph over this *maitre d'hotel,* cried I—and what then?—Then I shall let him see I know he is a dirty fellow.—And what then?—What then!—I was too near myself to say it was for the sake of others.—I had no good answer left—there was more of spleen than principle in my project, and I was sick of it before the execution.

---

[1] You see; look.

[2] Clonmell's marginal comment: "very nasty" (Franssen 181). Cf. *ASJ*'s final chapter, "The *Case* of Delicacy" (italics added).

[3] *OED*, s.v. reassume, 5.a, notes that the word was "very common" in the eighteenth century for "resume."

[4] And all that.

[5] In good faith.

In a few minutes the Grisset came in with her box of lace—I'll buy nothing however, said I, within myself.

The Grisset would shew me every thing—I was hard to please: she would not seem to see it; she open'd her little magazine,[6] laid all her laces one after another before me—unfolded and folded them up again one by one with the most patient sweetness—I might buy—or not—she would let me have every thing at my own price—the poor creature seem'd anxious to get a penny; and laid herself out to win me, and not so much in a manner which seem'd artful, as in one I felt simple and caressing.

If there is not a fund of honest cullibility[7] in man, so much the worse—my heart relented, and I gave up my second resolution as quietly as the first—Why should I chastise one for the trespass of another? if thou art tributary to this tyrant of an host, thought I, looking up in her face, so much harder is thy bread.

If I had not had more than four *Louis d'ors* in my purse, there was no such thing as rising up and shewing her the door, till I had first laid three of them out in a pair of ruffles.

—The master of the hotel will share the profit with her—no matter—then I have only paid as many a poor soul has *paid* before me for an act he *could* not do,[8] or think of.

---

[6] First example recorded in *OED,* s.v. 1.c: "A portable receptacle containing articles of value." Cf. *BJ,* p. 200, "Magazeens of Teas."

[7] *OED,* s.v.: "The quality of being cullible; gullibility." The first illustration is from Swift (1728), the second, this passage. Cf. Clonmell: "Cullibility is what may be found in Every Heart and sh[d] be sought constantly, tis . . . perhaps y[e] Most Amiable part of Man" (Franssen 184). One might also suspect a pun on *cul,* i.e., French: "backside."

[8] As Stout, 243, notes, this assertion marks a tendency in Sterne's life and writings, neatly summed up in James A. Work's pithy remark: "with a curiously perverse and possibly self-revelatory sense of the incongruous [Sterne] grins again and again over sexual impotence, the suspicion of which hovers like a dubious halo over the head of every Shandy male . . ." (Introduction to *Tristram Shandy* [New York: Odyssey Press, 1940], lx). Cf. *TS,* VII.29.624, where Tristram stands, "garters in my hand," while Jenny comforts him for "what had *not* pass'd." And we must puzzle over his account in *BJ,* pp. 184–85, of being treated for venereal disease, although he had had, he assures Eliza, "no commerce whatever with the Sex . . . these 15 Years."

THE RIDDLE.
PARIS.

WHEN La Fleur came up to wait upon me at supper, he told me how sorry the master of the hotel was for his affront to me in bidding me change my lodgings.

A man who values a good night's rest will not lay down with enmity in his heart if he can help it—So I bid La Fleur tell the master of the hotel, that I was sorry on my side for the occasion I had given him—and you may tell him, if you will, La Fleur, added I, that if the young woman should call again, I shall not see her.

This was a sacrifice not to him, but myself, having resolved, after so narrow an escape, to run no more risks, but to leave Paris, if it was possible, with all the virtue I enter'd in.

C'est deroger à noblesse, Monsieur,[1] said La Fleur, making me a bow down to the ground as he said it—*Et encore Monsieur,*[2] said he, may change his sentiments—and if (*par hazard*[3]) he should like to amuse himself—I find no amusement in it, said I, interrupting him—

Mon Dieu! said La Fleur—and took away.

In an hour's time he came to put me to bed, and was more than commonly officious—something hung upon his lips to say to me, or ask me, which he could not get off: I could not conceive what it was; and indeed gave myself little trouble to find it out, as I had another riddle so much more interesting upon my mind, which was that of the man's asking charity before the door of the hotel—I would have given any thing to have got to the bottom of it; and that, not out of curiosity—'tis so low a principle of enquiry, in general, I would not purchase the gratification of it with a two-sous piece—but a secret, I thought, which so soon and so certainly soften'd the heart of every woman you came near, was a secret at least equal to the philosopher's stone: had I had both the Indies,[4] I would have given up one to have been master of it.

I toss'd and turn'd it almost all night long in my brains to no manner of purpose; and when I awoke in the morning, I found my spirit as much troubled with my *dreams*, as ever the king of Babylon had been with his; and I will not hesitate

---

[1] That would be to lose face (literally, to depart from nobility—correctly, *déroger*); cf. above, p. 112, n. 4. Given the context, perhaps a bilingual pun, "de-*roger*," "rogering" being a cant term for "fucking"; Sterne uses it in his "Rabelaisian Fragment" (ed. M. New, *PMLA* 87 [1972]:1089, n. 16).

[2] And furthermore, Sir.

[3] By chance.

[4] That is, the East Indies and West Indies.

to affirm, it would have puzzled all the wise men of Paris, as much as those of Chaldea, to have given its interpretation.[5]

---

[5] Sterne alludes to Nebuchadnezzar's dream in Daniel 2:1–11; the Chaldean wise men are unable to interpret the dream (2:10).

LE DIMANCHE.[1]
PARIS.

IT was Sunday; and when La Fleur came in, in the morning, with my coffee and role and butter, he had got himself so gallantly array'd, I scarce knew him.

I had covenanted at Montriul to give him a new hat with a silver button and loop, and four Louis d'ors *pour s'adoniser,*[2] when we got to Paris; and the poor fellow, to do him justice, had done wonders with it.

He had bought a bright, clean, good scarlet coat and a pair of breeches of the same—They were not a crown worse, he said, for the wearing—I wish'd him hang'd for telling me—they look'd so fresh, that tho' I knew the thing could not be done, yet I would rather have imposed upon my fancy with thinking I had bought them new for the fellow, than that they had come out of the *Rue de friperie.*[3]

This is a nicety which makes not the heart sore at Paris.

He had purchased moreover a handsome blue sattin waistcoat, fancifully enough embroidered—this was indeed something the worse for the services it had done, but 'twas clean scour'd—the gold had been touch'd up, and upon the whole was rather showy than otherwise—and as the blue was not violent, it suited with the coat and breeches very well: he had squeez'd out of the money, moreover, a new bag and a solitaire;[4] and had insisted with the *fripier,* upon a gold pair of garters to his breeches knees—He had purchased muslin ruffles, *bien brodées,*[5] with four livres of his own money—and a pair of white silk stockings for five more—and, to top all, nature had given him a handsome figure, without costing him a sous.

He enter'd the room thus set off, with his hair dress'd in the first stile, and with a handsome *bouquet*[6] in his breast—in a word, there was that look of festivity in

---

[1] Sunday.

[2] To deck himself out (like an Adonis). Cf. Le Roux, *Dictionnaire,* s.v. *Adoniser:* "an invented word, only used in the familiar style. It means to dress well, to adorn oneself with art and effeminacy, to make oneself as handsome as Adonis, or at least to believe oneself to be so" (our translation).

[3] Street of second-hand clothes; cf. below, *fripier.* It was a real location in Paris, though probably more than one street, as in most great cities of the world.

[4] *OED,* s.v.: *bag:* "A silken pouch to hold the back-hair of a wig"; *solitaire:* "A loose necktie of black silk or broad ribbon"; Sterne italicizes "solitaire" on p. 154, suggesting the French fashion (and word) had not quite been anglicized, although *OED's* first illustration is dated 1731.

[5] Prettily embroidered.

[6] Cf. p. 147, where Sterne inserts a footnote defining *bouquet* as "Nosegay." *OED's* first illustration is dated 1716–1718, and this occurrence is the second; Sterne's footnote would suggest that the word was still not anglicized, while this occurrence, without definition, would suggest it was. *Bouquet* does not appear in Johnson's *Dictionary.*

A Sentimental Journey

every thing about him, which at once put me in mind it was Sunday—and by combining both together, it instantly struck me, that the favour he wish'd to ask of me the night before, was to spend the day, as every body in Paris spent it, besides. I had scarce made the conjecture, when La Fleur, with infinite humility, but with a look of trust, as if I should not refuse him, begg'd I would grant him the day, *pour faire le galant vis à vis de sa maitresse.*[7]

Now it was the very thing I intended to do myself *vis à vis* Madame de R****—I had retain'd the *remise* on purpose for it, and it would not have mortified my vanity to have had a servant so well dress'd as La Fleur was to have got up behind it: I never could have worse spared him.

But we must *feel,* not argue in these embarrassments—the sons and daughters of service part with liberty, but not with Nature in their contracts; they are flesh and blood, and have their little vanities and wishes in the midst of the house of bondage,[8] as well as their task-masters—no doubt, they have set their self-denials at a price—and their expectations are so unreasonable, that I would often disappoint them, but that their condition puts it so much in my power to do it.

Behold!—Behold, I am thy servant[9]—disarms me at once of the powers of a master—

—Thou shalt go, La Fleur! said I.

—And what mistress, La Fleur, said I, canst thou have pick'd up in so little a time at Paris? La Fleur laid his hand upon his breast, and said 'twas a *petite demoiselle*[10] at Monsieur Le Compte de B****'s.—La Fleur had a heart made for society; and, to speak the truth of him let as few occasions slip him as his master—so that some how or other; but how—heaven knows—he had connected himself with the *demoiselle* upon the landing of the stair-case, during the time I was taken up with my Passport; and as there was time enough for me to win the Count to my interest, La Fleur had contrived to make it do to win the maid to his—the family, it seems, was to be at Paris that day, and he had made a party with her, and two or three more of the Count's houshold, upon the *boulevards.*[11]

Happy people! that once a week at least are sure to lay down all your cares together; and dance and sing and sport away the weights of grievance, which bow down the spirit of other nations to the earth.[12]

---

[7] To play the lover; to court his mistress.

[8] A common scriptural phrase; see Exodus 13:3, 14, and 20:2; Deuteronomy 5:6, 6:12.

[9] Perhaps echoing Isaiah 42:1 (52:13): "Behold my servant, whom I uphold"; cf. 2 Samuel 9:6, 2 Kings 16:7.

[10] A young woman.

[11] Sterne's italics could indicate either that he considered the word foreign (*OED*'s first example is dated 1769), or simply that it had for him specific application to the large, tree-lined promenades of Paris, of a dimension not found in London or elsewhere.

[12] Cf. *TS,* VII.43, in Appendix below, pp. 246–48, Tristram's dance with Nannette.

140

THE FRAGMENT.[1]
PARIS.

LA Fleur had left me something to amuse myself with for the day more than I had bargain'd for, or could have enter'd either into his head or mine.

He had brought the little print of butter[2] upon a currant leaf; and as the morning was warm, and he had a good step to bring it, he had begg'd a sheet of waste paper[3] to put betwixt the currant leaf and his hand—As that was plate sufficient, I bad him lay it upon the table as it was, and as I resolved to stay within all day I ordered him to call upon the *traiteur*[4] to bespeak my dinner, and leave me to breakfast by myself.

When I had finish'd the butter, I threw the currant leaf out of the window, and was going to do the same by the waste paper—but stopping to read a line first, and that drawing me on to a second and third—I thought it better worth; so I shut the window, and drawing a chair up to it, I sat down to read it.

It was in the old French of Rabelais's time,[5] and for ought I know might have been wrote by him—it was moreover in a Gothic letter, and that so faded and gone off by damps and length of time, it cost me infinite trouble to make any thing of it—I threw it down; and then wrote a letter to Eugenius—then I took it up again, and embroiled my patience with it afresh—and then to cure that, I wrote a letter to Eliza.—Still it kept hold of me; and the difficulty of understanding it increased but the desire.

I got my dinner; and after I had enlightened my mind with a bottle of Burgundy, I at it again—and after two or three hours poring upon it, with almost as deep attention as ever Gruter or Jacob Spon did upon a nonsensical inscription,[6]

---

[1] Elizabeth W. Harries, "Sterne's Novels: Gathering Up the Fragments," *ELH* 49 (1982):35–49, suggests that for Sterne, "as for many of his contemporaries, the word 'fragment' was inextricably bound up" with Christ's command to "Gather up the fragments that remain, that nothing be lost" (John 6:12), and the miracle of plenty that follows (6:13–14).

[2] *OED*'s first illustration, s.v. *print,* B.5: "A pat of butter, moulded to a shape."

[3] Cf. Charles Johnstone's preface to *Chrysal: Or, The Adventures of a Guinea* (1760–1765), where the narrator discovers at a tea table "a piece of written paper, that served instead of a plate to hold their butter" and that appears "to be part of some regular work" (x).

[4] Restaurateur. *OED* gives examples from Smollett's *Peregrine Pickle* (1751) and *Travels* (1766): "a keeper of an eating-house (in France, Italy, etc.) who supplies or sends out meals to order."

[5] I.e., the sixteenth century; François Rabelais (c. 1494–1553), a satirist famed for his comic bawdiness, was a major influence on *TS* (see *Notes* 3:19–21); his absence in *ASJ* is one indication of the tonal difference between the two works.

[6] Jan Gruytère (1560–1627), Dutch historian, author of *Inscriptiones antiquae totius orbis Romanorum* (1603). Jacob Spon (1647–1685), French antiquarian and historian; Tristram refers to him in *TS,* VII.31.628, as an authority on Lyons, but Sterne probably never consulted him.

I thought I made sense of it; but to make sure of it, the best way, I imagined, was to turn it into English, and see how it would look then—so I went on leisurely, as a trifling man does, sometimes writing a sentence—then taking a turn or two—and then looking how the world went, out of the window; so that it was nine o'clock at night before I had done it—I then begun and read it as follows.

THE FRAGMENT.
PARIS.

——Now as the notary's wife disputed the point with the notary with too much heat—I wish, said the notary, throwing down the parchment, that there was another notary here only to set down and attest all this——

—And what would you do then, Monsieur? said she, rising hastily up—the notary's wife was a little fume[1] of a woman, and the notary thought it well to avoid a hurricane by a mild reply—I would go, answer'd he, to bed.——You may go to the devil, answer'd the notary's wife.

Now there happening to be but one bed in the house, the other two rooms being unfurnish'd, as is the custom at Paris, and the notary not caring to lie in the same bed with a woman who had but that moment sent him pell-mell to the devil, went forth with his hat and cane and short cloak, the night being very windy, and walk'd out ill at ease towards the *pont neuf.*

Of all the bridges which ever were built, the whole world who have pass'd over the *pont neuf,* must own, that it is the noblest—the finest—the grandest—the lightest—the longest—the broadest that ever conjoin'd land and land together upon the face of the terraqueous globe——

> By this, it seems, as if the author of the
> fragment had not been a Frenchman.[2]

The worst fault which divines and the doctors of the Sorbonne can allege against it, is, that if there is but a cap-full of wind in or about Paris, 'tis more blasphemously *sacre Dieu'*d[3] there than in any other aperture of the whole city—and with reason,[4] good and cogent Messieurs; for it comes against you without crying *garde d'eau,*[5]

---

[1] *OED*'s sole illustration; s.v. *sb.* 7.b: "One who is apt to get into a fume" (i.e., into "a fit of anger").

[2] Cole, among others, comments on French pride in their bridges: "The Bridges over the Seine at Paris are about 5 or 6, & nothing remarkable for their Beauty: tho' to hear the Descriptions of the Pont-Neuf, & the Pont-Royal, one would suppose that there were not two such Bridges to be met with any where" (*Journal* 48); see above, p. 73, n. 6.

[3] Cursed.

[4] Cf. *TS,* VII.41.644: "I think it wrong, merely because a man's hat has been blown off his head by chance the first night he comes to Avignon,——that he should therefore say, 'Avignion is more subject to high winds than any town in all France.'" The windiness of Avignon was proverbial.

[5] The warning cry in France (correctly, *gare l'eau*) and in Edinburgh before throwing dirty water, etc., out the window. *OED,* s.v. *gardyloo* (pseudo-French: *gare de l'eau*), lists Sterne's usage here as its first illustration; Sterne's phonetic rendering probably derives from his having heard the word in Britain.

and with such unpremeditable[6] puffs, that of the few who cross it with their hats on, not one in fifty but hazards two livres and a half, which is its full worth.

The poor notary, just as he was passing by the sentry, instinctively clapp'd his cane to the side of it, but in raising it up, the point of his cane catching hold of the loop of the sentinel's hat hoisted it over the spikes of the ballustrade clear into the Seine—

—'*Tis an ill wind,* said a boatsman, who catch'd it, *which blows no body any good.*[7]

The sentry being a gascon[8] incontinently twirl'd up his whiskers, and levell'd his harquebuss.

Harquebusses in those days went off with matches; and an old woman's paper lanthorn at the end of the bridge happening to be blown out, she had borrow'd the sentry's match to light it—it gave a moment's time for the gascon's blood to run cool, and turn the accident better to his advantage—'*Tis an ill wind,* said he, catching off the notary's castor,[9] and legitimating the capture with the boatman's adage.

The poor notary cross'd the bridge, and passing along the rue de Dauphine[10] into the fauxbourgs of St. Germain, lamented himself as he walk'd along in this manner:

Luckless man! that I am, said the notary, to be the sport of hurricanes all my days——to be born to have the storm of ill language levell'd against me and my profession wherever I go—to be forced into marriage by the thunder of the church to a tempest of a woman—to be driven forth out of my house by domestic winds, and despoil'd of my castor by pontific[11] ones—to be here, bareheaded, in a windy night at the mercy of the ebbs and flows of accidents—where am I to lay my head?[12]—miserable man! what wind in the two-and-thirty points

---

[6] *OED*'s sole example.

[7] Proverbial; Tilley, W421: "It is an ill WIND that blows no man good"; and *ODEP,* 401. This is another example of Sterne's penchant for literalizing a proverbial expression.

[8] Sterne predates *OED*'s first illustration (Smollett, "Song," 1771): "One who resembles a Gascon in character; a braggart, boaster (the natives of Gascony being notorious as such)."

[9] A beaver hat, i.e., a hat made from beaver fur, as was most common until the eighteenth century, when rabbit fur came into use and "beavers" became distinguished from "castors" or "demi-castors" (mixed beaver and rabbit); see *OED,* and Cunnington, 87.

[10] Correctly, Rue Dauphine.

[11] *OED* cites the usage here as a "*humorous nonce-use,*" i.e., "pertaining to a bridge." Milton, *Paradise Lost,* book 10, ll. 312–13, has a similar pun, where the intent is clearly anti-Catholic: "Now had they brought the work [the bridge between earth and Hell] by wondrous Art / Pontifical . . . ."

[12] Cf. Matthew 8:20 (Luke 9:58): "The foxes have holes, and the birds of the air have nests; but the Son of man hath not where to lay his head." Sterne seems to have liked this verse, using it in four sermons.

of the whole compass can blow unto thee, as it does to the rest of thy fellow creatures, good!

As the notary was passing on by a dark passage, complaining in this sort, a voice call'd out to a girl, to bid her run for the next notary—now the notary being the next, and availing himself of his situation, walk'd up the passage to the door, and passing through an old sort of a saloon,[13] was usher'd into a large chamber dismantled of every thing but a long military pike—a breast plate—a rusty old sword, and bandoleer, hung up equi-distant in four different places against the wall.

An old personage, who had heretofore been a gentleman, and unless decay of fortune taints the blood along with it was a gentleman at that time, lay supporting his head upon his hand in his bed; a little table with a taper burning was set close beside it, and close by the table was placed a chair—the notary sat him down in it; and pulling out his ink-horn and a sheet or two of paper which he had in his pocket, he placed them before him, and dipping his pen in his ink, and leaning his breast over the table, he disposed every thing to make the gentleman's last will and testament.

Alas! Monsieur le Notaire, said the gentleman, raising himself up a little, I have nothing to bequeath which will pay the expence of bequeathing, except the history of myself, which, I could not die in peace unless I left it as a legacy to the world; the profits arising out of it, I bequeath to you for the pains of taking it from me—it is a story so uncommon, it must be read by all mankind—it will make the fortunes of your house—the notary dipp'd his pen into his ink-horn—Almighty director of every event in my life! said the old gentleman, looking up earnestly and raising his hands towards heaven—thou whose hand has led me on through such a labyrinth of strange passages down into this scene of desolation, assist the decaying memory of an old, infirm, and broken-hearted man—direct my tongue, by the spirit of thy eternal truth, that this stranger may set down naught but what is written in that BOOK,[14] from whose records, said he, clasping his hands together, I am to be condemn'd or acquitted!—the notary held up the point of his pen betwixt the taper and his eye—

—It is a story, Monsieur le Notaire, said the gentleman, which will rouse up every affection in nature—it will kill the humane, and touch the heart of cruelty herself with pity—

---

[13] I.e., salon, a large room or hall, not, as in the United States, a beer hall or tavern.

[14] Cf. *TS*, VI.8.511: "The ACCUSING SPIRIT which flew up to heaven's chancery with the oath, blush'd as he gave it in;—and the RECORDING ANGEL as he wrote it down, dropp'd a tear upon the word, and blotted it out for ever." The Christian idea of a book of deeds being kept on every person perhaps derives from Revelation 20:12: "And I saw the dead, small and great, stand before God; and the books were opened: and another book was opened, which is the book of life: and the dead were judged out of those things which were written in the books, according to their works."

—The notary was inflamed with a desire to begin, and put his pen a third time into his ink-horn—and the old gentleman turning a little more towards the notary, began to dictate his story in these words—

—And where is the rest of it,[15] La Fleur? said I, as he just then enter'd the room.

---

[15] Sterne had played with incomplete stories in *TS*, including the mock continuation of "Slawkenbergius's Tale" (IV.1) and the "King of Bohemia and his seven castles" (VIII.19). Of course, he rarely brings any story to a traditional conclusion, including both *TS* and *ASJ*.

THE FRAGMENT
AND THE *BOUQUET.
PARIS.

WHEN La Fleur came up close to the table, and was made to comprehend what I wanted, he told me there were only two other sheets of it which he had wrapt round the stalks of a *bouquet* to keep it together, which he had presented to the *demoiselle* upon the *boulevards*—Then, prithee, La Fleur, said I, step back to her to the Count de B****'s hotel, and see if you canst get—There is no doubt of it, said La Fleur—and away he flew.

In a very little time the poor fellow came back quite out of breath, with deeper marks of disappointment in his looks than could arise from the simple irreparability of the fragment—*Juste ciel!*[1] in less than two minutes that the poor fellow had taken his last tender farewel of her—his faithless mistress had given his *gage d'amour*[2] to one of the Count's footmen—the footman to a young sempstress—and the sempstress to a fiddler, with my fragment at the end of it—Our misfortunes were involved together—I gave a sigh—and La Fleur echo'd it back again to my ear—

—How perfidious! cried La Fleur—How unlucky! said I.—

—I should not have been mortified, Monsieur, quoth La Fleur, if she had lost it—Nor I, La Fleur, said I, had I found it.

Whether I did or no, will be seen hereafter.

---

*Nosegay.

---

[1] Good heavens!
[2] Pledge of love.

The Act of Charity.
Paris.

THE man who either disdains or fears to walk up a dark entry may be an excellent good man, and fit for a hundred things; but he will not do to make a good sentimental traveller. I count little of the many things I see pass at broad noon day, in large and open streets.—Nature is shy, and hates to act before spectators; but in such an unobserved corner, you sometimes see a single short scene of her's worth all the sentiments of a dozen French plays compounded together[1]—and yet they are *absolutely* fine;—and whenever I have a more brilliant affair upon my hands than common, as they suit a preacher just as well as a hero, I generally make my sermon out of 'em—and for the text—"Capadocia, Pontus and Asia, Phrygia and Pamphilia"[2]—is as good as any one in the Bible.

There is a long dark passage issuing out from the opera comique into a narrow street; 'tis trod by a few who humbly wait for a *fiacre**, or wish to get off quietly o'foot when the opera is done. At the end of it, towards the theatre, 'tis lighted by a small candle, the light of which is almost lost before you get half-way down, but near the door—'tis more for ornament than use: you see it as a fix'd star of the least magnitude; it burns—but does little good to the world, that we know of.[3]

In returning along this passage, I discern'd, as I approach'd within five or six paces of the door, two ladies standing arm in arm, with their backs against the

---

*Hackney-coach.

---

[1] Cf. *Letters*, 162 (April 1762, to Garrick): "I have been these two days reading a tragedy . . . The Natural Son . . . [by Diderot]. . . . It has too much sentiment in it, (at least for me) the speeches too long, and savour too much of *preaching*—this may be a second reason, it is not to my taste—'Tis all love, love, love, throughout, without much separation in the character; so I fear it would not do for your stage, and perhaps for the very reason which recommend[s] it to a French one." Cf. *TS*, I.18.57: "Let me intreat you to study the pure and sentimental parts of the best *French* Romances;——it will really, Madam, astonish you to see with what a variety of chaste expression this delicious sentiment [of love] . . . is dress'd out."

[2] See Acts 2:9–10. Cf. *TS*, VI.30.551, Tristram's list of misogynists: "There was the great king *Aldrovandus,* and *Bosphorus,* and *Capadocius,* and *Dardanus,* and *Pontus,* and *Asius.*" Sterne obviously found this listing of geographical locations amusing, but for an exploration of how the second chapter of Acts, the story of Pentecost, may relate to *ASJ*, see Kraft, "Pentecostal Moment," 292–310.

[3] Cf. Thomas Pennant, *Tour on the Continent 1765*, ed. G. R. de Beer [London: Ray Society, 1948], 20: "The French think their streets better illuminated than any others in the universe; but those of London exceed them greatly. Paris is lighted by Lanthorns of a bad green glass in small panes set in lead. These are hung across the streets just in the middle by slender cords about sixteen feet above ones head; so that the lights are not of half the benefit to walkers as ours are."

wall, waiting, as I imagined, for a *fiacre*—as they were next the door, I thought they had a prior right; so edged myself up within a yard or little more of them, and quietly took my stand—I was in black, and scarce seen.

The lady next me was a tall lean figure of a woman of about thirty-six; the other of the same size and make, of about forty; there was no mark of wife or widow in any one part of either of them—they seem'd to be two upright vestal sisters,[4] unsapp'd by caresses, unbroke in upon by tender salutations: I could have wish'd to have made them happy—their happiness was destin'd, that night, to come from another quarter.

A low voice, with a good turn of expression, and sweet cadence at the end of it, begg'd for a twelve-sous piece betwixt them, for the love of heaven. I thought it singular, that a beggar should fix the quota of an alms—and that the sum should be twelve times as much as what is usually given in the dark. They both seemed astonish'd at it as much as myself.—Twelve sous! said one—a twelve-sous piece! said the other—and made no reply.

The poor man said, He knew not how to ask less of ladies of their rank; and bow'd down his head to the ground.

Poo! said they—we have no money.

The beggar remained silent for a moment or two, and renew'd his supplication.

Do not, my fair young ladies, said he, stop your good ears against me—Upon my word, honest man! said the younger, we have no change—Then God bless you, said the poor man, and multiply those joys which you can give to others without change!—I observed the elder sister put her hand into her pocket—I'll see, said she, if I have a sous.—A sous! give twelve, said the supplicant; Nature has been bountiful to you, be bountiful to a poor man.

I would, friend, with all my heart, said the younger, if I had it.

My fair charitable! said he, addressing himself to the elder—What is it but your goodness and humanity which makes your bright eyes so sweet, that they outshine the morning even in this dark passage? and what was it which made the Marquis de Santerre[5] and his brother say so much of you both as they just pass'd by?

---

[4] Cf. *TS,* IX.17.769, where Tristram relates his poverty: "I keep neither man or boy, or horse, or cow . . . or any thing that can eat or drink, except a thin poor piece of a Vestal (to keep my fire in) and who has generally as bad an appetite as myself." The vestal priestesses were virgins assigned to keep a perpetual fire burning in honour of Vesta, goddess of hearth and home.

[5] Milic, 121, n. 4, suggests a pun, "sans terres," i.e., without substance. Cf. Thicknesse, *Useful Hints,* 29: "[Smollett] and I are *sauntering* fellows [cf. below, p. 154, "Count de Faineant" and n. 12], a word I apprehend made . . . from two appertaining to this, i.e. *sans-terre,* men *without land* or property, and therefore live upon other mens labours, like soldiers and the *Reviewers,* because they have none of their own." Santerre is, however, a part of Picardie, south of Amiens, so Sterne possibly had in mind a real place or person.

The two ladies seemed much affected; and impulsively at the same time they both put their hands into their pocket, and each took out a twelve-sous piece.

The contest betwixt them and the poor supplicant was no more—it was continued betwixt themselves, which of the two should give the twelve-sous piece in charity—and to end the dispute, they both gave it together, and the man went away.

THE RIDDLE EXPLAINED.
PARIS.

I Stepp'd hastily after him: it was the very man whose success in asking charity of the women before the door of the hotel had so puzzled me—and I found at once his secret, or at least the basis of it—'twas flattery.

Delicious essence! how refreshing art thou to nature! how strongly are all its powers and all its weaknesses on thy side! how sweetly dost thou mix with the blood, and help it through the most difficult and tortuous passages to the heart!

The poor man, as he was not straighten'd for time, had given it here in a larger dose: 'tis certain he had a way of bringing it into less form, for the many sudden cases he had to do with in the streets; but how he contrived to correct, sweeten, concentre, and qualify it—I vex not my spirit with the inquiry—it is enough, the beggar gain'd two twelve-sous pieces—and they can best tell the rest, who have gain'd much greater matters by it.

PARIS.

WE get forwards in the world not so much by doing services, as receiving them: you take a withering twig, and put it in the ground; and then you water it, because you have planted it.[1]

Mons. Le Compte de B****, merely because he had done me one kindness in the affair of my passport, would go on and do me another, the few days he was at Paris, in making me known to a few people of rank; and they were to present me to others, and so on.[2]

I had got master of my *secret,* just in time to turn these honours to some little account; otherwise, as is commonly the case, I should have din'd or supp'd a single time or two round, and then by *translating* French looks and attitudes into plain English, I should presently have seen, that I had got hold of the *couvert** of some more entertaining guest; and in course, should have resigned all my places one after another, merely upon the principle that I could not keep them.—As it was, things did not go much amiss.

I had the honour of being introduced to the old Marquis de B****: in days of yore he had signaliz'd himself by some small feats of chivalry in the *Cour d'amour,*[3] and had dress'd himself out to the idea of tilts and tournaments ever since—the Marquis de B**** wish'd to have it thought the affair was somewhere else than in his brain. "He could like to take a trip to England," and ask'd much of the English ladies. Stay where you are, I beseech you, Mons. le Marquis, said I—Les Messrs. Anglois can scarce get a kind look from them as it is.—The Marquis invited me to supper.

Mons. P**** the farmer-general[4] was just as inquisitive about our taxes.— They were very considerable, he heard—If we knew but how to collect them, said I, making him a low bow.

---

*Plate, napkin, knife, fork, and spoon.

---

[1] Stout, 261, believes Sterne "may be indebted to the parable of the twig in Ezekiel 17:1– 10, which is planted and watered, and then withers."

[2] Sterne resided in Paris from January through mid-July 1762; cf. Cash, *LY,* 132*ff.* Except for Mons. P**** (the farmer-general; see n. 4), we cannot identify the other characters invoked.

[3] The Court of Love.

[4] Almost certainly an allusion to Alexandre-Jean-Joseph Le Riche de la Popelinière (1692– 1762), the "wealthiest of the *fermiers*" (see Cash, *LY* 132); and *Letters,* 155: "Monsieur Popelinière . . . is the richest of all the farmer[s general]; he did me the honour last night to send me an invitation to his house, while I stayed here—that is, to his music and table." The *fermiers généraux* (farmers general) were tax collectors, a lucrative enterprise in eighteenth-century France.

I could never have been invited to Mons. P*****'s concerts upon any other terms.

I had been misrepresented to Madame de Q*** as an *esprit*[5]—Madame de Q*** was an *esprit* herself; she burnt with impatience to see me, and hear me talk. I had not taken my seat, before I saw she did not care a sous whether I had any wit or no—I was let in, to be convinced she had.—I call heaven to witness I never once open'd the door of my lips.

Madame de Q*** vow'd to every creature she met, "She had never had a more improving conversation with a man in her life."

There are three epochas in the empire of a French-woman—She is coquette—then deist—then *devôte*:[6] the empire during these is never lost—she only changes her subjects: when thirty-five years and more have unpeopled her dominions of the slaves of love, she re-peoples it with slaves of infidelity—and then with the slaves of the Church.

Madame de V*** was vibrating betwixt the first of these epochas: the colour of the rose was shading fast away—she ought to have been a deist five years before the time I had the honour to pay my first visit.

She placed me upon the same sopha with her, for the sake of disputing the point of religion more closely.—In short, Madame de V*** told me she believed nothing.

I told Madame de V*** it might be her principle; but I was sure it could not be her interest to level the outworks,[7] without which I could not conceive how such a citadel as hers could be defended—that there was not a more dangerous thing in the world, than for a beauty to be a deist—that it was a debt I owed my creed, not to conceal it from her—that I had not been five minutes sat upon the sopha besides her, but I had begun to form designs—and what is it, but the sentiments

---

[5] See p. 19, n. 5. There is probably a bawdy play on "Madame de Q***," *cul* (backside, bottom), being the way Q sounds in French. Stout, 263, suggests two senses for *Bel Esprit*: a free-thinker, on the one hand, a "Genius refined by Conversation, Reflection, and the Reading of the most polite Authors" on the other—citing Addison, *Spectator* 160, ed. Bond, 2:127.

[6] Correctly, *dévote*, a religious enthusiast. Sterne seems to be using "coquette" and "deist" in a commonplace manner, marking the change from alluring with their faces to alluring with their freethinking. Cole's observation is pertinent, however: "the modish French Taste, in philosophizing Revelation out of Doors . . . is the *Ton des François* now almost universally among Men of Fashion, & not uncommon among the Ladies" (*Journey* 63–64). For *dévote*, cf. Smollett, *Travels*, letter 5, 1:74–75: "The character of a *devotee* . . . is very common here. You see them walking to and from church at all hours, in their hoods and long camblet cloaks, with a slow pace, demure aspect, and downcast eye." Tristram comments that Janatone "has a little of the *devote*: but that, sir, is a terce to a nine in your favour" (*TS* VII.9.590).

[7] Cf. sermon 45, "The ingratitude of Israel": "Charles the Second . . . has almost demolished the out-works of religion" (*Sermons* 4:421).

of religion, and the persuasion they had existed in her breast, which could have check'd them as they rose up.

We are not adamant, said I, taking hold of her hand—and there is need of all restraints, till age in her own time steals in and lays them on us—but, my dear lady, said I, kissing her hand—'tis too—too soon—

I declare I had the credit all over Paris of unperverting Madame de V***.—She affirmed to Mons. D***[8] and the Abbe M***,[9] that in one half hour I had said more for revealed religion, than all their Encyclopedia[10] had said against it—I was listed directly into Madame de V***'s *Coterie*[11]—and she put off the epocha of deism for two years.

I remember it was in this *Coterie*, in the middle of a discourse, in which I was shewing the necessity of a *first cause*, that the young Count de Faineant[12] took me by the hand to the furthest corner of the room, to tell me my *solitaire*[13] was pinn'd too strait about my neck—It should be *plus badinant*,[14] said the Count, looking down upon his own—but a word, Mons. Yorick, to *the wise*—

—And from the wise, Mons. Le Compte, replied I, making him a bow—*is enough*.

The Count de Faineant embraced me with more ardour than ever I was embraced by mortal man.

---

[8] Denis Diderot (1713–1784), philosopher, novelist, satirist, and dramatist; editor from 1745 of the *Encyclopédie,* to which he contributed articles in both art and science. For Sterne's acquaintance with him, see Cash, *LY,* 138–39. One doubts Diderot gave in as easily as Yorick suggests, but it is interesting to note that among the works Sterne instructed his bookseller to send to Diderot is "Tillotson's Sermons" (*Letters* 166); for Tillotson's importance to Sterne's theology, see *Notes to Sermons,* 5:24–25. Diderot's admiration of *TS* is best indicated by his posthumously published *Jacques le fataliste* (1796), perhaps the most significant aesthetic engagement with Sterne in the century.

[9] Usually taken to be Abbé André Morellet (1727–1819). Cash, *LY,* 139, notes that Sterne was less than fair to the abbé: "Morellet was a conservative in his theology. He wrote most of the theological articles in the *Encyclopédie,* such as those on 'God' and 'Soul,' maintaining an orthodox, though liberal position . . . ."

[10] I.e., *L'Encyclopédie, ou Dictionnaire raisonné des sciences, des arts et des métiers,* ed. by Diderot and d'Alembert in 35 volumes between 1751 and 1780. An outgrowth of one of Sterne's favorite sources, Ephraim Chambers's *Cyclopædia* (see *Notes to TS* 3:25 and passim), it can perhaps best be epitomized, in Keymer's fine phrase, as "the great dictionary-in-progress of Enlightenment thought" (158).

[11] See p. 70, n. 9.

[12] Loafer, lounger, idler (correctly, *fainéant*). Perhaps Sterne anticipates the fame the type would achieve in the nineteenth century, although *OED* lists examples from the early seventeenth century.

[13] See p. 139, n. 4.

[14] More loosely, with a lighter touch.

For three weeks together, I was of every man's opinion I met.—*Pardi! ce Mons. Yorick a autant d'esprit que nous autres.*——*Il raisonne bien,* said another.—*C'est un bon enfant,*[15] said a third.—And at this price I could have eaten and drank and been merry all the days of my life at Paris; but 'twas a dishonest *reckoning*—I grew ashamed of it—it was the gain of a slave—every sentiment of honour revolted against it—the higher I got, the more was I forced upon my *beggarly system*—the better the *Coterie*—the more children of Art—I languish'd for those of Nature:[16] and one night, after a most vile prostitution of myself to half a dozen different people, I grew sick—went to bed—order'd La Fleur to get me horses in the morning to set out for Italy.[17]

---

[15] By heaven! This Yorick's as witty as we are.——He reasons well . . . . He's a charming fellow.

[16] Cf. *Letters,* 179: "My wife and daughter are arrived [from England]—the latter does nothing but look out of the window, and complain of the torment of being frizled [curled].—I wish she may ever remain a child of nature—I hate children of art." It is a commonplace distinction of the age, and appears often in Sterne's writings.

[17] Stout, 267: "On his second trip abroad, Sterne left Paris to travel to Italy in late October or early November 1765"; see *Letters,* 260–62.

MARIA.
MOULINES.

I NEVER felt what the distress of plenty was in any one shape till now—to travel it through the Bourbonnois, the sweetest part of France—in the hey-day of the vintage, when Nature is pouring her abundance into every one's lap, and every eye is lifted up—a journey through each step of which music beats time to *Labour,* and all her children are rejoicing as they carry in their clusters—to pass through this with my affections flying out, and kindling at every group before me—and every one of 'em was pregnant with adventures.

Just heaven!—it would fill up twenty volumes[1]—and alas! I have but a few small pages left of this to croud it into—and half of these must be taken up with the poor Maria my friend, Mr. Shandy, met with near Moulines.[2]

The story he had told of that disorder'd maid affect'd me not a little in the reading; but when I got within the neighbourhood where she lived, it returned so strong into my mind, that I could not resist an impulse which prompted me to go half a league out of the road to the village where her parents dwelt to enquire after her.

'Tis going, I own, like the Knight of the Woeful Countenance,[3] in quest of melancholy adventures—but I know not how it is, but I am never so perfectly conscious of the existence of a soul within me, as when I am entangled in them.

---

[1] Cf. *TS,* VII.42.646, where Sterne describes rural abundance in similar terms: "There is nothing more pleasing to a traveller——or more terrible to travel-writers, than a large rich plain . . . ; and presents nothing to the eye, but one unvaried picture of plenty: for after they have once told you that 'tis delicious! or delightful! (as the case happens)—that the soil was grateful, and that nature pours out all her abundance, &c." Both travelers find more to write about by moving from the landscape to the people who inhabit it; see *TS,* VII.43, in Appendix below, pp. 246–48. And cf. *Letters,* 235 (March 16, 1765): "In the beginning of September I quit England, that I may avail myself of the time of vintage, when all nature is joyous, and so saunter philosophically for a year or so, on the other side the Alps."

[2] Cf. *TS,* IX.24, in Appendix, pp. 248–49. Moulins is in the historic province of Bourbonnais (the department of Allier today), on the river Loire, some 160 miles south of Paris. In mentioning "Moulines" Sterne, perhaps inadvertently, reminds us of the abrupt unsentimental ending of the meeting with Maria in *TS.*

[3] Cf. Stout, 270: "After his encounter with the funeral cortege, Don Quixote is dubbed by Sancho 'The Knight of the woeful Figure'" (*Don Quixote,* I.III.5; 1:171). The Motteux-Ozell translation that Sterne used (see *Notes* to *TS* 3:15), always translates Cervantes's "*Triste Figura*" as "woeful Figure"; the only literary appearance of "woeful countenance" we found is in Edward Ward's versification, *The Life and Notable Adventures of That Renown'd Knight, Don Quixote* (1710–1711), but the phrase may have already become commonplace. Sterne's identification with Don Quixote is evident in a letter he wrote in June 1760: "These . . . many Kicks, Cuffs & Bastinados . . . are begining to make me sick of this foolish humour of mine of sallying forth into this wide & wicked world to redress wrongs, &c. of wch I shall

The old mother came to the door, her looks told me the story before she open'd her mouth—She had lost her husband; he had died, she said, of anguish, for the loss of Maria's senses about a month before.—She had feared at first, she added, that it would have plunder'd her poor girl of what little understanding was left—but, on the contrary, it had brought her more to herself—still she could not rest—her poor daughter, she said, crying, was wandering somewhere about the road—

—Why does my pulse beat languid as I write this? and what made La Fleur, whose heart seem'd only to be tuned to joy, to pass the back of his hand twice across his eyes, as the woman stood and told it? I beckon'd to the postilion to turn back into the road.

When we had got within half a league of Moulines, at a little opening in the road leading to a thicket, I discovered poor Maria sitting under a poplar—she was sitting with her elbow in her lap, and her head leaning on one side within her hand—a small brook ran at the foot of the tree.[4]

I bid the postilion go on with the chaise to Moulines—and La Fleur to bespeak my supper—and that I would walk after him.

She was dress'd in white, and much as my friend described her, except that her hair hung loose, which before was twisted within a silk net.—She had, superadded likewise to her jacket, a pale green ribband which fell across her shoulder to the waist; at the end of which hung her pipe.—Her goat had been as faithless as her lover; and she had got a little dog in lieu of him, which she had kept tied by a string to her girdle; as I look'd at her dog, she drew him towards her with the string.—"Thou shalt not leave me, Sylvio," said she.[5] I look'd in Maria's eyes, and

---

repent as sorely as ever Sancha Panca did of his in following . . . Don Quixote thro thick & thin—but as the poor fellow apologised for it,—so must I. 'it was my vile fortune & my Errantry & that's all that can be said on't'" (*Letters*, 116; see also 233, where these words are repeated almost verbatim; the source is *Don Quixote*, II.III.33; 3:302).

[4] Perhaps no scene in eighteenth-century literature has been illustrated more than this meeting between Maria and Yorick. Cf. Tom Keymer, "Marvell, Thomas Hollis, and Sterne's Maria: Parody in *A Sentimental Journey*," *Shandean* 5 (1993):11: "Doleful images disseminated from the hands of such painters as Angelica Kauffmann and Joseph Wright of Derby combined to make Maria a veritable icon of sentimental distress, and her place in the public imagination is attested by the twenty representations of her plight that had been exhibited or engraved by 1819." See Gerard, "Benevolent Vision," 533–74; "Sterne in Wedgwood: 'Poor Maria' and the 'Bourbonnais Shepherd,'" *Shandean* 12 (2001):78–88; and "Sterne Illustrated," *Shandean* 14 (2003):76–80.

[5] Keymer, "Marvell," argues convincingly that the episode should be read as a parodic allusion to Andrew Marvell's "Nymph Complaining for the Death of Her Faun": "Sterne quite clearly plays on the specifically Marvellian precedent . . . ["in which lost love is poignantly recapitulated or renewed by the loss of a pet"]. Abandoned first by her lover and then by her goat, and now clinging obsessively to her lapdog 'Sylvio' [the unfaithful swain in Marvell], Maria suffers a comic intensification of the nymph's misfortune . . . . Once we take

saw she was thinking more of her father than of her lover or her little goat; for as she utter'd them the tears trickled down her cheeks.

I sat down close by her; and Maria let me wipe them away as they fell with my handkerchief.—I then steep'd it in my own—and then in hers—and then in mine—and then I wip'd hers again—and as I did it, I felt such undescribable emotions within me, as I am sure could not be accounted for from any combinations of matter and motion.[6]

I am positive I have a soul; nor can all the books with which materialists have pester'd the world ever convince me of the contrary.[7]

---

these hints, it becomes hard to think of Maria as simply an instance of picturesque distress, or even as the object of some mildly improper rapture. She becomes instead an instance of parody, an ironically debased version of the grieving nymph" (15–16).

[6] Keymer, "Marvell," 13–14, calls attention to the probable double entendre of "undescribable emotions" by comparing them to the "multiple 'Emotions' felt by Fielding's Parson Tickletext as he contemplates the eroticism of Richardson's *Pamela* [*Joseph Andrews and Shamela*, ed. Douglas Brooks (Oxford: Oxford UP, 1970), 322]" and also the "purient questioning with which Widow Wadman asks, of the wound to Toby's groin: 'Was motion bad for it?'" (*TS* IX.26.792). Cf. above, "little friction" (p. 5); and the "motion" of the *"Desobligeant,"* which attracts the attention of the *"inquisitive traveller"* (p. 17).

[7] See above, p. 5, and n. 3. Significantly, the same ambiguities inhere in both passages. The anonymous editor of the 1803 edition, always disturbed by Sterne's perceived immorality, comments: "In this instance our author's conviction . . . seems to arise more from the immediate impulse of sensibility, than a steady and well grounded belief and reliance on the important truths of revealed religion; had he thought more seriously, he would doubtless have drawn his conviction from a purer fountain" (186).

MARIA.

WHEN Maria had come a little to herself, I ask'd her if she remember'd a pale thin person of a man who had sat down betwixt her and her goat about two years before?[1] She said, she was unsettled much at that time, but remember'd it upon two accounts—that ill as she was she saw the person pitied her; and next, that her goat had stolen his handkerchief, and she had beat him for the theft—she had wash'd it, she said, in the brook, and kept it ever since in her pocket to restore it to him in case she should ever see him again, which, she added, he had half promised her. As she told me this, she took the handkerchief out of her pocket to let me see it; she had folded it up neatly in a couple of vine leaves, tied round with a tendril—on opening it, I saw an S mark'd in one of the corners.

She had since that, she told me, stray'd as far as Rome, and walk'd round St. Peter's once—and return'd back—that she found her way alone across the Apennines—had travell'd over all Lombardy without money—and through the flinty roads of Savoy without shoes—how she had borne it, and how she had got supported, she could not tell—but *God tempers the wind,* said Maria, to the shorn lamb.[2]

Shorn indeed! and to the quick, said I; and wast thou in my own land, where I have a cottage, I would take thee to it and shelter thee:[3] thou shouldst eat of my own bread, and drink of my own cup[4]—I would be kind to thy Sylvio—in all thy weaknesses and wanderings I would seek after thee and bring thee back—when the sun went down I would say my prayers, and when I had done thou shouldst

---

[1] For Tristram's encounter with Maria, see Appendix, pp. 248–49.

[2] Stout, 272–73: "a rendering of the French proverb 'A brebis tondue Dieu mesure le vent' (which George Herbert had translated, 'To a close shorne sheep God gives wind by Measure' *Outlandish Proverbs* [London, 1640], No. 861)." Cf. "Rabelaisian Fragment," 1090: "the aforesaid Tears, do you mind, did so temper the Wind that was rising upon the aforesaid Discourse."
Gerald P. Mander (*TLS* [July 17, 1937], 528), notes that the proverb was sufficiently well known in 1750 to be used in a card game for English children. And Keymer, 159, finds it recorded as a proverb ("Dieu mesure le froid à la brebis tondue") by Henri Estienne, *Les premices* (1593), 47, who adds that "aucuns disent *mesure le vent,* non pas *mesure le froid.*"

[3] Sterne several times pictures Eliza with him in his "thatched cottage," i.e., Shandy Hall, in Coxwold; e.g., *BJ,* April 16 and 27; and especially June 7 and 29, in which he describes improvements to the interior of his "cottage." Clearly he thought a "cottage" a romantic setting.

[4] Cf. p. 161 and n. 2. In what follows, Keymer, 159, seems correct in hearing echoes of Isaiah 56:7: "Even them will I bring to my holy mountain, and make them joyful in my house of prayer"; and Psalm 141:2: "Let my prayer be set forth before thee as incense; and the lifting up of my hands as the evening sacrifice."

play thy evening song upon thy pipe, nor would the incense of my sacrifice be worse accepted for entering heaven along with that of a broken heart.

Nature melted within me, as I utter'd this; and Maria observing, as I took out my handkerchief, that it was steep'd too much already to be of use, would needs go wash it in the stream.—And where will you dry it, Maria? said I—I'll dry it in my bosom, said she—'twill do me good.

And is your heart still so warm, Maria? said I.

I touch'd upon the string on which hung all her sorrows—she look'd with wistful disorder for some time in my face; and then, without saying any thing, took her pipe, and play'd her service to the Virgin—The string I had touch'd ceased to vibrate[5]—in a moment or two Maria returned to herself—let her pipe fall—and rose up.

And where are you going, Maria? said I.—She said to Moulines.—Let us go, said I, together.—Maria put her arm within mine, and lengthening the string, to let the dog follow—in that order we entered Moulines.

---

[5] A favorite image for both Sterne and the century, although its precise significance has been debated; see, esp., John A. Dussinger, "Yorick and the 'Eternal Fountain of our Feelings,'" in *Psychology and Literature in the Eighteenth Century,* ed. Christopher Fox (New York: AMS, 1987), 259–76. Among Sterne's other uses, see *TS,* II.12.131: "the action [Toby and the fly] set my whole frame into one vibration of most pleasurable sensation"; IV.1.326: "The moment I pronounced the words, I could perceive an attempt towards a vibration in the strings, about the region of the heart"; and IX.24.781: "I was in the most perfect state of bounty and good will; and felt the kindliest harmony vibrating within me, with every oscillation of the chaise alike," a moment Tristram describes just before hearing "the sweetest notes I ever heard" from Maria's pipe (see Appendix, p. 248).

Cf. the climactic statement of the image, p. 163, the "great SENSORIUM of the world! which vibrates, if a hair of our heads but falls upon the ground."

MARIA.
MOULINES.

THO' I hate salutations and greetings in the market-place,[1] yet when we got into the middle of this, I stopp'd to take my last look and last farewel of Maria.

Maria, tho' not tall, was nevertheless of the first order of fine forms—affliction had touch'd her looks with something that was scarce earthly—still she was feminine—and so much was there about her of all that the heart wishes, or the eye looks for in woman, that could the traces be ever worn out of her brain, and those of Eliza's out of mine, she should *not only eat of my bread and drink of my own cup,* but Maria should lay in my bosom, and be unto me as a daughter.[2]

Adieu, poor luckless maiden!—imbibe the oil and wine which the compassion of a stranger, as he journieth on his way, now pours into thy wounds—the being who has twice bruised thee can only bind them up for ever.[3]

---

[1] The scribes and Pharisees, according to the Gospel writers, "love salutations in the marketplaces" (Mark 12:38; see also Matthew 23:7, Luke 11:43, 20:46).

[2] Cf. 2 Samuel 12:3: "But the poor man had nothing, save one little ewe lamb, which he had bought and nourished up: and it grew up together with him, and with his children; it did eat of his own meat, and drank of his own cup, and lay in his bosom, and was unto him as a daughter." The verse (and Nathan's entire parable awakening David to his guilt in the murder of Uriah) was a favorite of Sterne. He had already paraphrased the verse twice in *ASJ;* see p. 159 and n. 4, and p. 58.

Lest we take the encounter with Maria too seriously, however, cf. Hester Thrale's comment: "I remember many years ago, when Susan & Sophia came home one Time from Kensington School . . . they used to repeat some Stuff in an odd Tone of Voice, & laugh obstreperously . . .—upon Enquiry we found out that 'twas the pathetic Passages in *Sterne's Maria* that so diverted & tickled their Spleen" (*Thraliana,* ed. Katharine C. Balderston, 2d ed. [Oxford: Clarendon, 1951] 2:823).

[3] See above, p. 25, n. 2.

THE BOURBONNOIS.[1]

THERE was nothing from which I had painted out for myself so joyous a riot of the affections, as in this journey in the vintage, through this part of France; but pressing through this gate of sorrow to it, my sufferings had totally unfitted me: in every scene of festivity I saw Maria in the back-ground of the piece, sitting pensive under her poplar; and I had got almost to Lyons[2] before I was able to cast a shade across her—

—Dear sensibility! source inexhausted of all that's precious in our joys, or costly in our sorrows![3] thou chainest thy martyr down upon his bed of straw— and 'tis thou who lifts him up to HEAVEN—eternal fountain of our feelings![4]— 'tis here I trace thee—and this is thy divinity which stirs within me——not that, in some sad and sickening moments, *"my soul shrinks back upon herself, and startles at destruction"*[5]—mere pomp of words![6]—but that I feel some generous joys

---

[1] I.e., the region and former province in southeast France.

[2] Yorick is traveling in a southeast direction; Lyons is about 90 miles from Moulins.

[3] Cf. *Letters*, 395–96 (September 27, 1767): "my Sentimental Journey will, I dare say, convince you that my feelings are from the heart, and that that heart is not of the worst of molds—praised be God for my sensibility! Though it has often made me wretched, yet I would not exchange it for all the pleasures the grossest sensualist ever felt."

[4] Cf. above, p. 63, n. 10. Sterne's fondness for the fountain metaphor may have a scriptural basis in "fountain of life" (Proverbs 13:14, 14:27, Psalm 36.9, Revelation 21:6).

[5] Sterne borrows from Cato's famous soliloquy on death in Addison's *Cato* (1713), (eds. Christine Dunn Henderson and Mark E. Yellin [Indianapolis: Liberty Fund, 2004], 88):

> It must be so—Plato, thou reason'st well!—
> Else whence this pleasing hope, this fond desire,
> This longing after immortality?
> Or whence this secret dread, and inward horror,
> Of falling into nought? why shrinks the soul
> Back on herself, and startles at destruction?
> 'Tis the divinity that stirs within us;
> 'Tis heav'n itself, that points out an hereafter,
> And intimates eternity to man. (V.i.1–9)

[6] Stout, 278, is useful in noting Johnson's comment on *Cato* in the "Preface to Shakespeare"—"its hopes and fears communicate no vibration to the heart"—but in doing so, he fails to recognize that Johnson shared with his age an enormously high regard for this play: "what voice or what gesture can hope to add dignity or force to the soliloquy of *Cato*. . . . We find in *Cato* innumerable beauties which enamour us of its authour, but we see nothing that acquaints us with human sentiments . . . . *Cato* affords a splendid exhibition of artificial and fictional manners, and delivers just and noble sentiments . . . but its hopes and fears communicate no vibration to the heart" (*Johnson on Shakespeare*, ed. Arthur Sherbo [New Haven: Yale UP, 1968], 1:79, 84).

Sterne's quarrel, in fact, seems not with Addison's style, but with Cato's argument that our fear of death creates our belief in God. Against this, Sterne argues that we bear witness

and generous cares beyond myself—all comes from thee, great—great SENSO-
RIUM[7] of the world! which vibrates, if a hair of our heads but falls upon the
ground, in the remotest desert of thy creation.[8]—Touch'd with thee, Eugenius
draws my curtain when I languish—hears my tale of symptoms, and blames the
weather for the disorder of his nerves.[9] Thou giv'st a portion of it sometimes to

---

to God in our generous feelings (for others) more than in our cringing fears (for ourselves).
While "pomp of words" is, perhaps, a commonplace, its appearance in Nicholas Rowe's
The Fair Penitent may have been in Sterne's mind along with *Cato*, since the context—
impending death and judgment—is similar; Calista is asked by her father: "Hast thou e'er
dared to meditate on death? / . . . 'Tis not the stoic's lessons got by rote, / The pomp of
words, and pedant dissertations / That can sustain thee in that hour of terror" (act V, ll. 77,
80–82; ed. Malcolm Goldstein [Lincoln: U of Nebraska P, 1969], 63).

That Sterne's argument—we awaken to God's presence through our generous feelings—
is well within orthodox boundaries is suggested by Sterne's connecting generosity to the
"*care*-fulness" of God, evidenced in the providentialist passage that immediately follows;
see below, n. 8.

[7] *OED* cites Sterne's use in *TS*, II.10.125, as its first example of playful usage: "in non-techni-
cal writing (sometimes for 'brain' or 'mind')." Sterne likes the word, repeating it in *TS*,
II.19.174.22, 178.21, III.38.273.10, and IX.26.793.21. His intent in this passage, however,
may be more serious. Useful contexts are provided by Addison, *Spectator* 565 (4:531–32),
recalling Newton's definition: "the noblest and most exalted way of considering this infinite
Space [that is God] is that of Sir *Isaac Newton*, who calls it the *Sensorium* of the Godhead.
Brutes and Men have their . . . little *Sensoriums*, by which they apprehend the Presence, and
perceive the Actions of a few Objects that lie contiguous to them. . . . But as God Almighty
cannot but perceive and know every thing in which he resides, Infinite Space gives room to
Infinite Knowledge . . ."; and Adam Smith's cogent summary of the Cartesian/platonic position in *The Theory of Moral Sentiments*, ed. D. D. Raphael and A. L. Macfie (Oxford: Oxford
UP, 1976), 300: "In the divine nature . . . benevolence or love was the sole principle of
action, and directed the exertion of all the other attributes. The wisdom of the Deity was
employed in finding out the means for bringing about those ends which his goodness suggested, as his infinite power was exerted to execute them. . . . The whole perfection and virtue
of the human mind consisted in some resemblance or participation of the divine perfections . . . . It was by actions of charity and love only that we could imitate, as became us, the
conduct of God . . . ." Sterne's point: God's "sensibility," manifested as providential care for
the weak and the pitiful, is a model for human virtue. See J. T. Parnell, "A Story Painted to the
Heart? *Tristram Shandy* and Sentimentalism Reconsidered," *Shandean* 9 (1997):122–35.

[8] Sterne alludes to the most fundamental providential assertion in Scripture, Matthew
10:29–31: "Are not two sparrows sold for a farthing? and one of them shall not fall on the
ground without your Father. But the very hairs of your head are all numbered. Fear ye not
therefore, ye are of more value than many sparrows" (cf. Luke 12:7). Behind the verses are
several Old Testament versions, e.g., 1 Samuel 14:45, 2 Samuel 14:11, 1 Kings 1:52.

[9] Cf. *TS*, I.12.33, where Yorick's deathbed is attended by Eugenius (i.e., Hall-Stevenson, for
whom see above, p. 75, n. 12): "A few hours before *Yorick* breath'd his last, *Eugenius* stept
in with an intent to take his . . . last farewell of him: . . . drawing *Yorick*'s curtain, and asking
how he felt . . . ."

Sterne also glances here at Hall-Stevenson's hypochondria; cf. Cash, *EMY*, 182–83; *Letters*, 139–41.

the roughest peasant who traverses the bleakest mountains—he finds the lacerated lamb of another's[10] flock—This moment I behold him leaning with his head against his crook, with piteous inclination looking down upon it—Oh! had I come one moment sooner!—it bleeds to death—his gentle heart bleeds with it—

Peace to thee, generous swain!—I see thou walkest off with anguish—but thy joys shall balance it—for happy is thy cottage—and happy is the sharer of it—and happy are the lambs which sport about you.

---

[10] The operative word is "another's," ensuring the lack of self-interest in the peasant's feelings.

THE SUPPER.

A SHOE coming loose from the fore-foot of the thill-horse,[1] at the beginning of the ascent of mount Taurira,[2] the postilion dismounted, twisted the shoe off, and put it in his pocket; as the ascent was of five or six miles, and that horse our main dependence, I made a point of having the shoe fasten'd on again, as well as we could; but the postilion had thrown away the nails, and the hammer in the chaise-box, being of no great use without them, I submitted to go on.

He had not mounted half a mile higher, when coming to a flinty piece of road, the poor devil lost a second shoe, and from off his other fore-foot; I then got out of the chaise in good earnest; and seeing a house about a quarter of a mile to the left-hand, with a great deal to do, I prevailed upon the postilion to turn up to it. The look of the house, and of every thing about it, as we drew nearer, soon reconciled me to the disaster.—It was a little farm-house surrounded with about twenty acres of vineyard, about as much corn—and close to the house, on one side, was a *potagerie*[3] of an acre and a half, full of every thing which could make plenty in a French peasant's house—and on the other side was a little wood which furnished wherewithal to dress it. It was about eight in the evening when I got to the house—so I left the postilion to manage his point as he could—and for mine, I walk'd directly into the house.

The family consisted of an old grey-headed man and his wife, with five or six sons and sons-in-law and their several wives, and a joyous genealogy out of 'em.

They were all sitting down together to their lentil-soup; a large wheaten loaf was in the middle of the table; and a flaggon of wine at each end of it promised joy thro' the stages of the repast—'twas a feast of love.[4]

The old man rose up to meet me, and with a respectful cordiality would have me sit down at the table; my heart was sat down the moment I enter'd the room;

---

[1] The horse between the shafts (thills) and closest to the carriage (i.e., to the wheels, hence also "the wheeler") in a team of horses.

[2] Mont Tarare, about 30 miles northeast of Lyons.

[3] Kitchen garden (correctly, *potager*).

[4] Sterne glances at the tradition of *agape* in the early church, communal meals known as love feasts that provided fellowship and charity for the poor. The core text is Jude 12; Robert Goadby, *An Illustration of the New Testament* (1760), provides a typical commentary: "*Tertullian* [*Apologeticus* 39] . . . describes these Love Feasts . . . : 'The Nature of our Supper may be known by its Name; for it is called by a Name which signifies *Love*. Whatever we spend therein, we look upon it as so much Gain, seeing we thereby refresh all our Poor. . . . Prayer also concludes the Feast.'" Goadby goes on to add that "the most antient Custom was to observe their Love Feasts towards the Evening" and that they "spread into all Places, wherever the *Christians* lived" as late as the thirteenth century.

Cf. R. F. Brissenden, *Virtue in Distress* (London: Macmillan, 1974); of this chapter and those following, he notes:

so I sat down at once like a son of the family; and to invest myself in the character as speedily as I could, I instantly borrowed the old man's knife, and taking up the loaf cut myself a hearty luncheon;[5] and as I did it I saw a testimony in every eye, not only of an honest welcome, but of a welcome mix'd with thanks that I had not seem'd to doubt it.

Was it this; or tell me, Nature, what else it was which made this morsel so sweet—and to what magick I owe it, that the draught I took of their flaggon was so delicious with it, that they remain upon my palate to this hour?

If the supper was to my taste—the grace which follow'd it was much more so.

The supper and the dance are a simple domestic manifestation of The Lord's Supper . . . in its earlier sense of the feast of love and fellowship. The word used by the Church Fathers to describe this occasion was *agape* . . . .

If *agape* is the informing spirit on this occasion and Yorick the priest its interpreter, *eros* is the inspirer of the next episode and Yorick the jester his attendant minister. . . .

The concluding episode . . . , like the book as a whole, emphasises that man is a sexual creature, and that if his capacity to love not only his fellow men and women but also his God is to be properly understood it must be seen in the light of his sexuality. . . . The incarnation is a sacred occurrence, but it is also, and inescapably, a carnal one. (239–40)

[5] "A thick piece . . . or a hunk" and obsolete, according to the *OED*, s.v. *lunch, sb*. 1.

THE GRACE.[1]

WHEN supper was over, the old man gave a knock upon the table with the haft of his knife—to bid them prepare for the dance: the moment the signal was given, the women and girls ran all together into a back apartment to tye up their hair—and the young men to the door to wash their faces, and change their sabots; and in three minutes every soul was ready upon a little esplanade before the house to begin—The old man and his wife came out last, and, placing me betwixt them, sat down upon a sopha of turf[2] by the door.

The old man had some fifty years ago been no mean performer upon the vielle[3]—and at the age he was then of, touch'd it well enough for the purpose. His wife sung now-and-then a little to the tune—then intermitted—and joined her old man again as their children and grand-children danced before them.

It was not till the middle of the second dance, when, from some pauses in the movement wherein they all seemed to look up, I fancied I could distinguish an elevation of spirit different from that which is the cause or the effect of simple jollity.—In a word, I thought I beheld *Religion* mixing in the dance—but as I had never seen her so engaged, I should have look'd upon it now, as one of the illusions of an imagination which is eternally misleading me, had not the old man, as soon as the dance ended, said, that this was their constant way; and that all his life long he had made it a rule, after supper was over, to call out his family to

---

[1] Cf. Thomas M. Curley, "Sterne's *A Sentimental Journey* and the Tradition of Travel Literature" in *All Before Them: 1660–1780,* ed. John McVeagh (London: Ashfield, 1990), 214: "The account of [Maria] and the Bourbonnais rises to mystical heights of beatific revelation. The sentimental parson becomes a Christlike Good Shepherd and Good Samaritan realizing an ecstatic communion with the 'great SENSORIUM of the world!' and engages in a secularized Eucharistic agape with a pastoral Maria Redemptorix ('thou shouldst eat of my own bread and drink of my own cup') and with peasants at a 'feast of love' . . . ."

[2] *OED*'s sole illustration of the transferred use of *sofa*.

[3] *OED* cites this passage as its first illustration: "A musical instrument with four strings played by means of a small wheel; a hurdy-gurdy."

dance and rejoice; believing, he said, that a chearful and contented mind was the best sort of thanks to heaven that an illiterate peasant could pay—

——Or a learned prelate either, said I.[4]

---

[4] Cf. *TS,* VII.43, and Sterne's description of the return of the Prodigal Son, in sermon 20, both reprinted in Appendix. The notion that religion's "ways are ways of pleasantness, and all her paths are peace" (Proverbs 3:17) is a consistent theme of the Restoration and eighteenth-century Anglican pulpit. Cf. William Burkitt's commentary on Luke 15:23: "upon this great Occasion . . . there was Musick and Dancing. *Learn hence,* That sincere Conversion brings the Soul into a joyful, into a very joyful State and Condition. The Joy that Conversion brings is an holy and spiritual Joy, a solid and substantial Joy, a wonderful and transcendent Joy, an increasing and never-fading Joy. Our Joy on Earth is an earnest of the Joys of Heaven" (*Expository Notes . . . on the New Testament,* 7th ed. [1719]); and W. B. C. Watkins, *Perilous Balance* (Princeton: Princeton UP, 1939), 119: "To a man of Sterne's quick and instinctive physical reactions to emotion it was inevitable that dancing should seem a perfectly natural expression of religious joy; after all, David danced before the Lord." Cash, *Sterne's Comedy of Moral Sentiments* (Pittsburgh: Duquesne UP, 1966), 97–98, sees both passages as reflective of Psalm 100:1–2: "Make a joyful noise unto the Lord, all ye lands. Serve the Lord with gladness: come before his presence with singing."

THE CASE OF DELICACY.

WHEN you have gained the top of mount Taurira, you run presently down to Lyons—adieu then to all rapid movements! 'Tis a journey of caution;[1] and it fares better with sentiments, not to be in a hurry with them; so I contracted with a Voiturin[2] to take his time with a couple of mules, and convey me in my own chaise safe to Turin through Savoy.

Poor, patient, quiet, honest people! fear not; your poverty, the treasury of your simple virtues, will not be envied you by the world, nor will your vallies be invaded by it.—Nature! in the midst of thy disorders, thou art still friendly to the scantiness thou hast created—with all thy great works about thee, little hast thou left to give, either to the scithe or to the sickle—but to that little, thou grantest safety and protection; and sweet are the dwellings which stand so shelter'd.

Let the way-worn traveller vent his complaints upon the sudden turns and dangers of your roads—your rocks—your precipices—the difficulties of getting up—the horrors of getting down—mountains impracticable—and cataracts, which roll down great stones from their summits, and block his road up.[3]—The peasants had been all day at work[4] in removing a fragment of this kind between

---

[1] Cf. Joseph Baretti, *An Account of the Manners and Customs of Italy* (1768), 2:314: "Apropos of mount Cenis, let no one be frightened by the dismal accounts, so frequent in the books of travel-writers, of the bad road over dangerous precipices through Savoy or the Appenines. Those dangerous precipices exist nowhere, but in the imagination of the timorous."

Sterne briefly mentions his own crossing in a letter from Turin (November 15, 1765): "After many difficulties I have got safe & sound—tho eight days in passing the Mountains of Savoy" (*Letters* 263). The weather encountered during the crossing would determine the danger.

[2] Cf. Sharp, *Letters from Italy,* 306–8:

> At *Lyons,* or *Geneva,* the Voiturins, (men who furnish horses for the journey over the *Alps*,) make their demands according to the number of travellers who are on the spot . . . . The price of a voiturin and pair of horses is, generally, from eight to ten or eleven louis (guineas) . . . .
>
> The voiturins, for this sum, defray your charges on the road; they pay for your dinner, supper, and lodging; so that the seven days journey from *Geneva* or *Lyons,* to *Turin,* costs little more than what you contract for with them . . . .

OED cites this passage in *ASJ* as its first illustration, s.v. *voiturin,* 1, but confuses matters when, s.v. *voiturin,* 2, Sterne is cited as the first to use the word to mean a "carriage for hire, a voiture." Sterne would seem to have distinguished between *voiture* and *voiturin,* although clearly they were becoming confused.

[3] Cf. *TS,* VII.29.623: "to behold upon the banks [of the Rhone] . . . vertiginous, the rocks, the mountains, the cataracts, and all the hurry which Nature is in with all her great works about her."

[4] See Constantia Maxwell, *The English Traveller in France 1698–1815* (London: George Routledge, 1932), 28: "In the seventeenth century the French roads were notoriously bad,

St. Michael and Madane;[5] and by the time my Voiturin got to the place, it wanted full two hours of compleating before a passage could any how be gain'd: there was nothing but to wait with patience—'twas a wet and tempestuous night; so that by the delay, and that together, the Voiturin found himself obliged to take up five miles short of his stage at a little decent kind of an inn by the road side.

I forthwith took possession of my bed-chamber—got a good fire—order'd supper; and was thanking heaven it was no worse—when a voiture arrived with a lady in it and her servant-maid.[6]

As there was no other bed-chamber in the house, the hostess, without much nicety, led them into mine, telling them, as she usher'd them in, that there was no body in it but an English gentleman—that there were two good beds in it, and a closet within the room which held another—the accent in which she spoke of this third bed did not say much for it—however, she said, there were three beds, and but three people—and she durst say, the gentleman would do any thing to accommodate matters.—I left not the lady a moment to make a conjecture about it—so instantly made a declaration I would do any thing in my power.

As this did not amount to an absolute surrender of my bed-chamber, I still felt myself so much the proprietor, as to have a right to do the honours of it—so I desired the lady to sit down—pressed her into the warmest seat—call'd for more wood—desired the hostess to enlarge the plan of the supper, and to favour us with the very best wine.

The lady had scarce warm'd herself five minutes at the fire, before she began to turn her head back, and give a look at the beds; and the oftener she cast her eyes that way, the more they return'd perplex'd—I felt for her—and for myself; for in a few minutes, what by her looks, and the case itself, I found myself as much embarrassed as it was possible the lady could be herself.

That the beds we were to lay in were in one and the same room, was enough simply by itself to have excited all this—but the position of them, for they stood parallel, and so very close to each other as only to allow space for a small wicker chair betwixt them, render'd the affair still more oppressive to us—they were fixed up moreover near the fire, and the projection of the chimney on one side, and a large beam which cross'd the room on the other, form'd a kind of recess for

---

but in the eighteenth century they were the best in Europe. . . . It was the corvée system, by which the labour of the peasants was conscripted for the upkeep and construction of the roads, which had been the salvation of the French highways."

[5] Stout, 285: "St. Michel and Modane, two towns (9–10 miles apart) on the river Arc, near the French-Italian border, southwest of Turin."

[6] According to John Macdonald's *Travels, in Various Parts of Europe, Asia, and Africa* (1790), something of this sort happened to John Craufurd of Errol (?1742–1814), a young Scot whom Sterne met in Paris in 1765. Stout, 355, quotes Macdonald's account, but adds that it may have been influenced by Sterne's version.

them that was no way favourable to the nicety of our sensations—if any thing could have added to it, it was, that the two beds were both of 'em so very small, as to cut us off from every idea of the lady and the maid lying together; which in either of them, could it have been feasible, my lying besides them, tho' a thing not to be wish'd, yet there was nothing in it so terrible which the imagination might not have pass'd over without torment.

As for the little room within, it offer'd little or no consolation to us; 'twas a damp cold closet, with a half dismantled window shutter, and with a window which had neither glass or oil paper[7] in it to keep out the tempest of the night. I did not endeavour to stifle my cough when the lady gave a peep into it; so it reduced the case in course to this alternative—that the lady should sacrifice her health to her feelings, and take up with the closet herself, and abandon the bed next mine to her maid—or that the girl should take the closet, &c. &c.

The lady was a Piedmontese of about thirty, with a glow of health in her cheeks.—The maid was a Lyonoise of twenty, and as brisk and lively a French girl as ever moved.—There were difficulties every way—and the obstacle of the stone in the road, which brought us into the distress, great as it appeared whilst the peasants were removing it, was but a pebble to what lay in our ways now—I have only to add, that it did not lessen the weight which hung upon our spirits, that we were both too delicate to communicate what we felt to each other upon the occasion.

We sat down to supper; and had we not had more generous wine to it than a little inn in Savoy could have furnish'd, our tongues had been tied up, till necessity herself had set them at liberty—but the lady having a few bottles of Burgundy in her voiture sent down her Fille de Chambre for a couple of them; so that by the time supper was over, and we were left alone, we felt ourselves inspired with a strength of mind sufficient to talk, at least, without reserve upon our situation. We turn'd it every way, and debated and considered it in all kind of lights in the course of a two hours negociation; at the end of which the articles were settled finally betwixt us, and stipulated for in form and manner of a treaty of peace—and I believe with as much religion and good faith on both sides, as in any treaty which as yet had the honour of being handed down to posterity.

They were as follows:

First. As the right of the bed-chamber is in Monsieur—and he thinking the bed next to the fire to be the warmest, he insists upon the concession on the lady's side of taking up with it.

Granted, on the part of Madame; with a proviso, That as the curtains of that bed are of a flimsy transparent cotton, and appear likewise too scanty to draw close, that the Fille de Chambre, shall fasten up the opening, either by corking

---

[7] Paper made transparent or waterproof by soaking in oil, a cheap substitute for glazing; OED's earliest illustration is from Dickens, Sketches by Boz (1836–1839).

pins,[8] or needle and thread, in such manner as shall be deemed a sufficient barrier on the side of Monsieur.

2dly. It is required on the part of Madame, that Monsieur shall lay the whole night through in his robe de chambre.[9]

Rejected: inasmuch as Monsieur is not worth a robe de chambre; he having nothing in his portmanteau but six shirts and a black silk pair of breeches.

The mentioning the silk pair of breeches made an entire change of the article—for the breeches were accepted as an equivalent for the robe de chambre, and so it was stipulated and agreed upon that I should lay in my black silk breeches all night.

3dly. It was insisted upon, and stipulated for by the lady, that after Monsieur was got to bed, and the candle and fire extinguished, that Monsieur should not speak one single word the whole night.

Granted; provided Monsieur's saying his prayers might not be deem'd an infraction of the treaty.

There was but one point forgot in this treaty, and that was the manner in which the lady and myself should be obliged to undress and get to bed—there was but one way of doing it, and that I leave to the reader to devise; protesting as I do it, that if it is not the most delicate in nature, 'tis the fault of his own imagination—against which this is not my first complaint.[10]

Now when we were got to bed, whether it was the novelty of the situation, or what it was, I know not; but so it was, I could not shut my eyes; I tried this side and that, and turn'd and turn'd again, till a full hour after midnight; when Nature and patience both wearing out—O my God! said I——

—You have broke the treaty, Monsieur, said the lady, who had no more slept than myself.—I begg'd a thousand pardons—but insisted it was no more than an ejaculation[11]—she maintain'd 'twas an entire infraction of the treaty—I maintain'd it was provided for in the clause of the third article.

---

[8] Sterne perhaps deliberately reminds us of *TS,* VIII.9.667, where Mrs. Wadman has the bottom of her night-shift fastened with a corking pin the second night of Uncle Toby's stay in her house, and kicks it out of Bridget's hands the third night.
"A pin of the largest size" (*OED*).

[9] Either the nightgown ("a long loose garment . . . with a wrap-over front and sometimes a roll collar . . . tied with a girdle or sash round the waist . . . . These gowns were worn for ease indoors instead of a coat or frock; never in place of the night-shirt which was the garment worn in bed") or the powdering jacket (gown), which was usually ankle-length or slightly shorter, and wrapped over in front (Cunnington, 73, 219–20); either would have served Madame's purpose.

[10] Cf. *Letters,* 403: "If [*ASJ*] is not thought a chaste book, mercy on them that read it, for they must have warm imaginations indeed!"

[11] Sterne had played on *ejaculation* in *TS,* IX.9.755, where the dramatic apostrophe to Jenny, on the passing of time, that concludes chapter 8 is dismissed in one facetious sentence: "NOW, for what the world thinks of that ejaculation——I would not give a groat."

The lady would by no means give up her point, tho' she weakened her barrier by it; for in the warmth of the dispute, I could hear two or three corking pins fall out of the curtain to the ground.

Upon my word and honour, Madame, said I—stretching my arm out of bed, by way of asseveration—

—(I was going to have added, that I would not have trespass'd against the remotest idea of decorum for the world)—

—But the Fille de Chambre hearing there were words between us, and fearing that hostilities would ensue in course, had crept silently out of her closet, and it being totally dark, had stolen so close to our beds, that she had got herself into the narrow passage which separated them, and had advanc'd so far up as to be in a line betwixt her mistress and me—

So that when I stretch'd out my hand, I caught hold of the Fille de Chambre's

END OF VOL. II.[12]

---

[12] Beginning with the "new" edition of 1768, a dash after "Chambre's" (as in the copyist's ms., it should be noted) marks those subsequent editions set from that version. As Stout notes, the dash, along with, in some instances, the omission of "END OF VOL. II," may tend to affect Sterne's final witticism. Many have written on Sterne's interest in the aposiopesis, which first emerges in the "Rabelaisian Fragment," and then in *TS,* II.6.115–16 (see *Notes* 3:146–47).

CONTINUATION OF
THE BRAMINE'S JOURNAL

This Journal wrote under the fictitious Names of Yorick & Draper—and sometimes of the Bramin & Bramine—but tis a Diary of the miserable feelings[1] of a person separated from a Lady for whose Society he languish'd—

The real Names—are foreigne—& the Acc^t a Copy from a french Mans^t—in M^r S——s hands—but wrote as it is, to cast a Viel over them[2]——There is a Counterpart—which is the Lady's Acc^t what transactions dayly happend—& what Sentiments occupied her mind, during this Separation from her Admirer—these are worth reading—the translator cannot say so much in fav^r of Yoricks—which seem to have little Merit beyond their honesty & truth——

---

[1] Cf. *ASJ*, p. 40, where Sterne labels Smelfungus's (Smollett's) travel-writing, "nothing but the account of his miserable feelings." And cf. below (August 4): "the History of my miserable feelings." That Sterne wrote this phrase at the end of the journal may suggest he was recalling his headnote, or, perhaps more likely, that the headnote was written at this later time, just before Sterne put his journal aside.

[2] Cf. *TS*, III.36.268, where Tristram comments on "the many opinions, transactions and truths which still lie mystically hid under the dark veil of the black [page]." As Cash notes, *LY*, 284–85, this preface is "curious," in that it pretends to anonymity, even while ensuring a clear knowledge of its author. This pseudo-masking has led some critics to believe the *Journal* was designed for publication. Cash believes this unlikely, as do we.

Continuation of
the Bramines Journal.

Sunday Ap: 13.[1]
wrote the last farewel to Eliza by Mʳ Wats (*he saild 23*)[2] who sails this day for
Bombay—inclosed her likewise the Journal kept from the day we parted, to
this——so from hence continue it till the time we meet again—Eliza does the
same, so we shall have mutual testimonies to deliver hereafter to each other, That
the Sun has not more constantly rose & set upon the earth, than We have
thought of & remember'd, what is more chearing than Light itself—eternal Sun-
shine! Eliza!—dark to me is all this world without thee! & most heavily will every
hour pass over my head, till that is come wᶜʰ brings thee, dear Woman back to
Albion. dined with Hall &c—at the brawn's head[3]—the whole Pandæmonium
assembled—supp'd together at Halls—worn out both in body & mind, & paid a
severe reckoning all the night.

Ap: 14.   got up tottering & feeble—Then is it, Eliza, that I feel the want of
thy friendly hand & friendly Council—& yet, with thee beside Me, Thy Bramin
would lose the merit of his virtue—he could not err—but I will take thee upon
any terms, Eliza! I shall be happy here—& I will be so just, so kind to thee, I will
deserve not to be miserable hereafter—a Day dedicated to Abstinence & reflection—& what Object will employ the greatest part of mine—full well does my
Eliza know.—

Munday.   Ap: 15.
worn out with fevers of all kinds but most, by that fever of the heart with wᶜʰ
I'm eternally wasting, & shall waste till I see Eliza again[4]—dreadful Suffering of

---

[1] As Curtis notes, *Letters,* 327, n. 1, Sunday fell on April 12th in 1767; Sterne's misdating
continues throughout the week.

[2] Eliza left London in March, but was still at anchor aboard the *Lord Chatham* in the
Downs, awaiting "the first fair Wind" (Cash, *LY* 280; quoting *Public Advertiser,* March 30).
The ship finally sailed on April 3 (*LY* 282–83). The parenthetical phrase seems to have been
inserted at a later time; we assume Sterne gave Mr. Wats (not identified) a packet to deliver
to Eliza in India and discovered later that he had sailed on April 23. Hereafter, "1767" is
assumed as the year of correspondence and will not be indicated.

[3] Hall-Stevenson was in London at this time, but we assume the "whole Pandæmonium"
(Sterne's usage predates the occasions of figurative use cited by *OED*) refers to Sterne's London acquaintances, similar to, but not identical with, his Yorkshire friends, labeled the
Demoniacs (see Cash, *EMY* 181–95). The "brawn's head," possibly a London tavern,
remains unidentified.

[4] This is the first of several passages in *BJ* that also appear in a letter Sterne may have written
to his wife (if we believe Lydia Sterne) more than twenty-five years earlier. For a discussion of

15 Months!—it may be more—great Controuler of Events! surely thou wilt proportion this, to my Strength, and to that of my Eliza. pass'd the whole afternoon in reading her Letters, & reducing them to the order in which they were wrote to me—staid the whole evening at home—no pleasure or Interest in either Society or Diversions—What a change, my dear Girl, hast thou made in me!—but the Truth is, thou hast only turn'd the tide of my passions a new way—they flow, Eliza to thee—& ebb from every other Object in this world— & Reason tells me they do right—for my heart has rated thee at a Price,[5] that all the world is not rich enough to purchase thee from me, at.   In a high fever all the night.

Ap: 16.   and got up so ill, I could not go to M[rs] James[6] as I had promissed her—took James's Powder[7] however—& leand the whole day with my head upon My hand; sitting most dejectedly at the Table with my Eliza's Picture[8] before me—sympathizing & soothing me—O my Bramine! my Friend! my——Help-mate![9]—for that, (if I'm a prophet) is the Lot mark'd out for thee,—& such I consider thee now, & thence it is, Eliza, I Share so righteously with thee, in all the

---

this problem, see the Introduction, pp. xv–xvi; *Letters*, 10–16; Margaret R. B. Shaw, *Laurence Sterne: The Making of a Humorist* (London: Richards Press, 1957); Duke Maskell, "The Authenticity of Sterne's First Recorded Letter," *N&Q* 215 (1970):303–7; and the detailed summary by Cash, *EMY*, 81–82. To the abundance of suppositions surrounding the issue, most involving accusations of either Sterne's or his daughter's dishonesty, we might suggest that a pleasure Sterne found in Eliza was reliving the romance of his youth. Hence, copying earlier letters was not intended to belittle Elizabeth or Eliza, but to regain the past.

[5] Perhaps echoing Proverbs 31:10: "Who can find a virtuous woman? for her price is far above rubies." If so, Sterne did not look at verse 11.

[6] See Introduction, pp. xii–xiv.

[7] *Letters*, 327, n. 6: "A nostrum, having a strong diaphoretic action, invented by Dr. Robert James (1705–1776), and sold exclusively by the bookseller Newbery and his agents." A contemporary apothecary, William Howes, *An Account of the Late Dr. Goldsmith's Illness*, 3d ed. (1774), 7–8, attributed Goldsmith's death to its overuse, and Sterne's physician also had some doubts: "I fell ill the moment I got to my lodgings," Sterne wrote to the Jameses on April 22; "[my physician] says it is owing to my taking James's Powder, and venturing out on so cold a day as Sunday—but he is mistaken, for I am certain whatever bears that name must have efficacy with me" (*Letters* 328). See, however, Sterne's advice to Hall-Stevenson, four months later (*Letters* 389): "You did well to discontinue all commerce with James's powder."

[8] See above, p. 4 and n. 7.

[9] Sterne first wrote "my future wife" and then deleted "future"; in different ink "wife" is deleted, the dash added, and "Help-mate!" inserted above the line. This is the first time Sterne uses the word *wife* in his *Journal*, although in one of his March letters he had certainly avowed his intention to marry Eliza, if ever she were widowed (see Appendix, p. 252). After June 28, when Sterne presumably abandoned all notions of sending his journal to India, he uses "wife" more freely.

evil or good which befalls thee—But all our portion is Evil now,[10] & all our hours grief—I look forwards towards the Elysium[11] we have so often and rapturously talk'd of—Cordelia's Spirit will fly to tell thee in some sweet Slumber, the moment the door is opend for thee—& The Bramin of the Vally, shall follow the track wherever it leads him, to get to his Eliza, & invite her to his Cottage.—[12]

5 in the afternoon—I have just been eating my Chicking, sitting over my repast upon it, with Tears—a bitter Sause—Eliza! but I could eat it with no other—when Molly spread the Table Cloath, my heart fainted with in me—one solitary plate—one knife—one fork—one Glass!—O Eliza! twas painfully distressing,—I gave a thousand pensive penetrating Looks at the Arm chair thou so often graced on these quiet, sentimental Repasts—& sighed & laid down my knife & fork,—& took out my handkerchief, clap'd it across my face, & wept like a child[13]—I shall read the same affecting Acc[t] of many a sad Dinner w[ch] Eliza has had no power to taste of, from the same feelings & recollections, how She and her Bramin have eat their bread in peace and Love together.

---

[10] Cf. *Letters,* 311 (to Eliza): "whatever measure of sorrow and distress is thy portion, it will be repaid to thee in a full measure of happiness"; and again, 316: "May poverty, distress, anguish, and shame, be my portion, if ever I give thee reason to repent the knowledge of me." The scriptural tinge of the language is noteworthy.

[11] See above, p. 120, n. 5.

[12] Sterne writes about "Cordelia's Spirit" in the letter (of disputed date) to a countess, later redirected to Eliza (see *ASJ* p. 62, n. 7). He describes his moonlit walks from Shandy Hall to the ruins of Byland Abbey (built in the twelfth century by Cistercian monks), two miles northeast of Coxwold, and visible from the back garden of Shandy Hall. Sterne relates to each of his multiple addressees how he remembers *her* most vividly when he is "in company with" his Nuns: "since I have got down to this all-peaceful and romantick retreat . . . my Love and my Devotion are ever taking me . . . to these delicious Mansions of our long-lost Sisters: I am just now return'd from one of my nightly visits [and] . . . cannot go to bed without . . . telling you how much, and how many kind things we have been talking about you these two hours . . ." (*Letters* 360). Sterne writes to Eliza about Cordelia or the Abbey again on June 12, July 27, and August 3.

Why Sterne chose the name *Cordelia* is not known; if Lear's loving daughter was in his mind, it might suggest the way in which both Eliza and Maria (if not the countess and a host of others) were to "*not only eat of my bread and drink of my own cup,* but . . . should lay in my bosom, and be unto me as a daughter" (*ASJ* p. 161 and n. 2). Or, *Cordelia* may simply have struck Sterne as an appropriate "monastic" name, based on cordeliers (a French term for Franciscans). Or, alternatively, he perhaps had had access to an unpublished poem by Mark Akenside, "To Cordelia" (1740): "From pompous life's dull masquerade, / From Pride's pursuits, and Passion's war, / Far, my Cordelia, very far, / To thee and me may Heaven assign / The silent pleasures of the shade." The poem continues in this vein for several more stanzas (see Robin Dix, ed. *The Poetical Works of Mark Akenside* [Madison, N.J.: Fairleigh Dickinson UP, 1996], 409, 521), a vein Sterne exploits with his sentimental visitations to the Abbey.

[13] Much of this appears in the disputed letter to Elizabeth Sterne (see *Letters* 10–11; and above, p. 177, n. 4).

April 17. with my friend M[rs] James in Gerard Street, with a present of Colours & apparatus for painting:[14]—Long Conversation about thee my Eliza— sunk my heart wth an infamous Acc[t] of Draper & his detested Character at Bombay—for what a wretch[15] art thou hazarding thy life, my dear friend, & what thanks is his nature capable of returning?—thou wilt be repaid with Injuries & Insults! Still there is a blessing in store for the meek and gentle, and Eliza will not be disinherited[16] of it: her Bramin is kept alive by this hope only—otherwise he is so sunk both in Spirits and looks, Eliza would scarse know him again. dined alone again to day; & begin to feel a pleasure in this kind of resigned Misery arising from this Situation, of heart unsupported by aught but its own tenderness— Thou owest me much Eliza!—& I will have patience; for thou wilt pay me all— But the Demand is equal;—much I owe thee, & with much shalt thou be requited.——Sent for a Chart of the Atlantic Ocean, to make conjectures upon what part of it my Treasure was floating[17]—O! tis but a little way off—and I could venture after it in a Boat, methinks—I'm sure I could, was I to know Eliza was in distress—but fate has chalk'd out other roads for us—We must go on with many a weary step, each in our separate heartless track, till Nature———— ——

Ap: 18.

This day, set up my Carriage,—new Subject of heartache, That Eliza is not here to share it with me.

Bought Orm's account of India[18]—why?—Let not my Bramine ask me—her heart will tell her why I do this, & every Thing—

---

[14] Cf. *Letters,* 412 (February 1768), where Sterne mentions the present again: "I presented her last year with colours, and an apparatus for painting, and gave her several lessons before I left town." Peter de Voogd has suggested to us that the "apparatus" could have been a "Claude glass," named after the French landscape painter Claude Lorraine (1600– 1682), "a small black convex glass used for reflecting landscapes in miniature" (*Oxford Companion to Art,* s.v.), but there were many such instruments in Sterne's day, including the pantograph and the camera obscura, both of which he mentions in *TS,* I.23.85.

[15] Cash, *LY,* 271–72, tries to substantiate the lover's opinion: "Eliza hated her husband. He was thirty-nine years old, exceedingly ugly, as we know from an existing portrait, and a man who knew nothing of the world except the colonial service to which he had been born. . . . Draper was determined to make a great fortune in the service, and to this end was brutally aggressive."

[16] Cf. Matthew 5:5: "Blessed are the meek: for they shall inherit the earth."

[17] Perhaps echoing *The Merchant of Venice,* I.i.8–10: "Your mind is tossing on the ocean, / There where your argosies with portly sail / Like signiors and rich burghers on the flood . . . ."

[18] I.e., Robert Orme, *A History of the Military Transactions of the British Nation in Indostan* (published serially, 1763–1778). Sterne told Lydia he was sending her a copy (of volume 1), so that she could read about Mr. James in it—and because "it is well worth your reading; for Orme is an elegant writer, and a just one; he pays no man a compliment at the expence of truth" (*Letters* 301–2). Orme (1728–1801) was a friend of the Jameses.

Ap: 19.   poor Sick-headed, sick hearted Yorick! Eliza has made a Shadow of thee[19]—I am absolutely good for nothing, as every mortal is who can think & talk but upon one thing!—how I shall rally my powers, alarms me; for Eliza thou has melted them all into one—the power of loving[20] thee—& with such ardent affection as triumphs over all other feelings—was with our faithful friend all the morning; & dined with her & James—What is the Cause, that I can never talk ab^t my Eliza to her, but I am rent in pieces—I burst into tears a dozen different times after dinner, & such affectionate gusts of passion, That She was ready to leave the room,—& sympathize in private for us——I weep for You both, said she (in a whisper,) for Elizas Anguish is as sharp as yours—her heart as tender— her constancy as great—heaven join Your hands I'm sure together!—James was occupied in reading a pamphlet upon the East India affairs—so I answerd her with a kind look, a heavy sigh,[21] and a stream of tears—What was passing in Eliza's breast, at this affecting Crisis?—something kind, and pathetic! I will lay my Life.

8 o'clock—retired to my room, to tell my dear this—to run back the hours^x of Joy I have pass'd with her—& meditate upon those wch are still in reserve for Us.—By this time Mr James tells me, You will have got as far from me, as the Maderas[22]—& that in two months more, you will have doubled the Cape of good hope—I shall trace thy track every day in the Map, & not allow one hour for contrary Winds, or Currents—every engine of nature shall work together for us—Tis the Language of Love—& I can speak no other. & so, good night, to thee, & may the gentlest delusions of love impose upon thy dreams, as I forbode they will, this night, on those of thy Bramine.

---

[19] Being reduced to a shadow is a common idea in Sterne's letters. Writing of himself in the third person to Mrs. James (?April 22), he claims "he is almost dead—yet still hopes to glide like a Shadow to Gerard Street in a few days" (*Letters* 328); and again in a letter to the Earl of Shelburne in May: "Death knocked at my door, but I would not admit him—the call was both unexpected and unpleasant—and I am seriously worn down to a shadow" (342); see further examples (408, 409), letters to the Jameses.

[20] In the ms. an "x" appears before "loving"; see the Introduction, p. xvi, n. 8, for a discussion of these "x" marks, assumed not to be in Sterne's hands. We have indicated all occasions hereafter with a superscript x; it is important to look at the entire context surrounding the "x'ed" word, especially the italicization of words close by, since underscoring may have been performed by the same unknown hand, now impossible to distinguish from Sterne's own underscoring.

[21] From "I burst . . .", a repetition of material from the disputed letter to his wife; see p. 177, n. 4. Sterne emended "heaven join" to "heaven will join," but after doing so, he deleted "will," thus restoring the words to their status as prayer rather than prediction.

[22] I.e., the Madeira Islands, Portugal's possession off the northwest coast of Africa (Morocco).

Ap: 20.   Easter Sunday.[23]

was not disappointed—yet awoke in the most acute pain—Something Eliza is wrong with me—you should be ill out of Sympathy—& yet you are too ill already—my dear friend—. all day at home—in extream dejection.

Ap: 21.[24]   The Loss of Eliza, and attention to that one Idea, brought on a fever—a consequence, I have for some time, forseen—but had not a sufficient Stock of cold philosophy to remedy—to satisfy my friends, call'd in a Physician— Alas! alas! the only Physician, & who carries the Balm of my Life along with her,[25]—is Eliza.—why did I suffer thee to go from me?—surely thou hast more than once call'd thyself, my Eliza, to the same Account.—twil cost us both dear! but it could not be otherwise—We have submitted——we shall be rewarded.

Twas a prophetic Spirit, wch dictated the Acc^t of Corp^l Trim's uneasy night when the fair Beguin ran in his head,[26]—for every night & almost every Slumber of mine, since the day We parted, is a repetition of the same description— dear Eliza! I am very ill—very ill for thee—but I could still give thee greater proofs of my Affection.[27]   parted with 12 Ounces of blood, in order to quiet what was left in me[28]—tis a vain experiment,—physicians cannot understand this; tis enough for me that Eliza does.—I am worn down my dear Girl to a Shadow, & but that I'm certain thou wilt not read this, till I'm restored—thy Yorick would not let the Winds hear his Complaints—   4 °clock—sorrowful Meal! for twas upon our old dish.—We shall live to eat it, my Dear Bramine, with comfort.

8. at night, our dear friend Mrs James, from the forbodings of a good heart, thinking I was ill; sent her Maid to enquire after me—I had alarm'd her on Saturday; & not being with her on sunday,—her friendship supposed the Condition, I

---

[23] Sterne is still a day ahead and is actually writing on Easter Sunday, April 19.

[24] Curtis, *Letters,* 327, n. 15, believed that Sterne wrote nothing on Monday, April 20, and resumed the journal on Tuesday, April 21, correctly dated. In actuality, the entry for "Ap:21" is Monday's entry, and the misdating continues through Tuesday and Wednesday. On Thursday, Sterne was "so ill" he only wrote a brief sentence, and continued the misdating, now April 24. On Friday, he started a new entry, misdating it April 25, "—So—Shall not depart . . . "; he then joined this Friday entry to the brief Thursday entry and overwrote April 25 with the correct date of April 24. Thereafter, the dating is correct.

[25] Cf. Jeremiah 8:22: "Is there no balm in Gilead; is there no physician there?" Cf. *Letters,* 307 (March 1767, to Lydia): "Friendship is the balm and cordial of life . . . ."

[26] Cf. *TS,* VIII.20.699: "My fever ran very high that night—her figure made sad disturbance within me—I was every moment cutting the world in two—to give her half of it."

[27] Cf. the final lines of a letter written from Naples to Lydia (February 3, 1766): "I have purchased you some little trifles, which I shall give you when we meet, as proofs of affection from Your fond father" (*Letters* 268).

[28] Cash, *LY,* 289: "such treatment quieted the patient by putting him in shock and bringing him to the verge of death."

was in—She suffers most tenderly for Us, my Eliza!—& We owe her more than all the Sex—or indeed both Sexes if not, all the world put together—adieu! my sweet Eliza! for this night—thy Yorick is going to waste himself on a restless bed, where he will turn from side to side a thousand times—& dream by Intervals of things terrible & impossible—That Eliza is false to Yorick, or Yorick is false to Eliza——

Ap. 22ᵈ—rose with utmost difficulty—my Physician order'd me back to bed as soon as I had got a dish of Tea—was bled again; my arm broke loose & I half bled to death in bed before I felt it. O Eliza! how did thy Bramine mourn the want of thee to tye up his wounds,²⁹ & comfort his dejected heart—still something bids me hope—& hope, I will—& it shall be the last pleasurable Sensation I part with.

4 o'clock/ They are making my bed—how shall I be able to continue my Journal, in it?—If there remains a chasm here—think Eliza, how ill thy Yorick must have been.—this moment recᵈ a Card from our dear friend, beging me to take care of a Life so valuable to my friends—but most so—She adds, to my poor dear Eliza.—not a word from the Newnhams!³⁰ but they had no such exhortation in their hearts, to send thy Bramine—adieu to em!—

Ap: 23.—a poor night. and am only able to quit my bed at 4 this afternoon—to say a word to my dear—& fulfill my engagement to her, "of letting no day pass over my head without some kind communication with thee"—faint resemblance, my dear girl, of how³¹ our days are to pass, when one kingdom holds us——visited in bed by 40 friends, in the Course of the Day—is not one warm affectionate call, of that friend, for whom I sustain Life, worth 'em all?——What thinkest thou my Eliza.——

---

²⁹ Sterne probably echoes a verse from one of his favorite scriptural stories, that of the good Samaritan, Luke 10:34: "And went to him, and bound up his wounds . . . and took care of him." Cf. *ASJ*, p. 25 and p. 161; and sermon 3, "Philanthropy recommended" (Appendix, p. 235).

³⁰ See Cash, *LY*, 278, and n. 58. The Newnhams were a family of "London merchants, lawyers and politicians," acquaintances of Eliza, and perhaps hostile to Sterne's interest in her: "The [Newnhams], by heavens, are worthless! I have heard enough to tremble at the articulation of the name. . . . For God's sake write not to them; nor foul thy fair character with such polluted hearts" (*Letters* 309; see also, 313–14). On the other hand, Sterne did not mind collecting subscriptions from them for *ASJ*: Miss Anne (imperial), Miss Honoria (imperial), Mr. T. (imperial), Mr. N. (two sets), Mr. W. (two sets).
For the extent of Sterne's efforts to separate Eliza from the Newnhams, see *Letters*, 369.

³¹ The word is marked with an "x&," differing from other instances (see p. 181, n. 20) in being underscored, with a caret below, and an ampersand following. Some editors have printed it as "of x & how."

Ap: 24.

So ill, I could not write a word all this morning—not so much, as Eliza! farewel to thee;—I'm going————am a little better——

——So—Shall not depart, as I apprehended—being this morning something
better—& my Symptoms become milder, by a tolerable easy night.—and now, if
I have strength & Spirits to trail my pen down to the bottom of the page, I have
as whimsical a Story to tell you,[32] and as comically disastrous as ever befell one of
our family—Shandy's Nose—his *name*—his Sash Window are fools to it.[33] It will
serve at *least* to amuse You. The Injury I did myself in catching cold upon James's
pouder, fell, you must know, upon the worst part it could,—the most painful, &
most dangerous of any in the human Body—It was on this Crisis, I call'd in an
able Surgeon & with him an able physician (both my friends) to inspect my
disaster—tis a venerial Case, cried my two Scientifick friends——'tis impossible
at least to be that, replied I—for I have had no commerce whatever with the
Sex[x]—not even with my wife, added I, these 15 Years—You are *****[34] however
my good friend, said the Surgeon, or there is no such Case in the world—what
the Devil! said I without knowing Woman—we will not reason ab' it, said the
Physician, but you must undergo a course of Mercury,—I'll lose my life first, said
I,—& trust to Nature, to Time—or at the worst—to Death,—so I put an end
with some Indignation to the Conference; and determined to bear all the torments I underwent, & ten times more rather than, submit to be treated as a *Sinner,* in a point where I had acted like a *Saint.* Now as the father of mischief w[d]
have it, who has no pleasure like that of dishonouring the righteous—it so fell
out, That from the moment I dismissd my Doctors—my pains began to rage
with a violence not to be express'd, or supported.—every hour became more
intollerable—I was got to bed—cried out & raved the whole night—& was got
up so near dead, That my friends insisted upon my sending again for my Physician & Surgeon—I told them upon the word of a man of Strict honour, They
were both mistaken as to my case—but tho' they had reason'd wrong—they
might act right—but that sharp as my sufferings were, I felt them not so sharp as

---

[32] Cf. *Letters* (to the Earl of Shelburne, May 21), 342–44: "I have as whimsical a story to tell
you as ever befel one of my family—Shandy's nose, his name, his sash window are fools to
it . . . ." Sterne then repeats, basically verbatim, the same account as here.

[33] The problems besetting Tristram Shandy in relation to his nose and his name are first
alluded to in the penultimate paragraph of the final chapter of volume II (19.180): "You
may raise a system to account for the loss of my nose by marriage articles,——and shew the
world how it could happen, that I should have the misfortune to be called Tristram." The
incident with the sash window occurs in volume V (17.449–50).

[34] Probably "clapt" or "poxed." Cash, *LY,* 290, suggests that the doctors were incorrect, and
that "Sterne suffered from tuberculosis of the fibrocaseous type, as evidenced by the recurrent bleeding of his lungs . . . . Moreover, tuberculosis often attacks other organs besides
the lungs, among them the genitals and the vocal chords. In short, one can unify all of
Sterne's known symptoms . . . under a diagnosis of tuberculosis."

the Imputation, wch a venerial treatment of my case, laid me under—They answerd that these taints of the blood laid dormant 20 Years—but that they would not reason with me in a matter wherein I was so delicate—but Would do all the Office for wch they were call'd in—namely, to put an end to my torment, wch otherwise would put an end to me.—& so have I been compell'd to surrender myself—& thus Eliza is your Yorick, y^r Bramine—your friend with all his sensibilities, suffering the Chastisement of the grossest Sensualist[35]—Is it not a most ridiculous Embarassm^t, as ever Yorick's Spirit could be involved in—

Tis needless to tell Eliza, that nothing but the purest consciousness of Virtue, could have tempted Eliza's friend to have told her this Story[36]—Thou art too good my Eliza to love aught but Virtue—& too discerning not to distinguish the open Character wch bears it, from the artful & double one wch affects it—This, by the way, w^d make no bad anecdote in T. Shandy's Life—however I thought at least it would amuse you, in a Country where *less Matters* serve.—This has taken me three Sittings—it ought to be a good picture—I'm more proud, That it is a true one. In ten Days, I shall be able to get out—my room allways full of friendly Visiters—& my rapper eternally going with Cards & enquiries after me. I sh^d be glad of the Testimonies—without the Tax.

Every thing convinces me, Eliza, We shall live to meet again—So—Take care of y^r health, to add to the comfort of it.

Ap: 25.   after a tolerable night, I am able, Eliza, to sit up and hold a discourse with the sweet Picture thou hast left behind thee of thyself, & tell it how much I had dreaded the catastrophe, of never seeing its dear Original more in this world—never did that Look of sweet resignation appear so eloquent as now; it has said more to my heart—& cheard it up more effectually above little fears & *may be's*—Than all the Lectures of philosophy I have strength to apply to it, in my present Debility of mind and body.—as for the latter—my men of Science, will set it properly a going again—tho' upon what principles—the Wise Men of Gotham[37] know as much as they—If they *act right*—What is it to me, how *wrong*

---

[35] Cf. *Letters*, 396 (September 27): "praised be God for my sensibility! Though it has often made me wretched, yet I would not exchange it for all the pleasures the grossest sensualist ever felt."

[36] Cf. the letter to Shelburne (see above, n. 32), *Letters*, 343–44: "Nothing but the purest conscience of innocence could have tempted me to write this story to my wife, which by the bye would make no bad anecdote in Tristram Shandy's Life—I have mentioned it in my journal to Mrs. [Draper.] In some respects there is no difference between my wife and herself—when they fare alike, neither can reasonably complain." Curtis, *Letters*, 344, n. 3, wittily compares this recycling of material to Yorick's rewriting La Fleur's all-purpose letter, *ASJ*, pp. 66–8.

[37] Proverbial, Tilley, M636, and *ODEP*, s.v. *wise;* it refers either to the apparent simplicity of the "wise men of Gotham," thought to conceal real shrewdness, or, alternatively, as here, real foolishness.

they think; for finding my machine[38] a much less tormenting one to me than before, I become reconciled to my Situation, and to their Ideas of it——but don't You pity me, after all, my dearest and my best of friends? I know to what an amount thou wilt Shed over Me, this tender Tax—& tis the Consolation springing out of that, of what a good heart it is which pours this friendly balm on mine, That has already, & will for ever heal every evil of my Life.   and What is becoming, of my Eliza, all this time!—where is she sailing?—what Sickness or other evils have befallen her? I weep often my dear Girl, for those my Imagination surrounds thee with—What w^d be the measure of my Sorrow, did I know thou wast distressd?—adieu—adieu. & trust my dear friend—my dear Bramine, that there still wants nothing to kill me in a few days, but the certainty, That thou wast suffering^x, what I am—& yet I know thou art ill—but when thou returnest back to England, all shall be set right.—so heaven waft thee to us upon the wings of Mercy—that is, as speedily as the winds & tides can do thee this friendly office.   This is the 7th day That I have tasted nothing better than Water gruel—am going, at the solicitation of Hall, to eat of a boild fowl—so he dines with me on it—and a dish of Macaruls—

7 o'clock—I have drank to thy Name Eliza! everlasting peace & happiness (for my Toast) in the first glass of Wine I have adventured to drink. my friend has left me—& I am alone,—like thee in thy solitary Cabbin after thy return from a tastless meal in the round house[39] & like thee I fly to my Journal, to tell thee, I never prized thy friendship so high, or loved thee more—or wish'd so ardently to be a Sharer of all the weights wch Providence has laid upon thy tender frame—Than this moment—when upon taking up my pen, my poor pulse quickend—my pale face glowed—and tears stood ready in my Eyes to fall upon the paper, as I traced the word Eliza. O Eliza! Eliza! ever best & blessed of all thy Sex! blessed in thyself and in thy Virtues—& blessed and endearing to all who know thee—to Me, Eliza, most so; because I *know more* of thee than any other—This is the true philtre by which Thou hast charm'd me & wilt for ever charm & hold me thine, whilst Virtue & faith hold this world together; tis the simple Magick, by which I trust, I have won a place in that heart of thine on wch I depend so satisfied, That Time & distance, or change of every thing wch might allarm the little hearts of little men, create no uneasy suspence in mine—It

---

[38] Sterne refers to his own body as a machine in several letters at this time; e.g., to Hall-Stevenson on May 25: "I know not what is the matter with me—but some *derangement* presses hard upon this machine" (*Letters* 346); and to Mrs. Montagu in March 1768: "excuse a weak brain for all this—and to strengthen this poor Machine, send me . . . a very few Jellies" (416).

[39] *OED* cites William Falconer, *An Universal Dictionary of the Marine* (1769): "a name given, in East-Indiamen, and other large merchant-ships, to a cabin . . . built in the after part of the quarter-deck, and having the poop for it's [*sic*] roof."

scorns to doubt—& scorns to be doubted—tis the only exception—When Security is not the parent of Danger.[40]

My Illness will keep me three weeks longer in town.—but a Journey in less time would be hazardous, unless a short one across the Desert wch I should set out upon to morrow, could I carry a Medcine with me which I was sure would prolong one Month of Y^r Life——or should it happen—— —— —— ————

—but why make Suppositions?—when Situations happen—tis time enough to shew thee That thy Bramin is the truest & most friendly of mortal Spirits, & capable of doing more for his Eliza, than his pen will suffer him to promise.

Ap: 26.   Slept not till three this morning—was in too delicious Society to think of it; for I was all the time with thee besides me, talking over the projess[41] of our friendship, & turning the world into a thousand Shapes to enjoy it. got up much better for the Conversation—found myself improved in body & mind & recruited beyond any thing I lookd for; my Doctors, stroked their beards, & look'd ten per C^t wiser upon feeling my pulse, & enquiring after my Symptoms—am still to run thro' a Course of Van Sweetens corrosive Mercury, or rather Van Sweeten's Course of Mercury is to run thro' me[42]—I shall be sublimated to an etherial Substance by the time my Eliza sees me—she must be sublimated and uncorporated too, to be able to see me—but I was always transparent & a Being easy to be seen thro',[43] or Eliza had never loved me nor had Eliza been of any other *Cast*[44] herself, could her Bramine have held *Communion*^{x} with her.   hear every day from

---

[40] This entire passage, beginning with "Than this moment," echoes the disputed early letter to his wife; see p. 177, n. 4.

[41] Possibly a misspelling of *progress,* but more likely Sterne's rendering of *projets,* French for "schemes," "projects."

[42] Cf. *Letters,* 339, n. 2: "Gerard Van Swieten (1700–1772), celebrated as the disciple of Boerhaave and physician to Maria Theresa." Venereal disorders in the eighteenth century were treated with a variety of dangerous compounds based on lead and mercury. However, as the first *Encyclopædia Britannica,* s.v. *Chemistry,* pointed out in 1771: "as lead is one of the most dangerous poisons we know . . . whoever uses such a pernicious drug deserves to be most severely punished."

[43] Cf. *TS,* I.11.27, where Yorick is said to be of "as mercurial and sublimated a composition . . . as the kindliest climate could have engendered"; and I.23.83, where Tristram argues that in the planet Mercury the intense heat may have "vitrified the bodies of the inhabitants . . . so that . . . all the tenements of their souls, from top to bottom, may be nothing else . . . but one fine transparent body of clear glass." And see also, *Letters,* 241 (?1765), to one of Sterne's "Mrs. F——"s: "I am moreover of a thin, dry, hectic, unperspirable habit of Body— so sublimated and rarified in all my parts That . . . I have not an ounce & a half of carnality about me." Sterne's "uncorporated" is unrecorded in *OED.*

[44] Cf. Parnell, 248, n. to 115: "a punning allusion to the division of Indian society according to hereditary castes, and the word's etymological relationship to 'casto,' meaning pure or chaste."

our worthy sentimental friend—who rejoyces to think that the Name of Eliza is still to vibrate upon Yoricks ear—

this, my dear Girl, many who loved me dispaird of—poor Molly who is all attention to me—& every day brings in the name of poor Mrs Draper, told me last night, that She and her Mistress had observed, I had never held up my head, since the Day you last dined with me—That I had seldome laughd or smiled—had gone to no Diversions—but twice or thrice at the most, dined out—That they thought I was broken hearted, for She never enterd the room or passd by the door, but she heard me sigh heavily—That I neither eat or slept or took pleasure in any Thing as before, except writing————[45]

The Observation will draw a Sigh, Eliza, from thy feeling heart—& yet, so thy heart w^d wish to have it—tis fit in truth We suffer equally—nor can it be otherwise—when the Causes of Anguish in two hearts are so proportion'd, as in ours.—Surely—Surely—Thou art mine Eliza! for dear have I bought thee!

Ap: 27.   Things go better with me, Eliza! and I shall be reestablish'd soon, except in bodily weakness; not yet being able to rise from thy[46] arm chair, & walk to the other corner of my room, & back to it again, without fatigue—I shall double my Journey to morrow, & if the day is warm the day after be got into my Carriage & be transported into Hyde park for the advantage of air & exercise—wast thou but besides me, I could go to Salt hill,[47] Im sure, & feel the Journey short & pleasant.—another Time!—the present, alas! is not ours. I pore so much on thy Picture—I have it *off by heart*—dear Girl—oh tis sweet! tis kind! tis reflecting! tis affectionate! tis——thine my Bramine—I say my matins & Vespers to it—I quiet my Murmurs, by the Spirit which speaks in it—"all will end Well my Yorick."—I declare my dear Bramine I am so secured & wrapt up in this Belief, That I would not part with the Imagination,[48] of how happy I am to be with thee, for all the Offers of present Interest or Happiness the whole world could tempt me with; in the loneliest Cottage that Love & Humility ever dwelt in, with thee along with me,

---

[45] Beginning with "poor Molly" this entire passage is paralleled in the letter to Sterne's wife; see p. 177, n. 4. Molly's mistress has been identified as Mary Fourmantel, "Hair Bag Maker to his Majesty," Sterne's landlady in Old Bond Street, where he took up residence in January 1767, and possibly as early as 1765, and where he eventually died when he returned to London in the winter of 1768 (*Letters*, 293, n. 1).

[46] Parnell, 115, emends to "my," but Sterne may be referring to a chair Eliza regularly occupied when visiting him, and thus "her" chair in their vocabulary; see above, p. 179.

[47] See below, p. 212, nn. 48, 49, where Sterne recalls just such a carriage ride with Eliza.

[48] It is to this power of imagination, as well as to Shakespeare, that Sterne pays tribute in his apostrophe to the "Sweet pliability of man's spirit" (*ASJ* p. 120). The entire passage, from establishing Eliza as the object of his matins and vespers, to his direct prayer to Jesus to bring about their union, perhaps shocks even modern readers, but it indicates the intensity of Sterne's passion or pathology at this time.

I could possess more refined Content, Than in the most glittering Court; & with thy Love & fidelity, taste truer[x] joys, my Eliza! & make thee also partake of more, than all the senseless parade of this silly world[49] could compensate to either of us— with this, I bound all my desires & worldly views—what are they worth without Eliza? Jesus! grant me but this, I will deserve it—I will make My Bramine, as Happy, as thy goodness wills her—I will be the Instrument of her recompense for the sorrows & disappointments thou has suffer'd her to undergo; & if ever I am false, unkind or ungentle to her; so let me be dealt with by thy Justice.

9 o'clock,/ I am preparing to go to bed my dear Girl, & first pray for thee, & then to Idolize thee for two wakeful hours upon my pillow—I shall after that, I find dream all night of thee, for all the day have I done nothing but think of thee—something tells me, that thou hast this day, been employd exactly in the same Way. good night, fair Soul—& may the sweet God of sleep close gently thy eyelids—& govern & direct thy Slumbers—adieu—adieu, adieu!

Ap: 28.   I was not decieved Eliza! by my presentiment that I should find thee out in my dreams; for I have been with thee almost the whole night, alternately soothing Thee, or telling thee my sorrows—I have rose up comforted & strength- end—& found myself so much better, that I orderd my Carriage, to carry me to our mutual friend—Tears ran down her cheeks when She saw how pale & wan[50] I was—never gentle Creature sympathiz'd more tenderly—I beseech you, cried the good Soul, not to regard either difficulties or expences, but fly to Eliza directly—I see you will dye without her—save y[r]self for her—how shall I look her in the face? What can I say to her, when on her return, I have to tell her, That her Yorick is no more!—Tell her my dear friend, said I, That I will meet her in a bet- ter world—& that I have left this, because I could not live without *her;* tell Eliza, my dear friend added I—That I died broken hearted—and that you were a Wit- ness to it—as I said this, She burst into the most pathetick flood of Tears—that ever kindly nature shed, you never beheld so affecting a Scene—'twas too much for Nature![51] Oh! she is good—I love her as my Sister!—& could Eliza have been

---

[49] A favorite expression of Sterne, from an early letter in 1750 to Archdeacon Blackburne: "this *silly* & uncertain World" (*Letters* 31); to a friend, Thomas Hesilrige in 1765: "how do you go on, in this silly world?" (252); to Ignatius Sancho in June 1767: "whatever befalls me in this silly world" (370). Cf. sermon 24 ("Pride"): "Simplicity is the great friend to nature, and if I would be proud of any thing in this silly world, it should be of this honest alliance" (4:234).

[50] Sterne comments elsewhere on his pallor (see *ASJ*, p. 114, n. 3), but perhaps he is also recalling the opening line of Sir John Suckling's famous song, "Why so pale and wan, fond lover?"

[51] Cf. Curtis's comment, *Letters,* 339, n. 4: "Affecting as was this scene with Mrs. James, it does not promote our regard for her common sense." See also Sterne's description of her to Lydia in February: "Mrs. James is kind—and friendly—of a sentimental turn of mind—and so sweet a disposition, that she is too good for the world she lives in" (*Letters* 302).

a witness, hers would have melted down to Death & scarse have been brought back, from an Extacy so celestial, & savouring of another world.—I had like to have fainted, & to that Degree was my heart & Soul affected, it was wth difficulty I could reach the Street door; I have got home, & shall lay all day upon my Sopha—& to morrow morning my dear Girl write again to thee; for I have not strength to drag my pen—

Ap: 29.

I am so ill to day, my dear, I can only tell you so—I wish I was put into a Ship for Bombay—I wish I may otherwise hold out till the hour We might otherwise have met—I have too many evils upon me at once—& yet I will not faint under them—Come!—Come to me soon my Eliza & save me!

Ap. 30.   Better to day—but am too much visited & find my Strength wasted by the attention I must give to all concern'd for me—I will go Eliza, be it but by ten mile Journeys, home to my thatchd Cottage—& there I shall have no respit—for I shall do nothing but think of thee—and burn out this weak Taper of Life. by the flame thou hast superadded to it—fare well My dear ****[52]—to morrow begins a new month—& I hope to give thee in it, a more sunshiny[53] Side of myself—Heaven! how is it with my Eliza————

May 1./

got out into the park to day—Sheba there on Horseback;[1] pass'd twice by her without knowing her—She stop'd the 3^d time—to ask me how I did—I w^d not have askd You, Solomon! said She, but y^r Looks affected me—for you'r half dead I fear—I thank'd Sheba, very kindly, but w^thout any emotion but what sprung from gratitude—Love^x alas! was fled with thee Eliza!—I did not think Sheba could have changed so much in grace & beauty—Thou hadst shrunk poor Sheba away into Nothing,—but a good natured girl, without powers or charms—I *fear* your Wife is dead, quoth Sheba—no, you don't *fear* it Sheba said I—Upon my Word Solomon! I would quarel with You, was you not so ill—If you knew the Cause of my Illness, Sheba, replied I, you w^d quarel but the more with me—You lie, Solomon! answerd Sheba, for I know the Cause already—& am so little out of Charity with You upon it—That I give You leave to come & drink Tea with me before You leave Town—you're a good honest Creature Sheba—no! you Rascal, I

---

[52] ?wife. See above, p. 178, n. 9; and Cash, *LY,* 285–86, on Sterne's use of *wife* when addressing Eliza. See most esp., his letter to Eliza in Appendix, pp. 251–52. The ms. has four *x*'s, which we have read as Sterne's usual asterisks.

[53] Cf. *Letters,* 185: "I rejoice . . . that you have snatch'd so many happy and sunshiny days out of the hands of the blue devils." The final sentence, "Heaven!, etc." is a later addition.

[1] See *ASJ,* p. 62, n. 7, the possible identification of Sheba as Lady Warkworth. Inevitably, Sheba's partner would be Solomon.

am not—but I'm in Love, as much as you can be for y^r Life—I'm glad of it Sheba!
said I—You Lie, said Sheba, & so canter'd away.—O My Eliza, had I ever truely
loved another (wch I never did) Thou hast long ago, cut the Root of all Affection
in me—& planted & waterd & nourish'd it, to bear fruit only for thyself—Continue to give me proofs I have had and shall preserve the same rights over thee my
Eliza! and if I ever murmur at the sufferings of Life, after that, Let me be num-
berd with the ungrateful.—I look now forwards with Impatience for the day thou
art to get to Madras—& from thence shall I want to hasten thee to Bombay^2—
where heaven will make all things Conspire to lay the Basis of thy health & future
happiness—be true my dear girl, to thy self^3—& the rights of Self preservation
which Nature has given thee!—persevere—be firm—be pliant be placid—be
courteous—but still be true to thy self—& never give up y^r Life,—or suffer the
disquieting altercations, or small outrages you may undergo in this momentous
point, to weigh a Scruple in the Ballance—Firmness—& fortitude & persever-
ance gain almost impossibilities—& "*Skin* for *Skin*," saith *Job*, "*nay all that a Man
has, will he give for his Life*"^{4}—oh My Eliza! That I could take the Wings of the
Morning,^{5} & fly to aid thee in *this* virtuous Struggle.   went to Ranelagh^6 at
8 this night, and sat still till ten—came home ill.

May 2^d
I fear I have relapsed—sent afresh for my Doctor—who has confined me to
my Sopha—being able neither to walk, stand or sit upright, without aggravating

---

^{2} Madras is on India's east coast; the *Lord Chatham* would then sail around the tip of India,
along the Malabar Coast up to Bombay on the west coast. After leaving St. Jago (i.e., Santiago in the Cape Verde Islands) the ship encountered a homeward-bound Dutch vessel and
transferred its mail, which included the second part of Eliza's journal, which Sterne
received at the end of July. Eliza would arrive at Madras in the middle of October, and at
Bombay in January 1768—in all, a nine-month voyage.

^{3} Probably a cliché, but Yorick does allude to Polonius's famous speech in *ASJ* (see p. 93
and n. 1), so perhaps another allusion to it (i.e., *Hamlet,* I.iii.78).

^{4} Not Job, but Satan; see Job 2:4: "And Satan answered the Lord, and said, Skin for skin,
yea, all that a man hath will he give for his life."

^{5} Cf. Psalm 139:9: "If I take the wings of the morning, and dwell in the uttermost parts of
the sea."

^{6} In the Chelsea borough of London, Ranelagh was a center of entertainment (often a bit
risqué) from May 1742 until it closed in 1803, and a place often frequented by Sterne. Cf.
Boswell's "A Poetical Epistle to Doctor Sterne, Parson Yorick, and Tristram Shandy" (1760):
"He runs about from place to place, / Now with my Lord, then with his Grace, / . . . In
Ranelagh's delightful round / Squire Tristram oft is flaunting found . . ." (*Boswell's Book of
Bad Verse*, ed. Jack Werner [London: White Lion, 1974], 136). See also *Letters,* 107, 140,
for mentions of Sterne's visits. Sterne was associated with Ranelagh in the public mind; a
pamphlet, *Tristram Shandy at Ranelaugh,* appeared in 1760, with a frontispiece showing
the gardens and the figure of a clergyman soliciting subscriptions for his sermons.

my Symptoms—I'm still to be treated as if I was a Sinner[7]—& in truth have some appearances so strongly implying it, That was I not conscious I had had no Commerce[x] with the Sex these 15 Years, I would decamp to morrow for Montpellier in the South of France, where Maladies of this sort are better treated[8] & all taints more radically driven out of the Blood—than in this Country; but If I continue long ill—I am still determined to repair there—not to undergo a Cure of a distemper I cannot have, but for the bettering my Constitution by a better Climate.—I write this as I lie upon my back—in wch posture I must continue, I fear some days—If I am able—will take up my pen again before night——

4 °clock.—an hour dedicated to Eliza! for I have dined alone—& ever since the Cloath has been laid, have done nothing but call upon thy dear Name—and ask why tis not permitted thou shouldst sit down, & share my Macarel & foul— there would be enough, said Molly as she place'd it upon the Table to have served both You & poor Mrs Draper—I never bring in the Knives & forks, added She, but I think of her—There was no more trouble with you both, than w^h one of You—I never heard a high or a hasty word from either of You—You were surely made, added Molly, for one another, You are both so kind so quiet & so friendly—Molly furnished me with Sause to my Meat—for I wept my plate full, Eliza! & now I have begun, could shed tears till Supper again—& then go to bed weeping for thy absence till morning. Thou hast bewitch'd me with powers, my dear Girl, from which no power shall unlose me—and if fate can put this Journal of my Love into thy hands, before we meet, I know with what warmth it will inflame the kindest of hearts, to receive me. peace be with thee, my Eliza, till that happy moment!—

9 at night/ I shall never get possession of myself, Eliza! at this rate—I want to Call off my Thoughts from thee, that I may now & then, apply them to some concerns wch require both my attention & genius, but to no purpose—I had a Letter to write to Lord Shelburn[9]—& had got my apparatus in order to begin—

---

[7] Cf. the account of this affair to Shelburne (*Letters* 343): "and determined to bear all the torments I underwent . . . rather than submit to be treated like a *sinner,* in a point where I had acted like a *saint.*"

[8] Cf. Smollett's account of the "celebrated professor F———, who is the Boerhaave of Montpellier. . . . He is said to have great practice in the venereal branch, and to be frequented by persons of both sexes infected with this distemper, not only from every part of France, but also from Spain, Italy, Germany, and England. . . . I have some reason to think the great professor F———, has . . . cured many patients that were never diseased" (*Travels,* letter 11, 1:175–76). Sterne had met both Dr. Antoine Fizès and Smollett in Montpellier in 1763; see Cash, *LY,* 160, 168. And see p. 194, n. 11, below.

[9] See above, p. 184, n. 32; if the letter of May 21 is the letter alluded to (the only letter to Shelburne that survives), it took Sterne almost three weeks to write it. Curtis identifies Shelburne as "William Petty (1737–1805), styled Viscount Fitzmaurice from 1753–1761, [who] had succeeded his father as Earl of Shelburne and was now Secretary of State for the South. . . . Sterne had 'played the good fellow' at Scarborough with him in 1764 . . ."

when a Map of India coming in my Way—I begun to study the length & dangers of my Eliza's Voiage to it, and have been amusing & frightening myself by turns, as I traced the path-way of the Earl of Chatham, the whole Afternoon—good god! what a voiage for any one!—but for the poor relax'd frame of my tender Bramine to cross the Line twice! & be subject to the Intolerant heats, & the hazards wch must be the consequence of em to such an unsupported Being!—O Eliza! 'tis too much—& if thou conquerest these, and all the other difficulties of so tremendous an alienation from thy Country, thy Children & thy friends, tis the hand of Providence wch watches over thee for most merciful purposes—Let this persuasion, my dear Eliza! stick close to thee in all thy tryals—as it shall in those thy faithful Bramin is put to—till the mark'd hour of deliverance comes. I'm going to sleep upon this religious Elixir—may the Infusion of it distil into the gentlest of hearts—for that Eliza! is thine—sweet, dear, faithful Girl, most kindly does thy Yorick greet thee with the wishes of a good night. &—of Millions yet to come————

May 3^d Sunday/   What can be the matter with me! Some thing is wrong, Eliza! in every part of me—I do not gain strength; nor have I the feelings of health returning back to me; even my best moments seem merely the efforts of my mind to get well again, because I cannot reconcile myself to the thoughts of never seeing thee Eliza more.—for something is out of tune in every Chord of me—still with thee to nurse & sooth me, I should soon do well—The Want of thee is half my distemper—but not the whole of it——   I must see Mrs James to night, tho' I know not how to get there—but I shall not sleep, if I don't talk of You to her—so shall finish this Days Journal on my return—/May 4th—
    Directed by Mr James how to write Over-Land to thee, my Eliza!—would gladly tear out thus much of my Journal to send to thee—but the Chances are too many against it's getting to Bombay—or of being deliverd into y^r own hands—— shall write a long long Letter—& trust it to fate & thee. was not able to say three words at Mrs James, thro' utter weakness of body & mind; & when I got home— could not get up stairs wth Molly's aid—have rose a little better, my dear girl—& will live for thee—do the same for thy Bramin, I beseech thee. a Line from thee now, in this state of my Dejection,—would be worth a Kingdome to me!—

May 4.   Writing by way of Vienna & Bussorah[10] to My Eliza.—this & Company took up the day.

(*Letters,* 344, n. 1). Cash, *LY,* 195–96, notes that Shelburne was "a friend to d'Holbach, Diderot, Hume, Johnson and Reynolds" and a great admirer of Sterne.

[10] Sterne presumably follows Mr. James's directions for overland mail. Bussorah, i.e., modern Basra in southern Iraq (at the northern end of the Persian Gulf), was a station of the East India Company from 1763.

5th   writing to Eliza.—& trying *l'Extraite de Saturne*[11] upon myself.—(a french Nostrum)—

6th   Dined out for the 1st time—came home to enjoy a more harmonious evening w[h] my Eliza, than I could expect at Soho Concert[12]—every Thing my dear Girl, has lost its former relish to me—& for thee eternally does it quicken! writing to thee over Land—all day.

7.   continue poorly, my dear!—but my blood warms, every mom[t] I think of our future Scenes.—so must grow strong, upon the Idea—what shall I do upon the Reality?——O God!——

8th   employ'd in writing to my Dear all day—& in projecting happiness for her—tho in misery myself. O! I have undergone Eliza!—but the worst is over—(I hope)—so adieu to those Evils, & let me hail the happiness to come.

9th 10th & 11th   so unaccountably disorder'd—I cannot say more—but that I w[d] suffer ten times more & with Smiles for my Eliza—adieu bless'd Woman!—

12th   O Eliza! That my weary head was now laid upon thy Lap[x]—(tis all that's left for it)—or that I had thine, reclining upon my bosome[x], and there resting all its disquietudes;—my Bramine—the world or Yorick must perish, before that foundation shall fail thee!—   I continue poorly—but I turn my Eyes Eastward the oftener, & with more earnestness for it—

---

[11] See Thomas Goulard, *A Treatise on the Effects and Various Preparations of Lead, Particularly of the Extract of Saturn, for Different Chirurgical Disorders* (1769; first pub. 1760, in French). Goulard was surgeon-major to the Royal and Military Hospital at Montpellier where the treatment of venereal disorders occupied much of his time (5). He praised his "extract of Saturn" (later called "Eau de Goulard") "for the cure of all disorders of the skin . . . [and] for the healing of ulcers, whether scrophulous, venereal, or cancerous." It was made by boiling lead in wine vinegar (6–7), and Goulard was aware of its dangers: "in general, the internal use of Lead is condemned; but may it not be deprived of its noxious quality by certain preparations, and administered in small doses? Does not Mr. Van Swieten [see above, p. 187, n. 42] (an author of great repute in the present age) give internally the corrosive sublimate with great success?" (4).

[12] Cf. *Letters,* 296, where Sterne comments on a Soho concert in January: "the concert at Soho top full—& was . . . the best assembly, and the best Concert I ever had the honour to be at." Curtis provides details, 297, n. 1, for these Wednesday evening concerts at Carlisle House for exclusive subscribers, "for whom Theresa Cornelys (1723–1797) directed her famous assemblies from 1760 until her failure in 1772. For those who preferred music to cards and dancing she inaugurated in 1765 a series of grand concerts of vocal and instrumental music, which were alternately conducted by Johann Christian Bach and Karl Friedrich Abel." Abel was a master of Sterne's own instrument, the viol da gamba.

Great God of Mercy! shorten the Space betwixt us,—Shorten the space of our miseries![13]

13th   Could not get the Gen[l] post Office to take charge of my Letters to You—so gave thirty shillings to a Merchant to further them to Aleppo & from thence to Bassorah—so you will receive 'em, (I hope in god) safe by Christmas—Surely 'tis not impossible, but I may be made as happy as my Eliza, by some transcript from her, by that time—If not I shall hope—& hope, every week, and every hour of it, for Tidings of Comfort[14]—we taste not of it *now*, my dear Bramine—but we will make full[x] meals upon it hereafter.[15]—Cards from 7 or 8 of our Grandies to dine with them before I leave Town—shall go like a Lamb to the Slaughter[16]—"*Man delights not me—nor Woman*"[17]

14.   a little better to day—& would look pert, if my heart would but let me—dined w[h] L[d] & Lady Bellasis.[18]—so beset wth Company—not a moment to write.

15—Undone with too much Society yesterday,—You scarse can Conceive my dear Eliza what a poor Soul I am—how I shall be got down to Coxwould—heaven knows—for I am as weak as a Child—You would not like me the worse for it, Eliza, if you was here—My friends like me, the more,—& Swear I shew more true fortitude & eveness of temper in my Suffering than Seneca,[19] or Socrates——I am, My Bramin, resigned.

---

[13] Sterne's invocation of God throughout *BJ* is paralleled in his letters to Eliza; e.g. *Letters*, 311, 312, and Appendix, p. 249, below. The desire to discover and assert a divine presence in his relationship with Eliza should not be dismissed merely as hypocrisy or self-deception.

[14] Sterne's mention of Christmas may have triggered his remembrance of the words of the eighteenth-century carol, "God rest you merry, gentlemen," with its refrain: "O tidings of comfort and joy." Cf. Luke 2:10: "behold, I bring you good tidings of great joy."

[15] Despite the "x" after "full" there seems little sensuality in the "taste . . . of full meals" Sterne promises himself, but rather a far more ethereal "tiding of comfort and joy"; Psalm 34:8 says as much: "O taste and see that the Lord is good: blessed is the man that trusteth in him."

[16] Cf. Isaiah 53:7: "He was oppressed, and he was afflicted, yet he opened not his mouth: he is brought as a lamb to the slaughter." Again, the image is summoned by the mention of Christmas.

[17] Cf. *Hamlet*, II.ii.309–10: "Man delights not me—nor women neither, though by your smiling you seem to say so."

[18] Henry, Lord Belasyse (1743–1802) and his wife, Charlotte; he was the son and heir of Thomas Belasyse, 4th Viscount and 1st Earl of Fauconberg (1699–1774), of Newburgh Priory, Coxwold, who granted Sterne his Coxwold living in 1760. Both Lord and Lady Belasyse subscribed to imperial copies of *ASJ*, and Lord Belasyse to vols. III and IV of the sermons as well.

[19] Annæus Seneca (c. 3 B.C.–A.D. 65) appears in Sterne's list of Stoics (taken from Chambers, *Cyclopædia*) in *TS*, III.4.190. Socrates' fortitude in facing death is famously chronicled in Plato's *Apology*.

16—Taken up all day with worldly matters, just as my Eliza was, the week before her departure—breakfasted with Lady Spencer[20]—caught her with the Character of y^r Portrait—caught her passions still more with that of y^{rs}elf—& my Attachment to the most amiable of Beings.[21]—drove at night to Ranalagh—staid an hour—returnd to my Lodgings, dissatisfied.

17.   At Court[22]—every thing in this world seems in Masquerade, but thee dear Woman—and therefore I am sick of all the world but thee—one^x Evening *so spent, as the Saturday's wch preceded our Separation—would sicken all the Conversation of the world—I relish no Converse*[23] *since*—when will the like return?—'tis hidden from us both, for the wisest ends—and the hour will come my Eliza! when We shall be convinced, that every event has been order'd for the best for Us—Our fruit is not ripend—the accidents of times & Seasons will ripen every Thing *together* for Us—   a little better to day—or could not have wrote this. dear Bramine rest thy Sweet Soul in peace!

18.   Laid sleepless all the night, with thinking of the many dangers & sufferings, my dear Girl! that thou art exposed to—from thy Voiage & thy sad state of health—but I find I must think no more upon them—I have rose wan and trembling with the Havock they have made upon my Nerves—'tis death to me to apprehend for you—I must flatter my Imagination, That every Thing goes well with You—Surely no evil can have befallen You—for if it had—I had felt some monitory sympathetic Shock within me, wch would have spoke like Revelation.— So farewell to all tormenting *May be's*, in regard to my Eliza—She is well—she thinks of her Yorick wth as much Affection and true esteem as ever—and values him as much above the World, as he values his Bramine——

---

[20] Margaret Georgiana, Countess Spencer, daughter of Stephen Poyntz, "a courtier and diplomat and favourite of George II" (Cash, *LY* 81–82), married John Spencer (1734–1783), great-grandson of the Duke of Marlborough, created Viscount Spencer of Althorp in 1761 and Earl Spencer in 1765. Sterne dedicated vols. V and VI of *TS* to him, and "the story of *Le Fever* in the sixth volume to her . . . ; for which I have no other motive, which my heart has informed me of, but that the story is a humane one" (*TS* V.Ded.[405]). The Spencers entertained Sterne again on May 21, just before he left London.

[21] A favorite eighteenth-century compliment. Cf. *Letters,* 301 (February 23): "one of the most amiable and gentlest of beings"; and again, 369 (June 30): "the most amiable of women reiterated my request." In both instances, Sterne refers to Mrs. James, not to Eliza.

[22] *Letters,* 342, n. 1: "Sterne had attended 'a very grand Court at St. James's, at which all the Royal Family except the Princess Dowager, of Wales, were present.' *Public Advertiser,* Monday, 18 May 1767 [p. 2]."

[23] While Sterne may be entirely innocent here, nevertheless, cf. *ASJ,* p. 13 and n. 5; see also p. 153, Madame de Q***'s "conversation."

19—Packing up, or rather Molly for me, the whole day—tormenting! had not Molly all the time talk'd of poor Mrs Draper—& recounted every Visit She had made me, and every repast She had shared with me—how good a Lady!—How sweet a temper!—how beautiful!—how genteel!—how gentle a Carriage—& how soft & engaging a look!—the poor girl is bewitch'd with us both—infinitely interested in our Story, tho' She knows nothing of it but from her penetration and Conjectures—She says however tis Impossible not to be in Love with her——

—In heart felt truth, Eliza! I'm of Molly's Opinion——

20—Taking Leave of all the Town, before my departure to morrow.

21.   detaind by Lord & Lady Spencer who had made a party to dine & sup on my Acc^t. Impatient to set out for my Solitude—there the Mind, Eliza! gains strength, & learns to lean upon herself,—and seeks refuge in its own Constancy & Virtue—in the world it seeks or accepts of a few treacherous supports—the feign'd Compassion of one—the flattery of a second—the Civilities of a third— the friendship of a fourth—they all decieve—& bring the Mind back to where mine is retreating—that is, Eliza! to itself—to thee (who art my second self) to retirement, reflection & Books[24]—When The Stream of Things, dear Bramine, Brings Us both together to this Haven—will not your heart take up its rest for ever? & will not y^r head Leave the world to those who can make a better thing of it—if there are any who know how.—Heaven take thee Eliza! under it's Wing— adieu! adieu.——

22^d/   Left Bond Street & London wth it, this Morning—What a Creature I am! my heart has ached this week to get away—& still was ready to bleed in quiting a Place where my Connection^x with my dear dear Eliza began—Adieu to it! till I am summon'd up to the Downs by a Message, to fly to her—for I think I shall not be able to support Town without you—& w^d chuse rather to sit solitary here, till the End of the next Summer—to be made happy altogether,—than seek for happiness—or even suppose I can have it, but in Eliza's Society.

—23^d   bear my Journey badly[25]—ill—& dispirited all the Way—staid two

---

[24] This passage is copied almost verbatim in the letter to the Earl of Shelburne (see above, p. 184, n . 32); Sterne's alteration of the tone—perhaps the sense—of a passage by means of apostrophe is noteworthy in comparing the journal version to the letter: e.g., "there the mind gains strength"; and again, "bring the mind back to where mine is retreating, to retirement, reflection, and books" (*Letters* 342).

[25] Cf. *Letters,* 346 (to Hall-Stevenson, May 25): "I have got conveyed thus far [Newark] like a bale of cadaverous goods consigned to Pluto and company—lying in the bottom of my chaise most of the rout, upon a large pillow which I had the *prevoyance* to purchase before I set out—I am worn out."

days on the road at the A-Bishops of Yorks²⁶—shewd his Grace & his Lady and Sister yᵉ portrait—wᵗʰ a short but interesting Story of my friendship for the Original—kindly nursed & honourd by both—arrived at my Thatchd Cottage the 28ᵗʰ of May

29ᵗʰ and 30ᵗʰ   confined to my bed—so emaciated, and unlike what I was, I could scarse be angry with thee Eliza, if thou Could not remember me, did heaven send me across thy way—Alas! poor Yorick!—*"remember thee! Pale Ghost—remember thee—whilst Memory holds a seat in this distracted World—Remember thee,"*—Yes, from the Table of her Memory, shall just Eliza wipe away all trivial men²⁷—& leave a throne for Yorick—adieu dear constant Girl—adieu—adieu.—& Remember my Truth and eternal fidelity—Remember how I Love—remember What I suffer.—Thou art mine Eliza by Purchace—had I not earn'd thee with a better price.²⁸———

/31/

Going this day upon a long course of Corrosive Mercury—wᶜʰ in itself, is deadly poyson, but given in a certain preparation, not very dangerous²⁹—I was forced to give it up in Town, from the terrible Cholicks both in Stomach & Bowels—but the Faculty thrust it down my Throat again—These Gentry have got it into their Noddles, That mine is an *Ecclesiastick Rhuem* as the french call it³⁰—

---

²⁶ Robert Hay Drummond (1711–1776) became Archbishop of York in October 1761. He was a native of Yorkshire and kept his residence at Brodsworth, five miles northwest of Doncaster, despite having available also the palace at Bishopthorpe in York. Of him, Cash, *LY*, 115, writes: "Drummond became Sterne's protector . . . simply by paying no attention to any criticism levelled against his celebrated subordinate." Cf. Judith Jago, *Aspects of the Georgian Church: Visitation Studies of the Diocese of York, 1761–1776* (Madison, N.J.: Fairleigh Dickinson UP, 1997), esp. 28–55. Curtis, *Letters*, 348, n. 1, identifies his wife as Henrietta (?1729–1773), daughter of Peter Auriol, Esq., of London.

²⁷ Sterne thus manages to include, yet again, his signature apostrophe: see *TS*, I.12.35–36, and *ASJ*, p. 70 and n. 5. Here he joins it to lines from elsewhere in *Hamlet*, viz., I.v.95–99: "Remember thee! / Ay, thou poor ghost, whiles memory holds a seat / In this distracted globe. Remember thee! / Yea, from the table of my memory / I'll wipe away all trivial fond records."

²⁸ Perhaps "bitter" price? As is often the case, Sterne ended his entry at an earlier point, with "my Truth," and then wrote "31/" on a new line before returning to "my Truth" and concluding with a greater flourish.

²⁹ Cf. Richard Mead, *A Mechanical Account of Poison*, 3d ed. (1745), 188–90, 200–201: "The effects of this poison [i.e., mercury sublimate] . . . are violent griping pains, with a distension of the belly; vomiting, . . . with cold sweats, tremblings, convulsions, *etc.*" Mead goes on to indicate a formula that diminishes the "corrosiveness" of the mixture "to a degree as to become not only a safe, but, in many cases, a noble medicine."

³⁰ *Dictionnaire historique de la langue française* (Paris: Robert, 1992), dates the term from 1718, a humorous circumlocution for the pox. We assume Sterne heard it in French (or English) society, rather than having a literary source.

god help em! I submit as my Uncle Toby did, in drinking Water, upon the wound he rec^d in his Groin—"*merely for quietness sake.*"[31]

June 1/
The Faculty, my dear Eliza! have mistaken my Case—why not Y^rs? I wish I could fly to you & attend You but one month as a physician—You'l Languish & dye where you are,—(if not by the climate)—most certainly by their *Ignorance of y^r Case,* & the unskilful Treatment you must be a martyr to in such a place as Bombay.—I'm Languishing here myself with every Aid & help—& tho' I shall conquer it—yet have had a cruel Struggle—W^d my dear friend, I could ease y^rs, either by my advice—my attention—my Labour—my purse—They are all at Y^r Service, such as they are—and that You know Eliza—or my friendship for you is not worth a rush.[1]

June 2^d/
This morning surpriz'd with a Letter from my Lydia—that She and her Mama, are coming to pay me a Visit——but on Condition I promise not to detain them in England beyond next April—when, they purpose, by my Consent, to retire into France, & establish themselves for Life—To all which I have freely given my parole of Honour—& so shall have them with me for the Summer—from Octr to April—they take Lodgings in York—When they Leave me for good & all I suppose.[2]—☞—Every thing for the best! Eliza.

This unexpected visit, is neither a visit of friendship or form—but tis a visit, such as I know you will never make me,—of pure Interest—to pillage What they can from me. In the first place to sell a small estate I have of sixty p^ds a year—& lay out the purchase money in joint annuitys for them in the french Funds; by this they will obtain 200 p^ds a year, to be continued to the longer Liver—and as it rids me of all future care—& moreover transfers their Income to the Kingdom

---

[31] Cf. *TS,* VIII.6.662, where Toby is said not to be a water-drinker, except "during the time he was under cure; when the surgeon telling him it would extend the fibres, and bring them sooner into contact——my uncle Toby drank it for quietness sake." See also the "Abuses of conscience" sermon, read by Trim in *TS,* II.17.164: "A bad life and a good belief are disagreeable and troublesome neighbours, and where they separate, depend upon it, 'tis for no other cause but quietness sake."

[1] A commonplace derived, supposedly, from the practice of spreading rushes on floors for guests, except those "not worth a rush."

[2] For a discussion of Elizabeth Sterne's actions, see Cash, *LY,* 294–95. Bitterly, Sterne wrote to an acquaintance a week later: "By heaven! I think mine is a life of the oddest and most tragi-comic incidents in nature; this very morning that I set about writing my Sentimental Journey through France,—have I received a letter from my wife, who is at Marseilles, advertising, that she is going . . . to make a Sentimental Journey through France, and post it a thousand miles, merely to pay me a visit of three months" (see Earl R. Wasserman, "Unedited Letters by Sterne, Hume, and Rousseau," *MLN* 66 [1951]:74).

where they purpose to live—I'm truely acquiescent—tho' I lose the Contingency of surviving them—but 'tis no matter—I shall have enough—& a hundred or two hundred Pounds for Eliza when ever She will honour me with putting her hand into my Purse——In the main time,[3] I am not sorry for this Visit, as every Thing will be finally settled between us by it—only as their Annuity will be too strait—I shall engage to remit them a 100 Guineas a year more, during my Wife's Life—& then, I will think, Eliza, of living for myself & the Being I love as much!—But I shall be pillaged in a hundred small Item's by them—wch I have a Spirit above saying, *no*-to; as Provisions of all sorts of Linnens—for house use— Body Use—printed Linnens for Gowns—Magazeens[4] of Teas—Plate, all I have (but 6 Silver Spoons)—In short I shall be pluck'd bare—all but of y^r Portrait & Snuff Box & y^r other dear Presents—& the neat furniture of my thatch'd Palace—& upon those I set up Stock again, Eliza. What Say You, Eliza! shall we join our *little Capitals together?*—will Mr Draper give us leave?[5]—he may safely—if y^r *Virtue* & Honour are only concernd,—'twould be safe in Yoricks hands, as in a Brothers—I w^d not wish Mr Draper to allow you above half I allow M^n Sterne— Our Capital would be too great, & tempt us from the Society of poor Cordelia[6]—who begins to wish for You.

By this time, I trust You have doubled the Cape of good hope—sat down to y^r writing Drawer,[7] & look'd in Yoricks face, as you took out y^r Journal; to tell him so[8]—I hope he seems to smile as kindly upon You Eliza, as ever—Y^r Attachment & Love for me, will make him do so to eternity—if ever he sh^d change his Air, Eliza!—I charge you catechize your own Heart.—Oh! twil never happen!——

June 3^d—Cannot write my Travels, or give one half hours close attention to them, upon Thy Acc^t, my dearest friend—Yet write I must, & what to do with

---

[3] ?mean time

[4] See above, *ASJ*, p. 136, n. 6.

[5] Probably at this time, Sterne tried writing to Daniel Draper, the result being an awkward, never forthright letter, littered with erasures, that tells Draper he is in love with his wife, but only with the same love he bears for his own daughter, and that he would like to help her; he concludes: "She is too good to be lost—& I would [?like] out [of] pure zeal to [?make] a pilgrimage to Mecca to seek a <specifick> Med[i]cine" (*Letters* 349–50; emended). One hopes Sterne dropped the entire idea. Parnell, 250, finds a pun on "Capitals," i.e., "suggesting both heads and accumulated wealth."

[6] See above, p. 179, n. 12.

[7] Not a combination recorded in *OED*.

[8] Sterne had given Eliza his portrait (Cash, *LY* 274, suggests a mezzotint by Edward Fisher of the original Reynolds portrait [see *EMY* 300–4]) early in their relationship; cf. *Letters*, 305 (March): "And so thou hast fixed thy Bramin's portrait over thy writing-desk; and will consult it in all doubts and difficulties.—Grateful and good girl! Yorick smiles contentedly over all thou dost; his picture does not do justice to his own complacency!"

You, whilst I write—I declare I know not—I want to have you ever before my Imagination—& cannot keep You out of my heart or head—In short thou enterst my Library Eliza! (as thou one day shalt) without tapping—or sending for—by thy own Right of ever being close to thy Bramine—now I must shut you out sometimes—or meet you Eliza! with an empty purse upon the Beach—pity my entanglements from other passions—my Wife with me every moment of the Summer—think w^t restraint upon a Fancy that should Sport & be in all points at its ease——O had I, my dear Bramine this Summer, to soften—& modulate my feelings—to enrich my fancy, & fill my heart brim full with bounty—my Book w^d be worth the reading——

It will be by stealth if I am able to go on with my Journal at all—It will have many Interruptions—& Hey ho's![9] most sentimentally utter'd—Thou must take it as it pleases God.—as thou must take the Writer—eternal Blessings be about You Eliza! I am a little better, & now find I shall be set right in all points—my only anxiety is about You—I want to prescribe^x for you, my Eliza—for I think I understand y^r *Case* better than all the Faculty.[10] adieu. adieu.

June 4.   Hussy!—I have employ'd a full hour upon y^r sweet sentimental Picture—and a couple of hours upon yourself—& with as much kind friendship, as the hour You left me—I deny it—Time lessens no Affections wch honour^x & merit have planted—I w^d give more, and hazard more now for your happiness than in any one period, since I first learn'd to esteem you—is it so with thee my friend? has absence weakend my Interest—has time worn out any Impression— or is Yoricks Name less Musical in Eliza's ears?—my heart smites me, for asking the question—tis Treason ag^st thee Eliza and Truth—Ye are dear Sisters, and y^r Brother Bramin Can never live to see a Separation amongst Us.—What a similitude in our Trials, whilst asunder!—Providence has order'd every Step better, than we could have order'd them,—for the particular good we wish each other—This you will comment upon & find the *Sense of* without my explanation.

I wish this Summer & Winter w^h all I am to go through with in them, in business & Labour & Sorrow, well over—I have much to compose—& much to discompose me—have my Wife's projects—& my own Views arising out of them, to harmonize and turn to account—I have Millions of heart aches to suffer & reason with—& in all this Storm of Passions, I have but one small anchor, Eliza! to keep this weak Vessel of mine from perishing—I trust all I have to it—as I

---

[9] Cf. *TS*, VIII.26.710, where Tristram compares his father's irascible approach to love to Toby's, who "blamed neither heaven nor earth . . . ; he sat solitary and pensive with his pipe——looking at his lame leg——then whiffing out a sentimental heigh ho! which mixing with the smoak, incommoded no one mortal." *OED*'s first example of "sentimentally" is dated 1784.

[10] Cf. Appendix (Yorick to Eliza), pp. 251–52. There is almost certainly a double entendre in "*Case*"; see above, *ASJ*, p. 135 and n. 2.

trust Heaven, which cannot leave me, without a fault, to perish.—may the same just Heaven my Eliza, be that eternal Canopy wch shall shelter thy head from evil till we meet—

Adieu—adieu. adieu.—

June 5./

I Sit down to write this day, in good earnest—so read Eliza! quietly besides me—I'll not give you a Look——except one of kindness.—dear Girl! if thou lookest so bewitching once more—I'll turn thee out of my Study[11]—You may bid me defiance, Eliza.—You cannot conceive how much & how universally I'm pitied, upon the Score of this unexpected Visit from france—my friends think it will kill me—If I find myself in danger I'll fly to You to Bombay—will Mr Draper receive me?—he ought—but he will never know What reasons make it his *Interest* and *Duty*—We must leave all all to that Being—who is infinitely removed above all Straitness of heart[12] . . . . . & is a friend to the friendly, as well as to the friendless.

June 6.—am quite alone in the depth of that sweet Recesse,[13] I have so often described to You—tis sweet in itself—but You never come across me—but the perspective brightens up—& every Tree & Hill & Vale & Ruin ab^t me—smiles as if you was amidst 'em—delusive moments!—how pensive[14] a price do I pay for you—fancy sustains the Vision, whilst She has strength—but Eliza! Eliza is not with me!—I sit down upon the first Hillock Solitary as a sequester'd Bramin—I wake from my delusion to a thousand Disquietudes, which many talk of—my Eliza!—but few feel[15]—then weary my Spirit with thinking, plotting, & project-ing—& when Ive brought my System to my mind—am only Doubly miserable, That I cannot execute it—

Thus—Thus my dear Bramine are we tost at present in this tempest—Some Haven of rest will open to us. assuredly—God made us not for Misery and

---

[11] Cf. Appendix, p. 251 (Yorick to Eliza).

[12] Cf. *TS*, II.27.150: "Another is sordid, unmerciful . . . a strait-hearted, selfish wretch"; *OED* cites this as its sole illustration (s.v. *strait*, a.,n., and adv. 17). See also Appendix, "Phi-lanthropy recommended," p. 234, where Sterne's "sordid wretch, whose straight heart is open to no man's affliction" is *OED*'s sole illustration: "Of a person's 'heart': Contracted in sympathies, narrow" (s.v. *strait*, 15.b).

[13] I.e., Byland Abbey.

[14] ?expensive

[15] Cf. *TS*, IV.S.T.319–20: "Julia had sunk . . . with the many disquietudes of a tender heart, which all talk of—but few feel . . ."; noted by Parnell, 250.

Ruin[16]—he has orderd all our Steps[17]—& influenced our Attachments for what is worthy of them—It must end well—Eliza!—

June 7.

I have this week finish'd a sweet little apartment[18] which all the time it was doing, I flatter'd the most delicious of Ideas, in thinking I was making it for you—Tis a neat little simple elegant room, overlook'd only by the Sun—just big enough to hold a Sopha,—for us—a Table, four Chairs, a Bureau—& a Book case.—They are to be all y[rs], Room & all—& there Eliza! shall I enter ten times a day to give thee Testimonies of my Devotion[x]—Was't thou this moment sat down, it w[d] be the sweetest of earthly Tabernacles—I shall enrich it, from time to time, for thee—till Fate lets me lead thee by the hand into it—& then it can want no Ornament.—tis a little oblong room—with a large Sash at the end—a little elegant fireplace—wth as much room to dine around it, as in Bond street.— But in sweetness & Simplicity, & silence beyond any thing—Oh my Eliza!—I

---

[16] This is a consistent theme in Sterne's sermons; see, e.g., sermon 22, "The history of Jacob" (4:212):

> We agree with the patriarch, that the life of man is miserable; and yet the world looks happy enough——and every thing tolerably at its ease. It must be noted indeed, that the patriarch . . . speaks merely his present feelings, and seems rather to be giving a history of his sufferings, than a system of them, in contradiction to that of the GOD of Love. Look upon the world he has given us,——observe the riches and plenty which flows in every channel . . . every place is almost a paradise, planted when nature was in her gayest humour.
>
> ——Every thing has two views. Jacob, and Job, and Solomon, gave one section of the globe,——and this representation another:——truth lieth betwixt—or rather, good and evil are mixed up together; which of the two preponderates, is beyond our enquiry;—— but, I trust—it is the good:——first, As it renders the Creator of the world more dear and venerable to me; and secondly, Because I will not suppose, that a work intended to exalt his glory, should stand in want of apologies.

[17] Cf. Psalm 37:23: "The steps of a good man are ordered by the Lord: and he delighteth in his way"; and Psalm 119:133: "Order my steps in thy word: and let not any iniquity have dominion over me."

[18] Cf. Cash, LY, 293–94: "Early in May, Sterne began directing extensive repairs and renovations of Shandy Hall. Most of the upstairs rooms were remodelled in 1767 . . . . But the most extensive work was the two-storey brick extension some six feet deep and topped by a parapet which was added to the western end so that from the garden the house would have a modest Georgian look." Eliza's suite was part of this renovation activity. See also, Kenneth Monkman, Shandy Hall's restorer and first curator: "the neat little simple elegant room does still exist identifiably as Sterne describes it: oblong, with a large sash window at one end facing south, and with a little elegant fireplace" (Quoted from correspondence in Eva C. van Leewen, Sterne's "Journal to Eliza": A Semiological and Linguistic Approach [Tübingen: Gunter Narr, 1981], 160).

shall see thee surely Goddesse of this Temple,[19]—and the most sovereign one, of all I have—& of all the powers heaven has trusted me with—They were lent me, Eliza! only for thee—& for thee my dear Girl shall be kept & employ'd.—You know *What*[x] *rights* You have over me—wish to heaven I could Convey the Grant more amply than I have *done*[x]—but tis the same—tis register'd where it will longest last—& that is in the feeling & most sincere of human hearts—You know I mean this reciprocally—& whenever I mention the Word Fidelity & Truth,—in Speaking of y[r] Reliance on mine—I always Imply the same Reliance upon the same Virtues in my Eliza.—I love thee Eliza! & will love thee for ever. Adieu.———

June 8.

Begin to recover, and sensibly to gain strength every day—and have such an appetite as I have not had for some Years—I prophecy I shall be the better, for the very Accident which has occasiond my Illness, & that the Medcines & Regimen I have submitted to, will make a thorough Regeneration of me, & y[r] I shall have more health and Strength, than I have enjoy'd these ten Years—Send me such an Acc[t] of thy self Eliza, by the first sweet Gale—but tis impossible You sh[d] from Bombay—twil be as fatal to You, as it has been to thousands of y[r] Sex—England & Retirement in it, can only save you—Come!—Come away—

June 9th   I keep a post Chaise & a couple of fine horses, & take the Air every day in it—I go out—& return to my Cottage Eliza! alone—'tis melancholly, what sh[d] be matter of enjoyment; & the more so for that reason—I have a thousand things to remark & say as I roll along—but I want You to say them to[20]—I could sometimes be wise—& often Witty—but I feel it a reproach to be the latter whilst Eliza is so far from hearing me—& What is Wisdome to a foolish weak heart like mine! Tis like the Song of Melody to a broken Spirit———You must teach me fortitude my dear Bramine—for with all the tender qualities w[ch] make you the most precious of Women—& most wanting of all other Women of a kind protector—yet you have a passive kind of sweet Courage w[ch] bears You up— more than any one Virtue I can summon up in my own Case—We were made

---

[19] Cf. Curtis, *Letters,* 353, n. 2: "Sterne's now frequent indulgence in whimsies such as he here describes should not excite our contempt. . . . [H]e was ill and . . . sought relief in playthings. In 1767 he divided his life between reality and daydreams. That he valued their efficacy in sheltering him from evils he suggested in the *Sentimental Journey*"; Curtis then quotes the "Sweet pliability" passage, *ASJ,* p. 120, which does seem acutely apropos.

[20] Twice in this sentence Sterne erased words, the first time so forcefully as to leave a hole, which was then patched with the almost total loss of the original word. The first "say" is inserted above this patch; the second "say" is inserted above a heavily overwritten word, which we tentatively read as "sing." Even in his journal, Sterne was an author fully aware of the stylistic importance of "the right word in the right place at the right time."

with Tempers for each other, Eliza! & You are blessd with such a certain turn of Mind & reflection—that if Self love does not blind me—I resemble no Being in the world so nearly as I do You[21]—do you wonder that I have such friendship for you?—for my own part, I sh^d not be astonish'd, Eliza, if you was to declare, "You was up to the ears in Love with Me".[22]

June 10th—
You are stretching over now in the Trade Winds from the Cape to Madrass— (I hope)—but I know it not. some friendly Ship You possibly have met wth, & I never read an Acc^t of an India Man arrived—but I expect that it is the Messenger of the news my heart is upon the rack for.—I calculate, That you will arrive at Bombay by the begining of October[23]—by February, I shall surely hear from you thence—but from Madrass sooner.—I expect you Eliza in person, by September—& shall scarse go to London till March—for what have I to do there, when (except printing my Books) I have no Interest or Passion to gratify—I shall return in June to Coxwould—& there wait for the glad Tidings of y^r arrival in the Downs—won't You write to me Eliza! by the first Boat?—would not you wish to be greeted by y^r Yorick upon the Beech?—or be met by him to hand you out of y^r postchaise, to pay him for the Anguish he underwent, in handing You into it?—I know your answers—my Spirit is with You.   farewel dear friend——

June 11.   I am every day negociating to sell my little Estate besides me—to send the money into France, to purchase peace to myself—& a certainty of never having it interrupted by Mrs Sterne—who when She is sensible I have given her all I can part with—will be at rest herself—Indeed her plan to purchase annuities in france—is a pledge of Security to me—That She will live her days out there—otherwise She could have no end in transporting this two thousand pounds out of England—nor w^d I consent but upon that plan—but I may be at rest!—if my

---

[21] Melvyn New, "Job's Wife," and Mark S. Madoff, "'They caught fire at each other': Laurence Sterne's Journal of the Pulse of Sensibility," in *Sensibility in Transformation* (Rutherford, N.J.: Fairleigh Dickinson UP, 1990), 43–62, agree in centering their discussion of *BJ* on the notion that "the correspondence" Sterne seeks between himself and Eliza "has at least as much to do with reflecting himself as with reaching another[;] . . . as he writes his journal, he must see Eliza at her desk writing hers. Indeed, the many references to sensibility and sentiment, sympathy and pathos in the 'Journal' all appear to come from this single urge, to find in another human being one's own self" (New 63; see also Madoff 59, n. 8).

[22] Cf. *TS*, VI.37.565: "to say a man is *fallen* in love,—or that he is *deeply* in love,—or up to the ears in love . . . carries an idiomatical kind of implication, that love is a thing *below* a man: . . . I hold [this] to be damnable and heretical"; and VIII.19.693, where Trim admits to having been in love "over head and ears" with the Beguine. Cf. Tilley, H268, and *ODEP*, s.v. *over*.
  Sterne's suggestion that Eliza had never used these words may tell us something.

[23] Sterne miscalculates by three months; see above, p. 191, n. 2.

imagination will but let me—Hall says tis no matter where she lives; If we are but separate, tis as good as if the Ocean rolld between us—& so I should Argue to another Man—but, tis an Idea wch won't do so well for me—& tho' nonsensical enough—Yet I shall be most at rest when there is that Bar between us—was I never so sure, I sh^d never be interrupted by her, in England—but I may be at rest I say, on that head—for they have left all their Cloaths & plate and Linnen behind them in france—& have joind in the most earnest Entreaty, That they may return & fix in france—to wch I have given my word & honour—You will be bound with me Eliza! I hope, for performance of my promise—I never yet broke it, in cases where Interest or pleasure could have tempted me—and shall hardly do it, now, when tempted only by misery.—In Truth Eliza! thou art the Object to wch every act of mine is directed—You interfere in every Project—I rise—I go to sleep with this in my Brain—how will my dear Bramine approve of this?—wch way will it conduce to make her happy? & how will it be a proof of my Affection to her? are all the Enquiries I make.—Y^r Honour, y^r Conduct, y^r Truth & regard for my esteem—I know will equally direct every Step—& movement of y^r Desires—& with that Assurance, is it, my dear Girl, That I sustain Life,—   But when will those Sweet eyes of thine, run over these Declarations?—how—& with Whom are they to be entrusted; to be conveyd to You?—unless Mrs James's friendship to us, finds some expedient[24]—I must wait—till the first evening I'm with You— when I shall present You w^th—them as a better Picture of me, than Cusway[25] Could do for You. .—have been dismally ill all day—oweing to my course of Medecines wch are too strong & forcing for this gawsy[26] Constitution of mine—I mend with them however—good God! how is it with You?——

June 12.   I have return'd from a delicious Walk of Romance,[27] my Bramine, which I am to tread a thousand times over with You swinging upon my arm—tis

---

[24] Cash, *LY*, 304 and n. 88, argues that the letters accompanying the manuscript of *BJ* (see Introduction, pp. xv–xvi) constitute prima facie evidence that the journal was placed in Mrs. James's hands before Sterne's death; it seems a valid assumption.

[25] I.e., Richard Cosway (1742–1821), whose portrait of Eliza is probably the painting described by Sterne in his letter to Eliza reprinted in Appendix, pp. 249–51; the *Oxford Companion to Art* (1970) labels him "by far the most fashionable miniature painter of his day." See also Stephen Lloyd, *Richard and Maria Cosway* (Edinburgh: Scottish National Portrait Gallery, 1995). In a rather odd sentimental turn, Sterne's great admirer, Thomas Jefferson, is reported to have had an affair with Cosway's young wife, Maria Hadfield Cosway (1760–1838), also a painter, while ambassador to Paris in the 1780s (Lloyd 50).

[26] Curtis, *Letters*, 359, n. 4, is almost certainly correct in suggesting "gauzy," i.e., flimsy, thin. However, in northern dialect "gawsy" means just the opposite; *OED*, s.v.: "Of persons: Well-dressed and jolly-looking. Of things: Large and handsome."

[27] Sterne's odd phrase may anticipate *OED*'s definition, s.v. *romance*, 5.b: "redolence or suggestion of, association with, the adventurous and chivalrous, spec. a love affair; idealistic character or quality in a love affair"; its first example is dated 1801.

to my Convent—& I have pluckd up a score Bryars by the roots wch grew near the edge of the footway, that they might not scratch or incommode you[28]—had I been sure of y^r taking that walk with me the very next day, I could not have been more serious in my employm^t—dear Enthusiasm![29]—thou bringst things forward in a moment, wch Time keeps for Ages back—I have you ten times a day besides me—I talk to You Eliza, for hours together—I take y^r Council—I hear your reasons—I admire you for them!—to this magic of a warm Mind, I owe all that's worth living for, during this State of our Trial—Every Trincket you gave or exchanged wth me, has its force—Y^r Picture is Y^{r}self—all Sentiment, Softness, & Truth—It speaks—it listens—'tis convincd—it resignes—Dearest Original! how like unto thee does it seem—& will seem—till thou makest it vanish, by thy presence—I'm but so, so— but advancing in health—to meet you—to nurse you, to nourish you agst you come—for I fear, You will not arrive, but in a State that calls out to Yorick for sup- port—Thou art Mistress, Eliza, of all the powers he has to sooth & protect thee— for thou art Mistress of his heart; his affections; and his reason—& beyond that, except a paltry purse, he has nothing worth giving thee—.

June 13.

This has been a year of presents to me—my Bramine—How many presents have I rec^d from You, in the first place?—Ld Spencer has loaded me with a grand Ecritoire of 40 Guineas[30]—I am to recieve this week a fourty Guinea-present of a gold Snuff Box, as fine as Paris can fabricate one—with an Inscription on it, more

---

[28] Cf. *ASJ*, p. 28, n. 6.

[29] That Sterne praises "enthusiasm" in the days immediately following Whitsuntide (Pente- cost), celebrated seven weeks after Easter, is perhaps associational, since Pentecost sermons would often dwell on the subject of visitation, as indeed in his own sermon 38, "On enthu- siasm." Sterne's attitude therein toward claims of "inspiration" remains steeped in Swiftian suspicion, but his usage here indicates the rehabilitation of the word in the course of the century, as in the poetry of William Collins; e.g., "Ode to Pity," ll. 28–30: "Its Southern Site, its Truth compleat / Shall raise a wild Enthusiast Heat, / In all who view the Shrine" (*Works*, ed. Richard Wendorf and Charles Ryskamp [Oxford: Clarendon, 1979], 26).

[30] Cf. *Letters*, 258–59 (October 1, 1765): "I wish I knew how to thank You properly for your obliging present; . . . I can only say to Lord Spencer '*That I thank him*' and promise him at the same time what I know will be more acceptable, That I will make his kind Wish in the Inscription as prophetic as the singularity of so odd a composition as I am made up of, will let me." The Latin inscription is offered at the bottom of the letter and may be translated: "To Laurence Sterne, A.M., John, Earl Spencer, prays to all the muses and in his love wishes that they may be propitious to you." Cash, *LY*, 226–27, seems correct in assuming that this is the gift Sterne alludes to here, despite its being given several years earlier. *Ecritoire*: a writing desk or ink stand.

The presenter of the "gold Snuff Box" is unknown; cf. *Letters*, 388 (to Mrs. James, in August): "I have just rec^d as a present from a right Honble——a most elegant gold Snuff [box] fabricated for me at Paris—I wish Eliza was here—I would lay it at her feet—however I will enrich my gold Box, with her picture . . . ."

valuable, than the Box itself—I have a present of a portrait, (which by the by, I have immortalized in my Sentimental Journey[31]) worth them both—I say nothing of a gold Stock buccle & Buttons[32]—tho' I rate them above rubies because they were Consecrated by the hand of Friendship, as She fitted them to me.—I have a present of the Sculptures upon poor Ovid's Tomb, who died in Exile, tho' he wrote so well upon the Art of Love—These are in six beautiful Pictures executed on Marble at Rome[33]—& these Eliza, I keep sacred as Ornaments for y[r] Cabinet, on Condition I hang them up.—and last of all, I have had a present, Eliza! this year, of a Heart so finely set—with such rich materials—& Workmanship—That Nature must have had the chief hand in it—If I am able to keep it—I shall be a rich Man;—If I lose it—I shall be poor indeed[34]—so poor! I shall stand begging at y[r] gates.—But what can all these presents portend—That it will turn out a fortunate earnest, of what is to be given me hereafter—

June 14./

I want you to comfort me my dear Bramine—& reconcile my mind to 3 Months misery—some days I think lightly of it—on others—my heart sinks down to the earth—but tis the last Trial of conjugal Misery—& I wish it was to begin this moment, That it might run its period the faster—for sitting as I do, expecting sorrow—is suffering it—I am going to Hall to be philosophizd with for a Week or ten Days on this point—but one hour with you would calm me more

---

[31] Cf. *ASJ*, p. 4: "the little picture which I have so long worn, and so often have told thee, Eliza, I would carry with me into my grave."

[32] Cf. Cunnington, 221: "*Stock buckles,* though generally concealed by the wig, were often costly and might be of gold, silver, plated, pinchbeck, worked or plain, and sometimes set with diamonds." For the *stock,* see *ASJ*, p. 129, n. 4.

[33] See *Letters,* 412 (February 1768), where Sterne thanks a correspondent for some prints: "I will decorate my study with them, along with six beautiful pictures I have already of the sculptures on poor Ovid's tomb, which were executed on marble at Rome.—It grieves one to think such a man should have dy'd in exile, who wrote so well on the art of love." Cf. Edward Wright, *Some Observations Made in Travelling through France, Italy, &c.,* 2d ed. (1764; first pub. 1730), 359–60:

> It is well known that Ovid died in banishment, in a country far distant from Rome, and was there buried. This sepulchre [in Rome], therefore, is not of Ovid himself, but of the *familia Nasonia,* descendants from him.
> . . . The designs of all the paintings, with which the rest of the niches, and all the other parts of the sepulchre were cover'd over, may be known by [Pietro Sante] Bartoli's prints, and [Giovanni Pietro] Bellori's illustrations, in their book of the *Grotte Antiche.*

We assume Sterne had prints copied or extracted from this work.

[34] Curtis, *Letters,* 359, n. 8, hears an echo of *Othello,* III.iii.159–61: "*Iago:* But he that filches from me my good name / Robs me of that which not enriches him, / And makes me poor indeed."

& furnish me with stronger Supports, under this weight upon my Spirits, than all
the world—put together—Heaven! to what distressful Encountres hast thou
thought fit to expose me—& was it not, that thou hast blessd me with a chearful-
ness of disposition—& thrown an Object in my Way, That is to render that Sun
Shine perpetual—Thy dealings with me, would be a mystery.—

June 15—from morning to night every momᵗ of this day held in Bondage at
my friend Lᵈ ffauconberg's[35]—so have but a moment.   left to close the day, as I
do every one—with wishing thee a sweet nights rest—would I was at the feet of yʳ
Bed—fanning breezes to You, in yʳ Slumbers—Mark!—you will dream of me this
night—& if it is not recorded in your Journal—Ill say, you could not recollect it
the day following—adieu.—

June 16.
My Chaise is so large—so high—so long—so wide—so Crawford's like,[36]
That I am building a coach house on purpose for it—do you dislike it for this
gigantick Size?—now I remember, I heard You once say—You hated a small post
Chaise—wᶜʰ you must know determined my Choice to this—because I hope to
make you a present of it—& if you are squeamish I shall be as squeamish as You,
& return you all yʳ presents—but one—wᶜʰ I cannot part with—and what that
is—I defy you to guess. I have bought a milch Asse this Afternoon—& purpose
to live by Suction, to save the expences of houskeeping—& have a Score or two
guineas in my purse, next September— — —

June 17/
I have brought yʳ name *Eliza!* and Picture into my work[37]—where they will
remain—when You & I are at rest for ever—Some Annotator or explainer of my
works in this place will take occasion, to speak of the Friendship wᶜʰ Subsisted so
long & faithfully betwixt Yorick & the Lady he speaks of—Her Name he will
tell the world was Draper—a Native of India—married there to a gentleman in
the India Service of that Name—, who brought her over to England for the
recovery of her health in the Year 65—where She continued to April the year
1767. It was abᵗ three months before her Return to India, That our Author's
acquaintance & hers began. Mʳˢ Draper had a great thirst for knowledge—was

---

[35] See above, p. 195, n. 18.

[36] Curtis, *Letters*, 359, n. 9, identifies him as John Craufurd of Errol (?1742–1814), whom
Sterne met in Paris in 1765. Supposedly, the "case of delicacy" in *ASJ* was an actual experience he imparted to Sterne (see *ASJ*, p. 170, n. 6). Sterne's comment is illuminated by Curtis's characterization of Craufurd's reputation: "Lavish, witty, eccentric, hypochrondriacal,
he was as much in love with pose as with play" (*Letters* 263, n. 7).

[37] See above, p. 4, n. 7. Possibly, Sterne is thinking of his second allusion to Eliza in *ASJ*,
pp. 62–3, when he twice names her.

handsome—genteel—engaging—and of such gentle dispositions & so enlightend an understanding, That Yorick, (whether he made much opposition is not known) from an acquaintance—soon became her Admirer—they caught fire[x] at each other at the same time—& they w[d] often say, without reserve to the world, & without any Idea of saying wrong in it, That their Affections for each other were *unbounded*[x]— —M[r] Draper dying in the Year *****[38]—This Lady return'd to England & Yorick the year after becoming a Widower—They were married—& retiring to one of his Livings in Yorkshire, where was a most romantic Situation—they lived & died happily—and are spoke of with honour in the parish to this day——[39]

June 18/

How do you like the History, of this couple, Eliza?—is it to your mind?—or shall it be written better some sentimental Evening after your return—tis a rough Sketch—but I could make it a pretty picture, as the outlines are just—we'll put our heads together & try what we can do. This last Sheet[40] has put it out of my power, ever to send you this Journal to India—I had been more guarded—but that You have often told me, 'twas in vain to think of writing by Ships w[ch] sail in March,—as you hoped to be upon y[r] return again—by their Arrival at Bombay— If I can write a Letter—I will—but this Journal must be put into Eliza's hands by Yorick only—God grant you to read it soon.—

June. 19.

I never was so well and alert, as I find myself this day—tho' with a face as pale & clear as a Lady after her Lying in, Yet you never saw me so Young by 5 Years— If you do not leave Bombay soon—You'l find me as young as Y[r]self—at this rate of going on— —Summon'd from home. adieu.

June 20/

I think my dear Bramine—That nature is turn'd upside down—for Wives go to visit Husbands, at greater perils, & take longer journies to pay them this Civility now a days out of ill Will—than good—Mine is flying post a Journey of a

---

[38] Daniel Draper died March 20, 1805, at his house in St. James's Street, London, long outliving both Sterne and Eliza. Sterne may have written "Year——" and then canceled the long dash with x's or vice versa.

[39] Sterne strikes the note of the conclusion of many novels of the period; e.g., Smollett's *Sir Launcelot Greaves:* "The perfect and uninterrupted felicity of the knight and his endearing consort, diffused itself through the whole adjacent country . . . . They were admired, esteemed, and applauded by every person of taste, sentiment, and benevolence; at the same time beloved, revered, and almost adored by the common people" (ed. David Evans [London: Oxford UP, 1973], 210); see also the conclusion of Fielding's *Tom Jones.*

[40] It is difficult to believe that up to the June 17 entry Sterne thought he had written nothing equally compromising.

thousand Miles—with as many Miles to go back[41]—merely to see how I do, & whether I am fat or lean—& how far are you going to see y' Helpmate—and at such hazards to y' Life, as few Wives' best affections w'd be able to surmount—But Duty & Submission Eliza govern thee—by what impulses my Rib[42] is bent towards me—I have told you—& yet I w'd to God, Draper but rec'd & treated you with half the courtesy & good nature—I wish you was with him—for the same reason I wish my Wife at Coxwould—That She might the sooner depart in peace.[43]—She is ill—of a Diarhea which she has from a weakness on her bowels ever since her paralitic Stroke—Travelling post in hot weather, is not the best remedy for her—but my girl says—she is determined to venture—She wrote me word in Winter, She w'd not leave france, till her end approach'd—surely this journey is not prophetick! but twould invert the order of Things on the other side of this Leaf[44]—and what is to be on the next *Leaf*—The Fates, Eliza only can tell us—rest satisfied.

June 21.

have left off all medcines—not caring to tear my frame to pieces with 'em—as I feel perfectly well.—set out for Crasy Castle[45] to morrow morning—where I stay ten days—take my sentimental Voyage—and this Journal with me, as certain as the two first Wheels of my Chariot—I cannot go on without them—I long to see Y'—I shall read it a thousand times over If I get it before y' Arrival—What w'd I now give for it—tho' I know there are *circumstances* in it, That will make my

---

[41] Sterne is equally wry in commenting to Mrs. James (August 16) about the impending visit: "Mrs Sterne & my daughter are coming to stay a couple of months with me, as far as from Avignion—& then return—Here's Complaisance for you[.] I went 500 Miles the last Spring, out of my Way, to pay my Wife a weeks Visit—and She is at the expence of coming post a thousand miles to return it—What a happy pair!—however, *en passant,* She takes back sixteen hundred pds into france with her——and will do me the honour, likewise to strip me of every thing I have— / — except Eliza's Picture" (*Letters* 389).

[42] Sterne uses this jocular term for a wife several times in his correspondence (*Letters* 52, 288) and in *TS,* I.16.48: "[Walter would] place his rib and self in so many tormenting lights."

[43] Cf. Luke 2:29: "Lord, now lettest thou thy servant depart in peace."

[44] I.e., Sterne's "prophecy," that Daniel Draper would die before Elizabeth Sterne.

[45] The name given, with the spelling "Crazy Castle," on the frontispiece depicting Skelton Castle, John Hall-Stevenson's home in Skelton, in North Yorkshire, close to Saltburn-by-the-Sea, which adorned the first edition of *Crazy Tales* (1762). For a full account of the circle of friends, known as the Demoniacs, who met there, see Cash, *EMY,* 181–95; his summation throws useful light on Sterne's visiting Hall-Stevenson at this time: "In the final analysis, the Demoniacs gave Sterne something far more valuable than literary influence: they gave him friendship. . . . Hall-Stevenson and the Demoniacs probably renewed Sterne's good spirits again and again during his years of poor health, marital difficulties and floundering career . . ." (195).

heart bleed & waste within me—*but if all blows over*—tis enough—we will not recount our Sorrows, but to shed tears of Joy over them[46]—O Eliza! Eliza!— Heaven nor any Being it created, ever so possessd a Man's heart—as thou possessest mine—use it kindly—Hussy—that is, eternally be true to it.—

June 22.[47] Ive been as far as York to day with no Soul with me in my Chase, but y^r Picture—for it has a *Soul,* I think—or something like one which has talk'd to me, & been the best Company I ever took a Journey with (always excepting a Journey I once took with a friend of Y^rs to Salt hill, & Enfield Wash[48]—The plea-sure^x I had in those Journies, have left *Impressions* upon my Mind, which will last my Life—You may tell her as much when You see her—she will not take it ill)— I set out early to morrow morning to see Mr Hall—but take my Journal along with me.

June 24th
as pleasant a Journey as I am capable of taking Eliza! without thee—Thou shalt take it with me, when time & tide serve hereafter, & every other Journey wch ever gave me pleasure, shall be rolled over again with thee besides me.— Arno's Vale[49] shall look gay again upon Eliza's Visit.—and the Companion of her

---

[46] The juxtaposition of Sorrow and Joy may recall John 16:20–22: "ye shall be sorrowful, but your sorrow shall be turned into joy. . . . And ye now therefore have sorrow: but I will see you again, and your heart shall rejoice, and your joy no man taketh from you." See also Job 41:22: "sorrow is turned into joy before him."

[47] As Cash, *LY,* 296–97, notes, Sterne first went to York on an errand, and then to Thirsk for "the archdeaconry visitation," where he probably visited with Dr. Francis Blackburne (1705–1787), Archdeacon of Cleveland, perhaps the most liberal cleric of the York estab-lishment; this would account for the missing entry on June 23. If the entries in the *Journal* are accurately dated, Sterne took a remarkably circuitous journey, heading south to York on June 22, returning to Thirsk, a few miles west of Coxwold, on the next day, and then travel-ing east-northeast across the moors to Skelton the day after that.

[48] It has been assumed that Eliza's children were at school at Salt Hill, just north of Slough and Windsor, on the western outskirts of London. In a second recall of the excursion at p. 223, however, "Enfield Wash" becomes "Enfield," and Sterne clearly indicates that the jour-ney was to see the children. But Enfield is on the northern edge of London, as in fact is Enfield Wash. This means that "Journies" signals trips to two different places, Salt Hill *and* Enfield (Wash), assuming "Salt Hill" is not a bawdy misdirection entirely; cf. *Letters,* 394 (September 19), alluding to a woman known only as "Hannah": "she is not the . . . lady who supp'd with me in Bond-street on scollop'd oysters, and other such things—nor did she ever go *tete-a-tete* with me to Salt Hill.—Enough of such nonsense . . . ." There is no Salt Hill in the Enfield area, which did have several reputable boarding schools in the eighteenth century.

[49] Cf. Appendix, letter to Eliza, p. 252, and *BJ,* p. 217, where Arno's Vale is clearly sexual in nature; Sterne may have associated the Arno with Petrarch and Laura, but it seems as well, perhaps, a private name for a location where they stopped in the vicinity of Salt Hill (or is "Salt Hill" itself suspect?) or Enfield. There was a popular song with the title "Arno's Vale."

Journey, will grow young again as he sits upon her Banks with Eliza seated besides him—I have this and a thousand little parties of pleasure—& systems of living out of the common high road, of Life, hourly working in my fancy for you—there wants only the *Dramatis Personae* for the performance—the play is wrote—the Scenes are painted—& the Curtain ready to be drawn up.—the whole Piece waits for thee, my Eliza—

June 25.—In a course of continual visits & Invitations here—*Bombay-Lascelles* dined here to day[50]—(his Wife yesterday brought to bed)—he is a poor sorry soul! but has taken a house two miles from Crasy Castle—What a stupid, selfish, unsentimental set of Beings are the Bulk of our Sex! by Heaven! not one man out of 50, informd with feelings—or endow'd either with heads or hearts able to possess & fill the mind of such a Being as thee, with one Vibration like its own[51]—I never see or converse with one of my Sex—but I give this point a reflection—how w^d such a creature please my Bramine? I assure thee Eliza I have not been able to find one, whom I thought could please You—the turn of Sentiment, with wch I left y^r Character possess'd—must improve, hourly upon You—Truth, fidelity, honour & Love mix'd up with Delicacy, garranteè one another—and a taste so improved as Y^{rs}, by so delicious fare, can never degenerate—I shall find you, my Bramine, if possible, more valuable & lovely, than when You first caught my esteem and kindness for You—and tho' I see not this change—I give you so much Credit for it—that at this moment, my heart glowes more warmly as I think of you—& I find myself more your Husband than contracts can make us—I stay here till the 29th—had intended a longer Stay—but much company & Dissipation rob me of the only comfort my mind takes, wch is in retirement, where I can think of You Eliza! and enjoy you quietly & without Interruption—tis the Way We must expect all that is to be had of *real* enjoyment in this vile world—which being miserable itself—seems so confederated agst the happiness of the Happy,—that they are forced to secure it in private—Variety must still be had;—& that, Eliza! & every thing wth it wch Yorick's sense, or generosity has to furnish

---

[50] I.e., at Skelton Castle. Cash, *LY*, 297: "Peter Lascelles [d. 1775], recently retired as a sea captain for the East India Company to an estate he had purchased near Hall's. Lascelles frightened [Sterne] by telling him about the terrible dangers that ships encountered in Indian waters . . . —pirates probably." Lascelles subscribed to *ASJ*, whatever Sterne's opinion of him might have been.

[51] Sterne's observations here parallel those in his famous letter to an American enthusiast, Dr. John Eustace (February 9, 1768), thanking him for his gift of a "*shandaic*" walking stick: "In *Tristram Shandy*, the handle is taken which suits their passions, their ignorance or sensibility. There is so little true feeling in the *herd* of the *world*, that I wish I could have got an act of parliament, when the books first appear'd, 'that none but wise men should look into them.' It is too much to write books and find heads to understand them. . . . [A true feeler's] own ideas are only call'd forth by what he reads, and the vibrations within" (*Letters* 411).

to one he loves so much as thee—need I tell thee—Thou wilt be as much a Mistress of—as thou art eternally of thy Yorick—adieu adieu.—

June 26.   eleven at night—out all the day—dined with a large Party—shewd yᵗ Picture from the fullness of my heart—highly admired—alas! said I—did You but see the Original!—good night.—

June 27.
Ten in the morning, with my Snuff open at the Top of this sheet,—& your gentle sweet face opposite to mine, & saying "what I write will be cordially read"—possibly you may be precisely engaged at this very hour, the same way— and telling me some interesting Story abᵗ yʳ health, yʳ sufferings—yʳ heartaches— and other Sensations wᶜʰ friendship—absence & Uncertainty create within You. for my own part, my dear Eliza, I am a prey to every thing in its turn—& was it not for that sweet clew of hope wᶜʰ is perpetually opening me a Way which is to lead me to thee thro' all this Labyrinth—was it not for this, my Eliza! how could I find rest for this bewilderd heart of mine?—I shᵈ wait for you till September came—& if you did not arrive with it—shᵈ sicken & die.—but I will live for thee—so count me Immortal—3 India Men arrived within ten days—will none of 'em bring me Tidings of You?—but I am foolish—but ever thine—my dear, dear Bramine.————

June 28.
O What a tormenting night have my dreams led me abᵗ You Eliza—Mʳˢ Draper a Widow!—with a hand at Liberty to give!—and gave it to another!—She told me—I must acquiese—it could not be otherwise—Acquiese! cried I, waking in agonies—God be prais'd cried I—tis a dream—fell asleep after—dreamd You was married to the Captain of the Ship—I waked in a fever—but 'twas the Fever in my blood which brought on this painful chain of Ideas—for I am ill to day— & for want of more cheary Ideas, I torment my Eliza with these—whose Sensibility will suffer, if Yorick could dream but of her Infidelity! & I suffer Eliza in my turn, & think my self at presᵗ little better than an old Woman or a Dreamer of Dreams⁵² in the Scripture Language—I am going to ride myself into better health & better fancies, with Hall—whose Castle lying near the Sea—We have a Beach as even as a mirrour of 5 miles in Length before it, where we dayly run races in our Chaises, with one wheel in the Sea, & the other on the Sand⁵³—O Eliza, wᵗʰ

---

⁵² A scriptural phrase; e.g., Deuteronomy 13:1: "If there arise among you a prophet, or a dreamer of dreams."

⁵³ Cf. *Letters,* 368–69 (June 30): "I am in still better health . . . than when I wrote last to you—owing I believe to my riding out every day with my friend Hall whose castle lies near the sea—and there is a beach as even as a mirrour, of five miles in length before it—where we daily run races in our chaises, with one wheel in the sea, and the other on the land."

w^t fresh ardour & impatience when I'm viewing this element, do I sigh for thy return—But I need no *memento's*[54] of my Destitution & misery, for want of thee—I carry them ab^t me,—& shall not lay them down—(for I worship & Idolize these tender sorrows) till I meet thee upon the Beech & present the handkerchiefs staind with blood wch broke out, from my heart upon y^r departure[55]—This token of what I felt at that Crisis, Eliza, shall never, never be wash'd out. Adieu my dear Wife[56]—you are still mine—notwithstanding all the Dreams & Dreamers in the World.—Mr Lascells dined wth us—Mem^d: I have to tell you a Conversation—I will not write it—

June 29. am got home from Halls—to Coxwould—O 'tis a delicious retreat! both from its beauty, & air of Solitude; & so sweetly does every thing ab^t it invite y^r mind to rest from its Labours and be at peace with itself & the world—That tis the only place, Eliza, I could live in at this juncture—I hope one day, you will like it as much as y^r Bramine—It shall be decorated & made more worthy of You—by the time, fate encourages me to look for you—I have made you, a sweet Sitting Room (as I told You) already—and am projecting a good Bed-chamber adjoining it, with a pretty dressing room for You, which connects them together—& when they are finishd, will be as sweet a set of romantic Apartments, as You ever beheld—the Sleeping room will be very large—The dressing room, thro' wch You pass into y^r Temple, will be little—but Big enough to hold a dressing Table—a couple of chairs, with room for y^r Nymph to stand at her ease both behind and on either side of you—wth spare Room to hang a dozen petticoats—gowns, &c— & Shelves for as many Bandboxes—Y^r little Temple I have described—& what it will hold—but if ever it holds You & I, my Eliza—the Room will not be too little for us—but We shall be *too big*^{x} for the Room.—

June 30—Tis now a quarter of a year (wanting 3 days) since You sail'd from the Downs—in one month more—You will be (I trust,) at Madras—& there you will stay I suppose 2 long long months, before you set out for Bombay—Tis there I shall want to hear from you,—most impatiently—because the most interesting Letters, must come from Eliza when she is there—at present, I can hear of y^r health, & tho' that of all Acc^{ts} affects me most—yet still I have hopes taking their Rise from that—& those are—What Impression you can make upon Mr Draper,

---

[54] Cf. *OED*, s.v., 3.a: "Something to remind one of a past event or condition, of an absent person, of something that once existed"; the first example is dated 1768; Sterne may still think of the word as foreign.

[55] Cf. Sterne's final letter to Eliza prior to her departure, *Letters*, 320 (March 30): "this poor, fine-spun frame of Yorick's gave way, and I broke a vessel in my breast, and could not stop the loss of blood till four this morning. I have filled all thy India handkerchiefs with it.—It came, I think, from my heart!"

[56] See above, p. 178, n. 9; after this, the term *wife* is used freely.

towards setting You at Liberty—& leaving you to pursue the best measures for Y^r preservation—and these are points, I w^d go to Aleppo,[57] to know certainly: I have been possess'd all day & night with an opinion, That Draper will change his behaviour totally towards you—That he will grow friendly & caressing—and as he knows y^r Nature is easily to be won with gentleness, he will practice it to turn you from y^r purpose of quitting him—In short when it comes to the point of y^r going from him to England—it will have so much the face, if not the reality, of an alienation on y^r side from India for ever, as a place you cannot live at—that he will part with You by no means, he can prevent—You will be cajolled my dear Eliza thus out of y^r Life—but what serves it to write this, unless means can be found for You to read it—If you come not—I will take the Safest Cautions I can, to have it got to You—& risk every thing, rather than You should not know, how much I think of You—& how much stronger hold You have got of me, than ever.—Dillon has obtain'd his fair Indian[58]—& has this post wrote a kind Letter of enquiry after Yorick and his Bramine—he is a good Soul—& interests himself much in our fate—I have wrote him a whole Sheet of paper ab^t us—it ought to have been copied into this Journal—but the uncertainty of y^r ever reading it, makes me omit that, with a thousand other things, which when we meet, shall beguile us of many a long winters night.—*those precious Nights!*—my Eliza!—You rate them as high as I do.—& look back upon the manner the hours glided over our heads in them,[59] with the same Interest & Delight^x as the Man you *spent them with*—They are all that remains to us—except the *Expectation* of their return—the Space between is a dismal Void—full of doubts, & suspence—Heaven & its kindest Spirits, my dear, rest over y^r thoughts by day—& free them from all disturbance at night adieu. adieu Eliza!—I have got over this Month—so fare wel to it, & the Sorrows it has brought with it—the next month, I prophecy will be worse—

---

[57] Although Aleppo was on the trade route Sterne seems to have been tracing, possibly the name stuck in his mind because of his recall of Othello's final speech before stabbing himself, V.ii.351–56 (see p. 208, n. 34, and p. 229, n. 42): "Set you down this; / And say besides, that in Aleppo once, / Where a malignant and a turban'd Turk / Beat a Venetian and traduc'd the state, / I took by th' throat the circumcised dog, / And smote him—thus."

[58] Curtis, *Letters*, 345, n. 1, identifies him as John Talbot Dillon (1734–1806); he had probably met Sterne at the Jameses'. Sterne's one surviving letter to him (May 22) calls him "my dear Dillon," and perhaps alludes to his courtship: "I am glad you are in so fair a road to [happiness]—enjoy it long, my Dillon" (*Letters* 344–45). Curtis also notes that the "'fair Indian,' who now became Dillon's bride, was certainly known to Mrs. Draper" and that she died a year later (*Letters* 368, n. 7). "Indian" here probably means an English woman from India. Dillon subscribed to an imperial copy of *ASJ*.

[59] Sterne perhaps recalls his beautiful apostrophe to Jenny in *TS*, IX.8.754: "every letter I trace tells me with what rapidity Life follows my pen; the days and hours of it, more precious, my dear Jenny! than the rubies about thy neck, are flying over our heads like light clouds of a windy day . . . ."

July 1.—But who can foretell what a month may produce—Eliza—I have no less than seven different chances—not one of wch is improbable—and any one of wch would set me much at Liberty—& some of 'em render me compleatly happy—as they w^d facilitate & open the road to thee—What these chances are I leave thee to conjecture, my Eliza—some of them You cannot divine—tho' I once hinted them to You—but those are pecuniary chances arising out of my Prebend[1]—& so not likely to stick in thy brain—nor could they occupy mine a moment, but on thy acc^t . . ; I hope before I meet thee Eliza on the Beach, to have every thing plann'd; that depends on me properly—& for what depends upon him who orders every Event for us, to him I leave & trust it—We shall be happy at last. I know—tis the Corner Stone of all my Castles—& tis all I bargain for. I am perfectly recoverd—or more than recover'd—for never did I feel such Indications of health or Strength & promptness of mind—notwithstanding the Cloud hanging over me, of a Visit—& all its tormenting consequences—Hall has wrote an affecting little poem upon it—the next time I see him, I will get it, & transcribe it in this Journal, for You.. He has persuaded me to trust her with no more than fifteen hundred pounds into—Franc[2]—twil purchase 150 p^ds a year—& to let the rest come annually from myself. the advice is wise enough, If I can get her Off with it—Ill summon up the Husband a little (if I can)—& keep the 500 p^ds remaining for emergencies—who knows, Eliza, what sort of Emergencies may cry out for it—I conceive some—& you Eliza are not backward in Conception^x—so may conceive others. *I wish I was in Arno's Vale!*^x—[3]

July 2^d—But I am in the Vale of Coxwould[4] & wish You saw in how princely a manner I live in it—tis a Land of Plenty—I sit down alone to Venison, fish or Wild foul—or a couple of fouls—with Curds, and strawberrys & Cream, and all the simple clean plenty wch a rich Vally can produce,—with a Bottle of wine on

---

[1] Cash, *LY*, 299, and n. 80, explains his expectations: "Sterne's annual income from the lease of North Newbald prebendal estate was about £12 per year, but he, as all prebendaries, counted upon the rare occasion when he would receive a fine, often £150 or more, for the renewal of the lease." This was about to happen.

[2] Sterne's intention is obscure; he may be indicating conversion into French denominations ("Franc") or foreshortening "Francs" or "France."

[3] See above, p. 212, n. 49. That the passage has a playful sexual undercurrent seems obvious.

[4] Cf. *Letters*, 353 (June 7): "I am as happy as a prince, at Coxwould—and I wish you could see in how princely a manner I live—'tis a land of plenty. I sit down alone to venison, fish and wild fowl, or a couple of fowls or ducks, with curds, and strawberries, and cream, and all the simple plenty which a rich valley under (Hambleton Hills) can produce—with a clean cloth on my table—and a bottle of wine on my right hand to drink your health. I have a hundred hens and chickens about my yard—and not a parishioner catches a hare, or a rabbet, or a trout, but he brings it as an offering to me." Sterne then adds, in a passage quite at odds with *BJ*, that he is "in high spirits—care never enters this cottage."

my right hand (as in Bond street) to drink y^r health—I have a hundred hens & chickens ab^t my yard—and not a parishoner catches a hare a rabbet or a Trout— but he brings it as an Offering—In short tis a golden Vally—& will be the golden Age when You govern the rural feast,^{5} my Bramine, & are the Mistress of my table & spread it with elegancy and that natural grace & bounty wth wch heaven has distinguish'd You.

—Time goes on slowly—every thing stands still—hours seem days & days seem Years whilst you lengthen the Distance between us—from Madras to Bombay—I shall think it shortening—and then desire & expectation will be upon the rack again—— come—come——

July 3^d/

Hail! Hail! my dear Eliza—I steal something every day from my sentimental Journey—to obey a more sentimental impulse in writing to you—& giving you the present Picture of myself—my wishes—my Love, my sincerity—my hopes— my fears—tell me, have I varied in any one Lineament,^{6} from the first Sitting—to this last—have I been less warm—less tender and affectionate than you expected or could have wish'd me in any one of 'em—or, however varied in the expressions of what I was & what I felt, have I not still presented the same air and face towards thee?—take it as a Sample of what I ever shall be—My dear Bramine— & that is—such as my honour, my Engagements & promises & desires have fix'd me—I want You to be on the other side of my little table, to hear how sweetly y^r Voice will be in Unison to all this—I want to hear what You have to say to Y^r Yorick upon this Text.—what heavenly Consolation w^d drop from y^r Lips & how pathetically you w^d enforce y^r Truth & Love upon my heart to free it from every Aching doubt—Doubt! did I say—but I have none—and as soon w^d I doubt the Scripture I have preach'd on—as question thy promises, or Suppose one Thought in thy heart during thy absence from me, unworthy of my Eliza.—for if thou art false, my Bramine—the whole world—and Nature itself are lyars— and—I will trust to nothing on this side of heaven—but turn aside from all Commerce with expectation, & go quietly on my way alone towards a State where no disappointments can follow me—you are grieved when I talk thus; it implies what does not exist in either of us—so cross it out, if thou wilt—or leave it as a part of the picture of a heart that *again* Languishes for Possession^x—and is disturbed at every Idea of its Uncertainty.—So heaven bless thee—& ballance thy passions^x better than I have power to regulate mine—farewel my dear Girl—I sit

---

^{5} Cf. *ASJ*, p. 165, and n. 4, where Sterne has portrayed a rural feast spread with "grace & bounty."

^{6} Sterne's usage is considered obsolete by *OED* (s.v. 2: "distinctive feature"), the last illustration being Henry Brooke's *Fool of Quality* (1760–1772); cf. *Letters*, 240: "I am a two footed animal without one Lineament or Hair of the beast upon me, totally spiritualized."

in dread of tomorrows post which is to bring me an Acc[t] when *Madame*[7] is to arrive.—

July 4th—Hear nothing of her—so am tortured from post to post, for I want to know certainly *the day & hour of this Judgment*[8]—She is moreover ill, as my Lydia writes me word—& I'm impatient to know whether tis that—or what other Cause detains her, and keeps me in this vile state of Ignorance—I'm pitied by every Soul, in proportion as her Character is detested—& her Errand known—She is coming, every one says, to flea[9] poor Yorick or slay him—& I am spirited up by every friend I have to sell my Life dear, & fight valiantly in defence both of my property & Life—Now my Maxim, Eliza, is quietly[10] in three words—"Spare my Life, & take all I have"—If She is not content to decamp with that—One kingdome shall not hold us—for If she will not betake herself to France—I will. but these, I verily believe my fears & nothing more—for she will be as impatient to quit England—as I could wish her—but of this—you will know more, before I have gone thro' this month's Journal.—I get 2000 pounds for my Estate[11]—that is, I had the Offer this morning of it—& think tis enough.—when that is gone—I will begin saving for thee—but in Saving myself for thee, That & every other kind Act is implied.

—get on slowly with my Work[12]—but my head is too full of other Matters— yet will I finish it before I see London—for I am of too scrupulous honour to break faith with the world[13]—great Authors make no scruple of it—but if they

---

[7] Sterne uses *Madame* for his wife on several occasions, almost invariably in postscripts to letters, where he finally seems to recall her; see, e.g., *Letters*, 187: "Madame keeps an excellent good house"; 201: "I can neither leave Madame with an empty purse"; and 300: "I suppose Md[lle] with Madame ma femme will negociate the Affair."

[8] Sterne's underscoring might indicate a scriptural allusion; e.g., Matthew 25:13: "Watch therefore, for ye know neither the day nor the hour wherein the Son of man cometh"; or Revelation 9:15: "And the four angels were loosed, which were prepared for an hour, and a day, and a month, and a year, for to slay the third part of men." Either allusion would be heavily ironic if intended.

[9] I.e., flay. Cf. *TS,* IV.S.T.302, where the sisters of Quedlingberg are "almost flead alive."

[10] ?quickly. Parnell, 252, hears an echo in the "Maxim" of George Farquhar's *The Beaux Stratagem* (1707), V.2: "Sir, spare all I have and take my Life" (ed. Eric Rothstein [New York: Croft Classics, 1967], 83). Sterne's inversion would be ironic.

[11] Cf. Cash, *LY,* 298–99: "By 4 July Sterne's negotiations to sell his estate had brought an offer of £2000—a fair price considering that six years earlier he had estimated its worth at £1800."

[12] Cf. *Letters,* 375 (July 6): "I am now beginning to be truly busy at my Sentimental Journey—the pains and sorrows of this life having retarded its progress—but I shall make up my lee-way, and overtake every body in a very short time."

[13] Sterne did, however, "break faith," as acknowledged in the Advertisement found in some copies of *ASJ*, apologizing for delivering two rather than the promised four volumes; see Introduction, p. vii.

are great Authors—I'm sure they are little Men.—& I'm sure also of another Point wch concerns y^rself—& that is Eliza, that You shall never find me one hair breadth a less Man than you—　　　farewell[14]—I love thee eternally—

July 5.　Two Letters from the South of France by this post, by which, by some fatality, I find not one of my Letters have got to them this month—This gives me concern—because it has the Aspect of an unseasonable unkindness in me[15]—to take no notice of what has the appearance at least of a Civility in desiring to pay me a Visit—my daughter besides has not deserved ill of me—& tho' her mother has, I w^d not ungenerously take that Opportunity, which would most overwhelm her, to give any mark of my resentment—I have besides long since forgiven her— & am the more inclined now as she proposes a plan, by which I shall never more be disquieted—in these 2 last, she renews her request to have leave to live where she has transfer'd her fortune—& purposes, with my leave she says, to end her days in the South of france—to all which I have just been writing her a Letter of Consolation & good will—& to crown my professions, intreat her to take post with my girl to be here time enough to enjoy York races[16]—& so having done my duty to them—I continue writing, to do it to thee Eliza who art the *Woman of my heart,* & for whom I am ordering & planning this, & every thing else—be asured my Bramine that ere every thing is ripe for our Drama,—I shall work hard to fit out & decorate a little Theatre for us to act on—but not before a crouded house—no Eliza—it shall be as secluded as the elysian fields—retirement is the nurse of Love and kindness—& I will Woo & caress thee in it in such sort, that every thicket & grotto we pass by, *shall* sollicit the remembrance of the mutual pledges We have exchanged of Affection with one another—Oh! these expecta- tions—make me sigh, as I recite them—& many a heart-felt Interjection! do they cost me, as I saunter alone in the tracks we are to tread together hereafter—still I think thy heart is with me—& whilst I think so, I prefer it to all the Society this world can offer—& tis in truth my dear oweing to this—That tho' I've rec^d half a dozen Letters to press me to join my friends at Scarborough[17]—that I've found

---

[14] This passage is heavily blotted after "you"; as it stands, the sentence exhibits Sterne's fondness for the aposiopesis.

[15] Cf. *Letters,* 385 (to the Jameses, August 2): "I had letters from France by last night's post, by which (by some fatality) I find not one of my letters has reached Mrs. Sterne. This gives me concern, as it wears the aspect of unkindness, which she by no means merits from me."

[16] Sterne frequently went to the summer race meeting at York, one of the more important in the English racing calendar. His attendance in 1766 and 1767 is recorded in the *York Courant;* we can assume he attended in previous years as well.

[17] Forty miles northeast of York, known for its races and waters. Sterne had not resisted the temptation in the autumn of 1764: "I am going to leave a few poor sheep here in the wil- derness for fourteen days," he wrote to Hall-Stevenson, "and from pride and naughtiness of heart to go see what is doing at Scarborough—stedfastly meaning afterwards to lead a new

pretences not to quit You *here*—and sacrifice the many sweet Occasions I have of giving my thoughts up to You—, for Company I cannot rellish *since* I *have tasted* my dear Girl, the *sweets^x of thine.*—

July 6/

Three long Months and three long days are pass'd & gone, since my Eliza sighed on taking her Leave of Albions cliffs, & of all in Albion, which was dear to her—How oft have I smarted at the Idea, of that last longing Look by wch thou badest adieu to all thy heart Sufferd at that dismal Crisis—twas the Separation of Soul & Body—& equal to nothing but what passes on that tremendous Moment.—& like it in one Consequence, that thou art in another World;[18] where I w^d give a world, to follow thee, or hear even an Acc^t of thee—for this I shall write in a few days to our dear friend Mrs James—she possibly may have heard a single Syllable or two ab^t You—but it cannot be;—the same must have been directed towards Yoricks ear, to whom you w^d have wrote the Name of *Eliza,* had there been no time for more. I w^d almost now compound wth Fate,—& was I sure Eliza only breathd—I w^d thank heaven & acquiesce. I kiss your Picture— your Shawl—& every trinket I exchanged with You—every day I live—alas! I shall soon be debarrd of that—in a fortnight I must lock them up & clap my seal & y^rs upon them in the most secret Cabinet of my Bureau—You may divine the reason, Eliza! adieu—adieu!

July 7.

—But not Yet—for I will find means to write to you every night whilst my people are here—if I sit up till midnight, till they are asleep.—I should not dare to face you, if I was worse than my word in the smallest Item—& this Journal I promised You Eliza should be kept without a chasm of a day in it. & had I my time to myself & nothing to do, but gratify my propensity—I sh^d write from sun rise to Sun set to thee—But a Book to write—a Wife to receive & make Treaties with—an estate to sell—a Parish to superintend—and a disquieted heart perpetually to reason with,

---

life and strengthen my faith" (*Letters* 225). A few weeks later, again to Hall-Stevenson, he writes: "I am but this moment return'd from Scarborough, where I have been drinking the waters ever since the races, and have received marvellous strength, had I not debilitated it as fast as I got it, by playing the good fellow" (226). Sterne finally returned to Scarborough in early September (Cash, *LY* 307–8).

[18] A traditional definition of death; cf. *TS,* II.19.174: "death . . . is nothing but the separation of the soul from the body"; and IV.S.T.309: "Death is the separation of the soul from the body." The image reappears, suspiciously enough, in a December 7 letter: "My heart bleeds . . . when I think of parting with my child—'twill be like the separation of soul and body—and equal to nothing but what passes at that tremendous moment" (*Letters* 406). Lydia, in editing her father's letters, may have, here as elsewhere, redirected a comment about Eliza to herself.

are eternal calls upon me[19]—& yet I have you more in my mind than ever—and in proportion as I am thus torn from y^r embraces^x—*I cling the closer to the Idea of you*—Your Figure is ever before my eyes—the sound of y^r voice vibrates with its sweetest tones the live long day in my ear[20]—I can see & hear nothing but my Eliza. remember this, when You think my Journal too short, & compare it not with thine, wch tho' it will exceed it in length, can do no more than equal it in Love and truth of esteem—for esteem thee I do beyond all the powers of eloquence to tell thee how much—& I love thee my dear Girl, & prefer thy Love to me, more than the whole world—

night./—have not eat or drunk all day thro' vexation of heart at a couple of ungrateful unfeeling Letters from that Quarter, from whence, had it pleas'd God, I should have lookd for all my Comforts—but he has will'd they sh^d come from the east—& he knows how I am satisfyed with all his Dispensations—but with none, my dear Bramine, so much as this—with wch Cordial upon my Spirits—I go to bed, in hopes of seeing thee in my Dreams.

July 8th./

—eating my fowl, and my trouts & my cream & my strawberries, as melancholly & sad as a Cat;[21] for want of you—by the by, I have got one which sits quietly besides me, purring all day to my sorrows—& looking up gravely from time to time in my face, as if she knew my Situation.—how soothable my heart is Eliza, when such little things sooth it! for in some pathetic sinkings I feel even some support from this poor Cat—I attend to her purrings—& think they harmonize me— they are *pianissimo* at least, & do not disturb me.—poor Yorick! to be driven, wth all his sensibilities, to these ressources—all powerful Eliza, that has had this Magic^l authority over him; to bend him thus to the dust—But I'll have my revenge, Hussy!

July 9.   I have been all day making a sweet Pavillion in a retired Corner of my garden—but my Partner & Companion & friend for whom I make it, is fled

---

[19] Cf. *Letters,* 369 (June 30): "I ought now to be busy from sun rise, to sun set, for I have a book to write—a wife to receive—an estate to sell—a parish to superintend, and what is worst of all, a disquieted heart to reason with—these are continual calls upon me."

[20] Cf. an earlier "love letter" to the bluestocking Elizabeth Vesey (June ?1761): "You are sensible, and gentle and tender—& from [one] end to the other of you full of the sweetest tones & modulations . . . in honest truth You are a System of harmonic Vibrations—You are the sweetest and best tuned of all Instruments—O Lord! I would give away my other Cassoc to touch you" (*Letters* 138). Sterne's tone to Eliza is much more serious than in this rather increasingly bawdy (and inappropriate) address to Mrs. Vesey.

[21] Curtis, *Letters,* 382, n. 2, points to Shakespeare, *I Henry IV,* I.ii.73–74: "*Falstaff:* 'Sblood, I am as melancholy as a gib cat . . . .'" Sterne mentions his cat to Hall-Stevenson, *Letters,* 390 (August 11): "I sit here alone as solitary and sad as a tom cat, which by the bye is all the company I keep—he follows me from the parlour, to the kitchen, into the garden, and every place"; and again, to Lydia, 391 (August 24): "My poor cat sits purring beside me."

from me, & when she returns to me again, Heaven who first brought us together, best knows—When that hour is foreknown What a Paradice will I plant for thee—till then I walk as Adam did whilst there was no help-meet found for it, and could almost wish a deep Sleep would come upon me till that Moment When I can say as he did—"*Behold the Woman Thou has given me for Wife*"[22] She shall be call'd La Bramine. Indeed Indeed Eliza! my Life will be little better than a dream, till we approach nearer to each other—I live scarse conscious of my existence—or as if I wanted a vital part; & could not live above a few hours. & yet I live, & live, & live on, for thy Sake, and the sake of thy truth to me; which I measure by my own,—& I fight ag^{st} every evil and every danger, that I may be able to support & shelter thee from danger and evil also.—upon my word, dear Girl, thou owest me much—but tis cruel to dun thee when thou art not in a condition to pay—I think Eliza has not run off in her Yoricks debt^x—

July 10.

I cannot suffer you to be longer upon the Water—in 10 days time, You shall be at Madrass—the element roles in my head as much as y^{rs}, & I am sick at the sight & smell of it——for all this, my Eliza, I feel in Imagination & so strongly— I can bear it no longer—on the 20th therefore Ins^t I begin to write to you[23] as a terrestrial Being—I must deceive myself—& think so I will notwithstanding all that Lascelles has told me—but there is no truth in him.[24]—I have just kiss'd y^r picture—even that sooths many an anxiety—I have found out the Body is too little for the head—it shall not be rectified, till I sit by the Original, & direct the Painter's Pencil,[25] and that done, we'll take a Scamper to *Enfield*[26] & see y^r dear Children—if You tire by the Way, there are *one or two* places to rest^x at.—I never stand^x out.[27] God bless thee. I am thine as *ever*

---

[22] Cf. Genesis 3:12: "And the man said, The woman whom thou gavest to be with me, she gave me of the tree, and I did eat." Sterne conflates the creation of Eve in Genesis 2:21–23 with the Fall—an interesting slip.

[23] Cf. *Letters,* 117: "pray is that Simile too warm? . . . I could easily mend it, by saying with the dull phlegm of an unfeeling John Trot . . . *That Y^{rs} of the 8th Inst^t came safe to hand.*"

[24] Cf. John 8:44: "there is no truth in him [i.e., the devil]."

[25] I.e., paintbrush.

[26] See above, p. 212, n. 48. Sterne seems to hint at a place to which the couple retired before completing their excursion; see following note.

[27] Cf. *OED,* s.v. *stand,* 99.c (*stand out*): "To resist, persist in opposition or resistance, . . . hold out"; or 99.f: "To haggle, make difficulties about striking a bargain," citing Goldsmith's *Vicar of Wakefield* (1766): "He always stands out and higgles." And cf. *TS,* VIII.15.674: "'tis certain from every day's observation of man, that he may be set on fire like a candle, at either end—provided there is a sufficient wick standing out." This may explain why the word is marked "x" in the manuscript.

July 11./

Sooth me—calm me—pour thy healing Balm Eliza, into the sorest of hearts[28]—I'm pierced with the Ingratitude and unquiet Spirit of a restless unreasonable Wife whom neither gentleness or generosity can conquer—She has now enterd upon a new plan of waging War with me, a thousand miles off—thrice a week this last month, has the quietest man under heaven been outraged by her Letters—I have offer'd to give her every Shilling I was worth, except my preferment, to be let alone & left in peace by her—Bad Woman! nothing must now purchase this, unless I borrow 400 p^{ds} to give her & carry into france more—I w^d perish first, my Eliza! e're I would give her a shilling of another man's, wch I must do—if I give her a Shill^g more than I am worth.

—How I now feel the want of thee! my dear Bramine—my generous unworldly honest Creature—I shall die for want of thee for a thousand reasons— every emergency & every Sorrow each day brings along with it—tells me what a Treasure I am bereft of,—whilst I want thy friendship & Love to keep my head up from sinking—Gods will be done. but I think she will send me to my grave.—She will now keep me in torture till the end of Sept^r—& writes me word to day—she will delay her Journey two Months beyond her 1st Intention——it keeps me in eternal Suspence all the while—for she will come unawars at last upon me—& then adieu to the dear sweets of my retirement.

How cruelly are our Lots drawn, my dear—both made for happiness—& neither of us made to taste it! In feeling so acutely for my own disapp^{t}ment—I drop blood for thine, I call thee in, to my Aid—& thou wantest mine as much—Were we together we sh^d recover^x—but never, never till then *nor by any other Recipe.*—

July 12.

am ill all day with the Impressions of Yesterdays account—can neither eat or drink or sit still & write or read—I walk like a disturbed Spirit ab^t my Garden— calling upon heaven & thee,—to come to my Succour—couldst thou but write one word to me, it would be worth the world to me—my friends write me millions—& every one invites me to flee from my Solitude & come to them—I obey the commands of my friend Hall who has sent over on purpose to fetch me—or he will come himself for me—so I set off to morrow morning to take Sanctuary in Crasy Castle—The news papers have sent me there already[29] by putting in the following paragraph.

---

[28] Cf. above, p. 25, n. 2, and p. 182, n. 25.

[29] Cf. Curtis, *Letters,* 382, n. 4: "The notice appeared in the *Public Advertiser* for Monday, 20 July 1767 [p. 2]: 'A Correspondent writes, that Skelton-Castle is, at present, the place of rendezvous of the most celebrated wits: The humourous author of Tristram Shandy, and Mr. G——, author of several ingenious pieces, have been there some time: some other persons of distinguished rank and abilities in the literary world, are daily expected." Cash thinks Sterne turned "G" into "Garrick" "only to impress Eliza," arguing that Garrick would not be

"We hear from Yorkshire, That Skelton Castle is the present Rendevouz, of the most brilliant Wits of the Age—the admired Author of Tristram—Mr Garrick &c. being there, & Mr Coleman & many other men of Wit & Learning being every day expected"—when I get there, wch will be to morrow night, My Eliza will hear from her Yorick—her Yorick—who loves her more than ever.

July 13.   Skelton Castle. . Your picture has gone round the Table after sup-per—& y^r health after it, my invaluable friend!—even the Ladies, who hate grace in another, seemd struck with it in You—but Alas! you are as a dead Person—& Justice, (as in all such Cases,) is paid you in course—when thou returnest it will be render'd more sparingly—but I'll make up all deficiencies—by honouring You more than ever Woman was honourd by man—every good Quality That ever good heart possess'd—thou possessest my dear Girl, & so sovereignly does thy temper & sweet sociability, which harmonize all thy other properties make me thine, that whilst thou art true to thyself and thy Bramin—he thinks thee worth a world—& w^d give a World was he master of it, for the undisturbed possession of thee—Time and Chance[30] are busy throwing this Die for me—a fortunate Cast, or two, at the most, makes our fortune—it gives us each other—& then for the World—I w^ll not give a pinch of Snuff.—Do take care of thyself—keep this prospect before thy eyes—have a view to it in all y^r Transactions, Eliza,—In a word Remember You are mine^x—and stand answerable for all you say & do to me—I govern myself by the same Rule—& such a History of myself can I lay before you, as shall create no blushes, but those of pleasure—tis midnight—& so sweet Sleep to thee the remaining hours of it. I am more thine^x, my dear Eliza! than ever—but that cannot be—

July 14.
dining & feasting all day at Mr Turner's[31]—his Lady a fine Woman herself, in love wth your picture—O my dear Lady, cried I, did you but know the Original—

---

referred to as the "author of several ingenious pieces" (*LY*, 300, n. 81). Sterne's other addi-tion to the newspaper account, "Mr Coleman," is George Colman the elder (1732–1794), manager of the Covent Garden Theater and prolific writer for the stage, including *Polly Honeycombe* (1760) and, with Garrick, *The Clandestine Marriage* (1766).

[30] Contingency is a favorite subject in Sterne's fiction; see, most obviously, his "chapter of chances" in *TS*, IV.9; and *ASJ*, p. 38, n. 4. In the *Sermons*, the phrase "time and chance" and variants such as "changes and chances" frequently recur; see, e.g., 4:94.15, 146.3, 210.22, 369.25–26, 389.19, etc. Significantly "time and chance" seem always to lead Sterne, in his sermons, to the doctrine of providence; see esp. sermon 8 ("Time and chance").

[31] Cf. *Letters*, 382, n. 5: "Charles Turner (?1726–[17]83), of Kirkleatham, Yorks., was a nephew of Cholmley Turner, whose campaign to be elected Knight of the Shire Sterne had successfully supported in 1741–[174]2. . . . [He] subscribed to Sterne's *Sermons*, i-iv, and to the *Sentimental Journey*." His wife, Elizabeth (1731–1768), was the daughter of William Wombwell, of Wombwell, Yorks. (n. 6).

but what is she to you, Tristram—nothing; but that I am in Love with her——
et cætera . . . said She—[32]   no I have given over dashes—replied I— —I
verily think my Eliza I shall get this Picture set, so, as to wear it, as I first pur-
posed—ab^t my neck—I do not like the place tis in—it shall be nearer my heart—
Thou art ever in its centre—good night—

July 15.   From home. (Skelton Castle) from 8 in the morning till late at Supper—I seldom have put thee so off, my dear Girl—& yet to morrow will be as
bad——

July 16.
for Mr Hall has this Day left his Crasy Castle to come and sojourn with me at
Shandy Hall for a few days—for so they have long christend our retired Cottage—we are just arrived at it—& whilst he is admiring the premises—I have
stole away to converse a few minutes with thee, and in thy own dressing room—
for I make every thing thine & call it so, before hand, that thou art to be mistress
of hereafter. This *Hereafter*, Eliza, is but a melancholly term—but the Certainty
of its coming to us, brightens it up—pray do not forget my prophecy in the Ded-
ication of the Almanack—I have the utmost faith in it myself—but by what
impulse my mind was struck with 3 Years—heaven, whom I believe it's author,
best knows—but I shall see y^r face before—but that I leave to You—& to the
Influence such a Being must have over all inferior ones—We are going to dine
with the Arch Bishop to morrow—& from thence to Harrogate for three days,
whilst thou dear Soul art pent up in sultry Nastiness—without Variety or change
of face or Conversation——Thou shalt have enough of both when I cater for thy
happiness Eliza—& if an Affectionate husband & 400 p^ds a year in a sweeter Vally
than that of Jehosophat[33] will do—less thou shalt never have—but I hope
more—& were it millions, tis the same—twould be laid at thy feet—Hall is come
in in raptures with every thing—& so I shut up my Journal for to day & tomor-
row for I shall not be able to open it where I go—adieu my dear Girl———

---

[32] Normally in Sterne, the first character after a dash is closed up to it; that "her——"
comes at the end of the line makes Sterne's intention here uncertain, but we left a space
after that dash, and again after "She—" in order to clarify the bawdy exchange taking place,
and because the ms. seems to call for spacing. Sterne's ellipsis may instead be read as three
hyphens. The passage exemplifies the age's typical usage of *et cetera* for the pudendum,
while the allusion to "dashes" recalls a particularly bawdy—and similar—passage in *TS*:
"'My sister, mayhap, . . . does not choose to let a man come so near her ****' Make this
dash,——'tis an Aposiopesis.—Take the dash away, and write Backside,—'tis Bawdy."

[33] See Joel 3:2 (and 3:12): "I will also gather all nations, and will bring them down into the
valley of Jehoshaphat . . . ." Sterne would have considered Jehoshaphat a (symbolic) place
of judgment, indicated more clearly, perhaps, in an earlier use: "When we find we can by a
shifting of places, run away from ourselves, what think you of a jaunt there [to Mecca],
before we finally pay a visit to the *vale of Jehosophat*" (*Letters* 140).

18——was yesterday all the day with our A-Bishop[34]—this good Prelate, who is one of our most refined Wits—& the most of a gentleman—of our order—oppresses me with his kindness—he shews in his treatment of me, what he told me upon taking my Leave—that he loves me, & has a high Value for me—his Chaplains tell me, he is perpetually talking of me—& has such an Opinion of my head & heart that he begs to stand Godfather for my next Literary production—so has done me the hon[r] of putting his name in a List which I am most proud of because my Eliza's name is in it[35]—I have just a moment to scrawl this to thee, being at York—where I want to be employd in taking you a little house, where the prophet may be accommodated with a "*Chamber[x] in the Wall apart, with a stool & a Candlestick*"—where his Soul can be at rest from the distractions of the world, & lean only upon his kind hostesse, & repose all his Cares, & melt[x] them *along with hers* in her sympathetic bosom.[36]

July 19.   Harrogate Spaws.[37]—drinking the waters here till the 26th—to no effect, but a cold dislike of every one of your sex—I did nothing, but make comparisons betwixt thee my Eliza, & every woman I saw and talk'd to—thou has made me so unfit for every one else—that I am thine as much from necessity, as Love—I am thine by a thousand sweet ties, the least of which shall never be relax'd—be assured my dear Bramine of this—& repay me in so doing, the Confidence I repose in thee—y[r] Absence, y[r] distresses, your sufferings; your conflicts;

---

[34] I.e., Archbishop Drummond; see above, p. 198, n. 26. Curtis recounts the story of a petition sent to Drummond by "Several well wishers" on March 30, 1767, asking him to censure Sterne in the face of his continued licentiousness in volume IX of *TS*, published two months earlier (*Letters* 300, n. 2., 383, n. 8; Cash, *LY* 266); as Curtis notes, it seems not to have "lessened his affection for Sterne."

[35] Drummond subscribed to an imperial copy of *ASJ*, Eliza to three copies, although one hopes they were Sterne's gift to her.

[36] Cf. the story of Elisha and the Shunammite woman (2 Kings 4:8ff.), upon which Sterne had commented in sermon 13 ("Duty of setting bounds to our desires"): "For after many repeated invitations and entertainments at her house, finding his occasions called him to a frequent passage that way;—she moves her husband to set up and furnish a lodging for him . . . 'let us make him a little chamber I pray thee on the wall, and let us set for him there a bed, and a table, and a stool, and a candlestick'" (4:124, quoting 2 Kings 4:10). Sterne's lesson is found in the disinterestedness of this act of charity.

Cash suggests, *LY*, 300, that Sterne had actually spent the day in York "looking for a house he could rent for Elizabeth and Lydia," his wife having demanded it as one of her conditions.

[37] The waters of Harrogate, twenty miles west of York, had been in use since the end of the sixteenth century. As Cash notes, *LY*, 301, despite the compliment to Eliza in this entry, Sterne "had begun to tire of writing every day, for he made no entries during his stay—the first large gap one finds in the *Journal*." Despite the July 19 dating, the entry would seem to have been written after his return, assuming that the use of the past tense accurately reflects the time of writing; i.e., "I did nothing . . . I saw and talk'd to . . . ."

all make me rely but the more upon that fund in you, wch is able to sustain so much weight—Providence I know will relieve you from one part of it—and it shall be the pleasure of my days to ease my dear friend of the other—I Love thee Eliza, more than the heart of Man ever loved Woman's—I even love thee more than I did, the day thou badest me Farwel!—Farewell!—Farewell! to thee again— I'm going from hence to York. Races.——[38]

July 27. arrived at York.—where I had not been 2 hours before My heart was overset[39] with a pleasure, wch beggard every other, that fate could give me—save thyself—It was thy dear Packets from Iago[40]—I cannot give vent to all the emotions I felt even before I opend them—for I knew thy hand—& my seal,—wch was only in thy possession—O tis from my Eliza, said I.—I instantly shut the door of my Bed-chamber, and orderd myself to be denied—& spent the whole evening, and till dinner the next day, in reading over and over again the most interesting Acc^t—& the most endearing one, that ever tried the tenderness of

---

[38] See below, n. 40.

[39] An unusual usage; *OED*'s meanings are primarily negative.

[40] I.e., St. Jago or Santiago, Cape Verde Islands, where Eliza landed in early May; see above, p. 191, n. 2. Sterne's response to the packets is well analyzed by Cash, *LY*, 301–2:

> At this juncture, when one might have expected him to return to the *Journal* with new inspiration, he ceased making entries for three weeks. He went home to Coxwold, worked on *A Sentimental Journey* and returned to York for Race Week, which was held on 16–23 August. During this holiday, he took up the *Journal* again. He began with a new paragraph added to his last: "I now want . . . ." Then he became worried about having said this with so little preparation. He went back to his entry for 19 July written from Harrogate, and doctored it by adding a single word, "Races" . . . . He had no worries about placing Race Week in July, for Eliza . . . would not see the *Journal* for years . . . . In that confidence he wrote three more entries during Race Week and possibly a fourth, antedating them in July and early August . . . .
> Then during Race Week he received a second set of letters, and lost heart again. . . . Sterne wrote under the date of 1 August, "what a sad Story" . . . . Eliza had done as Sterne had urged: she had written unstintingly about her illnesses. . . . Certainly he felt much sympathy. But he had not found in her letters what he longed to see, a declaration of her love for him.

Melvyn New, "Job's Wife and Sterne's Other Women," 64, reaches the same conclusion:

> As with many forms of obsessional behavior, one cure appears to be the granting of what the patient most believes he desires. On July 27 Eliza's "dear Packets" arrive . . . . Five entries later, Sterne ended the [*Bramine's Journal*]. Eliza's "Journal" . . . could not sustain the fiction he had created; whatever else Eliza Draper was, she was not "up to the ears" in love with Sterne as he had forced himself to believe . . . . The silence into which Sterne wrote from April through July was a sustaining space; Eliza's interruption of that silence scatters and disperses Sterne's animal spirits, and he wisely withdraws to . . . complete *A Sentimental Journey*.

man—I read & wept—and wept and read till I was blind—then grew sick, & went to bed—& in an hour calld again for the Candle—to read it once more—as for my dear Girls pains & her dangers I cannot write ab[t] them[41]—because I cannot write my feelings or express them any how to my mind—O Eliza! but I will talk them over with thee with a sympathy that shall woo thee, so much better than I have ever done—That we will both be gainers in the end—"*Ill love thee for the dangers thou hast past*"[42]—and thy Affection shall go hand in hand wth me, because I'll pity thee—as no man ever pitied Woman—but Love like mine is never satisfied—else y[r] 2[d] Letter from Iago—is a Letter so warm, so simple, so tender! I defy the world to produce such another—by all thats kind & gracious! I will entreat thee Eliza! so kindly—that thou shalt say, I merit much of it—nay all—for my merit to thee, is my truth.

I now want to have this week of nonsensical Festivity over—that I may get back, with thy picture w[ch] I ever carry ab[t] me—to my retreat and to Cordelia—

when the days of our Afflictions[43] are over, I oft amuse my fancy, wth an Idea, that thou wilt come down to me by Stealth, & hearing where I have walk'd out to—surprize me some sweet moon Shiney Night[44] at Cordelia's grave, & catch me in thy Arms over it—O My Bramin! my Bramin!————

July 31—am tired to death with the hurrying pleasures of these Races—I want still & *silent* ones—so return home to morrow, in search of them—I shall find them as I sit contemplating over thy passive picture; sweet Shadow! of what is to come! for tis all I can now[x] grasp—first and best of woman kind! remember me, as I remember thee—tis asking a great deal, my Bramine!—but I cannot be satisfied with less—farwell—fare—happy till fate will let me cherish thee myself.—O my Eliza! thou writest to me with an Angels pen—& thou wouldst win me by thy Letters, had I never seen thy face, or known thy heart.

Aug[st] 1/ what a sad Story thou hast told me of thy Sufferings & Despondences,[45] from S[t] Iago, till thy meeting wth the Dutch Ship[46]—twas a sympathy

---

[41] Sterne did write about them in a letter to Mrs. James (August 10): "I send you the contents w[h] I have rec[d]—and that is a melancholly history of herself and sufferings since they left Iago—continual & most violent rhumatism all the time—a fever brought on—with fits—and attended with Delirium: & every terrifying symptome: the recovery from this has left her low—and emaciated to a Skeleton" (*Letters* 388).

[42] Cf. *Othello*, I.iii.167: "She lov'd me for the dangers I had pass'd"; and *ASJ*, p. 40, n. 15.

[43] A biblical commonplace; cf. Job 30:16, 27, Jeremiah 16:19, Lamentations 1:7.

[44] Cf. *TS*, III.24.247, where Trim escorts Bridget to the bowling-green on a "moon-shiny night."

[45] *OED* does not record this plural form.

[46] Either this was a typical encounter along the sea route to India, or Sterne had been amazingly prescient, for in March he had written to Eliza: "Probably you will have an

above Tears—I trembled every Nerve as I went from line to line—& every moment the Acc[t] comes across me—I suffer all I felt, over & over again—will providence suffer all this anguish without end—& without pity?— *"it no can be"*[47]—I am tried my dear Bramine in the furnace of Affliction[48] as much as thou—by the time we meet, We shall be fit only for each other—& should cast away upon any other Harbour.

Aug[st] 2. my wife—uses me most unmercifully[49]—every Soul advises me to fly from her—but where can I fly If I fly not to thee? The Bishop of Cork & Ross[50] has made me great Offers in Ireland—but I will take no step without thee—& till heaven opens us some track—He is the best of feeling tender hearted men—knows our Story—sends You his Blessing—and says if the Ship you return in touches at Cork (w[ch] many India men do)—he will take you to his palace, till he can send for me to join You—he only hopes, he says, to join us together for ever—but more of this good Man, and his attachment to me—hereafter. and of a couple of Ladies[51] in the family &c. &c.

---

opportunity of writing to me by some Dutch or French ship, or from the Cape de Verd Islands" (*Letters* 315).

[47] Curtis, *Letters*, 384, n. 1, points to Sterne's similar phrase in a letter to Eliza in March: "*It can no be masser*" (315), and suggests an origin with Ignatius Sancho; however, no such phrase occurs in their correspondence. *OED*'s first example of "massa," a corruption of "master," is dated 1774; one suspects that the pidgin English has more to do with India than with Africa.

[48] Cf. Isaiah 48:10: "Behold, I have refined thee, but not with silver; I have chosen thee in the furnace of affliction."

[49] Sterne originally wrote: "my wife—& I wish I could not add my Daughter (for she has debauch'd her affections" and then deleted—or someone else deleted—the reference to Lydia. In the debate as to whether or not Lydia had access to the journal manuscript (see Introduction, p. xv), this erasure might lend credence to the affirmative side.

[50] Dr. Jemmett Browne (?1703–1782). Sterne probably met him during the York races (see Cash, *LY* 302, n. 85) and would spend time with him again in September; cf. *Letters*, 397–98: "I was ten days at Scarborough in September, and was hospitably entertained by one of the best of our Bishops; who, as he kept house there, press'd me to be with him . . . . I made in this time a connection of great friendship with my mitred host, who would gladly have taken me with him back to Ireland." Bishop Browne subscribed to an imperial copy of *ASJ*.

[51] As Cash, *LY*, 307, n. 5, points out, J. M. S. Tompkins, "Triglyph and Tristram," *TLS* (July 11, 1929):558, identifies one of the women as Lady Anne Dawson (1733–1769), daughter of the first Earl of Pomfret, who had married Elizabeth Vesey's cousin, Thomas Dawson, in 1754; and also establishes that Vesey (see above, p. 222, n. 20) had departed Scarborough before Sterne's arrival, so the second woman remains unidentified. Lady Anne's brother, George Fermor (1722–1785), second Earl of Pomfret, subscribed to Sterne's *Sermons* in 1769.

Augst 3^d

I have had an offer[52] of exchanging two pieces of preferment I hold here (but sweet Cordelia's Parish is not one of 'em) for a living of 350 p^{ds} a year in Surry ab^t 30 miles from London—& retaining Coxwould & my Prebendaryship[53]—wch are half as much more—the Country also is sweet—but I will not—I cannot take any step unless I had thee my Eliza for whose sake I live, to consult with—& till the road is open for me as my heart wishes to advance—with thy sweet light Burden in my Arms, I could get up fast the hill of preferment, if I chose it—but without thee I feel Lifeless^x—and if a Mitre was offer'd me, I would not have it, till I could have thee too, to make it sit easy upon my brow—I want kindly to smooth thine, & not only wipe away thy tears[54] but dry up the Sourse of them for ever—

—Augst 4[55]—Hurried backwards & forwards ab^t the arrival of Madame, this whole week—& then farewel I fear to this journal—till I get up to London—& can pursue it as I wish. at present all I can write would be but the History of my miserable feelings[56]—She will be ever present—& if I take up my pen for thee— something will jarr within me as I do it—that I must lay it down again—I will give you one gen^l Acc^t of all my sufferings together—but not in Journals—I shall set my wounds a-bleeding[57] every day afresh by it—& the Story cannot be too

---

[52] Cf. *Letters*, 406 (to an unidentified friend): "I have had an offer of exchanging two pieces of preferment I hold here, for a living of three hundred and fifty pounds a year, in Surry, about thirty miles from London, and retaining Coxwould, and my prebendaryship—the country also is sweet—but I will not, cannot come to any determination, till I have consulted with you, and my other friends . . . but I have rejected every proposal, unless Mrs. Sterne, and my Lydia could accompany me thither—I live for the sake of my girl; and with her sweet light burthen in my arms, I could get up fast the hill of preferment, if I chose it— but without my Lydia, if a mitre was offered me, it would sit uneasy upon my brow." Curtis, *Letters*, 387, n. 1, assumes Sterne substituted *Lydia* for *Eliza*, but it is quite possible that Lydia and not Sterne rewrote the passage, erasing Eliza's name and substituting her mother's and her own. Insofar as the letter is known only from her edition, it is suspect; see above, p. 217, n. 4, for another suspicious letter to the same correspondent.

For Sterne's typical quixotic invocation of "mitres" when discussing his clerical career, see *ASJ*, p. 102, n. 11.

[53] *OED*'s sole example is dated 1639. "Coxwould," i.e., "Cordelia's Parish"; see above p. 179, n. 12.

[54] Cf. *ASJ*, p. 61, n. 4.

[55] As Cash notes, *LY*, 303, Sterne actually wrote this entry in late September, when he was indeed "preparing Shandy Hall for the arrival of his family. . . . He then assigned a date of 4 August to this entry . . . ." Cash's reconstruction of the chronology of these final entries seems correct.

[56] Cf. above, p. 176, n. 1.

[57] Not recorded in *OED*.

short.—so worthiest, best, kindest & affect^te of Souls farewell—every Moment will I have thee present—& sooth my sufferings, with the looks my fancy shall cloath thee in.—Thou shalt lye down & rise up with me—ab^t my bed & ab^t my paths, & shalt see out all my Ways.[58]—adieu—adieu—& remember one eternal truth, My dear Bramine, wch is not the worse, because I have told it thee a thousand times before—That I am thine—& thine only, & for ever.

L. Sterne

Nov: 1st.[59]   All my dearest Eliza has turnd out more favourable than my hopes—M^rs S——— & my dear Girl have been 2 Months with me and they have this day left me to go to spend the Winter at York, after having settled every thing to their hearts content—Mrs Sterne retires into france, whence she purposes not to stir, till her death—& never, has she vow'd, will give me another sorrowful or discontented hour—I have conquerd her, as I w^d every one else, by humanity & Generosity—& she leaves me, more than half in Love wth me—She goes into the South of france, her health being insupportable in England—& her age, as she now confesses ten Years more, than I thought—being on the edge of sixty[60]—so God bless—& make the remainder of her Life happy—in order to wch I am to remit her three hundred guineas a year[61]—& give my dear Girl two thousand p^ds—wch wth all Joy, I agree to,—but tis to be sunk into an annuity in the french Loans——

——And now Eliza! Let me talk to thee——But What can I say, of What can I write—But the Yearnings of heart wasted with looking & wishing for thy Return—Return—Return! my dear Eliza! May heaven smooth the Way for thee to send thee safely . . . to us, & sojourn . . . for Ever.[62]

---

[58] Sterne reapplies to Eliza a favorite verse from the Psalter version of Psalm 139:3: "Thou art about my path, and about my bed: and spiest out all my ways"; see *Sermons*, 4:216.7–8, 290.6–7, and 321.1–2.

[59] Again, Cash, *LY*, 303, seems accurate in believing this date is factual; Elizabeth and Lydia moved to York in late October, but had been back in England one rather than two months.

[60] Elizabeth Sterne was born in 1714 and was fifty-three years old in 1767; it is doubtful that Sterne ever thought otherwise, since that would have made Elizabeth seventeen years old in 1741, the year they married.

[61] In June, Sterne had hoped for an agreement to remit "100 Guineas a year," and Cash, *LY*, 311, disputes his capacity to have paid 300 guineas at this time. Quite possibly, however, Sterne merely gives the total sum of monies he planned to provide, i.e., 200 pounds from annuities, and now 120 guineas to supplement the allowance.

[62] The last words of the *Journal* are written on a triangular fragment of paper; possibly they are the words of the rightmost edge of two additional lines and therefore are recorded to indicate hiatuses.

APPENDIX

Included here are several excerpts from Sterne's other writings that are particularly useful for contextualizing *A Sentimental Journey* and *Bramine's Journal*. *Tristram Shandy* and the sermons are reprinted from the *Florida Edition of the Works of Sterne*; the two letters to Eliza are reprinted from *Letters from Yorick to Eliza* (1773), edited by Melvyn New and Peter de Voogd, in *The Shandean,* 15 (2005). Fully annotated versions can be found in those texts.

1. Sermon 3: "Philanthropy Recommended" (excerpted).

Which now of these three, thinkest thou, was neighbour unto him that fell amongst the thieves?—And he said, he that shewed mercy on him. Then said Jesus unto him— Go, and do thou likewise.

Luke 10:36–37.

. . . A certain man, says our SAVIOUR, went down from Jerusalem to Jericho and fell among thieves, who stripped him of his rayment and departed, leaving him half dead. There is something in our nature which engages us to take part in every accident to which man is subject, from what cause soever it may have happened; but in such calamities as a man has fallen into through mere misfortune, to be charged upon no fault or indiscretion of himself, there is something then so truly interesting, that at the first sight we generally make them our own, not altogether from a reflection that they might have been or may be so, but oftener from a certain generosity and tenderness of nature which disposes us for compassion, abstracted from all considerations of self. So that without any observable act of the will, we suffer with the unfortunate, and feel a weight upon our spirits we know not why, on seeing the most common instances of their distress. But where the spectacle is uncommonly tragical, and complicated with many circumstances of misery, the mind is then taken captive at once, and, *were* it inclined to it, has no power to make resistance, but surrenders itself to all the tender emotions of pity and deep concern. So that when one considers this friendly part of our nature without looking farther, one would think it impossible for man to look upon misery, without finding himself in some measure attached to the interest of him who suffers it.—I say, one would think it impossible—for there are some tempers—how shall I describe them?—formed either of such impenetrable matter, or wrought up by habitual selfishness to such an utter insensibility of what becomes of the fortunes of their fellow-creatures, as if they were not partakers of the same nature, or had no lot or connection at all with the species.

Of this character, our SAVIOUR produces two disgraceful instances in the behaviour of a priest and a levite, whom in this account he represents as coming to the place where the unhappy man was—both passing by without either stretching forth a hand to assist, or uttering a word to comfort him in his distress.

And by chance there came down a certain priest!—merciful GOD! that a teacher of thy religion should ever want humanity—or that a man whose head might be thought full of the one, should have a heart void of the other!—This however was the case before us—and though in theory one would scarce suspect that the least pretence to religion and an open disregard to so main a part of it, could ever meet together in one person—yet in fact it is no fictitious character.

Look into the world—how often do you behold a sordid wretch, whose straight heart is open to no man's affliction, taking shelter behind an appearance of piety, and putting on the garb of religion, which none but the merciful and compassionate have a title to wear. Take notice with what sanctity he goes to the end of his days, in the same selfish track in which he at first set out—turning neither to the right hand nor to the left—but plods on—pores all his life long upon the ground, as if afraid to look up, lest peradventure he should see aught which might turn him one moment out of that straight line where interest is carrying him——or if, by chance, he stumbles upon a hapless object of distress, which threatens such a disaster to him—like the man here represented, *devoutly* passing by on the other side, as if unwilling to trust himself to the impressions of nature, or hazard the inconveniences which pity might lead him into upon the occasion.

There is but one stroke wanting in this picture of an unmerciful man to render the character utterly odious, and that our SAVIOUR gives it in the following instance he relates upon it. And likewise, says he, *a Levite, when he was at the place, came and looked at him.* It was not a transient oversight, the hasty or ill advised neglect of an unconsidering humour, with which the best disposed are sometimes overtaken, and led on beyond the point where otherwise they would have wished to stop.—No!—on the contrary, it had all the aggravation of a deliberate act of insensibility proceeding from a hard heart. When he was at the place, he came, and looked at him—considered his misfortunes, gave time for reason and nature to have awoke—saw the imminent danger he was in—and the pressing necessity of immediate help, which so violent a case called aloud for—and after all—turned aside and unmercifully left him to all the distresses of his condition.

In all unmerciful actions, the worst of men pay this compliment at least to humanity, as to endeavour to wear as much of the appearance of it, as the case will well let them—so that in the hardest acts a man shall be guilty of, he has some motives true or false always ready to offer, either to satisfy himself or the world, and, GOD knows, too often to impose both upon the one and the other. And therefore it would be no hard matter here to give a probable guess at what passed in the Levite's mind in the present case, and shew, was it necessary, by what kind of casuistry he settled the matter with his conscience as he passed by, and guarded all the passages to his heart against the inroads which pity might attempt to make upon the occasion.—But it is painful to dwell long upon this disagreeable part of the story; I therefore hasten to the concluding incident of it, which is so amiable that one cannot easily be too copious in reflections upon it.—And behold, says our SAVIOUR, a certain Samaritan as he journeyed came where he was; and when he saw him he had compassion on him—and went to him—bound up his wounds, pouring in oil and wine—set him upon his own beast, brought him to an inn and took care of him. I suppose, it will be scarce necessary here to remind you that the Jews had no dealings with the Samaritans—an old religious grudge—the worst of all grudges, had wrought such a dislike between both people, that they held themselves mutually discharged not only from all offices of friendship and kindness, but even from the most common acts of courtesy and good manners. . . . *Alas! after I have been twice passed by, neglected by men of my own nation and religion bound by so many ties to assist me, left here friendless and unpitied both by a Priest and Levite, men whose profession and superior advantages of knowledge could not leave them in the dark in what manner they should discharge this debt which my condition claims—after this—what hopes? what expectations from a passenger, not only a stranger,—but a Samaritan released from all obligations to me, and by a national dislike inflamed by mutual ill offices, now made my enemy, and more likely to rejoice at the evils which have fallen upon me, than to stretch forth a hand to save me from them.*

'Tis no unnatural soliloquy to imagine; but the actions of generous and compassionate tempers baffle all little reasonings about them.—True charity, in the apostle's description, as it is kind, and is not easily provoked, so it manifested this character here;—for we find when he came where he was, and beheld his distress,—all the unfriendly passions, which at another time might have rose within him, now utterly forsook him and fled: when he saw his misfortunes—he forgot his enmity towards the man,—dropped all the prejudices which education had planted against him, and in the room of them, all that was good and compassionate was suffered to speak in his behalf.

In benevolent natures the impulse to pity is so sudden, that like instruments of music which obey the touch—the objects which are fitted to excite such impressions work so instantaneous an effect, that you would think the will was scarce concerned, and that the mind was altogether passive in the sympathy which her own goodness has excited. The truth is,—the soul is generally in such cases so busily taken up and wholly engrossed by the object of pity, that she does not attend to her own operations, or take leisure to examine the principles upon which she acts. So that the Samaritan, though the moment he saw him he had compassion on him, yet sudden as the emotion is represented, you are not to imagine that it was mechanical, but that there was a settled principle of humanity and goodness which operated within him, and influenced not only the first impulse of kindness, but the continuation of it throughout the rest of so engaging a behaviour. And because it is a pleasure to look into a good mind, and trace out as far as one is able what passes within it on such occasions, I shall beg leave for a moment, to state an account of what was likely to pass in his, and in what manner so distressful a case would necessarily work upon such a disposition.

As he approached the place where the unfortunate man lay, the instant he beheld him, no doubt some such train of reflections as this would rise in his mind. "Good God! what a spectacle of misery do I behold—a man stripped of his raiment—wounded—lying languishing before me upon the ground just ready to expire,—without the comfort of a friend to support him in his last agonies, or the prospect of a hand to close his eyes when his pains are over. But perhaps my concern should lessen when I reflect on the relations in which we stand to each other—that he is a Jew and I a Samaritan.—But are we not still both men? partakers of the same nature—and subject to the same evils?—let me change conditions with him for a moment and consider, had his lot befallen me as I journeyed in the way, what measure I should have expected at his hands.—Should I wish when he beheld me wounded and half-dead, that he should shut up his bowels of compassion from me, and double the weight of my miseries by passing by and leaving them unpitied?—But I am a stranger to the man—be it so,—but I am no stranger to his condition—misfortunes are of no particular tribe or nation, but belong to us all, and have a general claim upon us, without distinction of climate, country or religion. Besides, though I am a stranger——'tis no fault of his that I do not know him, and therefore unequitable he should suffer by it:—Had I known him, possibly I should have had cause to love and pity him the more—for aught I know, he is some one of uncommon merit, whose life is rendered still more precious, as the lives and happiness of others may be involved in it: perhaps at this instant that he lies here forsaken, in all this misery, a whole virtuous family is joyfully looking for his return, and affectionately counting the hours of his delay. Oh! did they know what evil hath befallen him——how would they fly to succour him.—Let me then hasten to supply those tender offices of binding up his wounds, and carrying him to a place of safety—or if that assistance comes too late, I shall comfort him at least in his last hour—and, if I can do nothing else,— I shall soften his misfortunes by dropping a tear of pity over them."

'Tis almost necessary to imagine the good Samaritan was influenced by some such thoughts as these, from the uncommon generosity of his behaviour, which is represented by our SAVIOUR operating like the warm zeal of a brother, mixed with the affectionate discretion and care of a parent, who was not satisfied with taking him under his protection, and supplying his present wants, but in looking forwards for him, and taking care that his wants should be supplied when he should be gone, and no longer near to befriend him.

I think there needs no stronger argument to prove how universally and deeply the seeds of this virtue of compassion are planted in the heart of man, than in the pleasure we take in such representations of it: and though some men have represented human nature in other colours, (though to what end I know not) that the matter of fact is so strong against them, that from the general propensity to pity the unfortunate, we express that sensation by the word *humanity,* as if it was inseparable from our nature. That it is not *inseparable,* I have allowed in the former part of this discourse, from some reproachful instances of selfish tempers, which seem to take part in nothing beyond themselves; yet I am perswaded and affirm 'tis still so great and noble a part of our nature, that a man must do great violence to himself, and suffer many a painful conflict, before he has brought himself to a different disposition.

'Tis observable in the foregoing account, that when the priest came to the place where he was, he passed by on the other side—he might have passed by, you'll say, without turning aside.—No, there is a secret shame which attends every act of inhumanity not to be conquered in the hardest natures, so that, as in other cases, so especially in this, many a man will do a cruel act, who at the same time would blush to look you in the face, and is forced to turn aside before he can have a heart to execute his purpose.

Inconsistent creature that man is! who at that instant that he does what is wrong, is not able to withhold his testimony to what is good and praise worthy.

I have now done with the parable, which was the first part proposed to be considered in this discourse; and should proceed to the second, which so naturally falls from it, of exhorting you, as our SAVIOUR did the lawyer upon it, *to go and do so likewise:* but I have been so copious in my reflections upon the story itself, that I find I have insensibly incorporated into them almost all that I should have said here in recommending so amiable an example; by which means I have unawares anticipated the task I proposed. I shall therefore detain you no longer than with a single remark upon the subject in general, which is this, 'Tis observable in many places of scripture, that our blessed SAVIOUR in describing the day of judgment does it in such a manner, as if the great enquiry then, was to relate principally to this one virtue of compassion—and as if our final sentence at that solemnity was to be pronounced exactly according to the degrees of it. I was a hungred and ye gave me meat—thirsty and ye gave me drink—naked and ye cloathed me—I was sick and ye visited me—in prison and ye came unto me. Not that we are to imagine from thence, as if any other good or evil action should then be overlooked by the eye of the All-seeing Judge, but barely to intimate to us, that a charitable and benevolent disposition is so principal and ruling a part of a man's character, as to be a considerable test by itself of the whole frame and temper of his mind, with which all other virtues and vices respectively rise and fall, and will almost necessarily be connected. . . .

So that well might he conclude, that charity, by which he means, the love to your neighbour, was the end of the commandment, and that whosoever fulfilled it, had fulfilled the law . . . .

2. Sermon 20: "The Prodigal Son" (excerpted).

And not many days after, the younger son gathered all he had together, and took his journey into a far country.—

Luke 15:13.

I KNOW not whether the remark is to our honour or otherwise, that lessons of wisdom have never such power over us, as when they are wrought into the heart, through the ground-work of a story which engages the passions: Is it that we are like iron, and must first be heated before we can be wrought upon? or, Is the heart so in love with deceit, that where a true report will not reach it, we must cheat it with a fable, in order to come at truth? . . .

"A certain man, says our SAVIOUR, had two sons, and the younger of them said to his father, Give me the portion of goods which falls to me: and he divided unto them his substance. And not many days after, the younger son gathered all together, and took his journey into a far country, and there wasted his substance with riotous living."

The account is short: the interesting and pathetic passages with which such a transaction would be necessarily connected, are left to be supplied by the heart:——the story is silent——but nature is not:——much kind advice, and many a tender expostulation would fall from the father's lips, no doubt, upon this occasion.

He would dissuade his son from the folly of so rash an enterprize, by shewing him the dangers of the journey,——the inexperience of his age,——the hazards his life, his fortune, his virtue would run, without a guide, without a friend: he would tell him of the many snares and temptations which he had to avoid, or encounter at every step,——the pleasures which would sollicit him in every luxurious court,—the little knowledge he could gain—except that of evil: he would speak of the seductions of women,—their charms——their poisons:——what hapless indulgences he might give way to, when far from restraint, and the check of giving his father pain.

The dissuasive would but inflame his desire.——

He gathers all together.——

——I see the picture of his departure:—the camels and asses loaden with his substance, detached on one side of the piece, and already on their way:——the prodigal son standing on the fore ground, with a forced sedateness, struggling against the fluttering movement of joy, upon his deliverance from restraint:——the elder brother holding his hand, as if unwilling to let it go:——the father, ——sad moment! with a firm look, covering a prophetic sentiment, "that all would not go well with his child,"—approaching to embrace him, and bid him adieu.——Poor inconsiderate youth! From whose arms art thou flying? From what a shelter art thou going forth into the storm? Art thou weary of a father's affection, of a father's care? or, Hopest thou to find a warmer interest, a truer

238

counsellor, or a kinder friend in a land of strangers, where youth is made a prey, and so many thousands are confederated to deceive them, and live by their spoils?

We will seek no further than this idea, for the extravagancies by which the prodigal son added one unhappy example to the number: his fortune wasted, ——the followers of it fled in course,——the wants of nature remain,—— the hand of GOD gone forth against him,—— *"For when he had spent all, a mighty famine arose in that country."*—Heaven! have pity upon the youth, for he is in hunger and distress,——stray'd out of the reach of a parent, who counts every hour of his absence with anguish,——cut off from all his tender offices, by his folly,——and from relief and charity from others, by the calamity of the times.——

Nothing so powerfully calls home the mind as distress: the tense fibre then relaxes,——the soul retires to itself,——sits pensive and susceptible of right impressions: if we have a friend, 'tis then we think of him; if a benefactor, at that moment all his kindnesses press upon our mind.——Gracious and bountiful GOD! Is it not for this, that they who in their prosperity forget thee, do yet remember and return to thee in the hour of their sorrow? When our heart is in heaviness, upon whom can we think but thee, who knowest our necessities afar off,—puttest all our tears in thy bottle,——seest every careful thought,—hearest every sigh and melancholy groan we utter.——

Strange!—that we should only begin to think of GOD with comfort,—when with joy and comfort we can think of nothing else.

Man surely is a compound of riddles and contradictions: by the law of his nature he avoids pain, and yet *unless he suffers in the flesh, he will not cease from sin,* tho' it is sure to bring pain and misery upon his head for ever. . . .

Of all the terrors of nature, that of one day or another dying by hunger, is the greatest, and it is wisely wove into our frame to awaken man to industry, and call forth his talents; and tho' we seem to go on carelessly, sporting with it as we do with other terrors——yet, he that sees this enemy fairly, and in his most frightful shape, will need no long remonstrance, to make him turn out of the way to avoid him.

It was the case of the prodigal——he arose to go unto his father.——

——Alas! How shall he tell his story? Ye who have trod this round, tell me in what words he shall give in to his father, the sad *Items* of his extravagance and folly? . . .

——Leave the story——it will be told more concisely.—— *When he was yet afar off, his father saw him,*——Compassion told it in three words—*he fell upon his neck and kissed him.*

Great is the power of eloquence: but never is it so great as when it pleads along with nature, and the culprit is a child strayed from his duty, and returned to it again with tears: Casuists may settle the point as they will: But what could a parent see more in the account, than the natural one, of an ingenuous heart too open for the world,—smitten with strong sensations of pleasures, and suffered to sally forth unarm'd into the midst of enemies stronger than himself?

Generosity sorrows as much for the over-matched, as pity herself does.

The idea of a son so ruin'd, would double the father's caresses: every effusion of his tenderness would add bitterness to his son's remorse.———"Gracious heaven! what a father have I rendered miserable!"

And he said, I have sinned against heaven, and in thy sight, and am no more worthy to be called thy son. . . .

O ye affections! How fondly do you play at cross-purposes with each other! ——'Tis the natural dialogue of true transport: joy is not methodical; and where an offender, beloved, overcharges itself in the offence,——words are too cold; and a conciliated heart replies by tokens of esteem.

And he said unto his servants, Bring forth the best robe and put it on him; and put a ring on his hand, and shoes on his feet, and bring hither the fatted calf, and let us eat and drink and be merry.

When the affections so kindly break loose, Joy, is another name for Religion.

We look up as we taste it: the cold Stoick without, when he hears the dancing and the musick, may ask sullenly, (with the elder brother) What it means; and refuse to enter: but the humane and compassionate all fly impetuously to the banquet, given *for a son who was dead and is alive again,*——*who was lost and is found.* Gentle spirits, light up the pavillion with a sacred fire; and parental love, and filial piety lead in the mask with riot and wild festivity!——Was it not for this that GOD gave man musick to strike upon the kindly passions; that nature taught the feet to dance to its movements, and as chief governess of the feast, poured forth wine into the goblet, to crown it with gladness?

The intention of this parable is so clear from the occasion of it, that it will not be necessary to perplex it with any tedious explanation . . . .

These uses have been so ably set forth, in so many good sermons upon the prodigal son, that I shall turn aside from them at present, and content myself with some reflections upon that fatal passion which led him,——and so many thousands after the example, *to gather all he had together, and take his journey into a far country.*

The love of variety, or curiosity of seeing new things, which is the same, or at least a sister passion to it,——seems wove into the frame of every son and daughter of Adam; we usually speak of it as one of nature's levities, tho' planted within us for the solid purposes of carrying forwards the mind to fresh enquiry and knowledge: strip us of it, the mind (I fear) would doze for ever over the present page; and we should all of us rest at ease with such objects as presented themselves in the parish or province where we first drew our breath.

It is to this spur which is ever in our sides, that we owe the impatience of this desire for travelling: the passion is no way bad,——but as others are,——in it's mismanagement or excess;——order it rightly the advantages are worth the pursuit; the chief of which are——to learn the languages, the laws and customs, and understand the government and interest of other nations,——to acquire an urbanity and confidence of behaviour, and fit the mind more easily for conversation and discourse;——to take us out of the company of our aunts and grandmothers, and from the track of nursery mistakes; and by shewing us new objects, or old ones in new lights, to reform our judgments——by tasting perpetually the varieties of nature, to know what *is good*——by observing the address and arts of men, to conceive what *is sincere,*——and by seeing the difference of so many various humours and manners,——to look into ourselves and form our own.

This is some part of the cargo we might return with; but the impulse of seeing new sights, augmented with that of getting clear from all lessons both of wisdom and reproof at home——carries our youth too early out, to turn this venture to much account; on the contrary, if the scene painted of the prodigal in his travels, looks more like a copy than an original,—will it not be well if such an adventurer, with so unpromising a setting out,—without *carte,*—without compass,——be not cast away for ever,—and may he not be said to escape well——if he returns to his country, only as naked, as he first left it?

But you will send an able pilot with your son . . . .

[H]e shall be escorted by one who knows the world, not merely from books—but from his own experience:——a man who has been employed on such services, and thrice made the *tour of Europe, with success.*

. . . if he is such as my eyes have seen! some broken *Swiss valet de chambre,* . . . much knowledge will not accrue;——some profit at least,—he will learn the amount to a halfpenny, of every stage from Calais to Rome;——he will be carried to the best inns,——instructed where there is the best wine, and sup a livre cheaper, than if the youth had been left to make the tour and the bargain himself.——Look at our governor! I beseech you:——see, he is an inch taller as he relates the advantages.—— . . .

But when your son gets abroad, he will be . . . [educated] by his society with men of rank and letters, with whom he will pass the greatest part of his time.

Let me observe in the first place,—that company which is really good, is very rare——and very shy: but you have surmounted this difficulty; and procured him the best letters of recommendation to the most eminent and respectable in every capital.——

And I answer, that he will obtain all by them, which courtesy strictly stands obliged to pay on such occasions,—but no more.

There is nothing in which we are so much deceived, as in the advantages proposed from our connections and discourse with the literati, &c. in foreign parts; especially if the experiment is made before we are matured by years or study.

Conversation is a traffick; and if you enter into it, without some stock of knowledge, to ballance the account perpetually betwixt you,——the trade drops at once: and this is the reason,——however it may be boasted to the contrary, why travellers have so little (especially good) conversation with natives,——owing to their suspicion,—or perhaps conviction, that there is nothing to be extracted from the conversation of young itinerants, worth the trouble of their bad language,—or the interruption of their visits.

The pain on these occasions is usually reciprocal; the consequence of which is, that the disappointed youth seeks an easier society; and as bad company is always ready,—and ever lying in wait,—the career is soon finished; and the poor prodigal returns the same object of pity, with the prodigal in the gospel.

3. Sermon 29: "Our Conversation in Heaven" (excerpted).

For our conversation is in heaven.

Philippians 3:20.

THESE words are the conclusion of the account which St. Paul renders of himself, to justify that particular part of his conduct and proceeding,—his leaving so strangely, and deserting his Jewish rites and ceremonies, to which he was known to have been formerly so much attached, and in defence of which he had been so warmly and so remarkably engaged. . . .

The apostle, after this apology for himself,—proceeds, in the second verse before the text, to give a very different representation of the worldly views and sensual principles of other pretending teachers,—who had set themselves up as an example for men to walk by, against whom he renews this caution:—For many walk, of whom I have told you often, and now tell you even weeping, that they are the enemies to the cross of Christ,—whose end is destruction,—whose God is their belly, and whose glory is in their shame, who mind earthly things,--- Φρωνοῦντες,---relish them, making them the only object of their wishes,—taking aim at nothing better, and nothing higher.—But *our* conversation, says he in the text, is in heaven.—We christians, who have embraced a persecuted faith, are governed by other considerations,—have greater and nobler views;—here we consider ourselves only as pilgrims and strangers.—Our home is in another country, where we are continually tending; there our hearts and affections are placed; and when the few days of our pilgrimage shall be over, there shall we return, where a quiet habitation and a perpetual rest is designed and prepared for us for ever.— Our conversation is in heaven, from whence, says he, we also look for the Saviour, the Lord Jesus Christ, who shall change our vile body, that it may be fashioned like unto his glorious body, according to the working whereby he is able to subdue all things unto him.—It is observable, that St. Peter represents the state of christians under the same image, of strangers on earth, whose city and proper home, is heaven:—he makes use of that relation of citizens of heaven, as a strong argument for a pure and holy life,—beseeching them *as* pilgrims and strangers *here,* as men whose interests and connections are of so short a date, and so trifling a nature,—to abstain from fleshly lusts, which war against the soul, that is, unfit it for its heavenly country, and give it a disrelish to the enjoyment of that pure and spiritualized happiness, of which that region must consist, wherein there shall in no wise enter any thing that defileth, neither whatsoever worketh abomination.—The apostle tells us, that without holiness no man shall see God;—by which no doubt he means, that a virtuous life is the only medium of happiness and terms of salvation,—which can only give us admission into heaven.—But some of our divines carry the assertion further, that without holiness,—without some previous similitude wrought in the faculties of the mind, corresponding with the nature of the purest of beings, who is to be the object of our fruition hereafter;—that it is not morally only, but physically impossible for it to be happy,—and that an impure and polluted soul, is not only unworthy of so pure a presence as the spirit of God, but even incapable of enjoying it, could it be admitted.

And here, not to feign a long hypothesis, as some have done, of a sinner's being admitted into heaven, with a particular description of his condition and behaviour there,—we need only consider, that the supreme good, like any other good, is of a relative nature, and consequently the enjoyment of it must require some qualification in the faculty, as well as the enjoyment of any other good does;—there must be something antecedent in the disposition and temper, which will render that good a good to that individual,—otherwise though (it is true) it may be possessed,—yet it never can be enjoyed.—

Preach to a voluptuous epicure, who knows of no other happiness in this world, but what arises from good eating and drinking;—such a one, in the apostle's language, whose God was his belly;—preach to him of the abstractions of the soul, tell of its flights, and brisker motion in the pure regions of immensity;—represent to him that saints and angels eat not,—but that the spirit of a man lives for ever upon wisdom and holiness, and heavenly contemplations:—why, the only effect would be, that the fat glutton would stare a while upon the preacher, and in a few minutes fall fast asleep.—No; if you would catch his attention, and make him take in your discourse greedily,—you must preach to him out of the Alcoran,—talk of the raptures of sensual enjoyments, and of the pleasures of the perpetual feasting, which Mahomet has described;—there you touch upon a note which awakens and sinks into the inmost recesses of his soul;—without which, discourse as wisely and abstractedly as you will of heaven, your representations of it, however glorious and exalted, will pass like the songs of melody over an ear incapable of discerning the distinction of sounds.—

We see, even in the common intercourses of society,—how tedious it is to be in the company of a person whose humour is disagreeable to our own, though perhaps in all other respects of the greatest worth and excellency.—How then can we imagine that an ill-disposed soul, whose conversation never reached to heaven, but whose appetites and desires, to the last hour, have grovel'd upon this unclean spot of earth;—how can we imagine it should hereafter take pleasure in God, or be able to taste joy or satisfaction from his presence, who is so infinitely pure, that he even putteth no trust in his saints,—nor are the heavens themselves (as Job says) clean in his sight.—The consideration of this has led some writers so far, as to say, with some degree of irreverence in the expression,—that it was not in the power of God to make a wicked man happy, if the soul was separated from the body, with all its vicious habits and inclinations unreformed;—which thought, a very able divine in our church has pursued so far, as to declare his belief,—that could the happiest mansion in heaven be supposed to be allotted to a gross and polluted spirit, it would be so far from being happy in it, that it would do penance there to all eternity:—by which he meant, it would carry such appetites along with it, for which there could be found no suitable objects.—A sufficient cause for constant torment;—for those that it found there, would be so disproportioned, that they would rather vex and upbraid it, than satisfy its wants.—This, it is true, is mere speculation,—and what concerns us not to know;—it being enough for our purpose, that such an experiment is never likely to be tried,—that we stand upon different terms with God,—that a virtuous life is the foundation of all our happiness,—that as God has no pleasure in wickedness, neither shall any evil dwell with him;—and that, if we expect our happiness to be in heaven,—we must have our conversation in heaven, whilst upon earth,—make it the frequent subject of our thoughts and meditations,—let every step we take tend that way,—every action of our lives be conducted by that great mark of the prize of our high-calling, forgetting those things which are behind;—forgetting this world,---disengaging our thoughts and affections from it, and thereby transforming them to the likeness of what we hope to be hereafter.—How can we expect the inheritance of the saints of light, upon other terms than what they themselves obtained it? . . .

How inconsistent the whole body of sin is, with the glories of the celestial body that shall be revealed hereafter,—and that in proportion as we fix the representation of these glories upon our minds, and in the more numerous particulars we do it,—the stronger the necessity as well as persuasion to deny ourselves all ungodliness and worldly lusts, to live soberly, righteously and godly in this present world, as the only way to entitle us to that blessedness spoken of in the Revelations—of those who do his commandments, and have a right to the tree of life, and shall enter into the gates of the city of the living God, the heavenly Jerusalem, and to an innumerable company of angels;—to the general assembly and church of the first-born, that are written in heaven, and to God the judge of all, and to the spirits of just men made perfect,—who have washed their robes, and made them white in the blood of the Lamb.—

May God give us grace to live under the perpetual influence of this expectation,—that by the habitual impression of these glories upon our imaginations, and the frequent sending forth our thoughts and employing them on the other world,—we may disentangle them from this,—and by so having our conversation in heaven whilst we are here, we may be thought fit inhabitants for it hereafter;—that when God at the last day shall come with thousands and ten thousands of his saints to judge the world, we may enter with them into happiness, and with angels and arch-angels, and all the company of heaven, we may praise and magnify his glorious name, and enjoy his presence for ever. Amen.

4. *Tristram Shandy,* VII.1 (excerpted).

NO——I think, I said, I would write two volumes every year, provided the vile cough which then tormented me, and which to this hour I dread worse than the devil, would but give me leave——and in another place—(but where, I can't recollect now) speaking of my book as a *machine,* and laying my pen and ruler down cross-wise upon the table, in order to gain the greater credit to it—I swore it should be kept a going at that rate these forty years if it pleased but the fountain of life to bless me so long with health and good spirits.

Now as for my spirits, little have I to lay to their charge—nay so very little (unless the mounting me upon a long stick, and playing the fool with me nineteen hours out of the twenty-four, be accusations) that on the contrary, I have much—much to thank 'em for: cheerily have ye made me tread the path of life with all the burdens of it (except its cares) upon my back; in no one moment of my existence, that I remember, have ye once deserted me, or tinged the objects which came in my way, either with sable, or with a sickly green; in dangers ye gilded my horizon with hope, and when DEATH himself knocked at my door— ye bad him come again; and in so gay a tone of careless indifference, did ye do it, that he doubted of his commission——

"—There must certainly be some mistake in this matter," quoth he. . . .

But there is no *living,* Eugenius, . . . at this rate; for as this *son of a whore* has found out my lodgings——

—You call him rightly, said Eugenius,—for by sin, we are told, he enter'd the world——I care not which way he enter'd, quoth I, provided he be not in such a hurry to take me out with him—for I have forty volumes to write, and forty thousand things to say and do, which no body in the world will say and do for me, except thyself; and as thou seest he has got me by the throat (for Eugenius could scarce hear me speak across the table) and that I am no match for him in the open field, had I not better, whilst these few scatter'd spirits remain, and these two spider legs of mine (holding one of them up to him) are able to support me—had I not better, Eugenius, fly for my life? 'tis my advice, my dear Tristram, said Eugenius——then by heaven! I will lead him a dance he little thinks of—for I will gallop, quoth I, without looking once behind me to the banks of the Garonne; and if I hear him clattering at my heels——I'll scamper away to mount Vesuvius——from thence to Joppa, and from Joppa to the world's end, where, if he follows me, I pray God he may break his neck——

—He runs more risk *there,* said Eugenius, than thou.

Eugenius's wit and affection brought blood into the cheek from whence it had been some months banish'd—'twas a vile moment to bid adieu in; he led me to my chaise——*Allons!* said I; the post boy gave a crack with his whip——off I went like a cannon, and in half a dozen bounds got into Dover.

5. *Tristram Shandy,* VII.43 (excerpted).

I Had not gone above two leagues and a half, before the man with his gun, began to look at his priming.

I had three several times loiter'd *terribly* behind; half a mile at least every time: once, in deep conference with a drum-maker, who was making drums for the fairs of *Baucaira* and *Tarascone*—I did not understand the principles——

The second time, I cannot so properly say, I stopp'd——for meeting a couple of Franciscans straiten'd more for time than myself, and not being able to get to the bottom of what I was about——I had turn'd back with them——

The third, was an affair of trade with a gossip, for a hand basket of Provence figs for four sous; this would have been transacted at once; but for a case of conscience at the close of it; for when the figs were paid for, it turn'd out, that there were two dozen of eggs cover'd over with vine-leaves at the bottom of the basket—as I had no intention of buying eggs—I made no sort of claim of them—as for the space they had occupied—what signified it? I had figs enow for my money——

—But it was my intention to have the basket—it was the gossip's intention to keep it, without which, she could do nothing with her eggs——and unless I had the basket, I could do as little with my figs, which were too ripe already, and most of 'em burst at the side: this brought on a short contention, which terminated in sundry proposals, what we should both do——

—How we disposed of our eggs and figs, I defy you, or the Devil himself, had he not been there (which I am persuaded he was) to form the least probable conjecture: You will read the whole of it——not this year, for I am hastening to the story of my uncle Toby's amours—but you will read it in the collection of those which have arose out of the journey across this plain——and which, therefore, I call my

PLAIN STORIES.

How far my pen has been fatigued like those of other travellers, in this journey of it, over so barren a track—the world must judge—but the traces of it, which are now all set o'vibrating together this moment, tell me 'tis the most fruitful and busy period of my life; for as I had made no convention with my man with the gun as to time—by stopping and talking to every soul I met who was not in a full trot—joining all parties before me—waiting for every soul behind—hailing all those who were coming through cross roads—arresting all kinds of beggars, pil-

grims, fiddlers, fryars—not passing by a woman in a mulberry-tree without commending her legs, and tempting her into conversation with a pinch of snuff——
In short, by seizing every handle, of what size or shape soever, which chance held out to me in this journey—I turned my *plain* into a *city*—I was always in company, and with great variety too; and as my mule loved society as much as myself, and had some proposals always on his part to offer to every beast he met—I am confident we could have passed through Pall-Mall or St. James's-Street for a month together, with fewer adventures—and seen less of human nature.

O! there is that sprightly frankness which at once unpins every plait of a Languedocian's dress—that whatever is beneath it, it looks so like the simplicity which poets sing of in better days—I will delude my fancy, and believe it is so. . . .

——The sun was set—they had done their work; the nymphs had tied up their hair afresh—and the swains were preparing for a carousal . . . .

A sun-burnt daughter of Labour rose up from the groupe to meet me as I advanced towards them; her hair, which was a dark chesnut, approaching rather to a black, was tied up in a knot, all but a single tress.

We want a cavalier, said she, holding out both her hands, as if to offer them ——And a cavalier ye shall have; said I, taking hold of both of them.

Hadst thou, Nannette, been array'd like a dutchesse!

——But that cursed slit in thy petticoat!

Nannette cared not for it.

We could not have done without you, said she, letting go one hand, with self-taught politeness, leading me up with the other.

A lame youth, whom Apollo had recompenced with a pipe, and to which he had added a tabourin of his own accord, ran sweetly over the prelude, as he sat upon the bank——Tie me up this tress instantly, said Nannette, putting a piece of string into my hand——It taught me to forget I was a stranger——The whole knot fell down——We had been seven years acquainted.

The youth struck the note upon the tabourin—his pipe followed, and off we bounded——"the duce take that slit!"

The sister of the youth who had stolen her voice from heaven, sung alternately with her brother——'twas a Gascoigne roundelay.

VIVA LA JOIA!
FIDON LA TRISTESSA!

The nymphs join'd in unison, and their swains an octave below them——

I would have given a crown to have it sew'd up—Nannette would not have given a sous—*Viva la joia!* was in her lips—*Viva la joia!* was in her eyes. A transient spark of amity shot across the space betwixt us——She look'd amiable!——Why could I not live and end my days thus? Just disposer of our joys and sorrows, cried I, why could not a man sit down in the lap of content here—and dance, and sing, and say his prayers, and go to heaven with this nut brown maid? capriciously did she bend her head on one side, and dance up insiduous——Then 'tis time to dance off, quoth I; so changing only partners and tunes, I danced it away from Lunel to Montpellier——from thence to Pesçnas, Beziers——I danced it along through Narbonne, Carcasson, and Castle Naudairy, till at last I danced myself into Perdrillo's pavillion, where pulling a paper of black lines, that I might go on straight forwards, without digression or parenthesis, in my uncle Toby's amours——

I begun thus——

END of the SEVENTH VOLUME.

6. *Tristram Shandy,* IX.24 (Maria; excerpted).

. . . They were the sweetest notes I ever heard; and I instantly let down the fore-glass to hear them more distinctly——'Tis Maria; said the postilion, observing I was listening———Poor Maria, continued he, (leaning his body on one side to let me see her, for he was in a line betwixt us) is sitting upon a bank playing her vespers upon her pipe, with her little goat beside her.

The young fellow utter'd this with an accent and a look so perfectly in tune to a feeling heart, that I instantly made a vow, I would give him a four and twenty sous piece, when I got to *Moulins*——

———And who is *poor Maria?* said I.

The love and pity of all the villages around us; said the postillion——it is but three years ago, that the sun did not shine upon so fair, so quick-witted and amiable a maid; and better fate did *Maria* deserve, than to have her Banns forbid, by the intrigues of the curate of the parish who published them——

He was going on, when Maria, who had made a short pause, put the pipe to her mouth and began the air again——they were the same notes;——yet were ten times sweeter: It is the evening service to the Virgin, said the young man—— but who has taught her to play it—or how she came by her pipe, no one knows; we think that Heaven has assisted her in both; for ever since she has been unsettled in her mind, it seems her only consolation——she has never once had the pipe out of her hand, but plays that *service* upon it almost night and day.

The postillion delivered this with so much discretion and natural eloquence, that I could not help decyphering something in his face above his condition, and should have sifted out his history, had not poor Maria's taken such full possession of me.

We had got up by this time almost to the bank where Maria was sitting: she was in a thin white jacket with her hair, all but two tresses, drawn up into a silk net, with a few olive-leaves twisted a little fantastically on one side——she was beautiful; and if ever I felt the full force of an honest heart-ache, it was the moment I saw her——

——God help her! poor damsel! above a hundred masses, said the postillion, have been said in the several parish churches and convents around, for her,—— but without effect; we have still hopes, as she is sensible for short intervals, that the Virgin at last will restore her to herself; but her parents, who know her best, are hopeless upon that score, and think her senses are lost for ever.

As the postillion spoke this, MARIA made a cadence so melancholy, so tender and querulous, that I sprung out of the chaise to help her, and found myself sitting betwixt her and her goat before I relapsed from my enthusiasm.

MARIA look'd wistfully for some time at me, and then at her goat——and then at me——and then at her goat again, and so on, alternately——

——Well, Maria, said I softly——What resemblance do you find?

I do intreat the candid reader to believe me, that it was from the humblest conviction of what a *Beast* man is,——that I ask'd the question; and that I would not have let fallen an unseasonable pleasantry in the venerable presence of Misery, to be entitled to all the wit that ever Rabelais scatter'd——and yet I own my heart smote me, and that I so smarted at the very idea of it, that I swore I would set up for Wisdom and utter grave sentences the rest of my days——and never—— never attempt again to commit mirth with man, woman, or child, the longest day I had to live.

As for writing nonsense to them——I believe, there was a reserve—but that I leave to the world.

Adieu, Maria!—adieu, poor hapless damsel!——some time, but not *now*, I may hear thy sorrows from thy own lips——but I was deceived; for that moment she took her pipe and told me such a tale of woe with it, that I rose up, and with broken and irregular steps walk'd softly to my chaise.

——What an excellent inn at Moulins!

7. From *Letters from Yorick to Eliza* (1773; excerpted).

[London, March 1767]

My Dearest ELIZA,

I began a new journal this morning: you shall see it, for if I live not till your return to England, I will leave it you as a legacy: tis a sorrowful page, but I will write chearful ones, and could I write letters to thee, they should be chearful ones too, but few (I fear) will reach thee—however, depend upon receiving something of the kind by every post, till thou wavest thy hand, and bidst me write no more—Tell me how you are, and what sort of fortitude heaven inspires thee with. How are your accommodations my dear?—is all right?—scribble away any thing and every thing to me. Depend upon seeing me at Deal with the James's, should you be detain'd there by contrary winds. Indeed, Eliza, I should with pleasure fly to you, could I be the means of rendring you any service, or doing you any kindness—

"Gracious and merciful God, consider the anguish of a poor girl, strengthen and preserve her, in all the shocks her frame must be expos'd to, she is now without a protector but thee; save her from all the accidents of a dangerous element, and give her comfort at the last"—

My prayer, Eliza, I hope is heard, for the sky seems to smile upon me as I look up to it—

I am just return'd from our dear Mrs. James's, where I have been talking of thee these three hours—She has got your picture and likes it, but Mariot and some other judges agree, that mine is the better, and expressive of a sweeter character; but what is that to the original? yet I acknowledge her's a picture for the world, and mine only calculated to please a very sincere friend, or sentimental philosopher—

In the one you are dressed in smiles, and with all the advantages of silks, pearls, and ermine, in the other, simple as a vestal, appearing the good girl nature made you; which to me conveys an idea of more unaffected sweetness, than Mrs. Draper habited for conquest in a birth day suit, with her countenance animated and "dimples visible"—

If I remember right, Eliza, you endeavour'd to collect every charm of your person into your face with more than common care, the day you sat for Mrs. James, your colour too brighten'd, and your eyes shone with more than their usual brilliancy—

I then requested you to come simple and unadorn'd when you sat for me, knowing (as I see with unprejudic'd eyes) that you cou'd receive no addition from the silkworm's aid, or jeweller's polish—

Let me now tell you a truth, which I believe I utter'd before—when I first saw you, I beheld you as an object of compassion, and a very plain woman—

The mode of your dress (tho' fashionable) disfigur'd you—but nothing now cou'd render you such, but the being sollicitous to make yourself admir'd as a handsome one—

You are not handsome, Eliza—nor is your's a face that will please the tenth part of your beholders—

But you are something more; for I scruple not to tell you, I never saw so intelligent, so animated, so good a countenance; nor ever was there, nor will there be, that man of sense, tenderness, and feeling in your company three hours, that was not, or will not be, your admirer and friend in consequence of it, *i.e.* if you assume or assumed no character foreign to your own, but appear'd the artless being nature design'd you for—a something in your voice and eyes, you possess in a degree more persuasive than any woman I ever saw, read, or heard of:

But it is that bewitching sort of nameless excellence, that men of *nice sensibility* alone can be touch'd with—

Was your husband in England, I wou'd freely give him £500 (if money cou'd purchase the acquisition) to let you only sit by me two hours in the day, while I wrote my sentimental journey—I am sure the work wou'd sell so much the better for it, that I should be reimburs'd the sum more than seven times told—

I would not give nine-pence for the picture of you, that the Newnhams have got executed; it is the resemblance of a concerted, made up coquette—your eyes, and the shape of your face (the latter the most perfect oval I ever saw) which are perfections that must strike the most indifferent judge, because they are equal to any of God's works in a similar way, and finer than any I beheld in all my travels, are manifestly injured by the affected leer of the one, and strange appearance of the other, owing to the attitude of the head, which is a proof of the artist's, or your friend's false taste . . . .

I will write again to-morrow to thee, thou best, and most endearing of girls: a peaceful night to thee; my spirit will be with thee thro' every watch of it—Adieu.

8. From *Letters from Yorick to Eliza* (1773; excerpted).

[London, March 1767]

I wish to God, Eliza, it was possible to postpone the voyage to India for another year, for I am firmly persuaded within my own breast, that thy husband could never limit thee with regard to time—

I fear that Mr. B. has exaggerated matters,—I like not his countenance, it is absolutely killing thee—should evil befall thee, what will he not have to answer for—I know not the being that will be deserving of so much pity, or that I shall hate more; he will be an outcast alien; in which case I will be a father to thy children my good girl, therefore take no thought about them—But, Eliza, if thou art so very ill, still put off all thoughts of returning to India this year—write to your husband—tell him the truth of your case—if he is the generous humane man you describe him to be, he cannot but applaud your conduct—I am credibly informed, that his repugnance to your living in England arises only from the dread which has enter'd his brain, that thou mayest run him in debt, beyond thy appointments, and that he must discharge them—

That such a creature should be sacrificed, for the paultry consideration of a few hundreds, is too, too hard! Oh! my child, that I could with propriety indemnify him for every charge, even to the last mite, that thou hast been of to him! with joy would I give him my whole subsistence, nay, sequester my livings, and trust to the treasures heaven has furnish'd my head with for a future subsistence—

You owe much, I allow, to your husband; you owe something to appearances and the opinions of the world; but, trust me, my dear, you owe much likewise to yourself—Return therefore from Deal if you continue ill: I will prescribe for you gratis. You are not the first woman by many, I have done so for with success—

I will send for my wife and daughter, and they shall carry you in pursuit of health to Montpelier, the wells of Bancer's, the Spaw, or whither thou wilt; thou shalt direct them, and make parties of pleasure in what corner of the world fancy points out to you—

We shall fish upon the banks of Arno, and lose ourselves in the sweet labyrinths of it's vallies, and then thou should'st warble to us, as I have once or twice heard thee "I'm lost, I'm lost," but we would find thee again, my Eliza—

Of a similar nature to this, was your physician's prescription "ease, gentle exercise, the pure southern air of France, or milder Naples, with the society of friendly gentle beings"—

Sensible man, he certainly enter'd into your feelings, he knew the fallacy of medicine to a creature, whose illness has arisen from the affliction of her mind—Time only, my dear, I fear you must trust to, and have your reliance on: may it give you the health so enthusiastic a votary to the charming goddess deserves—

I honour you, Eliza, for keeping secret some things, which if explain'd, had been a panegyric on yourself—There is a dignity in venerable affliction which will not allow it to appeal to the world for pity or redress—Well have you supported that character, my amiable philosophic friend! And, indeed, I begin to think you have as many virtues, as my uncle Toby's widow—

I don't mean to insinuate, hussey, that my opinion is no better founded than his was of Mrs. Wadman; nor do I believe it possible for any Trim to convince me it is equally fallacious; I am sure while I have my reason it is not—

Talking of widows—pray, Eliza, if ever you are such, do not think of giving yourself to some wealthy nabob, because I design to marry you myself—My wife cannot live long—she has sold all the provinces in France already, and I know not the woman I should like so well for her substitute, as yourself—'Tis true, I am ninety five in constitution, and you but twenty-five; rather too great a disparity this! but what I want in youth, I will make up in wit and good humour—Not Swift so lov'd his Stella, Scarron his Maintenon, or Waller his Sacharissa, as I will love and sing thee, my wife elect—all those names, eminent as they were, shall give place to thine, Eliza.

Tell me in answer to this, that you approve and honour the proposal; and that you would (like the Spectator's mistress) have more joy in putting on an old man's slipper, than in associating with the gay, the voluptuous, and the young—Adieu, my Simplicia—

Yours
TRISTRAM.